FINNEGAN'S WEEK

Joseph Wambaugh

BANTAM BOOKS
NEW YORK · TORONTO · LONDON · SYDNEY · AUCKLAND

This edition contains the complete text
of the original hardcover edition.
NOT ONE WORD HAS BEEN OMITTED.

FINNEGAN'S WEEK
A Bantam Book/published by arrangement
with the author

PUBLISHING HISTORY
Morrow hardcover edition/December 1993
Bantam edition/August 1994

Excerpt from "MY WAY"
Music by Jacques Revaux & Claude François
French lyrics by Gille Thibault
English lyrics by Paul Anka
© 1967 Société Des Nouvelles Editions Eddie Barclay
© 1969 Management Agency & Music Publishing, Inc.
International Copyright Secured. All Rights Reserved. Used By Permission.
All rights reserved.
Copyright © 1993 by Wambaugh Family Trust.
Cover art copyright © 1994 by Paul Bacon.
Library of Congress Catalog Card Number: 93-24890

ISBN 0-553-76324-5

Published simultaneously in the United States and Canada

PRINTED IN THE UNITED STATES OF AMERICA

FINBAR FINNEGAN: A fortysomething aspiring actor who does more aspiring than acting, he has one hell of a day job—San Diego police detective. And this case is a truckload of trouble, involving several jurisdictions and putting him in the middle of two tenacious female investigators.

NELL SALTER: Working in the environmental crimes department of the San Diego D.A.'s office, she spends her time tracking down crimes that prosecutors and juries rarely take seriously. Now she has a chance to make a difference . . . if her attraction to Fin Finnegan doesn't get in the way.

"*Finnegan's Week* is a lot of fun; we should all have weeks like that."

BOBBIE ANN DOGGET: An all-American, mid-western sweetheart with the unlikely nickname Bad Dog, she's a navy investigator who's as stubborn as a dog with a shoe—in this case, two-thousand pairs of shoes. She's out to prove herself to her commander and to Fin and Nell, determined to crack the case . . . or die trying.

"Wambaugh has done a fine job of creating a fascinating mystery, then surrounding it with characters who are just close enough to the edge. This is a fast trip through places we might want to visit, but would never want to live."

JULES TEMPLE: His wealthy father gave him everything a boy could want . . . except a conscience. The owner of a fly-by-night waste hauling firm, he's out to make a fast fortune—no matter who dies along the way.

"Wambaugh's wit is in fine form . . . characters are sharply defined and the dialogue rings true."

ABEL DURAZO AND SHELBY PATE: Risking their miserable jobs to make a little profit of their own, the two hapless truckers think their load of stolen navy property is their ticket to wild life, great drugs, and fast sex—all without a price. But the cost will prove to be higher than they could have imagined. . . .

"If there is an American author who consistently provides bang for the buck, it's Joseph Wambaugh. . . . Wambaugh delivers."

Books by Joseph Wambaugh

Fiction

The New Centurions
The Blue Knight
The Choirboys
The Black Marble
The Glitter Dome
The Delta Star
The Secrets of Harry Bright
The Golden Orange
Fugitive Nights
Finnegan's Week
Floaters

Nonfiction

The Onion Field
Lines and Shadows
Echoes in the Darkness
The Blooding

For Detective Tony Puente,
San Diego Police Department

As usual, I have relied upon dozens of professionals for the expertise, anecdotes, and cop talk that inspired this story. Special thanks goes to Criminal Investigator Donna Blake and Deputy D.A. Mike Carleton, San Diego County District Attorney's Office; Security Director Roger Warburton and Detective Michael Newell, Naval Air Station, North Island; HazMat Specialist Nick Vent, San Diego County Environmental Health Services; Senior Investigator Barbara Naimark, State of California Health Services; Special Agent Gabrielle Carruth, Naval Investigative Service; Sergeant Bill Wolf, Office of Emergency Management, San Diego Police Department; and Private Investigator Manuel Smith, of the U.S.-Mexican border.

And many thanks to Dick and Janene Gant of the San Diego Yacht Club for the local lore and color.

FINNEGAN'S
WEEK

1

It was the face of a sociopathic killer. Granite eyes: gray, opaque, remorseless. The killer eyes narrowed, the jaw muscles bunched, the clenched lips whitened.

Fascinated, he watched as the killer began to belt out the sociopath's theme song: "Reee-grets . . . I've had a few . . . but then again . . . too few to mention."

An astonishing performance! Jack Nicholson doing Sinatra. No conscience, no regrets, Cobra Man. Or at least too *few* to mention.

Then he lifted a throw-away razor, five shaves past throwing, and shaved the killer face, nicking his chin dimple. He flicked the razor into the bathtub where it landed on the crumpled sports page, and he plastered toilet paper on the bloody cleft. He used to do a pretty fair Kirk Douglas impression, using the chin dimple to maximum advantage.

All this because *Harbor Nights*—a new late-night network melodrama—was shooting in San Diego, and they were casting for a contract-killer role. *Daily Variety* said that the killer might *appear* to get killed off in the first episode, but that he'd keep coming back at you, like Henry Kissinger or Elton John. So the job might be good for several episodes if *Harbor Nights* got a seven-show pickup.

After the shave he tried to summon forth the killer again, determined to at least read for the part. His worthless swine of an agent hadn't even called him about the role and yet there it was in yesterday's trades. That's what happens, he thought, when you have an out-of-town agent who couldn't make it in L.A., when you're an out-of-town actor who'd never even tried it in L.A. And once again he wondered if it could've all been different had he lived in L.A. instead of in *this* town.

Never believing stories about people being discovered, he believed that people discovered *it:* the opportunity to get out of your own miserable hateful body and *be* someone else for a while, without resorting to mind-altering, liver-killing drugs to accomplish the transformation.

For a moment he thought he'd found his man again while pulling on his socks, but when he ran to the mirror it told him he was wrong. Morning eye pouches caused momentary despair so he pressed a hot washcloth to the sockets, stimulating circulation. The contract killer was supposed to be in his thirties, and he'd just turned forty-five years old. Forty-five!

A wry thought: Maybe they could use a *middle-aged* sociopath. Gazing into the mirror he used an actor's trick and conjured images of middle-aged sociopaths: Fat Tony Salerno, Saddam Hussein, Ted Kennedy. Nothing worked, the killer had boogied.

The only way to catch his worthless swine of an agent was to get him when he came to the office at ten o'clock. That's what he planned to do, and he'd covered himself at his job by claiming he had a morning dental appointment.

The job. Maybe the face in the mirror could tell

him the truth about his job, a job he'd wasted himself on for twenty-three years when he should have been acting. Truth? Looking squarely in the mirror at the forty-five-year-old face, he decided there was not a single truth about which he was certain, so maybe he should run for office.

He spoke aloud to the mirror in a theatrical baritone: "Today, a typical day in Southern California, two thousand, three hundred and seventy-five unemployed actors will phone their agents. Three of them will receive callbacks, and I, I shall *not* be one of them." Then he added, "But maybe I'll catch him and tear the Velcro grin right off that smirky moosh!"

Then after jacking up his agent, he'd have to rush to work and begin the daily brain-slaughtering paper-shuffle that was his life. With a sigh that could blow out a bonfire, he adjusted his tie, brushed off his green-checked sport coat, collected his gun, badge, and handcuffs, and headed for the door. He hoped some junkie would burglarize his goddamn rathole of an apartment so he could make an inflated insurance claim.

It was 10:05 A.M. when he parked his Corvette on the street in North Park at the office of Orson Ellis Talent Unlimited. Orson was a failed talent agent, formerly of Hollywood, U.S.A., now living in San Diego, California, who'd made a "scientific" study of his failure as a Hollywood agent, scientifically concluding that it was the result of his mother not dubbing him Marty, Michael, Mort, or some other name beginning in M.

After locking his Vette, he noticed a passing coach full of elderly tourists, probably going somewhere like La Jolla, where they'd discover that they could spend two months at a timeshare at the Lawrence Welk Resort *with* unlimited golfing for what a simple "frock" would cost in a pricey La Jolla boutique. He knew that most of the seniors would be wearing walking shorts, and would have varicose veins like leeches clinging to their poor old legs. He also realized that the seniors were not *that* much older than himself. It made him think of polyps. Before entering Orson Ellis Talent Unlimited, he decided that Mother Nature is a pitiless cunt.

The agency was not impressive, but Thirtieth Street and University Avenue was not a trendy address. Orson had decorated the place to make you think you could actually get a job there, until you realized that all the inscribed photos of famous movie stars lining the walls weren't Orson's clients, only people to whom he'd sucked up during his twenty years of failure in Hollywood.

The new secretary was a lip curler, even more hostile than the last one. She wore her blond hair in a retro 1960's Afro, bigger than Danny DeVito. When she reached for the phone he noticed a clump of hair (brown) under her arms, and her toothy grin accentuated by cinnamon-brown lipstick could only be described as iguanalike, but not as warm. There was an X cap on her desk as well as a framed photo of movie director Spike Lee. He'd always had to spar with Orson's guard-dog secretaries, but this one looked like a fight to the death.

"I wanna see Orson," he said. "I don't have an appointment but I'll wait till he's *out of his meeting*. Or until he comes in through that front door, whichever happens first."

She shot him a look that could've reversed global warming, and said, "Mister Ellis is *not* in a meeting."

"Really? This must be my lucky day. I'd check my lottery tickets but I already did that three times."

"Your name?"

"Finnegan."

"First name?"

"I'm the Finnegan that calls here twice a week hoping to at least hear Orson say there's no work, except that you shine me every time, and I never hear him say anything at all."

"First name?"

"Finbar. Fin for short. Middle name, Brendan."

"It doesn't fit."

"Neither did General Schwarzkopf's little hat, but he kept that tiny thing perched on his bean anyway. I'd tell my mother you don't approve, but she's dead."

Like an eel this time: "I mean, Fin Finnegan's like John Johnson or Will Williams. Why don't you pick a professional name that fits? And if you're really a serious actor you *could* consider moving to L.A. where there's more work for *older* people."

Knowing how openly political and ethnically sensitive show biz was during this presidential campaign, Fin said, "Why don't *you* move to L.A. where your Afro fad might even last *hours* now that African American is Hollywood's craze *du jour*."

A tooth-and-claw counterattack was interrupted when Orson Ellis came panting into the office. He looked like he'd climbed ten flights of stairs, but Fin knew that Orson wouldn't use the staircase if the building was on fire. He wasn't a man to go vertical other than by mechanical means.

"*Jew*-lye! *Jew*-lye," Orson Ellis said to his secretary when he closed the door.

"Pardon me, Mister Ellis? Jew what?"

"That putz Ross Perot *had* to reenter the race!" Orson Ellis said. "*Jew*-lye. I thought he was making an anti-Semitic crack till I realized he was still apologizing for having withdrawn last July. *Jew*-lye. The cracker!" Then he noticed his client.

"Fin," Orson said, looking like his spaniel died, "Fin Finnegan. How *good* to see you, you old schlemiel."

Despite having done a thousand lunch meetings at Nate 'n Al's, Orson never got the Yiddish right. He said *kvel* when he meant *kvetch*, *schmutz* when he meant *schvitz* and *schlemiel* for *schlemazel*. Fin definitely considered himself a *schlemazel*, not a *schlemiel*.

"I thought you might call me next week if I started reminding you every night around midnight. I just dropped by to get your home address so I could start the night stalking."

"You been here long?" Orson asked.

"I been here so long her roots grew out," Fin said. Then to the secretary, "Really though, Albert Einstein did very well with that hairdo. I think you should keep it."

"I *love* this guy," Orson said to the young woman, who was glaring at Fin with a pair of scissors in her hand.

After Fin followed Orson Ellis into his private office, the fat man removed his size 52, double-breasted Armani knockoff, and plopped his bulk into an executive chair done in "blush" leather to complement the "pearl" client chairs, now that "pink" and "gray" had vanished from the designers' vocabulary.

"Want a drink? No, too early. Want an orange juice? Coffee?"

Fin was shocked by Orson Ellis's hair. All the side strands were about three feet long, and looped, swooped, and coiled across his naked skull, with some extra hair woven through it. The top hair was dyed the color of dead leaves, even though the sideburns were still gray.

"My new do," the agent said. "Whaddaya think?"

"Looks like a nest of tarantulas're eating your head. Why don't you just put a little minoxidil on your Froot Loops every morning?"

"Sensitive, that's what cops are," Orson Ellis said

to the wallpaper. Then he opened a cold Evian, since Perrier was out. "That's why I took you as a client, your sensitivity and compassion."

"And because I got your sister's kid outta that jam where he tried to punch out a whale trainer at Sea World because Shamu got his Rolex wet. By the bye, is the little prick still at large?"

"He's maturing. I think he'll eventually find himself."

"Yeah, in the gas chamber. Another victim of Doctor Spock."

"What's on your mind, Fin?" It wasn't really a question he wanted answered, and Orson Ellis punctuated it with a wet burp.

"What's on my mind? I haven't worked in fourteen months."

"Fin, you work every day," Orson Ellis reminded him, leaning back and raising his patent loafers to the top of the desk. "You're a cop, remember?"

"I was *trained* to be a cop," Fin said, "but . . ."

"You were *born* to act." Orson shook his head sadly. "You got it, kid, the addiction. I knew it first time I saw you. When was it? Five years ago?"

"Seven. In which time you got me four *one*-day jobs on that shitty private eye show, three *one*-line jobs on those movies they shot in Balboa Park that nobody but my sisters saw, and two dinner theater gigs. I got the *real* stage jobs on my own."

"How about the little theaters, Fin? Not to mention the one-act plays at the Gaslamp Quarter and the Sixth Avenue Playhouse and . . ."

"Nobody saw me there either. I need a *good* job. The last time you got me a good job that twinkle on your pinkie ring was still coal."

"It's a shame you ever got involved in that amateur theater group. Look how acting's made you dissatisfied with your real-life job. You *got* a good job. Civil service. With a pension and everything. You're a police detective, for chrissake!"

"I hate my job."

"I know, you wanna be a *movie* star. You're ready to quit the police force, move to Hollywood, right?"

"I'm not asking you to get me in something so hot you can only see it on cable, am I? This is just a crappy late night network melodrama!"

"What melodrama?"

"Don't you ever read the trades? *Harbor Nights!*"

"Oh, *that* melodrama."

"I'll bet even your new secretary knows about it and she doesn't have enough brains to churn butter. Do you hire them *with* an attitude or do you help them cultivate it, like slime mold?"

"But those tits'd raise Dracula outta his coffin at high noon, right?"

"Sure. And she's lugging enough silicone to raise the *Kitty Hawk* clear outta the water. You could lose your wristwatch in her cellulite and either she's doing a feminist armpit thing or that's a swarm of caterpillars under her arms."

"She's hot, Fin."

"You could find hotter ham in a meat locker."

"Bitter and cynical," the agent said sadly, "is what you are. Just because you got a chin dimple and a Cary Grant haircut *that I told you to get*, you ain't got what's in between. You got a pleasant Irish mug, but that's about it."

"Then get me a role playing Father O'Malley where I get to yell faith 'n begorrah and rescue street people."

"The camera looks for hope, not bitterness, Fin. Vulnerability, not cynicism. Haircuts don't matter."

"I shoulda kept my old hairdo *and* my Nehru coat. Everything comes around. Just ask your secretary."

"There was only one Elvis, Fin," the fat man informed him. "It wouldn'ta worked for you."

"I been thinking, maybe I should change my name. Fin Finnegan might not work for me. My old man's name was Timothy but everybody called him 'Fin,' so my mother decided that if they were gonna call me 'Fin' no matter what, it'd be because it was my Christian name, not my surname. But I been thinking, maybe it's too much like John Johnson or Ed Edwards?"

"Your name's not the problem, but I *have* noticed that your hair's receding. These days, your haircut looks more Clint Eastwood than Cary Grant. Have you considered a weave?"

"I don't need sensitivity or a haircut to play a contract killer. To get homicidal I only gotta think of shoulder pads Hillary picking out bad scarves and federal judges. You gonna help me or not?"

"What's an agent for? I'll make a call today. Is that acceptable?"

"As acceptable as a drive-by shooting. Get me the job."

"You think it's easy to book local actors in anything decent? This town's as avant-garde as your average Thursday night bowling league. I mean, around here a cultured person is one that don't drink dago red from a jar. Why do you think the San Diego Symphony's got more debt than Lithuania? You think I don't try? I can't even find anything to *eat* around here that don't look like a coroner's exhibit. A maggot in Musso and Frank's Hollywood garbage can eats better than the mayor of *this* burg. I'm malnourished, even!"

"Malnourished? Orson, Dennis Connor and his entire crew could sail you in the next America's Cup. Now listen, *Variety* said they're gonna use this contract killer in the episode they're prepping right *now*. Surely you can get me in to read this week."

"What age they looking for?"

"Thirties."

"Kee-rist, Fin!"

"I'm barely forty."

"You look suspiciously older."

"So do Filipino Little Leaguers but they get to play, goddamnit!"

"Okay, okay, I'll do what I can. Now go crush crime, for chrissake. Catch some crooks. Do what you do best."

"I act. *That's* what I do best. I'm only a cop by training. I was . . ."

"Born to act."

"No, I was born to sell my organs and live under bridges like a bum or wino—pardon me, now they're called *the homeless*—but I happened to take a police exam twenty-three years ago and here I am and now I hate police work and I hate cops above the rank of me which is just about everybody and I hate three ex-police wives, mine. And I got to do the fucking job five more years till I'm fifty years old or I won't get my pension and . . ."

"You're forty-five then," the agent said ruefully. "I *thought* so."

" . . . and I wish I could be immature irresponsible rich pampered spoiled and stupid with no hope of growing up or having a single sensible opinion. In short, I'd *love* to be a movie star. I'd even register Democrat and stop puking in my popcorn during Oliver Stone movies if I thought you could get me in the cultural elite. But I'll settle for a one-day bit as a contract killer in that chickenshit TV show before it gets canceled! Okay?"

"Okay okay, kid. Calm down," Orson said. "I'll get to work on it right away. I know who's casting that show. They'll like the idea, a real live San Diego cop playing a contract killer. Now I want you to do something for *me*, okay?"

"What?"

"I got a lawyer-pal. He's got a client. He wants to know what the DEA has on his client and . . ."

"Forget it. I still have five years to do. I'm not risking my pension."

"He's a respectable lawyer for God's sake."

"Sure. *Respectable* lawyer means he was never caught taking meetings with the Medellín Cartel, or doing lunch with BCCI bankers, and he hasn't been indicted by a federal grand jury. That's a *respectable* lawyer. Forget it."

"Okay okay. Let's you and me do lunch . . ."

"If you say *someday*, I'll kill you."

"I was gonna say *tomorrow*. Let's do lunch tomorrow."

"I'm too busy. Tomorrow's the day I fill my ice-cube trays. Look, Orson, I'm not asking for a movie with a Swedish director and subtitles, but I'm as serious as a tumor on your willy."

The agent studied his client thoughtfully for a moment and said, "I've seen this before, Fin. It's real tough for an actor to hit the benchmarks: forty, forty-five, fifty. You take it harder than normal sane people. Acting's an addiction, an obsession. Most of my clients, they need Prozac more than they need an agent."

"Well maybe I should just chuck it all and go sell derby hats to women in Bolivia."

"Just remember, no matter how down and depressed you get . . ."

"Yeah? What?"

"Tomorrow is another day."

"That one'll have me slapping my forehead for hours," the detective said, standing up to leave. "Why didn't I think of that? Now let's see if I can accomplish something *real* hard, like getting past your secretary without getting spit at."

Orson said, "If I can get them to let you read,

please wear a decent outfit. That sport coat's older than Hugh Hefner and even more tacky. Don't pick your teeth with a matchbook, and try to remember, Fin, tomorrow's another day."

Before the detective exited, he said: "Fuck you, Orson, and fuck Scarlett O'Hara."

2

The father of Jules Temple had always worried a great deal about Jules's emotional development, especially as his son neared adulthood. Jules's father had become conversant with certain clinical designations after Jules had been expelled from two private schools, and later when, as a college sophomore, Jules had been accused of what came to be called "date rape."

Jules's father, Harold Temple, was a corporate lawyer whose own father had been a San Diego superior court judge, so Jules's disgrace had been particularly hard to bear, but Jules's mother had been able to compartmentalize her feelings when it came to their only child. Harold Temple had been told by more than one of his son's therapists that Jules's mother lived in a world of denial, and it continued until her death in 1977.

Still, Jules Temple had managed to reach his twenty-fifth birthday in 1978 without having been convicted of a crime, thus satisfying the terms of his grandfather's trust. Jules then inherited $350,000 and had invested it and lived well as a real estate developer until after the Reagan years when the bottom dropped out of California's real estate–driven economy. Jules Temple then found himself broke, divorced, and back home living with his father in the Point Loma hilltop home overlooking the bay of San Diego.

Upon the approach of his thirty-fifth birthday, Jules had had a very significant conversation with his father. It took place in the study where Harold Temple spent most of his days. The floral chintz sofa in the study had been selected by his late wife, along with a nineteenth-century walnut bench decorated with elaborate needlepoint. Harold Temple hated all of his furniture except for the ugly old mahogany desk he'd inherited from his father, the judge.

Jules poured himself a double Scotch that evening, sensing he'd need it, and he sat down across the desk in a client chair. Jules thought it highly appropriate and very lawyerlike of the old boy to separate them with a desk. Jules couldn't remember ever having sat on his father's lap, even as a tot.

His father was dressed in pajamas, slippers and a silk robe. The old man's hair was wispy by then, and his back was bent from arthritis. His skin had thinned and grown transparent, and in the semi-darkness Harold Temple was as vivid as a Rembrandt. The older man had suffered a stroke that left him with paralyzed facial muscles and made his speech hard to understand.

"Son," his father had said to him on that fateful evening, "I'm extremely worried about you."

"Really?" Jules said with his trademark wry smile. "I wonder why."

For a moment, the father silently studied the son. Jules was blond like the Temples, tall and good-looking. Harold Temple was certain that his son was quite intelligent though he hadn't had decent grades since he'd been a seventh grader. Jules was a good golfer and sometimes played in tournaments at the La Jolla Country Club where Harold Temple had been a longtime member, and Jules frequently sailed at the San Diego Yacht Club. In short, Harold Temple believed that Jules had everything needed for success, but his son was a failure by any measure whatsoever.

"I've been reading a lot," Harold Temple began awkwardly.

"Hot novels, Dad?" Jules took a large swallow of Scotch and grinned wryly.

"This thing . . . this stroke that I've suffered, it's made me think a lot about you, about your . . . personality. In case . . . if something should *happen* to me I'd like to know that you'll be all right."

Then Harold Temple stared into his son's eyes, dreading that he'd see a flicker of *anticipation*. Fearing that Jules would say, "Is there any danger, Dad?" with mock concern.

But Jules said nothing. Jules was, as usual, non-committal, uninvolved.

His father continued: "I've had a certain worry for a long time, long before your marriage. Before your business went sour. About your personality and character."

"What about it?"

"You're clever and charming, but manipulative, Jules. You've always been like that. You were always the coolest one in the house every time you got into trouble, when your mother and I were yelling our heads off."

"A young man sowing wild oats," Jules said, finishing the Scotch and standing to refill his glass.

"Not always," his father said, thinking of the coed upon whom Jules had forced himself. That one had cost Harold Temple $50,000 through an intermediary, until the girl and her family agreed not to prosecute. "I think you've never had enough self-doubt to yell or get emotional about anything."

"What *are* you getting at?" Jules asked.

"It's that I've never sensed a feeling of . . . shame in you."

"Shame?"

"Or guilt or remorse. I must say, not ever."

"Shame about what? Guilt about what? About the fact that my development company went broke? Should I feel shame about hard economic times? I tried, didn't I? I risked my capital. What do you want from me?"

"I wasn't talking about that, son," Harold Temple said, and then his left leg started to shake. This had been happening a lot, a trembling of his limbs that he couldn't control.

"What then?"

"There are . . . terms for people who don't have empathy, who don't understand how their actions can hurt other people."

"Other people? What other people?"

"Your wife. Your child."

With a trace of a sneer: "*Ex*-wife, the bitch."

"She's the mother of your child."

"I see my child. I see Sally every chance I get," Jules said. "I'd send checks if I had any money!"

Harold Temple knew it was a lie, but he continued: "I worry that there's not a *complete* person inside you. You haven't outgrown a certain . . . incompleteness."

"I see," Jules said, looking past his father at the portrait of his grandfather on the wall. "What crimes am I guilty of? What have I done that's so terrible?"

"Call it a certain . . . moral insensitivity," the older man said, in great distress. "You haven't been involved in criminal activity, thank god, but . . ."

"You think I'm capable of it. That I'll disgrace *you*."

"Jules, I've heard stories about the investors in your development company. Your actions bordered on criminal fraud."

"They lost, I lost, we all lost. Sour grapes, hard times. What else, Dad? Let's get all my faults out *on your desk* so we don't miss anything."

"This isn't easy for me, son."

"For me this is a picnic, right? All this psychobabble."

"This isn't getting us anywhere, Jules," his father said, "so I might as well tell you that I've had my will rewritten. When I die you're getting an allowance of two thousand dollars a month for five years. And that's it."

"*And* the house?"

"No house, no property of any kind, no insurance. No more than two thousand a month for five years. You won't starve, but you'll have to get off your butt and make something of yourself."

"And where does the balance of your estate go?"

"To various charities."

Jules put the glass on his father's desk, then turned and headed for the door of the study. But he paused and said, "Thanks, Dad. Thanks for giving me everything, and then taking it away. You've been swell. And please don't tell me it's for my own good."

"I wouldn't tell you that, Jules," Harold Temple said. "Not anymore."

"Maybe I should just move out now," Jules said, and was shocked when his father replied, "That might be a good idea. Get out on your own and start scratching like everyone else has to do."

That evening Harold Temple wrote his son a check for $5,000. He called it "seed money." And that was that.

Jules packed his things and left the next morning, moving in with Margie, a divorced cocktail waitress he'd been dating. She said he could stay until he got on his feet. It was while living with her, after he'd grown desperate, that Jules Temple again became an entrepreneur.

The idea came to him when he was baby-sitting for Margie, who had the late shift at a nightclub in downtown San Diego's Gaslamp Quarter. He'd spent night after miserable night in front of the TV, drinking the cheap Scotch that Margie bought at discount outlets. Margie's seven-year-old daughter, Cynthia, had been begging him to play dolls with her when it happened: the idea!

He'd heard of the pedophile's motto: "Eight is too late." Cynthia was only seven, but she looked even younger. She was very pretty, but not a terribly bright child, not nearly as bright as Jules's own daughter had been at that age. Cynthia was a lot like her mother, he thought.

The next day Jules was in several adult magazine and book shops in downtown San Diego looking for chickenhawk and pedophile publications. When he got back to the apartment, he studied many photos of naked children in provocative poses. Then he homed in on the ads in those publications to learn how they were set up.

Later that evening when Margie was at work, Jules suggested to Cynthia that they play "movie star."

"You have to promise me that you won't tell Mommy," he said. "Cross your heart. It's *our* secret."

"Okay," the child said, and obeyed her director's instruction to the letter.

Jules did her makeup as best he could, using Margie's cosmetics. He believed that scant clothing would be more titillating than nudity, so he posed her in panties and ballet slippers, trying to imitate the young models. Essentially, he wanted a seven-year-old Madonna.

Jules knew that he didn't dare have more than one photo session because Cynthia might accidentally spill the beans. By the time that Cynthia *had* informed her mother of Jules's "movie star" game, Margie had already kicked him out for making long-distance calls, *lots* of long-distance calls all over the country that he said were "just business." Margie never understood that his business intimately concerned her daughter.

Jules had bought ad space in three pedophile publications. His ad included a photo of the child and listed a post office box in downtown San Diego. Within two weeks, more than sixty pedophiles had responded in letters directed to "Samantha's Uncle."

Almost all the pedophiles used post office boxes of their own, or general delivery, and within days each would receive glossy photos of the little girl. Along with the photos was a typed letter:

Dear Sir,

My name is Samantha. I am six years old and have been taught many things that will please you. If you would like to meet me and learn what I can do, please call my Uncle Desmond any time between 10:00 A.M. and 2:00 P.M. PST.

Love,
Samantha

Jules Temple went to the trouble of switching his answering service every two months during a year in which letters were exchanged with pedophiles as far away as Alaska. He ultimately received more than two hundred phone calls, and decided that nearly half of them were worth tape-recording surreptitiously.

During the pedophile's recorded conversations with "Uncle Desmond," Jules would usually manage to solicit a callback number, and surprisingly, the caller often gave his true name and address when asking for more photos, this after long and lascivious conversations with Uncle Desmond about Samantha.

Shortly thereafter, selected "Friends of Samantha" would receive a small parcel from Uncle Desmond which they would excitedly open, only to find an audiotape rather than more photos. On the audiotape would be the caller's own voice recorded during his lewd conversation with Uncle Desmond wherein he'd negotiated terms for the use of Samantha. The conversations included specific questions and answers about all the things Uncle Desmond had taught the little girl. There wasn't a caller who wasn't stunned to hear how explicit his own excited phone call had been.

At the end of the tape would be a message from Uncle Desmond that varied slightly, depending upon how much Jules had been able to learn during his conversation and correspondence with the pedophile, and how much Jules sensed the pedophile was worth. The message was:

> Hi (using the caller's name). *I have several more copies of this tape which I am considering sending to your local police department, as well as to the FBI and to your local newspaper. I might even include a copy to your closest relative. I think you know who I mean, don't you? I shudder to think what your family and friends will say when they hear your own voice telling me what you want Samantha to do to you and how much you are willing to pay for it.*
>
> *You are very lucky that I happen to need money at the moment. If you will immediately send cash in the amount of* (this would vary), *I will send you the duplicate audiotapes of your phone conversation telling Uncle Desmond what*

you intend to do to this helpless little six-year-old. I'd better hear from you by next week.

Jules Temple would often go so far as to hire a street person to pick up envelopes from his post office box and carry them to his car parked a safe distance away. But finally, Jules decided that he needn't have gone to such lengths. He was always overestimating people, and in this case he'd overestimated the authorities. About half a dozen pedophiles summoned up the nerve to go to the police and admit to being extortion victims, but the police and postal authorities had never got to a post office box that hadn't already been closed.

In that one year, Jules made $123,000 (tax free, of course) before the pedophile publications began printing warnings about Uncle Desmond. Cynthia's photos ended up in the files of several law enforcement agencies, but never were traced back to her or to her mother.

During that same year Jules Temple's father died after his second stroke, having kept his word to leave his son a stipend only. Jules did not visit his comatose father in the hospital, claiming he was too busy expanding his capital base. Having acted upon a hot tip from a country club acquaintance, Jules had invested the money in a mismanaged waste hauling company, a business field that was opening up with unlimited possibilities for someone like himself. Jules called his company Green Earth Hauling and Disposal.

One of Jules's first moves as a waste hauler was to form a corporation with a bogus president, in this case a former real estate agent of Mexican descent who'd worked for Jules in land development. Raul Medina drew a salary of $1,500 a month for doing nothing more than signing documents from time to time. Raul

Medina never set foot in Green Earth Hauling and Disposal, spending most of his time at home nursing a chronic back problem.

Jules owned forty-nine percent of the stock in the Green Earth corporation and the other fifty-one percent was "owned" by Raul Medina. All of the trucks, equipment, and material assets were transferred to the company by Jules, who took back a note from Raul Medina for twice the assets' value. Jules subleased the property to the company for twice what he paid to his landlord, and siphoned off all profits except for the $1,500 a month that Raul Medina received.

Because of Raul Medina's Hispanic surname, Jules had been able to secure government contracts that nonminority haulers could not get. And Jules was often contracted to haul hazardous material from military bases, some of which came from military facilities halfway around the world.

The generator of hazardous waste would list in the Environmental Protection Agency's "cradle to grave" numbered documents what the contents of the waste consisted of. The waste could then theoretically be easily traced from the generator of the waste, through the transporter, and finally to the disposal facility. Ultimately, the disposal facility was supposed to inform the EPA when the waste was incinerated or otherwise destroyed.

Four years later, after Jules found a promising buyer for his business, he and Raul Medina signed documents wherein the major stockholder paid off all notes and commissions to the minor stockholder, receiving nothing from the sale. But Raul Medina had no complaints. The $1,500 a month had been nice while it lasted, and Jules promised him that if his next commercial endeavor could benefit by minority preference, Jules and Raul Medina could make a similar arrangement.

Green Earth Hauling and Disposal had prospered because Jules Temple was a businessman who quickly discovered ways to cut corners in order to avoid the red tape inherent in this industry. Some of the ways in which he did that were exotic, some were quite simple, but Jules seldom tried to cut corners with military waste, not unless it could be ascertained that it could be safely mixed with other waste he was hauling. *Safely* for Jules only meant that it would be untraceable to him.

Sometimes, Jules just couldn't resist saving time and money with the waste generated by civilian companies, such as one called Southbay Agricultural Supply. The owner of the company was an ex-farmer named Burl Ralston who was making a lot more money selling supplies than he'd ever made on his sorry hundred-acre farm in the Imperial Valley. Burl Ralston was not a man for unnecessary paperwork and he was not one to ask a lot of questions, not when Jules Temple was consistently able to undercut the competition with his hauling bids, thus saving money for Burl Ralston.

Southbay Agricultural Supply and Green Earth Hauling and Disposal had just struck a deal whereby Jules Temple's employees would pick up a fifty-five-gallon drum full of something very toxic: Guthion. The pesticide had been consigned to a customer in Arizona, but had got mixed inadvertently with a small amount of weed oil, so it had to be disposed of ASAP. Jules Temple's low bid was for $500 to haul the Guthion, but as frequently happened with Jules, he wanted *cash* from Burl, to be given in an envelope to the driver. Green Earth's truckers were accustomed to receiving cash, and after successful transactions, Jules often would slip a $20 bill to the trucker as a "bonus" for good work.

From Jules's point of view, he could not afford to haul extremely hazardous waste if he had to transport it to a Texas incinerator for legal disposal, so he decided that item #11 on the manifest should list the Guthion as "waste flammable liquid." That way it could be hauled to a disposal site at a Los Angeles oil refinery when Jules had another load heading that way.

When the cash deal was struck, Jules said on the phone, "I'll do the manifest for you, Burl, so you just have to sign off and pay my driver. What's your EPA number?"

Thus, when truckers Abel Durazo and Shelby Pate showed up at Southbay Agricultural Supply in their twenty-four-foot bobtail van, Abel handed the completed and numbered seven-page manifest to the waste generator, Burl Ralston, who signed off without worrying about item #11 on the manifest. He could honestly say that "waste flammable liquid" was a legally correct description of a little oil and a lot of Guthion, if not morally correct. But Burl Ralston was confident that Jules would see that it got disposed of properly, with no harm done.

After the haulers left Southbay Agricultural Supply with the envelope containing $500, Burl Ralston put one manifest copy into an envelope to send by certified mail to Sacramento; then he filed his copy. The truckers had not asked Burl Ralston for a precise description of the material in the drum. In fact, *no* waste hauler had ever asked him. But Burl Ralston had informed Jules Temple that it was Guthion, hadn't he? And the skull and bones placard was on the drum, wasn't it? Burl Ralston went back into the warehouse to continue his inventory without giving that drum of poison another thought. It was Jules Temple's problem now, and probably would be the last deal they ever did together in that Jules was selling his business.

Trucker Shelby Pate folded the manifest copies around the money envelope, and put the packet in the zippered pocket of his leather jacket.

3

"Bad Dog" was not a respectable name for a young woman, her mother had said to her when she was home on leave.

"It's just navy, Mom," Bobbie had insisted. "Gimme a break!"

"Navy? I call it crude. That's the kinda brutal attitude toward women that caused the Tailhook scandal where all those horny pilots mauled the women in that Las Vegas nightclub."

"Hotel. The Las Vegas Hilton. And they're aviators. They land on carriers at night in pitching seas. They're *aviators*."

"Rapists is more like it. A hundred drunken rapists. I know what they land on at night."

"The navy's working on sexist attitudes," Bobbie had argued. "The secretary of the navy resigned, for crying out loud. Three admirals got stripped of their commands."

"The women were the ones got stripped. What'd the one admiral say? Female pilots . . . excuse me, *aviators* are like hookers or go-go dancers? I wish you'd consider leaving it. You don't belong in the navy. You're not even twenty-eight years old. Your life's *ahead* of you."

"I love the navy. I love my job."

"You love being called Bad Dog?"

"It's not meant in any mean or sexist way. It's my name. Bobbie Ann Doggett. B-A-D. Doggett. Bad Dog. It's natural."

Going home on leave to Kenosha, Wisconsin, had come to mean spending a few days with her parents, seeing her married brothers and their kids, and going out on the town with two high school girlfriends, both divorced. A surprising number of her classmates were gone from the Kenosha area, and before the leave was up, Bobbie was ready to go back to her *real* home. Back to the navy. At present, back to Naval Air Station, North Island, on the Coronado peninsula, across from downtown San Diego, where she served as a "command investigator."

Whenever she'd tried to explain to her mother what sweet shore duty it was, and how lucky, and yes, *honored*, she felt to have the job, her mother would heave a sigh. And as soon as it was tactful, her mother would bring up the name of some blind-date yuppie puppy who worked with Bobbie's brother at his insurance office.

Her father had given up long ago. Having served in Korea as a dogface grunt, he knew a lifer when he saw one. When Bobbie had made 2nd class petty officer during the Gulf War, her dad had sent a congratulatory telegram that caught up with her in Saudi Arabia where her tender serviced the fighting ships. That's the kind of ship women got put on, big ships like tenders, machine shops that float. The male personnel, both officers and enlisted men, made bets on how many pregnancies would occur during their sea tour, and what made Bobbie *really* mad was that there were quite a few. Dumb. Sailors of either sex could be so *dumb*.

Her defense of the navy to her mother was always upbeat. To other females, navy or civilian, Bobbie said that the Tailhook aviators who assaulted the women as they ran a "gauntlet" ought to be sent to federal prison. There they should have their pubic hair shaved into hearts after which they should be made to run a gauntlet in the shower room between two rows of only those psychopaths who'd been longest in solitary confinement. That's what Bobbie said to women other than her mother. Still, Bobbie Ann Doggett truly believed that in her present assignment she had the greatest job in the navy, and she wouldn't trade with any sailor on ship or shore.

On the day that Bobbie left home to return to the base, her teary-eyed mother gave her some cookies to take on the plane. Her mother was at least glad that Bobbie's weight was "just right." Her mother always thought Liz Taylor was "just right" before her diets, and "drawn and haggard" after them.

When Bobbie got harassed at the airport terminal by a persistent Krishna who couldn't've been stopped with a blowtorch, she tossed the homemade cookies to the skinhead, saying, "Phone your mom, Dribble-lips."

On her first day back, Bobbie decided to bicycle to work. She could bike it because she lived nearby in an over-the-garage apartment at the rear of a residence belonging to a pair of elderly sisters. It would've been a lot cheaper to live in the barracks and eat navy chow, and her off-base allowance didn't cover her rent and food by any means, but the freedom and privacy meant a lot to Bobbie. Another reason she rode her bike that day was because she had to shoehorn her hips into a mulberry slim-skirt that she'd worn comfortably before going home on leave.

Even without her sweet assignment as a command investigator, Bobbie Ann Doggett would've considered any shore duty at North Island to be primo. NAS North Island had a twenty-four-hour operational air field, the only one of its kind in the state of California, and was headquarters for the largest overhaul and repair organization in the world, as well as being home to two carriers: USS *Ranger* and USS *Kitty Hawk*, each ship bringing with it about 2,500 personnel.

North Island was the birthplace of naval aviation, the point from which Charles Lindbergh took off bound for St. Louis, New York, Paris and immortality. The air station covers about 2,800 acres and requires a force of 24,000 workers, both military and civilian. It is a small city within the small city of Coronado, across the harbor from the sixth-largest city in America, San Diego.

Like any small city, NAS North Island had its own police and fire departments and its own crime. Bobbie Ann Doggett was a plainclothes detective assigned to investigate those crimes, most of which were misdemeanors. When they were felony crimes, the Naval Investigative Service usually handled the cases.

Because she was a command investigator Bobbie was "designated" by the base commander to interrogate anyone regardless of rank. This meant that an E-5 like Bobbie could, theoretically, grill a command officer. She hadn't felt so powerful since those days when she'd first earned the "crow" of a petty officer, taking on the responsibility of command over subordinates.

Hers would be an exciting job for an E-5 of either sex, but was especially so for Bobbie, whose career hadn't been easy but *had* been interesting. She'd especially loved the schools: master-at-arms school where she'd learned about policing, and later, investigator's school.

There'd been two tours at sea, one of them in the Gulf War, and Bobbie had learned very quickly that master-at-arms is not a popular rate on a navy ship. She'd been made to feel like a cop from the very beginning, in a job that didn't attract the most feminine of females. A lot of the female masters-at-arms were butch and looked it. But it was easier for Bobbie to deal with them than with the male personnel who assumed *she* was gay because of her master-at-arms rate, and because she preferred to wear her blond curly hair loose, short and uncoiffed, avoiding eyeliner, skin toners, and excessive lipstick. Bobbie figured that was their problem.

The funny thing was, Bobbie Ann Doggett didn't mind feeling like a cop. She'd never dated a cop but had always wanted to, and like the rest of her generation she'd grown up watching television cop shows. The first time Bobbie got to introduce herself as "Detective Doggett," it was *awesome*.

Bobbie worked with two other investigators, both civilians, both men. She was the only military investigator in that nontraditional job. Like a city police detective, she wore civilian clothes, and unless something unusual occurred, she worked 7:30 A.M. to 4:00 P.M., Monday through Friday.

Her civilian colleagues were okay guys, but they *were* civilians, and much older. They didn't bring the same enthusiasm that a young military investigator brought to the job, and no wonder—they made about $1,000 less a month than their counterparts at nearby San Diego Police Department. In fact, when they factored in Bobbie's pay and her military fringe benefits, she cost the navy twenty-five thousand a year more than her civilian colleagues did.

Civilian investigators tended to stay on the job a long time except for one who'd recently resigned to take a position with a police department in northern

California. He was the one who took a look at Bobbie
Ann Doggett and said in a stage whisper to a senior
chief petty officer: "Bad Dog, my ass. Five foot three
in platforms. It's what the navy's come to: runts 'n
cunts!"

On the evening he'd said goodbye, Bobbie promised him she'd only sniffle, and try not to grieve
hysterically when she saw his taillights disappear.
The pissant!

Bobbie sometimes toyed with the fantasy of retir-
ing from the navy after twenty years and then joining
the San Diego P.D. She'd be only thirty-eight years
old, still young enough to do police work. But that
was almost eleven years away. Right now, Bobbie was
doing a job she loved, and she wanted to do it for the
full three-year tour and maybe even get an extension.
Sea duty she did *not* love.

When Fin Finnegan was busy learning that tomorrow is another day, Bobbie Ann Doggett had already
settled back into the office routine. The investigators
and all other security personnel worked out of one-
story wood-frame buildings just inside the main gate,
buildings that had served as the base hospital in the
1920's, as evidenced by the extra-wide doorways.

Both of her colleagues said they were glad to
see Bobbie back, but that it was mildly depressing
to have someone so happy and cheerful around the
office again. They asked her if Kenosha had changed
much. And did the kids still go to school with animal
traps in their book bags. And did they have credit
cards by now or did they still trade in pelts. The
female civilians gave her a welcoming hug with no
wisecracks.

Bobbie especially liked the oldest investigator,
Reggie Cole, who claimed he'd been at North Island
since aids were admirals' helpers, but the guy smoked
more than Kuwait in the war. During the lunch hour,

Bobbie told Reggie she was going to mosey over to the post office to buy some stamps, but really, she wanted to get some fresh air. Even though he'd taken to smoking outside at the insistence of everyone, Reggie reeked like an ashtray. It was in his hair and in his pores.

She had to hike up her skirt to mount the bike, and three sailors in civvies made the usual sounds of adolescent angst that teenagers make when they see the exposed thigh of an older woman. Bobbie looked at them and considered that in little more than two years she'd be *thirty*. Those sailors were children.

Bobbie decided to ride along the quay and sniff the ocean breeze blowing in from the sea on that warm October day. She thought that San Diego had America's most beautiful big-city harbor, maybe one of the world's most beautiful big-city harbors. It was incredibly clean, and the postmodern architecture looked acceptable in the slanting autumn light. Geometric glass buildings—hexes, octagons, emerald shapes—dominated the skyline. Bobbie didn't like smoked and mirrored windows, and there was a lot of that.

In fact, she didn't like much of the new architectural experiments. Horton Plaza, where she often shopped, was a multicolored set of mammoth Lego toys with a dizzying maze of walkways. She thought the upper level should post suicide-prevention signs for trapped patrons. Bobbie figured that San Diego must be a haven for architects who flunked drafting in their freshman year.

But the fortuitous geography of her adopted city defied the modern architects' efforts. Short of employing nuclear devices, nobody could compromise the site of San Diego, with its promontories, and the glorious harbor sparkling and glittering at twilight when the sun was setting beyond Point Loma.

Bobbie's favorite time was twilight when the city

view softened the geometry of the modern skyline and made the buildings glow in hues ranging from rose to burnt sienna. Even the sandstone color of the air station was warmed by that light, and the naval base then reminded Bobbie of an old California mission.

Bobbie was interested in nuclear-powered attack submarines, and several times had visited the sub base in the lee of Point Loma, even going aboard one of the huge boats that carried well over a hundred people. And when she was there she always visited the Cabrillo National Monument named for the Portuguese who discovered San Diego Harbor in the sixteenth century. From Point Loma, she could look south and see all of the twelve-mile harbor, and maybe take a tour through the old lighthouse.

That was the kind of San Diego architecture that Bobbie loved, the nineteenth-century lighthouse on top of the point, and the newer one down at the water's edge, still operated by the U.S. Coast Guard. She thought it would be interesting to be stationed out there and watch the migration of California gray whales. Certainly it'd be better than a tour of sea duty.

And Bobbie Ann Doggett loved the lighthouse because during the wars of the twentieth century it had represented the last look at their country for thousands of American sailors. The final look that some would *ever* have.

Now that she was back Bobbie had to make some short-term plans. First, she'd begin a rigorous aerobics program at the women's fitness center. Maybe she'd start swimming laps, anything to get rid of the disgusting blubber that delighted her mom. The thought made her pedal more vigorously.

While cruising along the quay, Bobbie saw that there were a large number of tractor-trailers and smaller vans loading and unloading at the monster warehouses, buildings huge enough to receive the contents of ships. She noticed an AOE docked at the quay wall. The big oiler had picked up two H-46 helicopters at Johnston Atoll, the U.S. possession just south of the Hawaiian chain. The choppers were in the process of being unloaded by crane, and they looked like huge larvae in white cocoons of rubberized plastic.

The ship had some other cargo that the skipper had picked up on Johnston Island in what the supply people called an "opportunistic lift." The "lift" consisted of drums with special flanged ring seals, the flange being constructed so that it could easily be handled by robot arms. Inside the big drums were smaller drums, vacuum-sealed like giant cans of peanuts. On each outer drum was a packing list and a port through which one could look to see the packing surrounding the inner peanut cans. The packing contained granules that would, with a change in color, inform the viewer of a toxic leak inside. At that point the outer drum would be gingerly handled and not opened except in a clean and protected environment. Some of the less hazardous waste such as two drums of contaminated fuel mixtures had been dollied into the warehouse to await the civilian contractor who would haul it away.

As Bobbie Ann Doggett bicycled, fretting about being ten pounds past bikini-secure, a navy bosun was bitching to another that there was nobody there to take control of all the waste they'd off-loaded.

The older bosun said, "The navy only knows how to make chemicals, not get rid a them. And there's never a civilian contractor comes when they're supposed to. You think a civilian contractor gives a shit?"

"If they want the goddamn navy contract they should give a shit," said the younger one.

"Scope those bazooms!" the older bosun said, as Bobbie cycled past. "Where's *she* work?"

"Careful," said the younger. "Nowadays they'll

give you brig time you even whistle at a babe. Either that or you end up with that whiny Congresswoman Schroeder going on TV and calling you a sex fiend like the Tailhookers. She's as worthless as Bill Clinton's war record. I'd rather sleep with an armadillo."

"Clinton'll fix her soon as he's elected," the older bosun said. "I don't give a shit if he never served a day in the Cub Scouts. It takes a bimbo boffer like him to straighten out all the bitches in Washington."

"Let's go get a hamburger," the younger one said. "These goddamn eighteen-wheelers around here? I got a headache already from all the fumes."

During lunch hour there were only a few riggers and warehouse personnel still by the quay wall when a bobtail van approached the truck gate of NAS North Island. The contractor had recently bought the twenty-four-foot bobtail van, and barely had time to paint GREEN EARTH HAULING AND DISPOSAL on the doors.

4

"You know where to go?" the navy sentry at the gate asked the Mexican driver who'd been given a temporary gate pass.

The Mexican had a lean handsome face and a wide friendly mouth. "We come here many times," he said to the sentry. "Many times."

The sentry waved the bobtail onto the base, then saluted a lieutenant commander who drove in behind the van.

Abel Durazo looked over at his companion Shelby Pate, and said, "Time to wake up."

He never used his partner's given name. With his accent it sounded like Chel-bee. Shelby Pate budged only to swipe at a string of spit dribbling down his unshaven chin.

The Mexican had spent his first year at Green Earth Hauling and Disposal feeling vaguely uncomfortable around gringo coworkers, although Abel spoke good English from having worked in the L.A. produce market for eleven years before coming back south to San Diego. But even the first time he'd slipped across the international border thirteen years ago as

a boy of sixteen, avoiding both Mexican bandits and
la migra, the Border Patrol—crawling through a no-
man's-land they called the Canyon of the Dead—even
then, he'd never have felt intimidated around gringos
like Shelby Pate.

Shelby Pate, whom the Mexican workers called
Buey—the ox—was comfortable to be with, and not
threatening to the Mexicans even though he was enor-
mous and biker-ugly. Shelby called him *Flaco*, because
the young Mexican was so thin.

"Wake up, Buey!" Abel said.

His companion's head bobbed and he sat upright.
"Huh?"

"Time to work."

The ox rooted in his nose, then wiped his finger
on his filthy black jeans. He was thirty-one, two years
older than Abel, and he talked so fast that the Mexican
understood him about half the time. The ox had four
tattoos on his arms, which were supposed to represent
a pack of killer cats: tiger, panther, lion, puma. To
Abel they looked like mongrel dogs, maybe coyotes.
Abel always wondered where the ox got such bad
tattoos, guessing it was in jail.

"When we gettin somethin to eat, dude?" Shelby
wanted to know, picking up his Mötley Crüe cap from
the seat of the cab and of course putting it on backwards, pulling his dead-straw hair down the back of
his neck. He used to have a dental bridge, but lost
it during a methamphetamine orgy that turned into a
barroom brawl. Abel thought the missing front tooth
actually improved the ox's looks, making him appear
more comical.

"Always eat," Abel said. "Eat drink eat. Joo too
fat, Buey."

Shelby had only been working at Green Earth
Hauling and Disposal for six months. He was big as a
forklift, blubbery fat, but very strong and willing. And

he'd take orders from anybody in the yard, Mexican, black or gringo. Abel didn't think the ox would ever be promoted to driver, but he didn't seem to care. Shelby came to work on time, did what he was told, then took his paycheck and spent it on methamphetamine and tequila in the biker bars in Imperial Beach and National City. The other workers underestimated the ox, but Abel did not. The Mexican sensed Shelby's cunning and street intelligence.

Once, Abel had stopped for a drink with the ox at his favorite biker hangout, Hogs Wild, but a redneck biker in the saloon said he didn't like drinking with a Mexican, so Abel turned and left. The ox left with him, but first he found out which Harley the redneck owned and slashed the leather seat with his buck knife.

"How long you figure it's gonna take us today?" Shelby asked, yawning.

"We finish by seex o'clock." Then Abel added, "Maybe later."

"How 'bout lendin me twenny bucks?"

"No way," Abel said. "I broke, Buey."

"Me, I'm *always* broke," Shelby said. "The boss is a cheap prick, ain't he? I'll be glad to see the last a that dude."

By seeing the last of the boss, Shelby Pate was referring to the fact that Green Earth Hauling and Disposal had recently been sold, and was about to close escrow. The new owner was cost-conscious, and had already said he'd have to lay off eight workers including Abel Durazo and Shelby Pate. Their boss, Jules Temple, had suggested that Abel and Shelby start looking for new jobs right away. Jules did not offer his assistance in relocation, or severance pay, or bonuses of any kind.

Abel Durazo was absolutely convinced that Jules Temple wouldn't know him if they passed on the street, he being just another Mexican who worked for a lot less money than a union driver.

"Boss all the same" was all the Mexican said.

"He pays you chump change. Know what a *real* driver gets for haulin poison waste?"

Abel knew that a *real* driver would be a gringo, not a former "Rodino" like himself, who felt lucky to have such a job. He'd been called a Rodino because of Congressman Rodino, who'd sponsored the legislation by which Abel had applied for and got permanent resident status. Under the plan, Mexican nationals had been allowed to avoid deportation by the Immigration and Naturalization Service if they could prove they'd been in the U.S. prior to January 1, 1981, and through May 1987. The "proof" often consisted of rent receipts, school records, work records, payroll stubs, utility receipts, birth or marriage records. Cynics said that it could also work if the Mexicans showed up with "Made in the U.S." clothing labels, ticket stubs from a Springsteen concert, whatever.

During the Rodino boom, American farmers and other employers often "sold names" to Mexicans, names of former employees who'd been in the U.S. for years, but who'd gone back south, or died, or disappeared. The future Rodinos could then apply under those names, and Mexican lawyers could supply bogus Social Security cards to match them. Lucky and smart Mexican nationals ended up with their resident "green cards" (which were no longer green, but blue) and were entitled to remain legally in the United States.

When the Green Earth van got to the quay there were other trucks already there, mostly eighteen-wheelers unloading at the mammoth warehouses on what was a very busy day.

Shelby said, "Look at all them lazy deck apes, smokin 'n jokin. Can't tell me anybody works in the navy. I shoulda been a swab."

"Een the navy?"

"Yeah, but they don't want guys that been in jail."

"Why een jail?" Abel asked.

"For GTA once," Shelby said. "Drove a hot Porsche for six months 'fore they nailed me. Wouldn'ta got me 'cept I was usin too much meth then. My brain got fried from snortin all that crank. Used to do a teener every night."

"Teener?"

"Teener means one sixteenth of an ounce. One eighth is called a eightball. You ever do cringe? That's what we called meth, *cringe*."

"No," Abel said. "Leetle marijuana sometime."

"Second time I got busted, I was workin for a guy had a big tanker rig. He figured a way to tap in to this oil line that went from California to Utah. When the line started operatin he installed a spigot and hose. The stupid oil company thought the atmospheric conditions caused the oil drop and never did figure it out. I got in on it toward the end. I use to sell the oil to guys at truck stops. A helicopter finally spotted a big spill in the desert and got suspicious and that's how it got shut down."

"Joo was caught?" Abel asked.

"Not for that. Only for stealin a goddamn Harley hog. Shoulda stayed in the oil business, but no, I had to steal that bike. Hard for the cops to get serial numbers off crude oil, right, Flaco?"

The ox snorted like a horse at that one, pausing to hawk up a lunger and spit it out the window. The Mexican didn't understand what he meant.

"Green Earth!" Abel shouted to a manifester in blue coveralls who was sitting on a pile of pallets beside the huge oiler at the quay wall.

"Okay," the manifester said. "Guess your paperwork's in the office."

Shelby followed Abel Durazo and the manifester, trying to check the time on a stainless-steel wristwatch that wasn't there anymore. On Saturday night in National City he'd traded it for some good crystal meth and bad black pussy. When he'd sobered up he began to worry about AIDS. She was a burned-out junkie, uglier than west Texas. Every time he looked at his wrist he thought about that junkie hose-bag and wondered if maybe he should get a blood test.

When he'd got to work on Monday and described his evening to a few of the guys, his foreman said, "Shelby, your cock takes you places I wouldn't go with a *gun!*"

Inside the monster warehouse was a little office off to the right. In it was a metal desk, a chair, a phone. The manifester entered, made a notation or two, and handed Abel the paperwork, saying, "We put the two pallets inside. We never know if you guys're gonna show this month or next."

"Not *our* company," Abel said. "We come on time."

There were pallets, boxes and crates stacked twenty feet high from one wall to the other. Abel saw the ox read the stenciled content markings on the nearest mountain of boxes.

"Man, jist imagine what they gotta store for those aircraft carriers," Shelby said. "Like, you gotta stash enough stuff for an army, right? I mean a navy. What's *in* all them boxes?"

Shelby looked at Abel when he said it, and Abel wondered if the ox could read his mind.

"We're loaded to the gunnels," the manifester said. "Got some big ships coming into port and they're taking on enough supplies to go out on the high seas for a ninety-day exercise. You got thousands of guys got to live a long time on all this, so we're prestaging."

"Uncle Sam takes care of his navy," Shelby said to Abel.

Then the manifester said, "Damn, I'm late for a lunch date with a lady. You guys can use a forklift, can't ya?"

"Use 'em all day long in our job," Shelby said.

The manifester pointed to a pair of yellow forklifts and said, "Don't take the one with the busted lift lever. The other one's better."

"Enjoy yourself," Shelby said, baring his gap-toothed grin. "And remember what the chaplain says: Don't take your most treasured possession and stick it in somethin that'd scare you to death if you was sober."

The manifester gave a thumbs-up, turned, and strode off along the quay, leaving the waste haulers alone. Lunch break lasted from 11:30 to 1:00. The warehouse was *theirs*.

Neither trucker spoke for a minute. Then Abel said, "Buey, our job gone een two, three week. We got *nada* then."

"And our boss is a cheap prick," the ox said, working himself into it, sensing what was going to happen here. "And I ain't paid in enough to be drawin much unemployment. I'm fucked!"

"I get the truck. You drive forkleeft down to the nex' loading bay. We don' take nothing from *this* bay."

"Excellent!" the ox said. "That manifester logged us in at this one, but there's dozens a truckers in and out a the rest a the bays all day long. The navy won't even miss whatever it is we take. Matter a fact, we're taxpayers, ain't we? We bought em all this shit in the first place, right? We got it comin to us, right, dude?"

It took them less than ten minutes to load the four fifty-five-gallon drums full of the U.S. Navy's contaminated fuel mixture that had been shipped from

Guam. They dollied the drums into the back of the van next to the drum they'd picked up from Burl Ralston at Southbay Agricultural Supply. By the time Abel got the rig backed up to the next open bay, yet another tractor-trailer was already parking alongside the oiler.

More *suspects*, Shelby thought. There was no way the navy would ever know which truckers to blame. That is, if anybody noticed there'd been a theft in the first place. Shelby had the forks hooked into a pallet of boxes when Abel ran inside the second warehouse bay.

The ox was so excited he looked like he was wired on methamphetamine. "Flaco!" he said. "There's some kinda computers and shit in these big boxes!"

"No," Abel said. "No computer. Too hard to sell."

Abel began running along the pallet stacks reading the military specifications on the boxes. Suddenly he stopped, took a knife from his pocket and cut open a box. He struggled for a moment, and pulled out a black, steel-toe, high-top, nonskid U.S. Navy flight-deck shoe. Then he grinned at Shelby.

"Leave that!" Shelby said. "There's TVs in them other boxes!"

"No TV," Abel said. "Serial number. Remember how you get caught before? These." He held up the navy shoes.

"Shoes? Who the fuck wants *shoes*?"

"Buey!" Abel said, grabbing the big man by his tattooed biceps. "I promise to you two thousand dollar! *Today!*"

"Today? How?"

"Get on forkleeft! Work, Buey!"

In less than twenty minutes the truckers had forklifted every pallet containing boxes marked "shoes" into the bobtail van. "They don't mees them. They got so much they don't mees the shoe," Abel said, pronouncing it *choo*.

Nobody inspected their load when they wheeled back through the gate. No one had *ever* bothered to inspect a load, not in the thirteen months that Abel Durazo had been hauling toxic waste.

When they were driving beside the Silver Strand State Beach, away from Coronado, the ox exploded. "I must be a fuckin moron! Shoes! I let you talk me into takin a million pair a useless fuckin *shoes!*"

"Two thousand," Abel said. He'd counted while Shelby had stacked. "We got two thousand. *Más o menos.*"

"Two thousand fuckin pair a shoes! *Now* what?"

"Joo going to see, Buey," Abel said, confidently.

The ocean along the Silver Strand reflected coral and turquoise in the sparkling light. Abel drove carefully, knowing that Coronado P.D. motor cops patrolled the boulevard because of sailors who piled up their cars on that dog tooth of a highway, returning drunk from Tijuana.

When the bobtail van left the strand and turned toward I-5, south toward Mexico, a flock of screaming gulls flew directly over them heading toward the Tijuana slough wildlife refuge that borders Imperial Beach on that southwestern tip of the United States. One of the reasons that geese, gulls, and other waterfowl frequented the estuary was because of the raw sewage that seeped into it from the Tijuana River that wound along the international border. Many a bird had plucked a morsel from the slough and died from it.

After driving silently for a while, Abel Durazo looked at his worried partner and said, "Do not worry, 'mano. Sometimes I borrow truck all night. But only when Mary say okay. See, I haul for guy een Tijuana. I haul for him vegetables and fruits back to San Diego. I make few dollar. Boss, he don't know, nobody know. The guy got paperwork for all produce. I go down, I come back through Otay Mesa crossing. No problem. Never."

"Don't nobody ever wonder why a waste disposal van's haulin produce?"

"Long as you got paperwork, nobody care what truck say on door. U.S. Customs peek eenside sometime. Sometime no. See fruits, vegetables, paperwork. Truck ain't stole. No problem."

Shelby studied the handsome young Mexican and said, "Fuckin her, ain'tcha? You're slippin Mary the ol' muscle missile, you little dickhead!"

Abel giggled and said, "I geev her nice present when I take truck to Tijuana. Perfume, sometime."

"I bet she'd like *my* pink projectile," Shelby said, showing his tooth-gap. "That bitch must be at least seven months pregnant, but I always did like little baby hands helpin me. Hey, that reminds me, you know how to paralyze a woman from the waist down? Marry her!"

"Huh?"

"Never mind. You Mexicans don't understand jokes. I guess if Mary's old man ever comes home early you can run outside and start mowin the lawn. Tell him you're the new gardener, right?"

"Huh?"

"Fergit it, dude. I'm wastin my fuckin humor."

The ox turned his cap bill forward to signify he meant *business*, and he said, "So how're you gettin me two grand today?"

"We go to Tijuana. My friend, he buy our shoe for three dollar a pair."

"What? These shoes must cost sixty!"

"Een Mexico, three dollar. Right *now*. Cash."

Shelby said, "Two thousand pairs times three bucks is *six* thousand. How come I only get *two*?"

Abel watched the big trucker nervously chew at a callus on his fat thumb. Filthy. The calluses were

filthy like the rest of him, but Abel liked the ox, filthy
or not.

"U.S. Customs, they don' worry about trucks
that go *south*, but we got to pay Mexican customs.
Mordida."

"What's that?"

"Bite. *Mordida.*" Abel made the motion of a fist
clamping shut.

"Graft?"

"Yes," Abel said. "We go through San Ysidro
gate. I know customs man. We borrow boss money
from last job. We put boss money back when we
collect for navy shoes."

The job to which Abel referred was the pickup
at Southbay Agricultural Supply where Shelby had
received an envelope containing $500. Shelby mulled
it over for a moment.

"Okay, how we gonna get back to the U.S. with
our drums full a who-knows-what kinda poison?"

"We don' come back weeth truck."

"What the fuck?"

"Our truck get stole. We go to San Diego police
to make report."

"Wait a minute! You're movin too fast."

"Look, Buey," Abel said. "I know how to do! We
sell shoe, we leave truck een Tijuana. We walk back
through border gate."

"We gonna tell the cops our truck got hijacked?
At gunpoint, or what?"

"No. We say we stop for burrito een Chula Vista.
Lunchtime. We eat, we come out, truck gone. We don'
care. Our job gone anyways."

"I got a bad feelin about this, dude," Shelby said,
"I got a bad feelin."

But he didn't object when the Mexican turned
south on Interstate 5 and headed toward the San
Ysidro crossing.

There were four lanes handling the southbound traffic at the international border. Unlike yellow caution signs at deer crossings that show antlered stags in black silhouette, the caution signs in *these* parts showed the silhouettes of a man, woman and child running. Every year, caution signs or not, many illegals were killed dashing across the freeway. Dying as they ran north to *survive*.

Abel pulled off the freeway at the Virginia Street truck gate, the gate used by commercial vehicles going into Mexico. As the van rumbled along the dusty hardpan road, Shelby saw several mobile homes, permanently on foundations, that served as offices for insurance and customs brokers. Before Abel wheeled the truck into the customs yard, the ox looked off to his right and saw two green and white U.S. Border Patrol Ford Broncos parked on top of the levee over the Tijuana River.

What made it an astonishing sight was that the uniformed Border Patrol officers were smoking and chatting and drinking soda pop, not thirty yards from a dozen Mexicans just on the other side of the broken-down border fence, who were preparing for their dash to *el norte* as soon as the opportunity presented itself. The Border Patrol knew they were coming. The Mexicans knew they knew. No hard feelings on either side.

Shelby Pate didn't want any part of this place. In his entire life, four years of it in the San Diego area, he hadn't been to Tijuana more than twice, once to buy meth and once to buy a hooker. One had been as bad as the other, so now he bought his cringe and pussy in San Diego.

When speaking of drugs or hookers, Shelby Pate always said, "Be a patriot. Buy American."

After they were inside the customs yard, Abel got out and approached a Mexican customs officer he knew well. Shelby watched Flaco jabber in Spanish to the guy, who wore a light-blue uniform shirt with epaulets, and a rakish cap with a sixty-mission crush.

At first, the customs officer turned away and shook his head, but finally he shrugged and nodded. Then the two Mexicans walked to the far side of the truck, away from traffic, and Shelby watched in the side-view mirror as Abel peeled off several twenty-dollar bills from the money they'd been given at Southbay Agricultural Supply.

When Abel came back to the truck he said, "I pay five hundred. Two-feefty my money, two-feefty from joo."

"You lyin little asshole!" Shelby said. "I saw you give him on'y two hunnerd at *most*!"

Abel grinned sheepishly and said, "Okay, no problem, no problem. I take one hundred from the two thousand I geev to joo."

"*Three* thousand. We're partners, goddamnit! Three fer you, three fer me. Fuck this!"

"Okay, Buey, okay," Abel said, shrugging his eyebrows.

"Ya know, dude," Shelby said, "we coulda jist dumped the drums out by Brown Field or somewheres. A *real* truck thief mighta did that before drivin south, right?"

"No," Abel said. "I cannot dump poison."

Shelby paused, then said, "Good call, dude. Neither can I."

There was something *else* troubling Shelby Pate after they got waved through the gate, after they were part of the sixty *million* who would cross north and south during the calendar year.

"Did you ever see that old movie on TV where three guys go hunt fer gold in Mexico? And this Mexican bandit with a gold tooth, he whacks one of em with a machete? And the greasers're too fuckin stupid to know the stuff he's carryin is gold dust? Ever see that movie?" the ox wanted to know.

"No, I like funny movie. Bugs Bunny."

"Those bandits stole his shoes. That's how come they got caught. They jist had to steal his fuckin shoes. I got a bad feelin about this." Shelby's little eyes widened as he looked around at all the brown faces on the Tijuana streets. "The bandits woulda got away," he continued, "if on'y they didn't have to stop and steal the *shoes*."

"So?" Abel was thoroughly puzzled. "So?"

"Them *shoes*. Them fuckin shoes got the Mexicans shot by a firin squad, dude!"

5

At every stoplight there were vendors selling ciga-prettes, soft drinks, tamales, flowers. Children scampered through traffic placing Chiclets on the window ledge of cars stopped for traffic signals. And if the motorist did not give the children a few coins for the gum, the waifs would snatch back the Chiclets just before the light changed to green, dodging the fast-moving traffic like tiny matadors.

"We early, Buey," Abel said, looking at his watch. "I drive aroun' for leetle while. Then we go see Soltero."

The traffic roundabouts made the ox uneasy, which Abel noticed when a smoking pickup truck cut them off and sped into a hub where streets fed out like spokes of a wheel.

"Thees called *gloriettas*," Abel said.

"How the fuck you know when it's your turn?" Shelby asked, just as a beat-up Oldsmobile, its side windows patched with plywood, zoomed across in front of the van and rattled off on one of the wheel spokes.

"They work good," Abel said. "Don' worry."

"Lotta squids around here," Shelby said.

"Wha's that?"

"Fast bad drivers. Squids," Shelby said nervously.

On nearly every street and highway around downtown Tijuana Shelby saw unfamiliar sights that made him anxious. A clown in sad white-face juggled balls and pocketed coins from motorists stopped for the traffic light. A fire-eater on the opposite corner performed for cars going the other way. Bony dogs prowled and rooted inside garbage containers, or just lay dangerously close to the endless traffic flow, inhaling noxious fumes from derelict cars.

"Man, I coulda crapped through a keyhole when you was givin a bribe to that Mexican cop," Shelby said as they inched through the city traffic. "My shit was syrup and I ain't scared to say it. I don't wanna go to stony lonesome, not down in *this* fuckin country."

"Wha's that, Buey?"

"Jail, man! The fuckin calaboose. A Mexican jail where they wake you up with cattle prods in your ass. And a course, they don't have no trouble findin your asshole 'cause some four-hundred-pound Indian convict from Sonora jist turned you into his pillow-bitin squaw. *That's* stony lonesome around these parts, dude!"

"I tol' you, 'mano, don' worry," Abel said. "That customs man, he jus' turn us back eef he don' take the *mordida*. But he like the money. They all like the *mordida*. They don' get paid *nada*."

But the ox wasn't reassured, Abel could see that. The hulking trucker was sweating. Beads dripped off his whiskers, and he was starting to smell, and not just from work sweat. Like in those drainpipes when Abel used to cross the frontier between Tijuana and San Diego at night, hoping that if anyone discovered him it would be *la migra*, the Border Patrol, and not Mexican bandits. The other *pollos* who crossed with him, they would smell like this while they waited in those drainpipes by the Canyon of the Dead.

"We going to be out een two, three hour, Buey," Abel said. "You don' got to worry."

It was the *multitudes* that Shelby didn't like. People walking, sitting, standing, driving. Shelby didn't like crowds. He never went to Jack Murphy Stadium even though he was a fan of both the Padres and Chargers. He watched his sports on TV to avoid the mobs. And *these* people, many were so small, so dark, so leathery: Indians, without a drop of European blood in them. Like burros, he thought, little Mexican burros, exceptionally strong for their size.

As a child, Shelby had seen lots of these little Indian migrants working in the lettuce fields near Stockton. And after getting the job at Green Earth he was often astonished at how they could muscle big drums onto the trucks, drums that he wouldn't move without a hand dolly, and he was twice the size of any of them.

This Tijuana peasant class, these leathery little Indians, made him very nervous and he couldn't explain it. Maybe it was those black eyes, fathoms deep, no way to read them. He might be indifferent to them when they were on *his* side of the border, but now, on *their* side he was unnerved and didn't know why.

"How many people live in this miserable fuckin town, Flaco?" asked Shelby, turning his cap around backwards to signify he wasn't really scared, not really.

Abel shrugged and said, "They say one, maybe two millions. They don' count when three, four families stay een one house. The peoples, they scared of taxes, see? They don' talk to the tax man. I theenk maybe two millions."

"Where we going anyhow?"

"*Colonia Libertad*," Abel said. "Soltero, he bought hees *mamá* a nice house there. Few minute away. Best house. Nice garage for cars, but no cars. When trucks come from the north they go to that garage. He pay cash. I know heem good."

By then, the van was moving along a more scenic highway, Paseo de los Héroes, where modern night-clubs and discos reassured Shelby.

"This is more like it," he said, looking around.

"Thees where reech peoples come," Abel said. "Dance. Dreenk. Very 'spensive."

Suddenly Shelby found himself gawking at a sixty-foot statue of an American president, right in the center of the roadway.

"Whoa!" he said. "That's Abraham Lincoln!"

"Uh huh," Abel said. "We crazy een Tijuana. We make statue of man who was president right after gringos steal our country." He giggled and said, "We crazy peoples!"

"That must be the biggest fuckin Lincoln outside a Mount Rushmore!" Shelby said.

They passed the huge concrete catch basin for the dry Tijuana River; then Shelby saw some of the many *maquiladora* factories: Kodak, Panasonic, Sony, G.E., and others.

Abel had told him that the *maquiladoras* were the hope of Mexican politicians now that the North American Free Trade Agreement was a strong possibility. But Abel, like most of the poor people of Mexico, wasn't looking for salvation from anything negotiated by the U.S. If the gringos wanted it, it must be bad for Mexico, was how the poor reasoned it out, no matter what their politicians said. Still, the *maquiladora* program could provide jobs in the short term. Jobs in the short term could buy them time. They were nothing if not patient.

Pointing to the modern factories, Abel said, "*Ma-quiladora* breeng money, they say. They say we make

new Hong Kong right here een Tijuana." Then he
looked at the ox and said, "But I don' theenk so,
Buey."

Abel's relaxed attitude was calming Shelby. "I
think we oughtta hold out fer more," he said. "Sixty-
dollar shoes oughtta bring us *ten* bucks a pair, even
down here."

But Abel shook his head and said, "Three dollar,
Buey. He pay three dollar, no more."

"How do ya know?"

"I know," Abel said, showing his large white
teeth in a grin. "I know."

"Wait a minute," Shelby said. "Jist a minute here!
You sure we *happened* to be in the right part a the
warehouse where these shoes was?"

Abel laughed and said, "Buey, joo no got, how
you say? Eemagine?"

"Imagination, asshole."

"See, I know many Mexican truck driver. Thees
guy I know, he go to North Island all the time. He
tell me what he see. I phone my friend een Tijuana.
He say, okay, navy boot. Weeth steel toe. *Good* boot.
Three dollar a pair. Cash. Many as we get!"

"You little whorehouse louse! You *planned* it!"

"Everybody steal from navy, Buey. Maybe after
boss sell company, you, me, we find *good* truck job.
Work hard, haul down to Tijuana. But we go back north
weeth our truck. No problem at San Ysidro gate weeth
empty truck. Today, no. Goddamn poison drum."

"Wonder if the boss'll fire us for letting his rig
get ripped off? Not that it matters since we're gettin
canned anyways."

"Ain't our fault. Somebody stole truck when we
eat lunch."

"Since you thought a everything, how'd the dirty
rotten thief steal our locked truck?"

"They break een, hot-wire."

"So you're gonna bust out the window when we ditch the truck?"

"Uh huh."

"And I'm gonna pop the ignition and wire it to make it look kosher?"

"You been to jail for steal car, Buey. You do job," Abel giggled. "Got to look good for when insurance company take truck back to boss."

"You're a ballsy little dude!" Shelby said. "I gotta give ya that. Hunnerd thirty pounds soakin wet, but all balls."

"I know my country," Abel said. "We got to sell, 'mano. *Everything* sell een Tijuana. Nobody worry about bees-ness license, no nothing. Nobody geev welfare check down here, Buey. You don' work, you don' sell, you don' *survive*."

"Yeah, these Mexicans got a lot to learn about handouts," Shelby said. "There's more moochers on one corner a downtown San Diego than in this whole town, I bet."

Colonia Libertad, one of Tijuana's numerous *colonias* or neighborhoods, was one of the poorest. Some streets were badly paved with asphalt, some were crudely cobbled, some were just hardpan that turned into slick water troughs when it rained. Shelby started worrying about their axle.

"Man, they got potholes that could swallow up Roseanne Barr," he said. "And why're these streets flooded? Water must be scarce this time a year, right?"

"Who know?" Abel shrugged. "Maybe somebody break water line. Somebody *always* break water line, 'lectric line, gas line."

The ox looked up and saw a cat's cradle of telephone and electrical lines dangling from poles, from roofs of clapboard shacks, even from trees! They seemed to be looped over anything, finally disappearing into flat-roofed dwellings that dotted the entire hillside. He saw children leaping onto propane tanks abutting those pathetic homes, the tanks being imaginary horses.

Shelby said, "A good stream a piss'd knock down the whole neighborhood."

The colors, particularly the colors of the commercial structures, many of which were built with corrugated aluminum, also made him nervous. The colors they used to infuse a little gaiety into the drab barrios—yellow, red, green, even purple—got him *down*, having the opposite of their intended effect.

Many of the houses had witches and skeletons dangling over doors and windows. Already they were preparing for *El Día de los Muertos*, the Day of the Dead. The witches and skeletons made Shelby especially uneasy. He found himself wishing he could relive that moment in the quayside warehouse when he'd decided to go along with this nutty scheme to steal *shoes*.

At the top of the hill was a twelve-foot-high barrier made of welded steel panels, originally designed to reinforce the tarmac on airstrips. Here the steel sheets were used to mark something other than a line between two countries; more accurately, it was between two *economies*. But even the steel barrier was a joke. It was rusted, chopped full of holes that even someone as big as Shelby Pate might crawl through. And in fact, tens of thousands of people had. Every day they breached that U.S. barrier in order to flock to the plateau on the American side. And when it was dark enough, the masses moved north. Toward *la migra*, and the bandits who waited in the dark.

Shelby was more tense by the time Abel parked the truck on an unpaved street in *Parte Alta*, the newer section of *Colonia Libertad*. He stayed in the truck when Abel disappeared behind a jumble of houses built from every material imaginable. Some houses were made of cinder block, some of wood, some of lathe and stucco. Some actually had four walls consisting of *all* those materials. If there was such a thing as a building inspector he lived on *mordida*, Shelby figured.

A falling leaf drifted in the air like a kite, making Shelby realize how few trees there were. And while watching that drifting leaf, he was startled by a little boy wanting to sell him chewing gum.

"*Chicle, chicle?*" The boy held four cellophane-wrapped pieces of gum in his palm.

The kid's hair was cropped very short because of a severe case of ringworm. Shelby was disgusted by it. Nobody was supposed to get ringworm or polio or cholera anymore. It made him *mad*. He shooed the kid away.

When Abel returned he'd lost that merry-Mex grin of his. He was frowning and looking at his watch.

"Gimme the bad news first," Shelby said, "but I got a feelin there ain't gonna be no good news to follow."

"Soltero no' here," Abel said. "Nobody here."

"Now what, dude? Now what the fuck we do?"

"We go to hees bees-ness. Down at *central de verduras*."

"What's that?"

"The fruits and vegetables market. Where they buy and sell the fruits and vegetables."

Fifteen minutes later, the truckers were wheeling the bobtail into the Tijuana produce market, but by then, Shelby was *very* unhappy. Even the hum and energy of the marketplace didn't lift his spirits, not a bit. Before leaving the van, Abel sliced into one of the boxes with Shelby's buck knife, and removed a pair of shoes to show to Soltero.

All the produce shops bore large colorful hand-painted signs. An explosion of color announced GUERRERO ABARROTES, and FRUTERÍA CARDENAS, FRUTERÍA

EL TEXANO, or FRUTERÍA EL CID. The painted signs were adorned with red parrots and yellow tigers with green eyes, and plump stalks of bananas, and ruby tomatoes. A cacophony of voices echoed through the square: men, women, children were haggling, buying, selling, *surviving*. Trucks were parked helter-skelter within the marketplace, all of it surrounded by low, two-story shops.

Somehow it worked. People managed. Which is what they did best, Abel said. The people of Mexico *managed*, against all odds. The lanky young Mexican hopped out of the van and disappeared behind one of the fruit stalls.

Shelby was fidgeting now. They'd wasted an hour. They should've had the deal done. They should've been ready to catch a cab back to the San Ysidro port of entry. Long moments passed before Abel climbed back into the truck and tossed the shoes onto the seat. Shelby noticed that he was sweating.

Abel said, "I find out where Soltero house ees. *Lomas de Agua Caliente.*"

"And where the fuck might that be?"

"Reech zone. Up over Caliente racetrack. Where reech peoples have homes."

This time they rode silently, as the van snaked its way up a residential street by the racetrack, past mansions made of concrete block and coated with colored stucco. Here there were new cars in the driveways. The battered rattletraps parked in front belonged to the help or to other workers, cars that were facing downhill in order to get them started.

"If you like concrete you'll love T.J.," Shelby said disgustedly.

He noticed that all the cars bearing FRONT BC license plates for "Frontera, Baja California" were American cars made by Ford, General Motors or

Chrysler. But as they climbed the hill heading toward Soltero's home he saw some new foreign cars in the driveways and motor courts of gated properties.

"How come most a the people drive American cars?" he wanted to know.

"Use to be we was not allow to eemport cars," Abel explained. "Chevies, Dodge, Buick, all U.S. car made een Mexico was all we get license for. And no four-wheel-drive car. None."

Shelby spotted a new four-wheel-drive Jeep Grand Cherokee and said, "Times must be changin."

"Oh yes," Abel said. "Soltero, he like four-wheel-drive."

Shelby didn't see any short leathery Indians up *here*, except for those who were wheeling small children in strollers and prams. And there were a lot of young people on the streets, leaning into cars, chatting, listening to boom boxes. Mostly they were tall and fair, well groomed, expensively clothed. Some of the boys had ponytails, and diamond studs in their ears. Most wore huge gold watches and leather bomber jackets.

"Juniors," Abel said, gesturing toward them. "We call them *Juniors*. They do what they wan'. They do sometheeng wrong, their father pay *mordida*. They got the life, Buey. No' like us."

"I ain't even gonna get to see the inside of a Tia-juana whorehouse!" Shelby moaned. "I knew I shouldn'ta got involved stealin shoes."

Abel stopped at a blue whale of a house constructed of concrete and Mexican terrazzo. It was situated near the top of *Lomas de Agua Caliente*, with a view of the city. The ox stayed in the truck while Abel got out, pushed the gate button, and spoke on an intercom. A moment later a middle-aged man emerged from the two-story mansion and stormed across the pebbled motor court toward the ten-foot wrought-iron gate where Abel waited.

Inside the motor court, held securely by a steel chain, was a snarling pit bull that looked like it wanted to *eat* the skinny Mexican. Abel kept looking from the dog to the man while they talked, but Shelby could see that Flaco wasn't about to win an argument with either of them. The man had a salt-and-pepper ponytail, and wore a lemon-colored guayabera shirt with epaulets on the shoulders. Shelby hated his guts without even knowing him.

When Abel started raising his voice the man turned toward the snarling tethered dog as though he was going to loose the chain. Then Abel walked away from the gated motor court, and the man in the guayabera shirt calmly reentered his house through a door twelve feet tall. Shelby wondered how many hinges that door needed.

"I come back here someday to keel that dog," Abel said.

"What's the story, dude? Don't keep me in suspense."

"Soltero say he geev money to guy from Ensenada to pay for cocaine cargo. He say he don' got our money now."

"No fuckin money! What're we gonna do with a million fuckin navy shoes?"

"He say we must leave them een garage at house of hees *mamá* back in *Colonia Libertad*. He say he geev us money nex' week."

"Fuck him! His goddamn front door's worth six grand! He ain't never gonna give us a penny!"

"Wha' we do, *'mano*?"

"What do *we* do? This is *your* fuckin country, remember? You're the one talkin big and makin all the plans! What do *we* do?"

"Maybe we go to hees *mamá*. Leave shoes. Get out of Tijuana."

"Shit!" the ox said, turning his Mötley Crüe hat around frontwards again. "I mighta known!" After a moment he said, "Okay, drive this piece a shit bobtail back to where that kid was."

"Where?"

"Back where Soltero's mother lives."

"We put shoes een her garage?"

"Yeah, what choice we got? But I wanna give that kid some shoes. Let him trade em fer some good dope or somethin."

"Okay, Buey," Abel said. "Okay."

"And let's leave this van as close to the border as we can," Shelby said. "Some fuckin mastermind!"

When they got back to *Colonia Libertad*, Shelby told Abel to drive around the streets for a few minutes until he spotted the kid with the chewing gum. When he did, he ordered Abel to stop.

"Hey, kid!" the ox yelled at the little boy. "C'mere!"

When the child came forward with a handful of gum, the ox said to Abel, "How you say shoe in Mexican?"

"*Zapato.*"

"*Zapato!*" Shelby said to the kid. "*Zapato!*"

Then he startled the boy by pushing open the door and heaving himself out. Shelby lumbered around to the back of the bobtail truck, opened the cargo door, climbed into the van and ripped open a carton.

Shelby tossed two dozen pair of shoes onto the dusty street, yelling: "*Zapato. Viva* fuckin *zapato!*"

Suddenly, a swarm of people emerged from the jumble of houses and began crawling all over the pile of shoes. By the time Abel got the truck turned around, the little boy was running off with his arms full.

"Like cock-a-roaches," Shelby said. "They jist crawl outta nowhere like cock-a-roaches."

The house of Soltero's mother was near the top of a promontory overlooking The Soccer Field, a desolate barren wasteland of relatively flat U.S. soil that served as a place for the poor of this *colonia* to play soccer unmolested by day, and to gather for their rush north by night. Scanning the soccer field as always was *la migra*, who captured only a fraction of the pilgrims and deported them just about long enough for them to gather themselves again for the *next* attempt. And so it went.

But after the soccer field lay *El Cañon de los Muertos*, better known to the U.S. cops as Deadman's Canyon, where Mexican bandits preyed upon the *pollos* coming across in the night. The house of Soltero's mother looked down on all that, on the misery of those border people who gazed across at *el norte*. Who could play soccer on U.S. soil anytime they wished.

The house was not a flat-roofed shack like the others. It had a pitched roof, the only one of its kind in the *colonia*, and a great deal of wood had been used in its construction, including wood siding. There were two mature cypress trees, one on each side of the asphalt driveway, and they too distinguished this home. The entire street had been blacktopped, probably as a result of Soltero paying *mordida* to the right street-maintenance supervisor, and the new blacktop extended from the curbless street in front, into a spacious two-car garage that was an unheard-of luxury in the *colonia*.

Abel backed the van into the driveway and walked to a side door that seemed to lead to a patio. No one answered his knock. Shelby discovered that the overhead garage door was not locked, so he swung it open.

When Abel raised the van's cargo door, Shelby said, "Somebody better get here quick and lock this fucker after we get them shoes inside."

"I theenk," Abel said, "somebody watch us now. Maybe *mamá* of Soltero. When we drive away somebody weel lock the door. Don' worry."

Abel climbed into the van and shoved the large cartons to Shelby, who eased them onto the ground, scooting them into the empty garage. The truckers were finished in minutes, and Shelby closed the overhead door, sliding an aluminum bolt in place.

"I ain't gonna run out and buy a new TV or nothin," the ox said, "if it depends on money from this."

"Soltero pay us," Abel said. "Or we come back and keel his dog."

"How 'bout *him*?" Shelby said. "*He's* the one we oughtta smoke if we don't get our money."

Abel said, "We take care of Soltero too."

Big talk, Shelby thought. If Soltero didn't pay them, what could they do? This was his town, his country, and he probably had his friends, plenty of them, to deal with the likes of Abel Durazo and Shelby Pate. Shelby knew that if they didn't get paid, they'd just have to slink back north.

But maybe they *could* at least snuff that red-assed dog. Shelby made a mental note to bring some poisoned hamburger when they returned to that big blue house up on rich man's hill overlooking the Caliente racetrack.

The haulers parked the truck in the Rio Zone, among other cars and trucks, in a parking lot three blocks from the border. Abel broke the driver's side

window with a crowbar; then the ox used it to pop
out the ignition. It took a few minutes to make a theft
look plausible to any American insurance agent.

As they walked to the pedestrian gate at the border, Shelby asked, "Whadda ya think the Mexican
cops'll do with the drums?"

Abel said, "They leave een truck. Maybe take
two, three week before they call San Diego police.
They don' move too fast down here."

They walked in silence until they got to the San
Ysidro crossing, where all twenty-four lanes of traffic
were backed up. On the Mexican side, the huge white
arched pedestrian bridge that spanned half a dozen
lanes and funneled into eighteen other lanes looked
to Shelby Pate like a set of animal ears, with fleas
swarming in one ear, crossing the curve of the skull,
and swarming out the other one. But these fleas were
human beings. People *swarmed* in this fucking town,
Shelby thought.

On the U.S. side, the building was conventionally
modern with a large flat brown roof resembling a
Hershey bar. A bite of chocolate didn't intimidate
Shelby Pate like animal ears did.

As they were going through the entrance to U.S.
Customs, they saw a female customs officer and a
dope-dog sniffing at the people walking past. Abel
turned and said, "Tell me, Buey, why you make me
find boy with *chicle*? Why?"

"Cause I was that poor when we lived in Stockton," Shelby said. "Only I didn't sell gum, I sold
turnips. And when I went to school for the first time
they all ran away like I was a goddamn leper. Cause
I had *ringworm*. Now let's get the fuck back to the
United States of America!"

That night, many in the adult male population
of *Colonia Libertad* were swapping, selling, trading,
brand-new, steel-toe, high-top, U.S. Navy shoes.

6

There were eight detectives working at the Southern Division substation, also called Southbay by the cops. One of those detectives subscribed to *The Hollywood Reporter*, and was trying to read it without much luck. That's because another detective who worked juvenile—a buxom female named Maya Tevitch—was outraged by a newspaper story concerning a fisherman in San Diego Harbor who had bill-chopped a pelican that stole his catch. That is, he'd cut off the pelican's bill and then nailed the wounded bird to a derelict sailboat "as a lesson to other pelicans."

Maya said she'd like to chop off the fisherman's nuts and nail them to the downtown fishing pier as a lesson to other bill-choppers. Maya was a tree-cuddler and animal rights vigilante, whose *secondary* mission in life was to liquidate all gun-toting rednecks who rode dirt bikes in "her" peaceful desert around Borrego Springs, shooting their rifles at everything larger than a computer mouse. Her *primary* mission was to prove that she was ballsier than any male cop in Southern Division, of which Fin Finnegan had no doubts.

Maya's voice invariably grew high-pitched when she was *this* excited so Fin couldn't concentrate on a semi-interesting story about a Screen Actors Guild wage dispute that might conceivably affect him *if* Orson got him that job.

At last, Maya's moral indignation made reading absolutely impossible so he got up and was heading for the station lobby when she said, "Fin, whadda *you* think they oughtta do about bill-chopping? Continue to treat it like some chickenshit misdemeanor or make it a felony?"

"Beats me," Fin said. "My thing is sea gulls. Last time out, I couldn't decide whether to crucify a sea gull or get a tattoo on my butt. I settled on the tattoo, but the guy ran outta ink after he wrote: 'Born to. . . . ' I told him to leave it like that. The tattoo described me perfectly. I'll show it to you sometime if you got a strong stomach, Maya."

With that he made his exit, and another detective said to Maya, "That's what happens to guys with three divorces after they turn forty-five. He sees everything in terms of his own misery. Fin thinks most pelicans live better than he does."

In Southern Division they worked in quasi-retirement, or so it was said around the police department. Fin called Southern Division "Sleepy Hollow," that southwestern corner of the United States, in a neighborhood called San Ysidro. The substation that housed Southern Division had 1950's architecture written all over it, both inside and outside. That is, there *was* no architecture. It was a nondescript rectangle constructed on the cheap, except that the inner walls were made of whitewashed concrete block that could probably withstand a direct hit from a mortar round. In somewhere like Los Angeles, a police station might have to do *just* that, some said, but not down in Sleepy Hollow.

They did get some action sometimes, being a block from the international border, the busiest port of entry in the world. But ordinarily it was quiet down there in San Ysidro. Except for one day in 1984 when James O. Huberty walked into McDonald's hamburgers carrying assault weapons and massacred twenty-one people including himself.

Eight detectives were jammed into one tiny office littered with metal desks, metal filing cabinets and one computer to fight over. Three worked crimes against persons, three including Fin worked crimes against property. One worked juvenile, and one worked diversion, which meant diverting young people from crime, a thankless and impossible task.

The front counter area was almost as bad off as the detective squad room. What should have been an adequate lobby had been turned into an open office, with three metal desks behind a counter. Two civilians did the division's paperwork, and a police officer manned a third desk as well as the counter itself, and had to deal with the walk-in traffic.

The parking lot had to be surrounded by a chain-link fence topped with barbed wire, or the police vehicles would've ended up in worse shape than the California budget. Unprotected police cars, like street hookers, were irresistible targets for violent acts. At 5:00 P.M. the front door got locked, and anyone needing a cop would have to use the telephone in front of the building.

Another of the detectives, Jimmy Estrada, worked crimes against property with Fin, and he did most of the Spanish-language translating. The others were, like Fin, middle-aged guys of European descent. Which meant that they didn't have a prayer in a Bill Clinton America, controlled by special-interest tribes and aggrieved ethnics. Or so they complained during the presidential campaign.

There were quite a few older cops working uniformed patrol at Southern Division, and at the front counter was one of them, a dinosaur who'd worked with Fin twenty-three years earlier when Fin was a rookie. Sam Zahn was fifty years old, on light duty from a heart attack, and biding his time till retirement. He was reading the sports page when Fin passed the counter seeking refuge from Maya's pelican lament.

Without lifting his gaze from the page he said, "Why're you guys working overtime? It's after six."

"They think our esteemed and slightly autistic vice president might show up for a photo op at the border. We gotta be available for security if he shows."

Sam Zahn just grunted, then said, "I see where the Dodgers're bringing Tommy Lasorda back for another year. They don't think he's too old to manage. Whadda *you* think is too old, Fin?"

Fin said, "I think it's when you couldn't pump up the old noodle with a cylinder of helium. *That's* when you're old."

Talking bravely, Sam Zahn said, "No problem here. But if it ever *does* happen there's always zinc. They say zinc makes it stiff."

"Only if you paint it on," Fin said sadly. "Mother Nature doesn't let us off that easy, the rotten bitch."

Just then Fin saw two guys come through the door: one a skinny Mexican, one a huge slob in a Mötley Crüe cap.

Abel Durazo said to the counter cop, "Sir, we got to make report for our truck."

"Our van got stolen," Shelby Pate said, "when we was havin a bite up on Palm Avenue. At Angel's Café? Know where it is?"

Sam Zahn said to the detective, "Fin, do *you* work persons or property?"

"Property," Fin said, "but as you *well* know, Sam, truck thefts are handled by the good folks downtown."

Since he was in his loafing-intensive mode, Sam
Zahn said, "Maybe *you'd* like to talk to them anyways.
They might need a detective."

"Was it hijacked?" Fin asked, which would make
it a crime-against-person, not property, and he could
easily kiss it off to *anybody* else. "Did somebody use
a gun or force?"

"No," Abel said. "We don' see thief."

"It was gone when we came outta Angel's," Shelby
said. "Jist wasn't there on the street no more."

"I'll do the fact sheet for you, Fin," Sam Zahn said
magnanimously. "You might wanna finish it?"

"Do the whole report, Sam," Fin said. "Then send
it downtown."

The counter cop sighed and fetched a blank report,
saying, "What's the name of the truck's registered
owner?"

"Green Earth," Shelby said. "Green Earth Hauling and Disposal."

"You drivers're *always* leaving your keys in your
trucks," Fin griped. "Somebody's forever stealing one
up there by Angel's."

"We didn', sir," Abel said. "The thief they pop
out ignition."

"How do you know they popped it?" Sam Zahn
asked.

"He means they *musta* popped it or somethin,"
Shelby said quickly, "cause he's got the keys in his
pocket."

Of course Fin was pleased that Central would get
this one. They had plenty of paper-shuffling detectives
up there, and they didn't have to battle for computer
access. Each central investigator had his or her own
cubicle instead of being jammed together like the refu-
gees in the Southern Division gulag. Fin didn't need
another piece of paper to file.

"Might end up in Mexico," Fin said. "They often do when they're stolen around these parts."

"Yeah?" Shelby said. "When you think the boss'll get it back?"

"They ain't in no hurry down in T.J.," Sam Zahn said. "Weeks, maybe. Could be a lot sooner if your boss's insurance company's on the ball. The Mexican cops like a 'reward' for finding hot cars. By the way, Angel's is four miles away. Did you boys *walk* clear down here or what?"

"Taxi," Shelby said. "Caught a cab."

"You coulda just phoned for a patrol unit," Sam Zahn grumbled. "They woulda come to you and took the report."

Shelby Pate said, "Oh yeah, I almost forgot. There was money in the glove box that we picked up on our last job. Five hunnerd bucks. Sure hope the thief don't look in there, but he prob'ly will."

"Five hundred bucks?" Fin said. "Why cash?"

"Don't ask us," Shelby said. "The guy at Southbay Agricultural Supply jist handed us an envelope with five big ones in it."

"Did you count it?"

"Yeah, we counted it. Fer our own protection in case it wasn't the right amount."

"You went in for a taco and left five hundred bucks of company money in the glove compartment?" Sam Zahn asked doubtfully, figuring correctly that they intended to scam the boss. He'd like to have strip-searched them both. "Hope you boys got another job to go to. Leaving cash in the truck? Your boss might not believe you."

Abel was the better actor and just smiled placidly. The ox started to twitch. He felt like turning his Mötley Crüe cap around backwards to show he wasn't worried. Suddenly, the remaining cash, still in the leather jacket with the manifests, felt heavy. He needed some methamphetamine.

"Anything else?" Fin asked. "Like maybe you left a fellow trucker sleeping in the van when you went to eat?"

"No, but there was somethin in there that we oughtta call to your attention," the ox said.

"What's that?"

"Hazardous waste. Five drums altogether. Four from North Island and one from Southbay Agricultural Supply."

"How hazardous?"

Abel shrugged, and Shelby said, "We ain't got no idea. We jist haul that shit. We don't know paint thinner from Agent Orange. We was supposed to bring it to our storage yard. The boss, Mister Temple, he handles it after that. He sends the real bad stuff outta state somewheres. To Texas or Arkansas, I think."

Now Fin was *really* glad that it would go downtown. He didn't want a case involving the Environmental Protection Agency or any other bureaucracy. "Will your boss know if the stuff is particularly dangerous?"

"Sure," Shelby said. "The description's there on the two manifests from the waste generators."

"Where're the manifests?" Fin asked. "In the truck, I suppose?"

"Een glove box," Abel said sadly. "Weeth five hundred dollar."

"The generators of the waste got *their* copies of the manifest," Shelby explained. "The navy at North Island and Southbay Agricultural Supply. Now we'd like to borrow your phone to call our dispatcher and have somebody pick us up, okay?"

"The thief musta only wanted your truck," Fin said. "He sure wasn't after your load."

"He get lucky," Abel said. "Get our boss money."

"Sure," Sam Zahn said. "Sure he did."

When Fin got off duty and was trudging toward the parking lot, he saw a truck with GREEN EARTH HAULING AND DISPOSAL painted on its doors pulling into the parking lot to collect the haulers. Then Fin almost panicked when he spotted something on his Vette until he realized that what appeared to be a ding in the left front fender was only a shadow made by the streetlight.

His 1985 Corvette was white with red leather, the second year of the major body-style change. His little beauty had a 240 h.p. fuel-injected engine with only 27,000 miles on it. It was the one thing of value that none of his three ex-wives had managed to confiscate.

When people asked Fin why the hell he'd got married *three* times, he always said, "Because they were *there*." When people asked if he was going to do it again, he always said, "Islam permits four wives and every Arab and Iranian in California drives a Mercedes, so maybe four's a magic number."

But to friends, Fin said he'd get married again when Cher had her new lips deflated. The pope would get married before Finbar Finnegan, he told them.

While he was driving back home to south Mission Beach in rush-hour traffic, Fin slipped a Natalie Cole tape into the deck and relaxed the instant he heard her father sing the first lyric of "Unforgettable." Fin had grown up listening to Nat Cole, Sinatra, Tony Bennett.

A baby boomer of the Bill Clinton/Al Gore generation, he had three older sisters, the youngest of whom was ten years older than himself. Their mother had become pregnant with him in her forty-first year, and two years after his father was killed in a boatyard accident, his mother died of breast cancer. Fin had been raised by his sisters, who treated him more like a son than a brother. He'd listened to *their* music, gone to *their* movies, read *their* books. And each of them felt free to kick his ass when she felt like it.

Finbar Finnegan had spent so many years being bossed around by women that as soon as he got old enough he joined the marines, even though it was a dangerous time, at the height of the Vietnam War. Like most people who'd been in that or *any* war, Fin hadn't fired a shot in anger. Near Danang there was the occasional incoming rocket, but being in a support battalion, he'd never even seen a live V.C. Only dead marines in body bags, being made ready for their trip home.

Although Fin hadn't had a John Wayneish marine career, although he'd bitched about the war as much as anybody, he was still vaguely uneasy about today's new breed of police officers, particularly the young sergeants and lieutenants with laptop computers and no military experience. Somehow they all looked too much like Bill Clinton. Finbar Brendan Finnegan was casting his November ballot for Ross Perot, mostly because of Perot's running mate, Congressional Medal of Honor winner James Stockdale.

That night, after eating some leftover meat loaf, Fin stared into the mirror and wondered if Orson Ellis would actually follow through and get him the part. This time, if he got to play a character who was going to be in future TV episodes, who knows, something *might* happen!

Fin slapped at the flesh between his chin and Adam's apple, wondering what a little tuck would cost, and whether he could make his medical insurance cover it. After all, he had legitimate acting credits, so why shouldn't cosmetic surgery be covered as a job-related medical expense?

Orson Ellis had been right. The benchmark birthdays *were* harder on actors than on normal sane people.

It was no consolation to remind himself that Clinton and Gore were considered young by every journalist in America. Forty-five was not young for a cop, and not young for a failed actor.

His middle sister, Bess, the most sympathetic of his three siblings, offered some advice on the subject after he'd mournfully confessed to her how he'd dreaded the last birthday.

Thirteen years older than Fin, and silently suffering the misery of hot flashes, Bess studied her baby brother for a moment and said, "Fin, honey, only sea anemones don't age. How many movie roles're out there for sea anemones? Now stop all this male menopause *bullshit* and have a piece of blueberry pie."

While Fin Finnegan was contemplating the injustice of being a human being and not an ageless anemone, a Mexican thief named Pepe Palmera had already spotted the abandoned bobtail van on the street in the Rio Zone just below *Colonia Libertad*. Within a few minutes the van was making its third trip of the day up the hill.

The first thing that Pepe did that evening, after he got near his house, was to park next to the mesquite-dotted canyon and get rid of the useless drums in the back. Pepe could not read English, nor Spanish for that matter, but he understood what the skull and bones meant on the drums. He ransacked the glove compartment but found nothing except registration and insurance papers, which he threw away. He found a pair of new steel-toe shoes on the front seat of the van, and would later profoundly regret not having put them on his feet.

The drums were very heavy, but Pepe was a determined thief. He managed to tip each drum and roll it on its edge to the cargo door, where he put his shoulder to it and pushed. But Pepe tipped the last drum a bit too far and it overturned, slamming onto his left foot before he could jump clear.

Pepe screamed and sat down while the big drum with the death's head placard rolled across the floor of the van and fell out onto the ground. Pepe knew at once that one toe was broken, perhaps two. He cursed and moaned, but eventually staggered to his feet and crawled out the cargo door.

The truck was parked one hundred meters from the row of shacks where he resided with his mother, and Pepe knew that there was a possibility that some *other* thief might steal the stolen truck, but that was the chance he had to take. His foot needed immediate attention.

His mother would know of a poultice or some other remedy that would control the swelling, and maybe tomorrow he could use the truck to earn enough money to go to a doctor. But then again, what could a doctor do with broken toes that nature couldn't do? Better to spend the money on some good marijuana, Pepe thought. *That* would help the pain better than anything.

Pepe's mother did her best to minister to her son that night, but the poultice didn't help very much. Pepe was in great pain from the fractures and didn't sleep well. And long before he got to sleep his van had been discovered by night prowlers.

The prowlers were not thieves like Pepe Palmera. They couldn't have stolen the van from Pepe even if they'd wanted to. The older of the pair, Jaime Cisneros, was ten years old. His companion, Luis Zúniga, was nine. But they were precocious in many ways, like most of the children of the border barrios.

Luis decided to run home and borrow some of

his brother's mechanic tools to open the drums. Jaime said there might be motor oil inside them, and if there was, it could be sold for more money than they had ever seen. Even reclaimed motor oil had great value, Jaime said. His father always bought used motor oil for his Plymouth.

While the thief, Pepe Palmera, slept fitfully, Jaime and Luis labored beside the van, working on the bung that was screwed into the drum. They both had to pull on the wrench handle with all their combined weight before they had success, working there by moonlight.

7

"We don't know how many pallets're gone, but we know there's been a major theft," the warehouse superintendent said to Detective Bobbie Ann Doggett. "We'll have to do a complete inventory."

"When did somebody last see pallets in this spot?" Bobbie asked, indicating the only vacant space in that part of the quayside warehouse.

"Five days ago," he said. "One of our people can definitely say they were here then."

"And you're sure the pallets contained boxes of shoes?" Bobbie asked, glancing at the report she'd received from a patrolman.

"Flight-deck shoes," the supervisor said. "Like these." He pulled up his right trouser leg and showed Bobbie his steel-toe high-top shoe. "I could be wrong, but I think there's hundreds of pairs missing. Maybe more. We'll soon know."

"How many civilian truckers would you say had access to this warehouse during the past five days?" Bobbie asked. "Both day and night?"

"Well, we're prestaging," he said, "so I'd say a dozen. Maybe a dozen haulers."

"A dozen. No more than that?"

"Could be more, I don't really know," the supervisor said.

It was the same story every time: no suspects, uncertainty as to what was stolen, not sure when the crime occurred. At least this time it was narrowed down to the past five days.

When Bobbie was leaving, the supervisor said, "Guess our security around here ain't too good, huh?"

"I'd rank it with domestic beer and the House Armed Services Committee," Bobbie replied.

After returning to the office Bobbie notified Naval Investigative Service of the grand theft, figuring they'd want to deal with it due to the large amount stolen. She got a female special agent on the phone, and after explaining the case to the woman, Bobbie said, "Guess we could handle it if you want us to. A dozen different civilian haulers coulda done it. Maybe more."

"A dozen? Hopeless," the special agent said. "We're still snowed under around here. The Tailhook business is taking forever. Tailhook's turning into the thing-that-wouldn't-die. *Halloween*, part ten!"

"I don't mind working on this one," Bobbie said eagerly. "It's pretty dead around here right now."

"You got it, honey," the special agent said. "Let us know if you come up with a suspect."

After Bobbie hung up she had other things to think about besides navy shoes. Tomorrow night was quarterly qualification with her .45 automatic. They'd be using the North Island pistol range for the night shoot instead of the Border Patrol range. Bobbie liked it when she got to shoot the practical weapons course. She enjoyed the challenge of speed-loading, running, dropping to her knee to shoot multiple targets. But night shooting also had its charms. The smell of cordite and the muzzle flash were thrilling. And it was a relief to discover that the navy's trusty 1911 model .45 didn't kick all that much, not like a .357 magnum.

An instructor had said to her: "It's a great old handgun. When you got a big punkin ball going at your target from that huge black hole, you know that if you hit what you're aiming at *nothing's* gonna be coming back at you. Very reassuring, this old gun."

It was a big pistol for such a small woman, but Bobbie Ann Doggett had surprised everyone including herself by being a very competent shooter.

By the time that the thief, Pepe Palmera, awoke before dawn, his toes were black and swollen, but not quite as painful as before. Still, he was too sore to wear his new shoes, so using a broom as a cane he hobbled barefoot down the pothole-studded street to the stolen van.

When he got to the truck he stumbled into a pool of liquid. He used his flashlight and saw that a drum had been pried open and tipped over, spilling onto the road. The oily liquid had a horrible odor, but wasn't scorching his feet, so he knew it wasn't acid. It smelled something like the D.D.T. they used when he was a boy.

Pepe wiped off some of the stinking stuff in the weeds by the road. He'd felt some discomfort when that slime slithered between his toes and bathed the deep fungal cracks in his skin—that dermal absorbent slime.

After going home and drinking coffee, he found his broken toes felt better, so Pepe eased into the steel-toe shoes, not bothering to wash his feet. If *only* he'd been wearing those shoes when the drum had toppled over! Then Pepe drove the van to a pottery maker named Rubén Ochoa who sold his goods to customers in San Diego and Los Angeles. Rubén was always in need of a truck.

The pottery maker was happy to see the thief

that morning. It seemed that he had a consignment of pottery that had to get to San Diego, and the truck he'd planned to use had transmission problems. Pepe had a *pasaporte*, a laminated border-crossing card good for seventy-two-hour visits to the U.S. but not good more than twenty-five miles from the border. Since the delivery was to San Diego, Pepe could do the job for him, and when Pepe returned to Tijuana, Rubén would pay him top price for the delivery, *and* take the stolen truck off his hands for a good price.

Striking a deal was a sure thing, so while the two men haggled over details, one of Rubén Ochoa's workers carried the pottery consignment to the van while another spray-painted the doors to obliterate GREEN EARTH HAULING AND DISPOSAL.

Still another worker drove to a nearby junkyard to buy an ignition with a key that worked, to replace the damaged one. While en route, he stole a pair of Mexican license plates from a truck parked on the street.

The U.S. Customs officers might check license plates, but they'd seldom do a check on vehicle identification numbers, and if they did, Pepe was prepared to say that he couldn't find his vehicle registration card. And he could even produce bogus documentation claiming that he was the owner/hauler of the pottery.

By the time that Pepe was ready to leave for the Otay Mesa border gate, he wasn't feeling well. The little thief was perspiring, and had a terrible headache. Also, he had to keep swallowing saliva that kept forming in his mouth. He ran to the toilet and vomited, feeling a little better afterward.

Influenza was going around *Colonia Libertad*, and the other *colonias* as well. He'd been stricken by it a week ago and, until now, thought he was getting better. Pepe hoped that the wait at U.S. Customs would not be a long one. He wanted to deliver the pottery, get back to Tijuana, buy some marijuana, and go to bed until the fever passed.

Luis Zúniga, though younger, had always been stronger than his friend Jaime Cisneros. Jaime had asthma and had been sickly all his life, but even Luis got nauseated after they'd tipped over the drum full of oily liquid. The liquid was slimy and smelled terrible. Both children knew it was not motor oil, new or reclaimed. Luis got splashed with the stuff, but Jaime got absolutely drenched. It splashed onto their faces, hands and clothing, and they ran to Luis's house to rinse it off as best they could in a tub of water outside.

Luis got very sick to his stomach when he went to bed that night, and he developed the worst headache of his life. His mother gave him aspirin but it didn't help. Jaime got what his mother thought was his worst asthma attack *ever*. In the middle of the night she gave him some medicine but he couldn't hold it down. He tried his inhaler but it didn't seem to have any effect.

The mother of Jaime Cisneros became extremely frightened when her son began to salivate. He started drooling like a hungry dog. He also got very short of breath, but the most frightening thing of all was that his pupils seemed to bounce!

Jaime's mother got a flashlight and looked into her son's eyes. One pupil looked small, one looked large. Then they seemed to trade sizes! Within fifteen minutes he was convulsing. By the time the uncle of Jaime Cisneros drove the boy to the Hospital Civil, Jaime was not conscious.

Later that morning Luis Zúniga was admitted to the same hospital with symptoms similar to Jaime's.

He had lost control of bowels and bladder during the night. He had tried to get up to get a drink of water, but his vision was so blurred that he tripped over a kitchen chair and fell. His father found him on the floor and drove him to the hospital.

After examining Luis Zúniga a doctor asked the boy's mother what her son had had to eat the night before. His symptoms were similar to a person who had been poisoned, the doctor said. He asked if the rest of the family was all right.

She told the doctor that her family was well, but then she remembered that Luis had been playing with his friend Jaime Cisneros all evening, and they had come home very late. She suspected that the boys had bought tamales from a street vendor. She'd always warned Luis about street vendors. They used cat and dog meat in their tamales, she'd always told her son.

8

No sex appeal is what they always said about cases involving hazardous waste. By that they meant no *jury* appeal.

"How do you take a bubbling vat of hazardous waste before a jury?" a deputy district attorney had once rhetorically asked D.A.'s Investigator Nell Salter when she'd wanted a criminal complaint against a waste hauler.

"Well, what if we drape a little silk and lace on the acid drum and hang a dildo on the flange?" Nell had suggested, before calling it a day and giving up on a case that had cost her at least one hundred investigative hours.

That was everybody's attitude when it came to environmental crime. Nobody cared about it because nobody knew much about it, least of all the cops. The field was too new, too esoteric, too unsexy, and there was almost no case law. Clint Eastwood would never ask the owner of a dioxin-producing paper company to "make his day."

When Nell had been assigned to the unit back in 1985, she and another investigator, Hugh Carter, had simply shaken hands and said, "Now what?"

The District Attorney's Fraud Unit had been given the job of investigating environmental crimes. There were about fifty of them in the unit: attorneys, accountants, investigators and assistants, all sharing a floor in a downtown bank building because the county building was not large enough. The Fraud Unit could be housed in a privately owned high rise because their clientele wouldn't frighten the other tenants of the building as ordinary street criminals might do.

Their quarters were cramped, and Nell's view was of the downtown homeless. She had a cubicle containing a small desk, two chairs, a computer, a bookshelf and a file cabinet. Investigators were not entitled to a full wall so she had to settle for a three-quarter divider, but she also had an unobstructed view of the common bathroom in a nearby residential hotel. Nell learned that both men and women had some *weird* bathroom rituals.

There'd been no training and very little information available on the subject of environmental crime back when Nell was assigned. In the early years most cases dealing with the illegal disposal of toxic waste merely involved lawsuits by the county. Then dumping became a misdemeanor, and sometimes a "wobbler" felony that could be prosecuted as a misdemeanor, depending upon the circumstances.

But at last the laws had been given teeth, fangs in fact. For a hazardous waste hauler who "should have known" of intentional dumping there were new felony provisions for a determinate sentence of sixteen months, twenty-four months, or thirty-six months in prison, and a fine of up to $100,000 per *day* per offense, with a mandatory minimum of $5,000 per day. If someone suffered great bodily injury as a result of the dumping, the perpetrator could get thirty-six months added to his sentence, along with a fine of $250,000 for every day that the material was actively exposed.

The county's share from *that* kind of money made the bureaucrats and politicians pay attention to environmental crime.

When Nell Salter and Hugh Carter started out they referred to all hazardous waste as "methyl-ethyl bad-shit," until gradually they began to learn a thing or two. Once, an EPA Super Fund team of chemists and waste handlers had made an error cleaning up a dump site that involved a large quantity of nitric acid. A lot of workers ended up with a snootful of acid and cyanide fumes, the very thing used to *execute* people within the walls of San Quentin Prison. That made Nell and Hugh more anxious to read all they could about any methyl-ethyl bad-shit they might encounter, so as not to get up-close-and-personal to suspicious containers with strange contents.

"Beware of BFRC!" is how they put it: Big Fucking Red Cloud.

Many of their investigations consisted of tracking down knowing disposers. Plating companies were among the worst offenders, and their acids were dumped everywhere, much of it in southeast San Diego. Nell knew of one particularly egregious case where fifty 55-gallon drums were transported to Mexico by a waste disposal company that had bribes in to a Mexican customs official. The de-headed drums were dumped into the Tijuana River and the empty ones were sold to squatters who used them to haul drinking water. And there were other horror stories involving Mexico as a dump site; one involved the casting of re-bars used in cheap Mexican concrete housing with metal that had been made *radioactive* in the United States.

Presidential candidate Bill Clinton had recently *sort of* approved of the North American Free Trade Agreement, his approval being subject to more environmental safeguards from the Mexican side, but

Mexicans said that their citizens had suffered from U.S. toxic waste in ways that no one would ever know about. In that poor Mexicans had a high mortality rate from diseases long since eradicated in the U.S., who could say if hazardous waste contributed to it?

That was the way of things in a Third World country, or so the Mexicans said. And nobody south of the border thought that the Americans would sign the NAFTA agreement unless it greatly favored the U.S. It had always been thus, ever since the gringos stole their land in the Mexican War, or so the Mexicans said.

Of course Nell's job stopped at the international border, but she often thought about the people down there. She frequently took holidays on the Baja peninsula, and had been to Mexico City twice, as well as to Acapulco. She was interested in the Mexican culture, liked the people, and hoped to be able to afford a decent specimen of pre-Columbian sculpture someday, like those she'd admired in the shops of Mexico City.

If Finbar Finnegan thought it was tough staring down the muzzle at the forty-five-year benchmark, Nell Salter could have told him that it wasn't a lark turning forty-three, which she had accomplished in July. Unlike Fin, she hadn't managed to chalk up three divorces during her twenty years in law enforcement; one was enough, when she was twenty-two, then working as a civilian crime-scene photographer for the San Diego P.D.

The job of crime-scene photographer hadn't been exactly what she'd envisioned. During young Nell's second day on the job she'd found herself literally cheek by jowl with a dead drug dealer who'd had his throat cut, and was discovered inside the trunk of his own Mercedes two weeks after his murder. Nell's civilian husband had made her strip naked before she was allowed into the house after that one. Her clothes smelled, her hair smelled, her *fingernails* smelled. For months she could whiff that dead drug dealer. It might happen when she'd walk into an unfamiliar room, or when she'd open the trunk of her own car. Once it happened when she was cooking dinner. Keeping a small can of aerosol in her purse helped her to get her imagination under control.

"This isn't what I expected from corpse photography," she'd explained to her boss.

He said, "Did you expect they'd resemble mannequins that you could dress up like dolls?"

Nell's fourteen-month marriage to her high school sweetheart deteriorated quickly after that. His boozing, aggravated by a job layoff, made things worse. One night after a drunken row, he'd punched her in the face, breaking her nose and blackening both eyes.

As a civilian employee of the S.D.P.D. Nell had known what to do, but didn't. She didn't call the police and didn't prosecute, but she *did* try a gag that a cop had told her about. While he was packing his clothes, vowing to leave forever, she put tiny pebbles inside the valve stems on his tires, then screwed the caps back on, while she bled on her $50 silk blouse. Then she watched him drive away, hoping that the tires wouldn't go flat until he got on the freeway.

It was a pots 'n pans divorce, and she sent him a check for his half of all they owned. As far as Nell knew, her ex was still living in Miami, where he'd gone to work for an uncle at a Cadillac dealership. After she'd taken back her maiden name and joined the San Diego P.D., he'd called her late one night to suggest that they consider reconciliation, asking if she missed him.

Nell said she missed him like a yeast infection,

and that she no longer got misty remembering their high school homecoming dance, and that if he ever crossed her path again she was going to show him a few tricks she'd learned at the police academy, like ripping out his fucking eyeballs and feeding them to the cat.

As it turned out, breaking her nose was the only good thing he ever did for her. As she matured physically during her eleven years as a San Diego cop—after she'd got into jogging and regular workouts—her face narrowed and her cheeks hollowed, giving her a more refined look. And with that refinement a slightly bent nose was sexy indeed. In those days other female cops told her that if they could get a nose like that they'd date Norman Mailer. In more recent years they changed it to Mike Tyson.

Nell regularly jogged along the Embarcadero in those days, loving the spangled sunlight that ricocheted off the bay and caressed her bare legs. No headset for Nell; she liked to hear the groans of sailboats straining at their moorings, and the zing of halyards against metal masts. Jogging along the Embarcadero was an utterly sensual experience.

Later in her S.D.P.D. career when she'd worked as a detective, Nell began to dress better. In winter she liked cable turtlenecks, and double-pleated trousers worn with blazers or tweed jackets. A loyal Nordstrom's customer since the chain opened in the San Diego area, she wore slim-girl things off duty: stirrup trousers and walking shorts.

Nell promised herself that she was always going to dress well and live well, and that no son of a bitch was *ever* going to punch her in the face again, not without wearing handcuffs and getting some big-time payback before she got him to jail. And for sure he'd be wearing the cuffs with his palms *outward*, because once Nell had the misfortune to arrest a Plastic Man clone whom she cuffed palms inward for his comfort. While she was outside her patrol car completing her report, he'd managed to jackknife his body and pull his cuffed hands around his legs and feet. Then he drove off, crashing ten minutes later during a high-speed pursuit by the Highway Patrol. Her *most* humiliating day. After that, Nell Salter wasn't the kind to worry a whole lot about a male prisoner's comfort.

Other events began to change her in subtle ways, as inevitably happens to young people in law enforcement. One of these changes resulted from a phone call by a parole board representative who wanted her opinion concerning the impending release of a man she'd arrested for battering his family. The man had not only broken his wife's nose, but had cracked four of her ribs. During his rampage he'd also managed to fracture the skull of his eight-year-old daughter and puncture the child's spleen.

He had not served even half of his sentence, but it turned out that his kidney disease was causing the state to have to pay for dialysis treatments, and what with the budget crunch, the parole board thought about springing him. Despite premonitions, Detective Nell Salter had allowed herself to be persuaded not to oppose the release. She was told how, like everyone from Manson murderers to Watergate conspirators, he'd found Jesus perched on his bunk in that little prison cell.

What really made Nell assent, despite misgivings, was that he'd broken his wife's *nose* during the assault. Nell worried that at a subconscious level, she might be transferring feelings about her ex-husband onto this man, so she did not vigorously oppose the parole. Three weeks after his release, he located his wife's new home, broke in, shot her to death, then his daughter, then himself.

The murdered child had given Nell a photo of herself in a Girl Scout uniform, and on a few occasions during the weeks following the killings, Nell had surprised herself by breaking into sobs. Always when she was alone, of course, because unlike TV cops, real cops don't wear their hearts on their sleeves. And the one thing that female police officers absolutely could not do under *any* circumstance was to cry. Not in the presence of a male cop, nor in any situation where a male cop might hear about it.

Male cops. That was a big problem, as far as the females were concerned. It was never enough to be as good *as*, not if a woman wanted total acceptance. The woman had to be at least as good as, and not let the men know it. It was a very dicey business, the care and handling of male cops.

All the females talked about how, during stressful, emotion-packed moments, male and female police partners would bond and lose track of the "other" world, the civilian world. That bonding, those moments, could be sexually supercharged.

More than a few hard-nosed, veteran cops had walked into their lieutenant's office to say: "My wife won't let me work with females anymore!"

Nell had tried living with a male cop she thought she was in love with. Confident and competent professionally, he was a personal and emotional *mess*, just like almost every male cop she'd ever known.

Finally one day she said to him: "I'm *not* your mommy. I'll never *be* your mommy. You should go back to your mommy."

He'd seemed stunned, and said, "But I thought we had something together! I was thinking about . . . *marrying* you!"

"Go marry a nurse," Nell told him. "That's what you guys do, marry nurses and other care givers. But please, leave my life so I can chisel the crud out of my oven and scrape my kitchen table with a putty knife."

The day he left, she went to Nordstrom's and bought a new dress, after which she'd had her brown hair touched up with chestnut highlights. And she made a vow to date civilians.

That seemed like a good idea, and at first it was lots of fun regaling civilians with cops 'n robbers tales. They loved it, most of them: a dentist (sexy whiner), a flight engineer (unsexy whiner), a carpenter (great buns, no brains), a lawyer (seldom changed his underwear), and a mall developer (never wore any) who went broke and left town just ahead of subpoenas.

There was one common denominator: Most of the civilians were fascinated by her gun. She was always playing Mister Rogers show-and-tell with her 9mm Sig Saur.

"This is a Sig semi-automatic! Can you say Siiiig? It holds sixteen rounds and can make a biiiiig mess!"

She finally decided that the shrinks were right about pistols and penises. Mainly though, they just didn't *get* it, those civilians. They didn't understand what it is that cops see: i.e., not just the worst of people, but ordinary people at their worst. They didn't understand the cynicism, and the gross-out gallows humor. They couldn't understand dealing with horror by smacking it in the face with a cream pie full of maggots.

Nell finally decided that marrying a civilian couldn't work, not anymore, not even if she found one she liked. And marrying a cop was unthinkable, unless she wanted to be tied to a forty-year-old infant with chest hair. Gilbert and Sullivan didn't know the half of it about a policeman's lot. They should've known a few *female* cops, or so her colleagues always said.

At last, Nell Salter decided that she needed a

change. Not a huge change, not out of law enforcement
entirely. So, Nell left the San Diego Police Department
in favor of the District Attorney's Office, and became
one of two people investigating environmental crimes.
And there she'd stayed, and there she'd learned to
identify methyl-ethyl bad-shit and Big Fucking Red
Clouds.

On the day that Fin Finnegan visited his agent with
malice aforethought, Nell Salter, having had three cups
of coffee with her morning poached egg, had to run
to the john the moment she arrived at work. And as
often happened with female investigators who were
in a hurry, she forgot all about her handcuffs when
she sat down to pee.

A few minutes later, when she entered her own
office, her older partner, Hugh Carter, looked up over
his bifocals and said, "Three more days and I'm gone.
Three whole weeks. Salmon. Pine cones. Clean air . . ."

"Mosquitoes," Nell said. "Psychotic hermits in
camouflage fatigues with M-sixteens. Snakes!"

"Hope you can manage without me, and . . ."
Suddenly Hugh Carter noticed that she was shaking
the water out of her handcuffs. *Again.* He said, "Nell,
you know how fastidious I am. Would you not shake
those nasty drops all over the floor. Aim for my coffee
cup, please."

"Hugh," Nell said, "I don't know if it's a good
time for you to go on vacation. You know how we
always talk about some evil and ugly genetic monster
emerging from all the contaminants in places like the
Tijuana River and the Rio Grande?"

"Yeah?"

"Some uncontrollable mutant life-form that'll
raise its horrible snout from the toxic muck and slime
of California or maybe Texas, and flap its scaly ears,

and terrify the entire nation with its wicked bellowing screams?"

"Yeah, yeah?" her partner said.

"It's happened!" Nell cried. "Ross Perot is gaining in the polls!"

9

When Fin came to work on Monday he discovered that Sam Zahn had neglected to make any hazardous material notifications on the van that was stolen at Angel's Café. Because Sam had the day off, Fin thought he'd better cover his old pal's ass by making the notifications. Sam had a short-timer's attitude.

Nell Salter's partner had only been gone on vacation for one day when she received the unusual call from San Diego P.D.

"This is Nell Salter," she said to a somewhat familiar telephone voice identifying himself as Detective Finnegan.

Salter? He used to know a female cop named Salter. Was she the chubby one that could've used a Thighmaster if they'd had them in those days? "Did you have a sister with S.D.P.D. at one time?" he asked.

"I don't have a sister, brother," Nell said. "I left the P.D. in nineteen eighty-five."

"I worked Central then," he said. "Fin Finnegan?"

She couldn't place him, and said, "I'd probably know you if I saw your face. How can I help you?"

"I gotta talk to a sludge drudge," he said. "You know, a goop cop. Are you one of them?"

Sludge drudge. She hadn't heard that one. "Yeah, I work environmental crimes. What's up?"

"On Friday, a van got stolen down near Imperial Beach. Had some drums of toxic junk in it. Belongs to Green Earth Hauling and Disposal. Ever heard of them?"

"No, there're quite a few hauling contractors around town. What'd the waste consist of?"

"All I know is the trucker picked up some stuff from the navy at North Island and from a place called Southbay Agricultural Supply down here in San Ysidro. I've notified our office of emergency management and HazMat and the county health department and now you. I'm all tuckered out."

"Any suspects?"

"Nope. May've been a try at a cargo theft if they couldn't read 'hauling and disposal' on the door of the cab. Just thought I'd let you know. In case the drums get found you'll know where they belong."

"Can you send me a copy of the report?" she asked. Then she added, "Where was the truck stolen from exactly?"

"Angel's Café. Know it?"

She thought she knew Angel's, and said, "As I recall, a lotta guys wearing shades hang around there. They're either astronomers waiting for a solar eclipse or drug dealers, right?"

Fin said, "They sell dime bags of smoke. Truckers sprinkle it on their hamburgers."

"If you hear anything about the truck, call me."

Fin said, "We don't handle truck thefts here at Southern. And if the truck's recovered with the sludge still in it, I wouldn't go near it anyway. Waste from the navy is probably the kinda stuff that makes an insect turn in circles and die from one whiff. That's what the military wants *people* to do."

Suddenly his voice had a face: chin dimple, nice

soft gray eyes. A smallish guy with a smart mouth. Nell said, "I used to work with your ex-wife. She was a police officer, right? A sergeant? Worked Northern?"

"My *first* ex-wife. The good sergeant. That experience taught me not to marry above my station. She put bruises on my psyche that bled into my hat. I learned what police brutality really means being married to that Nazi. I hope she wasn't a *close* friend of yours?"

"No, I just remember how she used to complain to the other women about *you*. You're the amateur actor, right?"

The line went dead for a few seconds. "I act, yeah," Fin said icily. *Amateur?*

"The hazardous waste could very well turn up somewhere in Southbay," Nell said. "If you hear anything, gimme a call, huh?"

Then he was able to put a face on "Salter." She was the one that actually jogged to work, sometimes in shorts and a T-shirt. On cold misty mornings her nipples would pop out, so the male cops called her "Foglights" behind her back. He wondered if her fog lights were on today. He wondered how well she'd *aged*.

It had been a long wait at U.S. Customs. Pepe Palmera had breezed through Mexican customs, but now the U.S. officers were letting their dog sniff very carefully around all the trucks as though they'd received a tip.

Pepe had confidence in his cold plates. The yellow FRONT BC license, and the PEPE'S POTTERY that Rubén's workers had stenciled on the doors, made it absolutely plausible that he was hauling his own merchandise to the U.S. market. He was fairly confident that no one would give him any trouble about a missing registration, but then, he'd only taken stolen trucks through on two other occasions. Usually he was driving cold cars or cold trucks when he did business on the U.S. side, criminal business in most cases.

Pepe had a record with the San Diego police. He'd been arrested twice for petty theft and once for a commercial burglary that had got him ninety days in the county jail. He wasn't very worried that a U.S. Customs officer would give him trouble but he *was* worried about his health. The sweating had gotten ferocious, and the headache was actually causing his vision to blur. Pepe couldn't stop swallowing, and while waiting in the line at U.S. Customs he had to get out of the truck to vomit.

Just before it was his turn, he had a bit of luck. The drug dog scored a hit on an eighteen-wheeler in front of him. The dog started barking wildly and clawing at the mud flaps behind the rear wheels. A customs officer crawled under the truck and emerged with a large taped bundle.

While one officer was handcuffing the driver, the other gave Pepe a perfunctory check and he was waved through. Two miles inside the U.S., Pepe felt like renting a motel room and waiting out the fever. But he kept driving north.

Jules Temple was not happy when he gave orders that Abel Durazo and Shelby Pate come immediately to his second-floor office at Green Earth Hauling and Disposal. A dispatcher had tried to inform Jules of the truck theft on Friday, but Jules was at a Thai restaurant in Hillcrest, telling an exotic dancer named December Doolan that as soon as his hauling business closed escrow, he planned to open a topless bar and would use her as a star attraction.

Jules had had to spend $200 on the bitch, all for naught. She ate like a Charger defensive lineman and drank more than he did, yet when it came time for his payoff he got a good-night kiss and that was it. He'd been too frustrated and tired to listen to his messages when he'd got home, so he didn't learn about the truck until he came to work on Monday.

Any theft but this one would've irritated Jules, but *this* one made him furious. Because the manifest from Southbay Agricultural Supply did *not* match the missing load!

His hazel eyes were glittering when his two employees entered. "Close the door behind you," he said, letting them both stand in front of his desk while he remained seated.

Jules was the only boss that Shelby Pate had ever seen in a blue-collar business who dressed like this. His boss was wearing a suit the color of curdled cream, and a forest-green shirt buttoned at the throat. Shelby absolutely hated yuppie shirts buttoned at the throat. Jules Temple had even rolled up the cuffs of his jacket to hip-it-up.

All the Mexican workers and most of the others took off their hard hats when they entered the boss's private office; therefore Shelby Pate left his cap *on*, turned around backwards. Shelby wore a blue Public Enemy T-shirt.

Jules studied them. Abel Durazo waited patiently, but Shelby Pate stared back at him, like the redneck monster he was. Jules hated them because they'd been careless with his truck, and because he was positive they'd stolen his money.

He surprised them both when he said, "If I'd have heard about this on Friday night, I'd have asked the cops to search you. I don't believe you left my five hundred dollars in the glove compartment. You wouldn't do something that stupid."

"We sorry, Boss," Abel said contritely. "We thought money was more safe een glove box."

Shelby Pate said, "If you're gonna fire us, go ahead, but I don't appreciate being accused a stealin your money, Mister Temple."

"I only got twel' dollar, Boss," Abel said. "I show eet to you."

"I just want you to know that I'm not fooled," Jules Temple said. He was trying so hard to maintain control that his mouth barely moved when he spoke, and it made it hard for Abel to understand him.

"You ain't gonna believe us," said Shelby Pate, "so I guess this means we're fired, huh?"

Jules kept quiet for a moment and stared into his coffee cup. Then he said, "I'm willing to give you the benefit of the doubt. Abel, you've worked for me for some time and you've always been honest." He looked at Shelby and said, "By the way, where's the manifest from the navy?"

"Een glove box," Abel said.

It was all Jules could do to maintain his voice level then. "And Mister Ralston's manifest. Where . . . is . . . *that* manifest?"

"Gone," Abel said, and both young men were shocked when Jules Temple smacked his coffee cup across the desk, spilling it on the carpet.

But they weren't as shocked as Jules Temple was. He'd *lost* it! Always so cool, his late father had said. Cool when others were not cool, to the extent that the old man had suspected pathology, a personality disorder of some kind. And he'd knocked his cup across the desk. He'd *lost* it. In front of these cretins.

"I'm sorry, guys," Jules said. "It's just that everything's coming down on me. Selling my business and not wanting anything to go wrong? You can understand, can't you?"

Abel said, "Okay, Boss," but Shelby Pate just stared at Jules Temple.

Then Shelby said, "The navy's manifest was in the glove compartment, the other one wasn't."

"Where was it then?" Jules Temple asked, *much too quickly.*

"On the seat," Shelby said, unable to understand why it was so vital. "Probably it'll jist get tossed out by the thief."

Jules Temple nodded and said, "You're right. The thief probably threw them away and dumped the drums somewhere. But I hate to lose those manifests. They have EPA numbers on them. Strict controls, you understand."

"Was eet *real* bad poison, Boss?" Abel asked.

"It's all bad," Jules Temple said. "Our job is to protect the public from it. You can go back to work now."

Abel smiled and said, "Thanks, Boss."

Shelby just nodded, and Jules Temple didn't like the insolent smile on that big bastard. Not a bit. After his haulers were gone, Jules immediately called Burl Ralston at Southbay Agricultural Supply.

"Burl," he said, when the old man answered, "it's Jules. Did you mail the EPA manifest copy from Friday?"

"No, I got it right here," Burl Ralston said.

"And your file copy?"

"Yes."

"Don't do anything with them," Jules said. "Put them in your desk. I'll be *right* there."

Pepe Palmera could hardly focus when they unloaded the pottery at Huerta's Pottery Shed in Old Town. This wasn't the tourist season, but there were plenty of people roaming through the shops and buying souvenirs.

Pepe entered and stumbled right into a hanging

clay pot shaped like a pig, but he didn't even feel it. His face was numb. After they off-loaded, Pepe was told by Alberto Huerta that payment would be by mail per agreement, so Pepe got back into the truck to leave. He scraped against the fender of a parked car as he pulled away from the curb.

When Pepe reached the freeway on-ramp he was utterly confused, and turned north instead of south. He began to drive fast, and it was very hard to steer because the lane lines had begun to undulate. Then he saw someone standing beside a car that had pulled off the freeway. The someone was his sister, Blanca!

Pepe Palmera jerked the wheel, and crossed three lanes of traffic. Brakes screamed. Tires smoked. Two cars hit the center divider and screeched to a stop.

Pepe stopped the van in the traffic lane, leaped out, and waved wildly to his sister. Then he began to weep and ran to embrace the beautiful girl who had been dead for seven years.

He was calling to her: "Blanca! Blanca!" when a 1989 BMW struck, rocketing Pepe through space, where he was hit in flight by a Toyota and then run over by a Greyhound bus.

Pepe Palmera had jetted out of his shoe, the left one, loosely laced because of his swollen toes. But the right shoe stayed securely attached to his foot, which was severed and catapulted into the still-flowering ice plant growing up the bank of the I–5 freeway.

10

When Jules Temple arrived at the office of Burl Ralston he thought he was in command of his emotions, yet Jules was unaccountably warm on an October day when the cool offshore air signaled the end of a long summer. His forest-green shirt was open at the throat now, and one of his neatly rolled coat sleeves had come unrolled.

"Something wrong with Friday's pickup?" Burl Ralston asked, the moment Jules entered his office.

The old man had just come in from the warehouse and was still wearing a blue hard hat. He was a big man, a bit stooped, but still a hard worker. He removed his trifocal glasses and wiped them when he sat down, noting that Jules's smile was less smarmy than usual.

"Can I see the EPA copy of the manifest?" Jules asked. "And your copy?"

Burl Ralston opened his desk drawer and removed an envelope, using a scissor blade to cut it open. "I was going to mail this today. What's wrong, Jules?"

"My truck got stolen a few hours after my haulers picked up your drum. There was some North Island waste in it as well as yours."

"Too bad about the truck," Burl Ralston said. "But I don't see what . . ."

"You *did* read the manifest on Friday, didn't you, Burl?" Jules asked, pressing his fingertips together in that annoying way of his.

"I glanced at it, sure," Burl Ralston said, pretending he didn't know what Jules was driving at.

Jules's smile darkened then, and the light through the office window made Burl Ralston realize how much he disliked Jules Temple's affectations. Jules wasn't as young as he dressed, not as young as his haircut. Fortyish, he seemed too old for the little yellow sports car he drove, and Burl Ralston didn't even like Jules's rich-boy *teeth*.

Then Jules said, "Of course you read it. You signed it in the presence of my two haulers."

"*You* prepared it," Burl said, taking off his hard hat, baring a bald splotchy scalp.

"I don't deny that I prepared it," Jules said. "You asked me to. You said you were too busy with your own paperwork."

"I asked you to? No, you *offered*. You asked for my EPA identification number and I gave it to you over the phone. Remember?"

"Why quibble?" Jules said, delicately tugging at his trouser creases before crossing his legs. Jules had a prissiness that always made Burl Ralston uncomfortable. Jules had once hinted that he'd been a Green Beret in Vietnam, but Burl Ralston didn't believe that he'd even been in the military.

"What difference does it make if you typed the manifest or if I typed it?" Burl asked. "I admit I signed it."

"Admit that you *read* it then," Jules said. "Particularly item eleven."

Burl picked up the EPA's copy of the uniform hazardous waste manifest and read aloud: "Waste flammable liquid." Then he said, "Okay, that's maybe a technically correct description for Guthion that's been accidentally mixed with a little weed oil."

"Technically correct?" Jules said.

"But it's not morally correct because I *told* you it was Guthion. You should've described it as Guthion. I think I see where you're going with this conversation, Jules."

"I described it exactly like you described it to me."

"That's a *lie*."

"Burl, you signed off on the manifest. Look at your signature. Is Sacramento going to accept that you didn't go along with a *morally* incorrect description of the hazardous waste?"

"I think you better leave, Jules."

"Even if the EPA believed that you told me it was Guthion, you obviously went along with the *morally* incorrect description because you got a very good bid from me to haul and dispose of the stuff. For which you paid *cash* to my haulers. Didn't you read item nine? Look at the designated facility: a refinery in Los Angeles. Since when can Guthion be disposed of at a refinery in L.A.? Someone'd say you went along because you got a good deal from me and even paid cash under the table."

"What happened, did the drum turn up somewhere? Did someone get hurt? What happened?"

"Nothing happened," Jules said. "And I don't think the drum will ever turn up. But *if* it does, and if somebody from HazMat or the EPA should test the contents and find out that the waste flammable liquid headed for Los Angeles was really Guthion, I'd say you're in a lot more trouble than I am. In fact, as I see it, I'm not in trouble at *all*. I don't work for the I.R.S. so I don't question my customers if they're trying to cheat Uncle Sam by doing *cash* transactions."

"You little son of a bitch," Burl Ralston said, twisting the manifest copy like a chicken neck. "You been doing cash business with me for two years."

"That's it, Burl," Jules said, "destroy those copies. Both of them. I'm here to protect you."

"You're here to *protect* me?"

"Sure. After my truck got stolen it suddenly occurred to me: What if there was something besides oil or solvent or something like that in Burl's drum? What if there was something like, oh, malathion, or paraquat, or even Guthion? If it gets dumped, found and tested, old Burl could get in trouble. So I just thought I'd come by and tell you about the theft of the truck. And that you *probably* have nothing to worry about. The drums might never turn up. Maybe the truck went to Mexico. Down there, they'll empty the drums and use them to barbecue baby goats in. So you probably have nothing to worry about."

"I'm going to call the EPA right now and tell them the truth. That I told you it was Guthion in that drum."

"That's exactly why I came by here!" Jules said. "I *thought* you might panic and do that if you heard my truck got stolen. I thought you might try to put it off on old Jules. I just want you to think about it, Burl. *Who* signed the manifest? The contents're listed right there as flammable waste bound for L.A. *Who* signed it? *Who* paid cash to my driver?"

"We could both go to prison if somebody's hurt. Do you understand that, you shit-sucking little prick?" Burl Ralston clenched his big fists on the desktop.

"Put a customer's order form, or a credit-card receipt, or a note to your sister Mabel, or any goddamn piece of paper you have into an envelope and send it certified to the EPA. When they finally contact you about it, just say, 'What? You mean I didn't send you the manifest copy of the Guthion that Green Earth was going to take to *Texas* for disposal with some other hazardous waste? Well, land o' goshen!' "

"And my generator's copy. Does that get *misplaced*?"

"Of course. Your files're a mess. How old're you, seventy-something? Tell them you're lucky if you can file your nails. And that you know it's time to retire but you just can't let go. And that you'll look everywhere for the manifest copy. But you'll never find it, will you? And don't worry about my two haulers. I doubt that either of them can read anything more complex than the label on a beer can. They just knew to pick up the two loads and bring them to our yard. Period."

"The thief might get caught with the manifest in his possession."

"No truck thief is gonna keep owner documents lying around. He'd toss them away. The manifest doesn't exist, not after you destroy those two copies in your hands. Now we're both going to tell *anyone* who contacts us that the waste was indeed Guthion and that it was correctly manifested as Guthion and it was heading for incineration in Texas within three days. That's in case the waste ever *does* show up and gets tested. I'm trying to help you, Burl."

"You're trying to help *yourself*, you snake."

"I want my business to close escrow with no problems. If the EPA or the D.A. starts going over all my past manifest copies, who knows what mistakes they might find in some of my other cash transactions? Even some I've done with *you*."

"If that manifest is in the truck when the cops finally find it, then what?"

"It won't be."

"But if it is?"

"The cops don't know from jelly donuts about

manifests or hazardous waste. They'll notify me if the truck gets recovered and I'll run down to their tow yard and destroy the manifest. But it won't happen like that."

"I never wanna see your smarmy face again," Burl Ralston said. "You're never doing business with me after this."

"Not with anyone," Jules Temple said. "Not *this* business anyway. You know, Burl, I got a very good price for my company, recession and all, but maybe I shouldn't've sold. With Al Gore as vice president and all those ecology groupies flocking to Washington, waste hauling might become a very good business indeed. Environmental protectors, that's who we are."

"Get outta my office," Burl Ralston said. "You got what you came for."

When Jules headed for the door, he said, "It was okay for two years, wasn't it, Burl? All those low bids I gave you? All those manifests you signed, not caring how I described your waste or where I was taking it? Now when something goes wrong you give me sanctimonious bullshit. Well, just remember that at your age any jail time could be a *life* sentence. That'll stop your sniveling, old man."

When Fin got home that evening with too much booze in him, he checked his messages and found a call from Orson Ellis, who said, "This is the world's greatest agent calling to inform you that tomorrow morning you're going to read for Ms. Lenore Fielding, co-executive producer of *Harbor Nights*! Finbar, my son, you have but to command me. Remember, be yourself. Good luck. And dress *tall*. The professional killer is probably a formidable specimen."

After Fin turned off the machine he was excited.

He ran to a mirror and looked for the face of a contract killer. But he saw nothing but a flushed middle-aged civil servant with *fear* in his eyes!

Fin went to the medicine cabinet and grabbed a vial of Halcion that a nurse he used to date had given him for nights like this. He knew he shouldn't mix the drug with all the happy-hour booze, but what the hell, George Bush took them and hadn't expired yet. But Bush was close to expiration, being ten points behind Clinton with only a few days left.

When Fin got under the covers he tried to relax every muscle and fiber. He almost succeeded until he thought about that earthworm of an agent telling him to dress *tall*.

11

Fin only had twenty minutes to rehearse before going to work, but he made the best of it. He had to find the eyes of a killer. Instead, they looked like tide pools of disgusting red plankton, and he used half a bottle of eyewash trying in vain to clear them.

When he got to the office he had trouble keeping his mind on the mound of paperwork: the reports requiring follow-up calls, license and VIN numbers to be checked, the glorified *secretarial* work that made up his job and his life. He was surprised when his thoughts kept flashing to Nell Salter, of the long-ago fog lights, and long legs, and the sexy broken nose.

But on this day he had other things to worry about. He'd shaved as closely as he could, and he'd worn his best dress shirt, and a herringbone sport coat with an understated paisley tie. He thought he should dress *against* type. He was the professorial, calculating, professional hit man, someone who had it in the *eyes.*

Fin hoped they wouldn't videotape the reading. That had happened to him twice before and his performances had suffered. Of the dozen or so tricks he'd used so unsuccessfully during thirteen years of amateur and professional acting, the one that helped him most was to start an argument with somebody just before a reading, to elevate his energy level. John McEnroe used that gag in every successful tennis match.

It'd been easy to find something to get mad at when he was still married, but now that he was single he had to search for sufficient aggravation to motivate a performance. Just before leaving for his reading, he settled on Maya Tevitch. You could rely on her to fly into a rage simply by confessing that you'd spanked your puppy with a newspaper.

In addition to animal rights advocacy, Maya was one of the few cops he'd ever known who was an outspoken liberal Democrat, having championed Clinton from the moment he did the saxophone gig for Arsenio Hall. So when the time arrived, Fin looked over at Maya, who'd just hung up the phone, and said to her, "Maya, did you hear the latest medical report on Clinton's laryngitis? They say it's just an excuse to let Hillary make all the speeches, since all he is, is her *beard* anyway."

"He's got allergies," Maya said disgustedly. "My god, the poor guy was *dripping!*"

"I hope it's his nose," Fin said. "With *him* you never know."

Because Fin was a Perot supporter, Maya retorted, "Did you get a load of Perot Monday night? You still think there's a genius imprisoned in that grotesque little body? Like Toulouse-Lautrec maybe?"

Another Perot man, Detective Jimmy Estrada, said, "At least Perot responds. Clinton'd just stand there and nod understandingly if you pissed on his leg. If he wins he's a one-termer, then he'll be out pounding nails for the street people, with Jimmy Carter."

Maya said, "At least he won't be shooting birds

in Texas like George Bush and all his cowboy pals. The same guys that buy special licenses to blow away peaceful grazing buffalo since it's illegal to shoot *cows*. Clinton'll heal the wounds of this country!"

"Heal the wounds!" Fin scoffed. "That's all I hear from the guy. Heal the wounds. Does he wanna be a president or a paramedic? And what's all this about investing in infrastructure? What the hell's infrastructure? Where do I buy some of this infrastructure he's so hot to invest my money in?"

"Yeah," Jimmy Estrada piped up. "And lucky for him the press overlooks his yuppie spokesman's slight reluctance to tell the truth. What's that kid's name? Stephen Lollipops?"

"Stephanopoulos is his name!" Maya's voice was soaring toward falsetto when she said, "I suppose Bush tells the truth?"

"None to top 'Gennifer Flowers was just a casual friend,'" Fin said. "But I'm no Bush guy. They oughtta put that geek's missing pronouns on a milk carton. If butchering our language was a crime he'd be in the electric chair."

"How can you vote for a guy like Clinton that's never met a trial lawyer he didn't *owe*," Jimmy Estrada wanted to know. "And your middle class tax cut won't buy a new toothbrush, Maya."

"He'll bring us all *together*!" Maya cried.

Since all San Diegans feared "Los Angelezation," Fin said, "With all groups living in perfect harmony just like in L.A., huh? Better known as the Balkans West where you gotta pass through metal detectors to get in airports, courthouses and kindergarten classrooms."

Casper Johns, the oldest detective at Southern Division—ten years past when he *should* have retired—uttered the first political statement anyone had ever heard him make. He chewed on his pipestem, a habit he couldn't break even though he no longer smoked, and said, "Maybe it's time for old guys like me *and* George Bush to retire. We're both confused. He can't tell there's a recession going on and I can't tell a homeless unshaven unbathed schizophrenic hobo from Andre Agassi. They look alike to me."

Jimmy Estrada said, "Speaking as a member of the testosterone-producing gender, I can tell you, Maya, Willie Weasel's newfound celibacy has a definite shelf life."

"Sure," Maya said, "and those slippery Republican hatchet men're out there beating the bushes for another smoking bimbo in a spaghetti-strap. Is that any way to win an election?"

And so forth. The political debaters had exhausted themselves by the time Fin got up, energized, to drive to the production office and reveal the chilling visage of a killer. To show them a roaring force of nature!

Before he exited he said to the steaming detective, "Tell me Maya, was it good for *you*?"

The production office of *Harbor Nights* was in the Hillcrest district of San Diego, a logical location because Hillcrest passed for San Diego's Greenwich Village. In Hillcrest there were several cinemas showing art-house films and lots of places to hang out and drink coffee or juice. There were offbeat bookshops and a multitude of ethnic restaurants. Basically, it was nouveau hippie in a town that had for decades been known as the admirals' graveyard.

The production staff of *Harbor Nights* had done its best to glitz up the second story of a commercial building that had begun its life as an apartment house. There were cheaply framed, one-sheet movie posters hanging in every room, most of them from old Hollywood classics that had never been seen by any human being who worked for Harbor Nights Productions. The oldest member of the staff was the co-executive producer, Lenore Fielding, age twenty-nine.

Everyone was hoping that the network would order additional episodes, but the members of the company weren't holding their breath. *Harbor Nights* looked like a mid-season casualty; still, like the forty-first president of the United States, each person was praying for a November miracle.

The moment he entered, Fin's heart sank. This receptionist was all pout. She wore a coral tunic over spandex pants, and you could've served a family of four on the platters hanging from her ears. She was playing a U2 tape on a ghetto blaster, and deliberately ignored him until he'd said his name twice.

"What'd you say?" she asked, after switching off the tape to hear what he'd said.

Accustomed to war with show-biz receptionists, and being *in* character, all locked-and-loaded, so to speak, Fin said, "I don't know *what* I said. But what I was thinking was, that music sounds like a pack a coyotes falling off a cliff."

"Can I help you?" Her lip wriggled upward. He saw that those beautiful violet irises were really beautiful violet lenses.

"I'm here to read," he said.

"To read *what*?"

He pulled back the jacket of his herringbone, showed her the badge on his belt, and said, "To read you your *rights*! When was the last time you bought a quarter of flake? Empty your purse on the desk!"

"What?" Her scarlet pout fell open. "What?"

"Point one milligram of white can kill you!" Fin said.

"What?" she sputtered. "What?"

Then he grinned and said, "Well, I passed the *first*

audition. Just get on the phone and tell Ms. Fielding I'm here. The name's Finnegan. I'm reading for the part of a hit man."

The girl kept both eyes on Fin as she punched the intercom button saying, "Lenore, there's a . . . Mister Finnegan here."

When she put the phone down, she tossed her head toward the inner office and said, "Is that badge *real*?"

As he passed her desk, he said, "I'm a costume cop. I do drive-by fashion checks, and that Betty Boop hairdo's about as up-to-the-minute as an abacus."

When he entered the little office of the co-executive producer of the dying TV show, he tried to walk with a confident stride, but not a swagger. He'd learned that if you start over the top, there's nowhere to go but *down*.

"Mister Finnegan," she said, holding out her hand, palm toward the floor.

He didn't know whether to shake it or kiss her ring, but he kept his killer gaze fixed on the bridge of her candy-colored eyeglasses. She wore an environmentally correct shirt grown from green organic cotton with no chemical dyes. Ditto for the jeans. Draped over the chair was a $600 jacket made from cork that was "shed from trees."

"Hello," he said. "Good to meet you."

She motioned toward a rock-hard sofa, and she sat in a straight-back chair with her head a foot higher than his.

She studied him while Fin continued to dead-stare her. Then she said, "Orson tells me you're a real policeman?"

He showed a hint of a smile and said, "That should give me an advantage playing a contract killer, shouldn't it?" Then he lied and said, "I've known my share of hit men."

"Have you really? Can you talk about it?"

Fin shifted on the sofa and cocked his head as if to say, "Sorry, you know how it is."

She said, "We're thinking of changing the script so that our killer is actually a renegade FBI agent, or maybe a member of the CIA."

Fin figured that would make it the 1,532nd TV show where an agent of the government is the bad guy. Because every member of the Hollywood Elite liked to claim that his phone had been tapped, or a hit squad had tailed him when he was: 1) a student during Vietnam, 2) making a movie about Chile, 3) investigating the Kennedy assassination.

That's what Fin was thinking, but what he said was, "What a great idea! And given my law enforcement experience, I'd be ideal for that role!"

"Orson sent me a list of your credits, Fin," she said. "You haven't done much TV. And I didn't see *anything* in features."

"I did some extra work in two features," he said. "Did you see . . ."

She interrupted him to say, "Do you have formal training?"

"Well, not formal formal," he said. "I've done a lotta stage work . . ."

"Locally?"

"Locally," he said. "I mean, I'm not the type to move to Hollywood and join one of those actors' studios where you learn to imitate a ripe cantaloupe. I'm more of a *natural* actor."

"Right," she said. "Well, would you read this for me, please?"

She handed him a page of a script. *One* page. There was dialogue on the page involving three characters: Renfro, Skaggs and Gonzales.

"Which character?"

"Skaggs," she said. "I think, Skaggs."

He read the dialogue. "He's toast?" Fin looked from the dialogue to the co-executive producer.

"It's not a question," she said. "You read it like a question."

"Is this it?" he asked. "The dialogue? *One* line? *Two* words?"

She said, "Try it again. Remember, you're a . . . let's say a CIA man gone bad. You're referring to our hero who you've been contracted to kill. You're responding to Renfro who said, 'Can you finish him?' And you say . . ."

"He's toast?" Fin asked.

"You did it again," she said patiently. "You delivered your line as a question. It's *not* a question, Skaggs. I mean, Fin. It's a very definitive statement."

Fin gathered himself, studied his dialogue, closed his eyes for a moment, and when he opened them they were slits. "He's *toast*," Fin said.

"Try it again."

"*He's* toast," Fin said.

"Once more."

"He's . . . toast," Fin said.

"That's close."

"I can throw it away," Fin offered. Then he threw it away, mumbling, "He's toast."

"I'm not sure," she said.

"I could play him as an Aussie," Fin suggested. "I do Aussies."

"No Aussies, no."

"He's toast, mate!"

"I said no Aussies."

"A Canadian, then! He's toast, eh?"

"That's enough. Thanks."

"I can Bogart the line for you!" Fin said desperately. "I can put so goddamn much menace in it you'll hear background music from Alfred Hitchcock!"

"No, that's fine," she said. "That was very good. Thank you, Fin. We'll be in touch."

He stood when she did and took her dry hand in his clammy one. Then he asked, "Will the character be coming back? I mean, I was led to believe he'll get killed or *seem* to get killed but he'll come back?"

"We hope he'll come back," she said. "We hope we're *all* coming back. We'll be in touch."

As he was about to open the door, she said, "Fin, do you have a moment to advise me about something?"

"Sure," he said.

She went to a desk that still had the rental-company sticker on one leg, and took out a clipped stack of parking citations.

"There's no place to park," she explained. "And our production van's been collecting these. Would you know someone downtown who could . . . show us *consideration* and perhaps take care of these? After all, San Diego wants movie and TV companies to shoot down here. Would you be able to help us?"

Fin shook his head and said, "I could pay them for you, but I think I'd need to have a thirteen-show contract from the looks of that stack. Sorry, we can't fix tickets in this town."

"Of course," she said, and her smile melted like a snow cone on Ocean Beach.

"Does this mean *I'm* toast?" Fin asked bleakly.

"We'll be in touch," she said with a papal gesture, closing the door behind him.

The snotty little receptionist couldn't have looked happier if she'd been masturbating to music. She knew he was toast.

Fin glanced at the eight-by-ten glossies on her desk, local male actors in their twenties. Each had at least a three-day stubble on his unlined boyish face.

Each probably read his lines in a whispery voice, both wise and sensual. *Toast. Toast!*

"Guess you can't expect a job if you shave every day," he muttered.

"Are you a cop?" the receptionist asked before he exited. "Are you a *real* cop?"

Fin felt used, defeated, humiliated, *old*. He said, "I ain't sure anymore, kid, but I got handcuffs older'n you."

It had been a tough day for Bobbie Ann Doggett too. In the first place, it was hard getting Captain Fontaine, the deputy director of security, to give her permission to use investigative time for a theft that Naval Investigative Service was too busy to bother about.

"A dozen trucking companies and waste haulers?" the marine officer said doubtfully. "And *no* leads of any kind?"

"But I don't have much going on, sir," she told him. "And this is a pretty big felony. We now think there might be as many as fifteen hundred pairs stolen. Maybe a lot more."

"Okay," he said reluctantly, "but just work on it when you can spare the time. Make it your *hobby* for a week or two. And don't tie up the Chevy all day. The boss might need the car."

"Okay, Captain, thanks," she said, noticing that her civilian counterparts rolled their eyes at each other.

She knew what they were thinking: a dozen trucking crews to check out? And every trucker a thief. Good luck, Bad Dog.

The hauling companies that were located outside San Diego County would have to be contacted by telephone; not that they were any less likely to be the perpetrators, but there was only so much she could do with a clueless case. Seven of the contractors whose rigs had been at or near the warehouse during the period in question *were* in San Diego County. Just to see how it would go, she decided to do the first one as a cold interview, without a preliminary phone call.

Zimmer Transport was owned by Roger (call me Speed) Zimmer, who was highly amused and delighted to be questioned by a detective from the navy, particularly by a female detective. In the past he'd always been contacted by San Diego P.D. detectives who were *never* cute little blondes. Speed Zimmer loved how she filled out that white cotton blouse, and he asked right away if she'd like to take off her jacket on such a warm day.

It was a teal-colored, wool-blend melton blazer with deep lapels. She'd shopped for three days until she found one on sale for $39. Bobbie was wearing stone-washed jeans, but she never wore jeans without dressing them up with a blazer, and with a no-nonsense cotton shirt, and mid-heel pumps.

Speed Zimmer thought she was adorable. Bobbie Ann Doggett thought the fat old creep was *gross*, especially when, after she asked to interview the truckers who'd been to the quayside warehouse, he said, "Sure, sure, but lemme ask, do you dig Paula Abdul? I'm tryin to get tickets to a concert in L.A. and I'd hate to go alone."

"Sorry, *sir*," Bobbie said. "I think I'll be too busy for the rest of the year helping N.I.S. investigate people who sexually harass women."

That caused Speed to call his truckers into the office. Bobbie figured he only knew about Paula Abdul from that Diet Coke commercial. Speed Zimmer reeked of Polo cologne, which always smelled to her like chocolate gone rancid.

When she finally got to talk to each trucker,

Bobbie found one surly and one confused. They were both capable of stealing anything, but they were so stupid she felt sure they'd be *wearing* the stolen shoes, since their own looked like something a dock worker in Guam wouldn't be caught dead in.

The dumber of the two spotted the bulge of the .45 automatic under her jacket, and asked, "Do you carry a *loaded* gun? I mean, being a girl and all?"

She remained only long enough to see that no other employee was wearing flight-deck shoes.

At the next stop of the day no one tried to take her to concerts or ask questions about her sidearm, but the owner of Haulright Vans had gone on vacation and the shift foreman didn't have the faintest idea who'd made the run to North Island.

And so it went all afternoon. She didn't want to go back to the office and confess to her co-workers that they were right about the waste of time, so she didn't return to the base until 4:45 P.M., after they'd gone home.

That evening, Bobbie Ann Doggett soaked in the bathtub and thought about giving up on the shoe investigation, but she was convinced that just about any hauler she'd encounter would feel so confident or be so stupid that he'd wear, or sell to a co-worker, a pair of black, steel-toe, high-top, nonskid U.S. Navy shoes. She decided to visit as many of the trucking companies as possible just to have a look at everyone's *feet*.

12

After Bobbie had her eggs, toast and orange juice the next morning, and after she'd studied the list of truckers she was going to try to contact, she decided to wear a skirt instead of jeans with her blazer. Maybe a more businesslike look would help discourage rock concert invitations, but actually, she wouldn't mind seeing Paula Abdul if somebody halfway acceptable had asked her.

Until the month before Bobbie had gone home on leave she'd been kept pretty busy by a neighbor whom she'd met through her landlady. The guy was a paving contractor, older than Bobbie, but still in his thirties, and recently separated from his wife. A guy in that state of utter turmoil where he continually waffled between reconciliation and divorce.

He'd finally kissed off Bobbie by telling her that for the sake of the children he had to go back home. As they *all* did eventually, every married or separated guy she'd ever dated. They always got that message across, apparently thinking it was unique, that they were only staying with or returning to a wife "for the sake of the children." It got very boring.

After the paving contractor had reconciled, Bobbie

missed the weekly dinner date, the box seat at Jack
Murphy Stadium, and the pretty good sex. The contractor had a nice sense of humor, and she'd actually enjoyed him as a friend and companion. Bobbie
believed that she'd learned sooner than most wom-
en her age that young guys were selfish lovers, yet
she'd never had the chance to go to bed with a man
over forty.

One of the women on her last ship had a boyfriend sixty-three years old, and she claimed that he
was so adept sexually, he could just "talk her off."
The trouble with young sailors was, they didn't talk at
all; they just rutted like buffaloes. Bobbie wasn't sure
about a guy sixty-three, but if she met an older guy
she liked she'd be very curious, no doubt about it.

The third waste hauler on her list was Reggie's
Truck Line. She didn't get to the company in Mira
Mesa until 10:30 A.M., discovering that Reggie was a
cop-hater who wasn't anxious to cooperate with anyone connected to law enforcement. And he complained
to her that he'd been unable to get navy contracts,
except for the one job in question, because of ethnic
contractors who were beating him out. After twenty
minutes of bitching about how Americans were losing
out to spics, spades, and slopeheads, he grudgingly
gave Bobbie permission to interview the employees
who'd made a pickup at North Island.

The first was a Mexican national, fifty years old.
His partner was a Honduran, about the same age.
Neither spoke English, so Reggie had to supply
Bobbie with a bilingual secretary from his office.
Both truckers were so intimidated they could hardly talk. The Honduran wore tennis shoes with soles
that flipflopped when he walked. The Mexican wore
huaraches with soles made of truck tires. Bobbie felt
sure that they *hadn't* stolen the flight-deck shoes.

After having a burger for lunch, Bobbie noted

that the next contractor on the list was Green Earth Hauling and Disposal in Chula Vista. When she got there she found that it was one of the larger hauling companies. There was a yard behind the building that encompassed a square block, and the whole property was surrounded by an eight-foot chain-link fence, topped with razor wire. In this type of business it was more to protect the public from the product than the other way around.

The company office was upstairs in a U-shaped stucco building, but before going to meet the owner Bobbie stood outside the yard and counted ten workers loading and off-loading. Two vans and an eighteen-wheeler drove out during the time she remained there observing. Business was good.

Bobbie was met in the upstairs office by a very pregnant, fortyish dispatcher with a hairdo that said, Wake me up early for the curling iron. On a woman her age and in her physical condition the hairdo looked all right to Bobbie, but being twenty-seven years old, she couldn't help wondering why, the older they got, the harder they worked on their hair, instead of lightening up on themselves.

The pregnant dispatcher said, "Can I help you?"

Bobbie showed her navy credentials and said, "I'm Detective Doggett from North Island. I'd like to speak to the owner, please."

The pregnant dispatcher (Abel Durazo's sometimes squeeze, who wasn't sure if her baby was going to look like her carrot-top husband or a papoose) picked up the phone, punched a key, and said, "Mister Temple, there's a naval person here from North Island."

Jules Temple stood up when Bobbie entered his office, and showed her his Rotary luncheon smile: "How can I help my favorite customer, the United States Navy?"

Bobbie thought he was a good-looking guy, but she wasn't fond of his blond hairdo, long on top but stopping halfway down the sides. It looked like something an F-14 could take off from. He was tall and had great teeth, but he dressed like a Manila car dealer in one of those ice cream suits with a black shirt buttoned all the way up. The other waste haulers she'd met wore khakis or coveralls.

His office was surprising too. There was a glazed cabinet with bookshelves, and glass shelves for decanters of liquor, as well as two leather wingback chairs divided by a lacquered occasional table. His desk was a large glass-topped, art-deco copy. This was the office of a man who hauled *waste*?

After she was seated in a wingback, Jules said, "Coffee? A soft drink? How about some macadamia coconut cookies? My secretary's crazy about them."

"Nothing, thanks."

She knew by the way he was looking her over that he could be her first older sex partner if she but said the word. She would not be saying it, not to this guy. She could imagine him rubbing his legs together like a happy insect.

"We had a large theft at one of our warehouses," she said to Jules. "We can narrow it down to a period last week when one of your trucks was there picking up two drums of hazardous waste. I'd like to talk to your employees and see if maybe they saw something or could help me in some way."

"May I ask what was stolen?"

"We're not sure," Bobbie said.

Jules showed his wry smile and said, "Then how are you sure there *was* a theft, Detective? Shall I call you Detective or . . ."

"That's fine," Bobbie said, "or *Ms.* Doggett if you like."

Wryer yet, and not at all discouraged, he said,

"I guess you're saying you don't wanna tell me too much about the crime?"

"Not unless you were in the truck, sir."

Jules *loved* girls like this. He figured she was the chunky cheerleader in high school. Every school had one. She'd blossomed and lost most of it, but there was just enough still showing. Maybe in the thighs, maybe under that slim little skirt. "I understand, *Detective*," Jules said.

Now the brazen son of a bitch was staring at her tits! And being obvious about it. "I won't keep them from their jobs for very long, sir," Bobbie said. "I just got a few questions. I'd like to go out to their workplace, if you don't mind."

"I don't mind," Jules said. "If you don't mind wearing a hard hat. Can't have anything falling on that pretty blond head, can we?"

"Whatever you say, sir," Bobbie said. "Where can I get a helmet?"

He loved it. Young girls never called anybody "sir" anymore. This sailor cop was *just* the kind of all-American girl he'd envisioned as a hostess, when he opened his topless dancing club.

After Jules allowed Bobbie to write down the names, addresses, and phone numbers of haulers Durazo and Pate for her records, he told her that she'd find them in the yard washing down equipment.

He added, "I don't *think* any of my employees would commit a theft, but you never know, do you? I should tell you that less than an hour after they left North Island, their van was stolen from them. If there was something of yours inside, it's gone. I don't believe they're dishonest people. Dumb, but not dishonest. I don't believe they're thieves."

"Thank you," Bobbie said, and headed for the yard.

Abel Durazo was puzzled to see the young gringa in a company hard hat approaching them. The ox was inside a trailer hosing it out while Abel wiped down the tractor. Both wore gray coveralls and rubber Wellington boots.

Abel liked her looks very much until she said, "Mister Durazo? I'm Detective Doggett from North Island. Mister Temple's given me permission to talk to you and Mister Pate. Separately and privately, if you don't mind."

When the ox gawked down at her from the trailer bed, Bobbie said, "Mister Pate, you can continue what you're doing for now. Thank you."

Bobbie and Abel Durazo left the yard and sat at a Formica table in a shed that served as a lunchroom. There were coin-operated machines for soft drinks, coffee, and junk snacks.

"Can I buy you a soda?" Bobbie asked the handsome young Mexican.

"No thanks, lady," he said.

"Can you guess why I'm here?" she asked.

"No, lady," he said.

"When you came to North Island to pick up the drums containing hazardous waste, you were in the quayside warehouse. Something happened there, Abel."

She paused, but he just smiled quizzically. Then he said, "Yes?" It sounded like "Jas?"

"There were some boxes taken from the warehouse," Bobbie said. "We hope you can help us."

Abel shrugged and said, "Yes, lady?"

"We know that truckers took the boxes," Bobbie said. Then she tried a ploy and said, "We have a *witness*."

The Mexican didn't bat an eye. "Yes?"

"Have you ever been arrested, Abel?"

"Me? No, lady. Never."

"Has your co-worker Shelby Pate ever been arrested?"

"I don' know," Abel lied. "Maybe joo ask him?"

"Yes, I will," Bobbie said. "Our witness may be able to identify the truckers. It'd be better if they came forward *before* that happens. Do you understand?"

Abel shrugged again. "Yes, lady?"

"Sometimes one person is mainly responsible for taking something and the other person just goes along with it. Maybe the person who goes along is . . . *afraid* of the stronger person. That could be what happened in this case."

Abel continued smiling, not bothering to say: Yes, lady?

"We do have a pretty good witness who saw something," Bobbie repeated.

"You could bring your witness here and let him look at us," Shelby Pate said, waddling into the lunch area, wiping his salami fingers with an orange rag. Now he was wearing his Mötley Crüe cap instead of a hard hat. His coveralls were unzipped, revealing a Guns 'n' Roses T-shirt.

He didn't look diffidently at Bobbie the way Abel Durazo did. He shot her a look that said, "I ain't afraid of some little navy cop."

"Thanks," Bobbie said. "I might do that. I guess you're here most every day?"

"Except Saturday and Sunday," Shelby said. "Better hurry though. The boss is sellin the business, and as soon as the new owner shows up, we're history."

"Anything more, lady?" Abel asked.

"If you got a camera with you we don't mind if you take our pitchers, do we, Flaco?" Shelby said. "You could show them to your witness and maybe save yourself another trip. So what was taken outta the warehouse anyways?"

"Boxes," Bobbie said, wishing they weren't wearing rubber Wellingtons. She wanted to see their shoes. "Where're your lockers?"

"You're gonna search our lockers?" Shelby asked.

Then Bobbie watched him turn his cap around backwards and give her an in-your-face grin, crossing huge arms that were covered with amateurish skin-ink.

"I didn't say that," Bobbie said.

"Tell you what," Shelby said, winking at Abel. "I'll give you permission to search my locker if you'll have a beer with me after work. I know a place in Imperial Beach. Lotta sailors hang out there. *Female* sailors even. You might meet some old shipmates."

Dropping her professional demeanor with this asshole, Bobbie said, "Cut me some slack, Jack. I wasn't dissing you, so don't dis me. Okay?"

She stood up then, and Abel Durazo said, "Joo can look een my locker, lady."

"Some other time," Bobbie said, glaring at Shelby Pate, who turned his back and dropped some coins in a junk-food machine only slightly wider than he was. She wished she could see their *shoes*!

"What time's your shift end?" Bobbie directed the question to Abel, but Shelby answered, "Five. Change your mind 'bout the beer?"

"How many of you leave here at five?"

" 'Less they work overtime, maybe ten, twelve," Shelby said. "But I ain't invitin *them* for the drink. Jist you, me and maybe Flaco here."

Abel thought it was rude and stupid to talk like this to her. He understood that the ox was using insolence to show a lack of concern, but to Abel it could have the result of indicating *guilt*, not innocence. He wished the ox would shut up and let this woman leave. "We not thiefs, lady," Abel said. "Call me when joo wan' my photo."

"You kin call me at home," Shelby Pate said. "I wanna see *more* a you!"

"You're gonna see more of me, Creepy Tooth," she muttered, feeling their eyes on her when she walked back across the yard to the company building. The hard hat made her self-conscious so she took it off and ran her fingers through her bob. She heard Shelby Pate say something to Abel and chortle at his own remark.

When Bobbie had first been assigned as detective at North Island, the director of security, a former San Diego P.D. cop, said to her, "Police work is very frustrating sometimes, especially investigation. And for a woman there're special little miseries and no man can help you with them. But when you do succeed in developing a case based entirely on your own diligence and intuition and luck, the feeling is *incredible.*"

Bobbie Ann Doggett could define what "incredible" would mean to her in this instance: snapping those steel ratchets around the fat wrists of that feloniously ugly sonofabitch!

He'd taken his act too far, way too far. She had more than a hunch that these two had stolen the navy shoes. But if so, what did the later stealing of the van signify? Was it just a coincidence? An unknown thief *happening* to steal the stolen navy cargo?

This was not a case she could talk about to her colleagues, nor even to her boss. Not yet. It was all based on instinct, and they'd just rag on her about women's intuition, and roll their eyes, and smirk. Be that as it may, her investigator's instinct told her that Shelby Pate and Abel Durazo were her thieves.

13

The bobtail van belonging to Green Earth Hauling and Disposal had not been in the stolen vehicle system for long. The day after it went missing, traffic on I-5 north had been backed up for two miles because of that van, and the remains of its driver, less his right foot, had been taken to the county morgue in Kearny Mesa.

A CHP officer discovered that it was a stolen San Diego van by calling in the VIN number as well as the Mexican license number. He then allowed the van to be hauled to the tow yard because his radio operator was late in informing him there was a HazMat notification on that stolen vehicle. Otherwise it would've stayed where it was until a HazMat team in protective clothing and breathing apparatus could get to the scene and make sure it was safe.

Urgent calls were eventually made, and in less than an hour a fire department HazMat team wearing moon suits arrived at the tow yard to check the bobtail van for any sign of a toxic spill. The truck was found to be clean and was cleared for release to the owner, and CHP agency-to-agency computer messages so informed all interested parties includ-

130

ing Nell Salter and the San Diego P.D. And because Fin had made the HazMat notifications, he too was informed of the truck's status.

Long after the bobtail van had been hauled away, a CHP rookie, whose training officer didn't want to be walking around out there at night, searched for a missing item that his partner didn't want to find. Pepe Palmera's left shoe was not on his foot, and for all they knew, was on the bumper of a car bound for San Francisco. The right shoe and the foot inside it had not been found either. The rookie thought he should search for it as a humanitarian gesture.

The young officer spent twenty minutes slogging through the ice plant on the steep bank of earth on the west side of the freeway, shining his light on every piece of refuse and trash trapped beneath the flowering ground cover. By the time he finally spotted the shoe, swarming with ants, his tan uniform was a mess.

"Here it is!" he hollered to his training officer, who shook his head in disgust. Now, instead of going for a tasty beef-dip they'd be taking a stinking bug-covered human foot to the morgue!

The rookie slid and scrambled down the bank, holding the shoe and foot aloft like a tennis trophy, yelling: "We *got* it!"

"I hope you're satisfied," the training officer said to him. "Now what're you gonna do with it? Have it bronzed?"

The next day, Fin was worried that he might have to assist on a drive-by homicide that had occurred the night before. He said to his co-worker Maya Tevitch, "I don't need dead bodies complicating my life. The theme on my favorite talk show is, will Mia take Woody back? I was all set to call in and say that

she'll let the devil knock her up again before she gives
Woody another crack. I gotta stay *available* today!"

"Are *you* gonna go to the morgue?" Maya asked
gleefully, knowing Fin's reputation for squeamish-
ness.

Fin responded to the animal rights advocate,
"Why don't you go for me, Maya? You people like
to hold wakes for road kills. So pretend it's a gerbil
and get indignant. You'll *enjoy* yourself."

While Fin Finnegan fretted about going to the
place where former human beings are sawed, sliced,
diced, and leave the premises a lot lighter than when
they entered, Nell Salter made a call to the CHP and
got all the information she wanted from the officer
who did the traffic report.

"What do his fingers look like?" Nell asked the
Chip. "Is he gonna be printed for I.D.?"

"His fingers were kibbled," the officer said, "but
we're very satisfied with his I.D. His border crossing
card and driver's license say his name is José Palmera,
twenty-five years old, resident of Tijuana. And he's
got a minor arrest record with S.D.P.D. In the truck
there was a bill of lading for a delivery he made to
Huerta's Pottery Shed in Old Town."

"Is HazMat through with the truck?"

"Everyone's done with it," the Chip said. "The
San Diego P.D. oughtta follow up on the pottery deliv-
ery. The shop in Old Town might be in cahoots with
Tijuana thieves who steal trucks and cold-plate them."
Then he added, "Of course I'm not the detective."

"Okay," Nell said. "I'm concerned about the hazardous waste."

Before Nell could hang up, the CHP officer said,
"Wait a minute, there's an officer here who wants to
talk to you."

It was the young officer who'd found Pepe Palmera's shoe and foot. He said, "Hello? This is Officer Tim Haskell? I just wanted you to know that I found the deceased's foot in the ivy?"

"Very good," Nell said. "Good work."

"I just wanted you to know?" the kid said.

"Know what?"

"Well, when I found the foot it was covered with hungry ants."

"Can't blame them," Nell said.

"Anyways, the ants were swarming."

"I can understand that," Nell said.

"But by the time I gave it to the meat wagon, the ants had bought it!"

"Whaddaya mean bought it?"

"Croaked. All the ants went tits-up." Then he added, "Sorry, ma'am. Belly-up."

After Nell thanked the kid for the info, she called San Diego P.D. and received the message loud and clear from a detective at Central that if they could get the time to do a follow-up at the pottery shop they'd *try* to get around to it.

Nell hung up, thinking, sure, in this decade or the next? Somehow she believed that the hazardous waste could be located. Or did she just want to talk to Detective Finnegan again? She wasn't sure.

It turned out that Fin didn't have to help with the drive-by homicide after all, so he said to Maya Tevitch, "I *thought* this was my lucky day. I might even get another one of those letters from Publishers Clearing House telling me I won enough to save Somalia."

Fin had thought several times about Nell Salter's fog lights, and was truly curious to see how well she'd aged. He believed that babes who're looking down the barrel at forty-something are anxious to prove they've still got it. He dialed her number.

"Nell Salter," she said, when she answered. He

liked babes with full-throated voices, but he hoped it didn't mean she had a neck like Maya Tevitch, which was a size larger than his own.

"It's Finnegan," he said. "I got some news about the stolen van."

"I was just thinking about calling *you*," she said. "I already phoned the CHP and found out all about it."

"Yeah? So what happened?"

"Yesterday on I-five near Mission Bay, the driver of the van jumped out and got dusted running across the freeway."

"Was it a high-speed pursuit or what?"

"Nope, he just parked by the center divider and jumped out yelling and running. Right into a Greyhound bus, among other vehicles. Like he was out of his head."

"Any hazardous material in the truck?"

"Like a lawyer's conscience, meaning there was none."

"No leads at all?"

"He had paperwork for some pottery he'd hauled from Tijuana to Huerta's Pottery Shed in Old Town. I can't convince anybody at Central to check it out right away, so I'm going up there. Might find a lead as to where he dumped the stuff."

"How's about if I stop by your office and pick you up?" Fin suggested. "I'll go *with* you."

Nell Salter figured correctly that his motive was not investigation but seduction. She said, "My partner's on vacation. I got a lotta work to do today, but how about tomorrow?"

"Yeah, I'm busy too," Fin said. "Ain't civil service hell? Tomorrow's perfect. I know a German bar that makes their own beer. They play Barry Manilow tapes, and if that ain't bad enough, they just discovered potato skins. The cutting edge of hip if you're from a farm in Bavaria. The place is so depressing your own misery disappears for a while. Whaddaya say we check out the pottery shop and go have a beer?"

The phone line was quiet for a moment; then she said, "I can't resist an enticing invitation like that. I'll meet you in Old Town at four-thirty tomorrow afternoon." Before she hung up, Nell said, "There's one more bit of news that might mean something. The dead guy's foot was cut off and the ants tried to take it home. Except they all *died*. And anticipating your avid interest in all this I've asked that the medical examiner send blood and tissue samples to a specialty lab ASAP to discover why the ants died. And I'm gonna phone the hauling company and find out exactly what they were hauling in case tomorrow we get a lead on where the thief dumped it."

"Okay," Fin said, wondering if he'd made a mistake. This babe was actually interested in doing police work!

Late that afternoon Jules Temple crawled all *over* his bobtail van like a live ant on a dead foot. He'd gone to the tow yard with Abel Durazo to pick up the van, and before he'd even completed the paperwork Jules had looked in the glove compartment, under the seat, behind the seat, under the rubber floor mats and inside the cargo area before he was satisfied that the manifest was not there.

He was particularly elated to learn from the police that the driver of the van, presumably the thief who stole it, was a Mexican national with a police record. Which meant that the waste was probably in Mexico!

As the cops saw it, the stolen van had been driven south of the border, cold-plated, crudely painted to get rid of the company name, and used to haul merchandise for a Tijuana pottery maker who was no doubt aware of the truck theft because the invoice found in the van wrongly showed that the pottery was owned by the deceased.

"Are you sure there were not *any* documents of mine in the truck?" Jules asked the detective who'd notified him.

"Like your registration? No, they got rid of that," the detective said.

"But was there *anything* of mine?"

"Like what?"

"Any paperwork? Anything at all?"

"There was nothing in the truck to tie it to Green Earth Hauling and Disposal," the detective said. "Naturally, the thief didn't want U.S. Customs to make that connection when the van came back north."

"He must've thrown away my manifests," Jules said.

"Of course he'd throw away *any* paperwork."

"That'll cause me some extra trouble," Jules Temple said. "But never mind, I'm just happy to get the van back."

"I doubt you'll ever hear from the Mexican side about your hazardous waste if that's where it got dumped," the detective said.

"Of course not," Jules said, cheerfully. "Somebody'll dehead the drums and make barbecue ovens for pigs. They might even cut them horizontally and use them for tubs to bathe their babies in. Well, thanks again. I'll write a letter of commendation to your boss."

After Jules hung up, he thought about calling Burl Ralston to assuage his fears. But then he thought, fuck him, let the old bastard percolate. He deserved it for even *thinking* about ratting off Jules Temple to the Environmental Protection Agency.

For the rest of the afternoon Jules went to a topless bar down on Midway. There was a new dancer he'd heard about who could set off the Richter scale. Jules was dead serious about taking the $743,000 he was going to net from the sale of his business and investing it in a club that would drive every other joint out of business. There was a market for upscale clientele including Asian businessmen, not just for the MTV generation who seemed to frequent those places. Jules had *lots* of ideas.

The strange odyssey of the bobtail van was the topic of conversation most of that day at Green Earth Hauling and Disposal. Of course, the majority of the conversation concerned Abel Durazo and Shelby Pate, who were enjoying the attention. Both were happily surprised that Jules Temple had no intention of firing them even though he'd as much as accused them of stealing his $500.

Abel kept his share of the cash at home in a bedroom that he rented from a Guatemalan family. On Saturday night, Shelby lost most of his in a bikers' bar in National City, too fried on crystal meth to be gambling on a game of pool, but doing it nonetheless.

Shelby and Abel had speculated privately about *why* the boss hadn't fired them, finally deciding that, until escrow closed, Jules Temple didn't want to make personnel changes that might send a signal to the future owner that there were problems at Green Earth. He wouldn't want the guy to rethink the purchase.

It was during one of these conversations that Abel said to Shelby, "Tell me, Buey, was joo berry much scared when we make the report? And the cop he say, '*Sure.* Money een glove box. *Sure.*' Was joo scared like me?"

"I ain't scared a *no* cops," Shelby bragged. "They can't jist search people without a good reason. This ain't Mexico, dude. He mighta figgered the money was on us but he couldn't do nothin about it."

"I was scared, *'mano*," Abel said. "That money feel like a bomb een my pocket!"

For the first time, Shelby remembered that on Friday night he'd had the money in the pocket of his leather jacket. *With* the manifests from North Island and Southbay Agricultural Supply. For the first time he realized that the manifests were still in the pocket of the jacket.

"I fergot to toss them manifests away," he said to Abel. "They'll still be in my jacket."

"Toss them," Abel said.

"I'll toss 'em tonight," Shelby said. "The jacket's in my bitch's closet."

And he would've done that if he hadn't decided to stop for *one* drink in Imperial Beach, where a biker he knew sidled up and said, "I can let you have a quarter a go-fast for twenny bucks. This special sale can't be repeated."

Shelby couldn't resist. He bought a quarter of a gram of methamphetamine, got zombied-out, and forgot *all* his good intentions.

A day that had started well for Jules Temple ended on a troubling note when the phone rang just as he was leaving for home.

"Mister Temple," the telephone voice said. "This is Nell Salter. I'm an investigator with the District Attorney's Office, investigating environmental crimes."

"Yes, and what can I do for you?"

"It's about your stolen van," Nell said. "The thief who was killed in it may've had a toxic substance in his body."

"I wouldn't doubt that," Jules said. "Probably a doper, huh?"

"Organophosphate poisoning might cause some of the things observed."

"Like a pesticide?"

"Possibly," Nell said. "What I'm wondering is, could he have been contaminated when he dumped your hazardous waste? What *exactly* were your people hauling?"

Jules's mind was racing! The goddamn waste just *might* turn up somewhere! That fucking Mexican thief! Jules said calmly and truthfully, "The navy's waste was contaminated diesel fuel. And one drum from Southbay Agricultural Supply contained Guthion."

"Guthion," Nell said. "That's a dangerous insecticide."

"It sure is," Jules said.

Nell said, "That'd explain his bizarre behavior when he ran wildly into freeway traffic. He was probably hallucinating."

"This case is interesting," Jules said. "What're you gonna do now? Search for the missing drums?"

"Since the truck got to Tijuana, the drums might be there," Nell said. "*Unless* he dumped them somewhere between Imperial Beach and the border. The police and sheriffs have been notified, of course. I'll make a few calls to Tijuana."

"I see," Jules said. "To trace the dead man's activity?"

"As best I can," Nell said. "There's a remote possibility I might come up with something. Somebody else may've been contaminated."

"This is *very* interesting!" Jules said. "I've never been part of an investigation before. Please let me know what's going on and if I can help you in any way, you only have to call."

Jules Temple hung up the phone without telling Nell Salter that Detective Bobbie Ann Doggett had questioned his haulers about a separate crime entirely!

Jules didn't know why, but his instinct told him he should not put Bobbie Ann Doggett and Nell Salter together. He sensed that it'd be better for him if the two investigators pursued separate criminal inquiries, and never crossed paths. For the first time, Jules Temple seriously considered the possibility that his employees *might* be responsible for the theft at North Island.

14

San Diego's Old Town—wildly popular with the city's vital tourist industry—was never one of Fin's favorite haunts, even though a lot of cops frequented an Old Town restaurant that served pretty fair carnitas, homemade tortillas, and decent margaritas, all of which tended to attract happy-hour working women.

There wasn't much left in Old Town of the Spanish period when Father Junípero Serra and the soldiers of the Presidio brought the Gospel to the local Kumeyaay whether the Indians liked it or not. There was some evidence that they didn't, in that the peace-loving Kumeyaay destroyed the friars' original mission.

The early nineteenth century brought the Mexican period and with it large adobes, including some impressive haciendas with whitewashed walls, tile roofs, patios and fountains. One of those old haciendas, actually built for a rich Peruvian, had been transformed into a restaurant with courtyard dining, and it packed in the tourists. But most of the surrounding shops sold items that could be purchased more cheaply in Tijuana.

A grassy square in the middle of Old Town Plaza was the best part of the whole shebang, as far as Fin was concerned. It was there in the pedestrian area where he'd strolled with ex-wife number two and made the disastrous mistake of proposing marriage, after guzzling five margaritas. He'd never enjoyed margaritas since.

Huerta's Pottery Shed was larger than the other shops, in that the pots required large display space. Alberto Huerta, the second-generation owner of the shop, sold glazed pottery for cookware and serving, and decorative pottery for plants and flowers, specializing in cactus pots with watering ports. Some of his pottery was designed in the shape of chickens, pigs, sheep, and of course, bulls.

Nell Salter was late, so Fin decided to go it alone and get it over with. He figured that any acquaintance of the late thief José Palmera wasn't about to confess and beg for leniency.

Alberto Huerta was surprised that afternoon when a rather slight man in a herringbone sport coat entered his shop and showed him a badge.

"You took delivery of a truckload of pots a couple of days ago," Fin said to the shop owner.

"Yes, that's right."

Alberto Huerta didn't look like somebody who'd know dick about a hot van and a cold thief, but since it was a bogus investigation anyway, Fin said, "The driver got killed in an accident after he left you."

"He did? My god!"

"Did you know him well?"

"He told me his name was Pepe Palmera. I never saw him before, but we've done business with Rubén for years. That's who makes the pots in Tijuana, Rubén Ochoa."

"The paperwork indicated that the driver was the *owner* of the pottery business."

"They do that down there," Alberto Huerta explained. "They make up all kinds of paperwork to get past U.S. Customs and deliver their loads up here. It's a hard life down there so they learn to cut through the U.S. red tape. That driver didn't own a single pot, I promise you."

"That was a *special* van," Fin said. "It was loaded with drums of toxic waste when it got stolen last Friday. I've got a colleague who wants to know where the thieves dumped the waste."

"I can't help you with that," the shopkeeper said. "A stolen truck? You might try Rubén Ochoa in Tijuana. Maybe he can help you." Then he added, "Toxic waste? Those people have enough to worry about without us giving them our poison. Let me get Rubén's address and phone number for you. I don't think he'd *knowingly* do business with a truck thief."

"You *sure* about that?"

"Well . . ." Alberto Huerta shrugged apologetically. "They're *poor* people, aren't they?"

He went into the back room and when he returned he gave Fin a piece of paper with the pottery maker's Tijuana address and phone number on it.

"Here's my card," Fin said. "If you hear anything that I should know, gimme a call."

Alberto Huerta nodded, anxious to help the customer standing in the doorway. She was a tall woman in a red cable-knit turtleneck. She had shapely legs revealed to advantage in a long skirt with a front slit. Alberto Huerta liked the way her hair had that I-just-got-out-of-bed look. She looked boldly at everyone in the shop. And her nose, it was slightly bent, obviously having been broken. On a fine-looking woman, the broken nose was strangely exciting, the shopkeeper thought.

After Fin spotted Nell, his thoughts were instantly similar to Alberto Huerta's—about the long legs, and the go-to-hell hairdo—but especially about the *nose.* In 1984, when acting jobs were more plentiful, he'd done a local TV commercial with a model whose nose had been broken in a jet-ski accident. Her agent had tried to persuade her to leave it as is but she got it fixed, after which her modeling career went nowhere. Fin told her to rebreak it.

"Yo, Nell!" Fin said, and her firm handshake gave him goose bumps.

"Sorry I was late," Nell said, as they walked toward his car after a quick briefing.

She'd offered to drive, but he wanted her to see his Vette. "He didn't seem to know diddly," Fin said. "I bet your toxic goop got dumped in T.J."

"Nothing unusual in that," Nell said. "The next generation in that town's gonna be Ninja Turtles."

"This is mine," he said, when they got to the Vette. He unlocked the door on her side and offered his hand as she settled into the leather seat.

Decent manners, Nell thought. And he was kinda cute, but pretty small for a cop. This actor was *not* the leading-man type, a second banana, maybe. The guy that doesn't get the girl, hard as he tries. Still, he had soft gray eyes and didn't have a macho cop mustache, thank god.

She hadn't found a man worth sleeping with in seven months, not since St. Patrick's Day after a boozy party for D.A. investigators. Then, after five dates with the guy, she'd found out that the lying bastard *was* married.

When Fin fired up the Vette he revved the engine to let her feel the power. Then he said, "Now that all the hard police work's done, do you really want a beer or shall I take you someplace nice?"

"To that German saloon," she said. "You made it sound slightly better than an emergency call to a shrink."

"I was kinda lying about the beer," Fin confessed.

"Actually their suds is the kinda stuff they use in Germany to kill potato bugs with. Lemme take you somewhere else."

"Speaking of bugs," Nell said, "I think we're gonna get a lab report from the medical examiner saying that Palmera had been exposed to an organophosphate."

"What's that?"

"In this case an insecticide called Guthion. That's what they were hauling when the truck got ripped off."

"Poetry in that," Fin said. "The thief steals poison and it poisons him."

"I just wanna know if it got somebody else. And where the hell *is* it, that's what I wanna know."

He took the Garnet turnoff to Pacific Beach, saying, "You've held up real well in the years since I last saw you."

"They say that about old buildings."

"That didn't come out right," Fin said. "I'm nervous. You're the first woman that's been in my Vette since last June."

"Your dance card can't look *that* bad."

"It's because of my last divorce," Fin said. "I'm a three-time loser. Every time somebody rides in my Vette I marry her. I've learned to ask dates if they mind riding the bus."

"So where're we going for the beer?"

"Pacific Beach," Fin said. "I know a place on the sand where we can get a free sunset with an overpriced beer."

"I live in P.B.," she said.

"Yeah? Then you've probably been everywhere in town."

Nell decided that a sunset drink was about all this guy was good for. *Three* divorces? No way! To make conversation, she said, "Got any kids?"

"Never had kids," Fin said. "Would it be too forward of me to explain that I have a very low sperm count? *Negligible* in fact."

"I didn't ask," she said.

"Sorry if that was too intimate a revelation. It's been several months since I talked to a date, not that this is a date. But let's talk about *me*. Did you happen to catch my gig at Blackfriars' Theatre? Or maybe at North Coast Rep? Or at Lamb's Players Theatre last season?"

"I've never seen you perform," she said. "But I think I read a small story in the paper a couple years ago about local actors. You were mentioned, right?"

"It wasn't *that* small," he said. "My picture was used in the story, though not one of my best. I'm, uh, being considered for a part in *Harbor Nights*."

"What's that, a play?"

"No, a TV series they're shooting down here."

"That should be interesting."

"A contract killer. Can you see me as a killer?"

She turned and looked at him then, and he turned away from the traffic to face her. He was definitely one of them, Nell Salter thought. He had Peter Pan Policeman written all over him. Only he was worse than most: an *actor* to boot!

She said, "If you're a real actor, you can be a killer or anything else."

"That's exactly right!" Fin said. "You're smarter than all the yuppie casting agents I've read for in the past five years. 'Not the type we're looking for,' they usually say. I say, 'Was John Malkovich the type to play a world-class seducer in *Dangerous Liaisons*?' "

"I don't know," she said. "I didn't see it."

"Okay, let's talk about *me*," Fin said. "Do you like Irish types? My full name is Finbar Brendan Finnegan."

Was it an omen? "As a matter of fact, I just had

a passing thought about last St. Patrick's Day," she admitted.

"Really? What?"

"Not important. Yeah, I like the Irish except for the Kennedys and all their cousins including pets and live-stock. I don't like people that treat women like . . ."

"Like Marilyn Monroe?"

"You got it."

"I'm the opposite," Fin said. "I've been victimized by women all my life. My sisters were so protective they thought Jerry Lee Lewis was the devil's step-child. And they were so unbelievably cruel they made me learn the words to every song Patti Page ever recorded. Would you like me to sing 'How Much Is That Doggie in the Window'?"

"I don't think so," Nell said, catching herself wondering if his little body held any interesting surprises, like a nice ass. His chatter *was* a bit disarming.

"Anyway, that's *my* life story until I joined the marines and went to Vietnam and came home and joined the San Diego P.D. and got my own place just so I didn't have to hear the Von Trapps yodeling in the Alps about the sound of mucous. My sisters think that's the greatest musical ever made. They're very Catholic. Then I met and married that sergeant you used to know who was the reincarnation of the Bitch of Buchenwald. Never marry somebody who thinks her handcuffs are a fashion statement."

"Me, I learned about marriage the first time I tried it," Nell said. "If I ever get real lonely I'll buy a parrot. Better conversation than I get from most guys."

"That's 'cause you people're more verbal than we are," Fin said. "*And* more mature. Little boys stay lit-tle boys till they're forty-something; little girls're just sawed-off women."

"And you?" Nell turned and looked at him. "Are you finally mature?"

"I haven't got married since I was forty-two," Fin said. "That might mean I'm growing up."

Nell found herself wondering about his buns again. Then he wheeled the Vette into a parking lot across from the oceanfront.

The restaurant was by the Crystal Pier, one of the last structural relics of Southern California's Golden Age of The Beach. It was a charming, seedy period piece. The main street of Pacific Beach, or "P.B.," as the locals called it, fed right onto the pier, under a two-story arch that joined two whitewashed, teal-shingled buildings belonging to the Crystal Pier Hotel. Farther out on the wooden pier were twenty-one cottages lining both sides of the pier, where cars could park in front of their rooms, over a sandy beach and white water.

Beyond the cottages, the pier narrowed into a wide pedestrian boardwalk that opened up again onto a spacious fishing platform guarded by a white railing, one hundred yards out over blue water. From above, the pier looked like a sand shovel that had drifted away from a giant child and floated on the ocean.

The restaurant was a typical California chain. The emphasis was not on food but on drinks, expensive enough to justify the rent, but affordable enough not to completely discourage the locals who'd be needed when winter came and tourists went.

Fin and Nell were lucky to get a window table, where they ordered tropical drinks served in ceramic coconut shells by a waitress in a sarong. They looked out on a "boardwalk" made of concrete that stretched four miles south to Mission Beach. And because autumn was late in arriving, the boardwalk was loaded with joggers, walkers, rollerbladers and skateboarders draped in bag-rags out for their evening exposure. Most of the hardbodies wore combinations of Day-Glo shorts, tank tops, T-shirts, swimsuits and cutoffs. There was a bit of hip-hop and grunge, but not like at L.A.'s Venice Beach.

Continuing with his obsessive chatter, Fin said, "I've been around women all my life. You'll find I'm easy to be with. In fact, women are very comfortable with me. I'm the sensitive artistic type. I wouldn't hurt a Medfly."

The weird thing was, whatever the guy was doing, it was starting to work on her. He was starting to look a little cuter, even after only *one* drink. Cute little guys could be dangerous though. She asked, "Did you bring your ex-wives here?"

"No, they preferred those trendy places in La Jolla where you can watch the sunset, but you're surrounded by a lotta wealthy gentlemen from countries where camels're still beasts of burden and occasional lovers. But enough about my ex-wives. Let's talk about *me*."

Then they didn't talk much about anything for a few minutes, because of the impending sunset. Sitting there at the fake monkeypod cocktail table, drinking from a fake coconut shell, being brushed lightly by a fake potted-palm branch, they were getting caught up in the nostalgia. A hint of the way it *was*, the way it *must* have been, in bygone days when summer never ended along California's coast. Because life was different then, or so they said, all who'd lived it.

Fin was delighted to see that it was going to be a great sunset, guaranteeing that people in the bar beside the windows would "Oh!" and "Ah!" the instant the fireball disappeared into the eternal sea. No matter how many times he'd seen it, Fin never stopped feeling exhilaration, followed by a sense of loss when the sky momentarily blazed crimson from the afterglow of the heavenly light.

By the time it happened, Fin and Nell had already finished their second drink. He turned to her and she looked as sad as he felt after all the fire had vanished.

She gazed into his eyes for a moment, and she astonished him by reading his mind. By saying what he felt.

"I *know*," Nell said, nodding. "For a little while, before it disappears, you can really pretend, can't you? That life's a beach, after all."

Fin was awfully glad he'd matured. In the old days he'd have married her for that.

15

After work that day, Jules Temple sipped Chablis and soaked in the hot tub until sunset, the hot tub belonging to the apartment building in Sunset Cliffs, an old residential area by Point Loma where he rented a two-bedroom unit. He had the hot tub all to himself, and from the hillside vantage point, he watched as the sky blazed and fired the sandstone cliffs below, burnishing them to the color of old gold. Those golden cliffs at sunset reminded him of his mother's antique-jewelry collection: *another* small treasure his father had given to charity rather than to his only child.

Jules was not a worrier and never had been, but the phone call from Nell Salter was troubling. There was so much riding on the sale of his company that the most remote threat to the negotiations was of concern. He'd been mulling a few scenarios involving the theft of his truck and the toxic exposure to the Mexican driver, but no scenario made sense.

Jules had never been one to project, nor to fret unduly as to the consequence of actions, even impulsive ones—as his father had often pointed out—so he decided to stop fretting for now. Tomorrow he'd go to the yacht club and get some free legal advice about some vexing scenarios he'd conjured. For now he was just going to enjoy the view, the wine, and the tub.

One day soon, he'd have his *own* house with a view of the Pacific, and his *own* hot tub where he could soak naked, either with or without female companionship. And he'd also have a decent car, like a red Mercedes 560SL, instead of a yellow Mazda Miata that he was almost ashamed to drive. Then he could start to live the way he'd been meant to live, if his father hadn't taken his only child's birthright to the grave.

Jules wasn't sure if he'd truly hated his father, but he loathed the old man's memory. The only time he wished the old man was alive was when he'd accomplished something, such as selling a business that had increased his cash investment tenfold in only a few years, and in the teeth of a global recession. It reminded Jules that he'd have to hide the capital gain or his ex-wife would be after him for more child support.

It pleased him to compare himself to his father, a man who'd never been able to accomplish much, content to be a salaried lawyer at a law firm. Jules believed that he'd got the entrepreneurial spirit from his grandfather, but what had happened to his grandfather's legacy? Gone to charities, because the grandfather had trusted *his* son to do right by his descendants.

What could he have accomplished, Jules wondered, if only he had inherited his father's house? It had fetched more than two million dollars because of the glorious bay view, and the executor, an old friend and colleague of Harold Temple, had seen to it that Jules did not so much as get his mother's silver coffee service. He got his five-year monthly stipend and nothing more.

So Jules wished that Harold Temple could be alive if only to see what his son had accomplished, all alone, from his own hard work and quick mind. The old man never would have believed it: a blue-collar industry of the worst kind. But the *right* industry for someone as imaginative as Jules Temple.

It'd been easy to beat out his competition, childishly easy. Just as it would be when he put the profits—not all, but a good portion—into a topless dancing establishment that would be the talk of San Diego. He'd show the doubters an amazingly profitable operation.

His reveries were interrupted when one of his neighbors, an elderly woman in a puckered pink swimsuit, dropped her towel on a lounge beside the hot tub, and said, "Mind if I join you?"

Her flesh was dead white and veined, like his father's during those last years. Jules had never introduced himself to any of his neighbors and wasn't about to start. Now he couldn't enjoy the view or the wine or even the jasmine-scented evening air. She disgusted him.

"It's all yours," he said.

After having been awed into silence by the sunset, Fin and Nell got back to chatting, and gave their table to a pair of diners, a twenty-something pair of lovebirds who did more kissing than dining. Fin and Nell moved closer to the bar and perched on high stools at a little cocktail table. By then, they'd switched to vodka martinis, and after he'd completely lost count of his drinks Fin decided they were more bombed than Bosnia.

His chin kept slipping off his hand as he listened to her whine boozily about the sexual harassment she'd endured throughout her tenure in law enforcement. That was after she'd listened to him whine boozily about the injustices he'd suffered at the hands of ex-wives and talent agents.

When his dimpled chin fell out of his hand for the *third* time, she said, "How many martinis've you had, anyway?"

"As many as you."

"We shoulda stuck to piña coladas."

"Too sugary."

"You gotta drive soon," she said, slurring slightly. "Maybe we oughtta get something to eat."

"Certainly," he said, slurring worse.

"I don't usually drink like this," Nell said. "I don't usually *talk* like this. So much, I mean."

"I know," Fin said, his eyelids drooping. "It's because I'm so easy to talk to. Women tend to talk to me like I'm one of the girls."

Nell blew a puff of breath upward because her hair kept falling across her eyes. "Why?" she asked. "Are you gay or something?"

"I probably am," Fin said somberly, "except for the sex part."

"Nobody cares what *anybody* is," Nell said, spilling some booze on the table. "You get to a certain age, all you care about is, does the guy have AIDS. And does he cuddle good."

"I know how that is," Fin said, sympathetically. And this time his elbow slipped clear off the cocktail table. "When I used to go to singles bars, I'd wear my San Diego Blood Bank T-shirt just to show all the lonely nurses and schoolteachers that I'm a clean donor."

"I *knew* you'd go for nurses and schoolteachers," Nell said, accusingly. "The care givers, right?"

"*I'm* the cuddly care giver," Fin said, defensively. "Remember my first ex-wife, the good sergeant? She wore those confrontational stockings with seams in them even before Madonna did. And call me a silly goose if you want to, but I don't think it's romantic when a female wears scary eye makeup and does one-arm pushups in her teddy just before she jumps in bed at night. The most tender thing she ever said to me was 'Let's get it on.' "

"Was she like that?" Nell was genuinely shocked.

"When we got divorced she got all the dishes she hadn't thrown at me. Living with her was more risky than clerking in a Seven-Eleven store."

"I really didn't know her very well," Nell assured him.

Fin said, "I think I married my second ex-wife because she was the opposite of the sergeant. She loved the great indoors and prescription drugs, but hated people and avoided them. The Witness Protection Program has better mixers. It was because of her that I had a test done and found out that I have a very low sperm count. I was glad 'cause any baby *she* gave birth to would end up being Howard Hughes. Compared to her Salman Rushdie is a party animal. Did I mention my practically nonexistent sperm count? That *nobody* has to worry about?"

"Yeah, yeah, you said." Nell licked some spilled martini off the back of her hand.

The sight of her tongue gave Fin a semi-woody! He *adored* her broken nose! "I give blood every month, so I'm always getting tested."

"Yeah yeah yeah," she mumbled, signaling to the waitress for another round.

"You know what I hate about young actors?" Fin said. "Most of them don't even drink."

"Know what I hate about all male cops?" Nell said. "They *do*."

"It doesn't pay to tomcat around in singles bars, not in these times," Fin said. "I mean, some of the cops I work with? When they sober up they have to sit in a tub full of chlorine bleach for two days. I mean, if you caught a rear view of them in the shower you'd run and call the orangutan wrangler at the San Diego Zoo."

"Yeah yeah yeah," she said, sitting up tall and crossing her legs, causing her skirt-slit to reveal her entire thigh.

"You sure are in good shape for your . . . you sure are in good shape," he said. "Do you jog or something?" Of course he well remembered her back in her youthful jogging days: Foglights Salter!

"I'm in good shape for *any* age, bucko!" she said, truculently.

"You sure are," he said, slumping a bit, figuring that submissive gestures are best when boozy babes get pugnacious.

When the waitress put the drinks down she looked doubtfully at the two dipsos.

Nell said to Fin, "You're *not* very tall, are you?"

"None of us actors are as tall as you imagined," he said, with a hiccup. "Excuse me," he said, and did it again.

"I guess you're right," Nell said. "Bogart stood on a milk crate when he did love scenes with Ingrid Bergman."

"James Cagney was even shorter," Fin said earnestly. "None of us are tall."

"If I was wearing tall heels, would you be embarrassed to dance with me?"

He thought it'd be tricky to walk, let alone dance, but he said gallantly, "Just *tell* me if you wanna dance. We could go somewhere. I do all the Latin steps."

"No, I don't wanna dance!" she said, exasperated, and this time *her* elbow slipped. "I just wanna know how secure you really are. I never met a secure male cop in my whole entire life!"

"My third ex-wife was six foot one," Fin explained. "Barefoot. She taught me to tango and I was never embarrassed with my face pressed to her bosom. But being married to her was like *Fatal Attraction Two.* Before we split up she accused me of dating other babes, and she started putting cockroaches in the toaster. I don't know where she got the cockroaches because she was a clean person, I have to give her that much. Life with her was a game of Dungeons and Dragons. If we'd had a kid that turned out like her, I'd've had it put to sleep."

"I don't believe all this!" Nell said, much louder than she realized.

The bartender shook his head at the cocktail waitress: No more booze!

"That's paranoid," she said. "Cockroaches! You're just proving you're a typical insecure male cop!"

"I'm not paranoid," he said, gravely. "She turned the toaster into a cockroach condo. I checked every inch of the apartment and there were no cockroaches anywhere else. It *had* to be her. I think maybe she was trying to justify sleeping with half the San Francisco Giants one afternoon before a double-header with the Padres. There were a lotta tired puppies on the field *that* night, I can tell you."

"Was she good-looking?"

"Actually, my conscious mind no longer remembers anything about her physical appearance. She went the way of my seventh-grade French."

"Fin!" she cried suddenly. "I got a flash for you. We're hammered. Smashed. Fried. Tanked. *Both* of us. I haven't been like this in years!"

"That doesn't scare me," he said, fumbling for the money in his wallet and holding a bill up to the light, not wanting her to see that he had to wear reading glasses. "Every time I got married I was cold sober, so being drunk doesn't scare me."

"Take me to my car," she said. "I can't have dinner. I'm not feeling well."

"We could go to my apartment," he said. "It's very close. Want a nightcap?"

"No! I can't drink any more!"

"You could have a crème de menthe," he suggested. "And pretend it's prom night."

Suddenly she grabbed him by the lapel and put her bent nose inches from his, saying, "Don't . . . you . . . get it? We are *blitzed*! How did this happen to me?"

"I don't know," he said, unable to stop hiccuping. "I'm not that much of a drinker. I think it's probably our age. I'm forty-five, Nell. All I can see in my future is answering those TV commercials where they give a free prostate check to volunteers over forty-five. Do you know how frightening it is? Turning forty-five?"

She leaned into him and they grabbed each other's shoulder bravely, but unsteadily. Then they stood up and that was tricky too.

The bartender whispered to the waitress: "Perfect friendship, alcohol-induced."

"I'd *like* to go to your apartment, Fin," she confessed to him. "But I can't do that on a first date."

"I understand," he said, feeling queasy, doubting that he could handle this babe anyway, under the circumstances.

"And it's none of my business," she continued, as they lurched to the parking lot, "but I don't think you should get involved with me or that I should get involved with you. You're kinda cute, but *very* neurotic."

"I understand," he said, and the perfect pals were in the camaraderie mode now, standing beside his Vette, holding each other by the biceps. Foreheads pressed together in a bonding gesture. Perfect pals butting each other like rams.

"I don't think you should *ever* get married again, Fin," she said gravely.

"The whole goddamn College of Cardinals will graduate with their MBAs and drive their kids to school in a Volvo wagon before I get married again," Fin pledged.

"Let's go home," she said, "before you gotta call nine-one-one."

He managed to drive back to Old Town while Nell dozed. After he arrived, he parked and opened the door for her, noticing that she was getting green around the gills.

But she got out and gamely gave him a peck on the cheek, saying, "You give great blarney. I'll bet you get lots 'n lots of sleepovers."

Fin wanted to show her his stage flourish, but he was listing too far and almost toppled over. He settled for his leading-man salute; then he said, "Nell, the unvarnished truth is that my orgasms are so infrequent they oughtta be Roman-numeraled like British monarchs and Rocky movies. But I'm a very sincere person. And an above-average cuddler."

16

The first thing that Nell Salter did after arriving at work the next day was to take two aspirin with her coffee, her fifth cup of the morning and her fourth aspirin.

One of the other investigators passed her in the hallway and said, "You don't look too good."

"Too much caffeine," Nell said. "I'm so amped I could jump-start Frankenstein's monster."

Nell kept going to the mirror to check for signs of life. Her tongue needed a shave. That goddamn little neurotic got her wasted!

Late in the morning when she felt better she phoned the office of the county medical examiner and spoke with a pathologist, a navy doctor who moonlighted at the morgue when he was not on duty with Uncle Sam.

"FedEx just arrived," he told Nell. "The specialty lab worked at record speed. What did you tell them?"

"Only that the deceased had expired after a five-minute swim at La Jolla cove. That's believable considering all the toxic spills around here."

"Really?"

"No, I forget what I told him. Look, I got a head-ache today, Doctor. Can you give me the bottom line?"

"Well, it appears that you were right. Of course, we suspected you were, given the inhibiting of cho-linesterase."

"What?"

"Has to do with the nerve enzyme level. The pesticide destroys the enzyme."

"What did the toxicology tests say? The *bottom* line."

"That his death is consistent with organophos-phate poisoning, specifically, azinphos methyl. I think we could give an opinion that the exposure to Guthion could've caused the behavior that contributed to his accident."

"*Indirectly* led to his death, you mean."

"I'm not a lawyer. You'll have to talk to the dis-trict attorney about all that directly and indirectly stuff."

"How long does it take that kind of insecticide to kill a person?"

"Depends on the exposure. One of the textbook cases tells about a preacher who decided to take a few gulps of malathion and read the Twenty-third Psalm to his flock. He got to 'the shadow of death' and fell into the collection plate. Another one concerns a woman who died in ten minutes after soaking her tampon in paraquat."

Nell was silent for a second, then said, "Wait a minute! Why would anyone . . ."

"I know, I know," the pathologist said. "They never say *why* anyone would."

After talking to the body snatcher, Nell wasn't sure whether she'd be better off trying to upchuck or work. With march-order grit, she opted for work and located a Spanish-speaking secretary to help with a call to the Hospital Civil in Tijuana, where any emergency case would be taken.

After three calls over a period of an hour, they were able to reach a Doctor Velásquez. He spoke excellent English and confirmed that there was not one but *two* patients, both young boys, who were brought into the hospital on Saturday, and who showed every symptom of pesticide poisoning.

After Nell explained the case she said, "Doctor, we know the truck was carrying Guthion. That's an organophosphate."

"I am familiar with it," he said to Nell. "There are a great many insecticides still being used in our country, including some very dangerous ones that you have banned."

"Could you send blood and tissue samples to our lab in San Diego? We could verify if it's Guthion. And if possible, we'd like someone to talk to the boys and find out how they got contaminated."

"As to talking with the boys it will not be possible," Doctor Velásquez said. "One child is in a coma and the other one is very ill. Perhaps in a day or two he will be able to talk to us."

"If you could get the samples to us as soon as possible, I'd appreciate it."

"We are perhaps not as primitive as you might think, Ms. Salter," the doctor said. "We do have a somewhat reliable laboratory. And now that you have identified the substance I would wager that our people might even be able to verify it."

"Of course, Doctor," Nell said. "I didn't mean to . . ."

"That is all right," Doctor Velásquez said. "I am grateful for your call. And I shall personally see to it that the laboratory work is done at once. *Personally.*"

After she hung up, Nell said to the secretary, "I just offended him. I'll bet he does a real job on this one so he can show a thing or two to this patronizing gringa bitch."

Shelby Pate was even more hung over than Nell Salter that morning, but he had ingested his drugs of choice in far greater quantities. During the lunch break, the ox was at last able to hold down his food, and was munching his second bag of Fritos when Abel suggested that they go rest in the shade by a stack of waste drums.

When they were sitting alone, Abel said, "Joo throw away paperwork?"

Shelby looked puzzled for a moment, and then said, "Oh, you mean the manifest? Tell the truth, I didn't get home till two-thirty in the morning, and my old lady was seriously bummed. I couldn'ta chilled her out with tickets on a love-boat cruise. She says to me, she says, 'Through your nasal canal has passed more white than they see at the Pillsbury Mills.' And me, her sugar man, I says to her, 'I'm on'y tryin to do my part fer local lab workers.' She's a hardworkin bitch though. I gotta give her credit fer that much."

"Throw away papers, Buey."

"Yeah, sure," the ox said. "There ain't nothin to worry about. Don't let that little navy cop scare ya."

"I don' know, Buey," Abel Durazo said. "Remember when joo get bad feeling? Now I got bad feeling about shoes. *Bad.*"

If the San Diego Yacht Club had lost its America's Cup cachet, Jules Temple might've resigned his membership. He never would've had it in the first place were it not for the fact that his father had been a longtime member. However, keeping up the membership only cost $70 a month, and Jules always hoped that he could use club connections to help in business.

When he was a teenager, Jules used to steal snatch blocks from other members' sailboats docked at the club marina, and sell them to weekend sailors. Other members' sailboats were also good places to steal liquor, and even binoculars, since most boat owners kept a good pair on board.

The San Diego Yacht Club was perhaps an unlikely keeper of the America's Cup. It was a laid-back club, far more egalitarian than the tony New York Yacht Club where the cup had resided for so long amid blazers and white ducks. In San Diego the cup lived with flipflops and Levi's, and yachtsmen talked a lot more about prime rates than crime rates, as in New York.

The San Diego Yacht Club occupied several acres across from Shelter Island on the end of the channel. The members had a swimming pool and other amenities, but the main attraction was the large private marina where millions of dollars' worth of pleasure craft floated, and no doubt distressed their owners during hard economic times. It was a square structure, two sides of which faced the marina. The building was functional but not unattractive, with a modified pagoda roof, and a crow's nest on top that added a nautical touch.

San Diego Yacht Club member Dennis Conner had probably done more than anyone to put the esoteric gentleman's sport onto America's sports pages by the introduction of financial syndicates, corporate sponsors, television coverage, and greed. His successor, millionaire Bill Koch—the Donald Trump of yacht racing—showed promise of doing the same, proving that you *could* buy an America's Cup if you were willing to scuttle more treasure than Hitler's U-boats.

Occasionally, Jules would go out for a beer-can race on a sailboat owned by an old school friend, and once in a while he'd be invited for booze-cruises on large powerboats. Jules didn't own a boat of his own and didn't want one, using the club as a place to get a decent meal and some business gossip in a high-tech city that was feeling the ominous recession as much as anywhere. San Diego was overdeveloped, at least as far as hotels and office buildings were concerned, and in the California real estate–driven economy, people were nervous. What Jules often got from his visits was free legal advice from the many lawyers who were part of the yachting community.

Jules found that the club wasn't particularly busy that weekday afternoon. There were a few visitors gawking at the old black-and-white photos of past commodores that lined one wall along the peg-and-groove corridor. And a few kids were pressing their noses to the glass case that housed the America's Cup, at least until the next regatta, when a Japanese billionaire would probably be ready to take it.

Jules walked into the bar, acknowledging a few people at the cocktail tables. There was a fair-sized luncheon crowd out on the back deck seated at tables under blue umbrellas. A sixty-foot Bertram convertible sportfisher was side-tied to the dock just below the porch. Jules saw that her name, painted across the transom, was *Peligrosa*.

He knew that *Peligrosa* belonged to a middle-aged couple he'd met in August at the Jewel Ball in La Jolla, one of San Diego's glitzier events. Jules had escorted a sixtyish widow named Barbara Gump whom he'd mistakenly thought would be easy pickings if he needed a willing investor in some future scheme, but she'd spent the evening knowledgeably discussing her blind trusts, and killed any hopes Jules may have had. She was a good friend of Willis and Lou Ross, owners of *Peligrosa*.

Jules had thought it wouldn't be all that easy to find the right legal advice because he needed counseling on a potential *criminal* matter, and criminal law was not the specialty of most yachting attorneys. But Jules was aware that Willis Ross headed a law firm that had represented an investment group that bilked a thousand people out of $180 million in a Ponzi scheme by promising a thirty percent annual income from foreign investments. Moreover, the law firm had got the lucrative job of defending the corporate head of a savings and loan that had scammed *another* thousand or so people out of their savings, for many of them their life savings, so Willis Ross was more than qualified to advise.

The lawyer, like Jules Temple, had an eye for the ladies, *young* ladies. Jules discovered that on the night they'd met, when he and Willis Ross were not taking turns dancing with each other's escorts. Since then, Jules and Willis had had a few discussions about Jules's idea to open an up-market topless dancing club.

Jules waited at the bar for a few minutes, then headed down to the dock where Willis Ross was idling his twin 1400-horsepower diesels. Willis wore baggy knee-length shorts and Topsiders, and an America's Cup Nautica jacket. He spotted Jules and waved.

"C'mon aboard!" he yelled from atop the fly bridge.

The big sportfisher had a marlin tower and outriggers for big fish. Jules had been told that the boat had cost 1.3 million dollars.

"Looks like you're ready to cast off."

"Waiting for Lou," Willis Ross said. "That woman's never on time."

Willis Ross was sixty-three, and had scars from

skin cancer surgeries all over his face and neck, and across his hairless scalp. He'd even lost a piece of his lip to the knife, but despite all this he'd never given up the sun and sea.

"Going fishing?" Jules asked.

"Naw. She just needs blowing out and it's a beautiful day. Who wants to bill clients on a day like this?"

"Any lawyer who ever lived," Jules said, grinning.

"Actually I've been scrubbing down the hull," Willis Ross said. "My boat cleaner's been sick for the past month. I hate to let him go, but I'm looking around for a new one."

"Buy you a drink?" Jules asked.

"C'mon aboard. I'll supply the drinks," Willis Ross said.

"Why not. Got a beer?"

Jules hopped aboard and sat in the fighting chair while Willis Ross headed to the wet bar inside the main saloon. When he returned with cocktails, Jules said, "Hey, I wanted a beer. It's kinda early for heavy booze."

"Try it," Willis Ross said. "The best rum money can buy."

The lawyer removed his white floppy hat and sat on a locker in the shade.

His bald scalp looked even worse than the last time Jules had seen it. The lawyer wore hats now, and ladled on the sunscreen, but it was too late. Crusty patches of white mingled with fiery splotches of red. The cumulative effect of all those years of harsh California sun had done its worst. His flesh was alive with skin cancers from the neck up. Even his hands and forearms were badly scarred from surgeries.

The lawyer said, "You still drive that yellow Miata, don'tcha, Jules? I been thinking about buying one for a . . . *friend*. She thinks they're cute."

"Yeah," Jules said. "I had an auto security system installed in mine. It arms and disarms by remote control. It can even unlock the door. And get this: It can start the engine from a distance of three hundred feet! That way your car's cooled off or warmed up before you get in it. That system set me back a thousand bucks."

"Isn't that overkill for a cheap little car?"

"Maybe," Jules said, "but I won't be driving a cheap little car much longer. I'll be glad to show it to your friend if she's interested." Then he thought: *cheap* car. The *nouveau* shyster!

After the first rum, Jules didn't have any trouble convincing himself to have another. When they were working on the second, Jules said, "I'm getting nearer to close-of-escrow, and when I close, I'll be looking for that spot I told you about."

"What spot?"

"The topless club, remember? With the most beautiful girls this town's ever seen?"

"Oh yeah," Willis Ross said, smacking his lips when he licked off the rum. "You gonna sell memberships like the place down on Midway?"

"That might be one way to set things up," Jules said. "It keeps out the riffraff. I might decide to take a few investors, the *right* people, of course. Interested?"

"I'm interested in being a member," the lawyer said.

"You'll get membership-card number one," Jules said. "Can I ask you a couple questions about the law?"

"For membership number one? Fire away."

"Do you know anything about environmental law? You know, for dumping hazardous waste, that sort of thing?"

"Probably not as much as you know," the lawyer

said. "It's a new field. There really isn't much case law out there when it comes to environmental crimes."

"You know about the penalties, don't you? Like, a hundred grand a *day* and prison time for certain kinds of violations."

"It can top two hundred thousand a day," the lawyer said. "And there's a provision for some big jail time. Why do you ask? I hope you're not in trouble?"

"No, no," Jules said. "It's just that this guy that's buying my business, he's having some problems. I'm scared to death something could happen to him and make me lose my deal."

"What problems?"

"Well, it seems that his employees might've dumped a load of very hazardous waste when they should've properly disposed of it. And somebody got sick from it. *Very* sick."

Before Jules could continue, Lou Ross came flouncing along the dock shouting, "Ahoy, Jules!"

Jules didn't like her but she liked him and she'd made it clear the first night they'd met at the ball in La Jolla. Every time he'd danced with her she'd done more pelvic thrusts than Michael Jackson in concert. But Lou Ross was getting on, and multiple face-lifts hadn't worked, not as far as Jules was concerned. Her body was okay for her age, but unless she had more to offer by way of business, he wasn't interested.

Every time Jules saw her at the club she never missed the opportunity to tell him when Willis was going on a fishing trip. Once she'd left a message at Green Earth saying she'd be having lunch at the club and begged him to be her guest. He'd declined, claiming that he had to go to L.A. to negotiate the purchase of two new bobtails. Still, he didn't want to shut the door because her husband was important.

And at this crucial time in Jules's business life, Willis Ross could become *very* important, if any of Jules's worst fears were realized.

He held out his hand to help Lou Ross aboard. She was wearing a glittery T-top decorated with red, white, and blue sequins that formed a small American flag and a large elephant. Her tinted henna hair said hot rollers and hairdressers, and she was ten pounds past looking good in red stirrup pants.

"It's for George Bush," she explained, indicating the T-shirt. "The Republican elephant? I had it made special when we met Mrs. Bush at the fund-raiser. You like?"

She thrust out her chest when she said it, and he had to admit she had pretty nice hooters. His eyes told her that, and she smiled, brushing the back of her hand against his fanny when she walked by him to the saloon.

"About time," her husband complained. "I can't just sit at the guest dock all day."

"Tut tut," she said. "Old grump wants his baby to look nice, doesn't he?"

Lou Ross turned and winked at Jules, then disappeared inside the saloon to pour herself a generous noontime shot of rum on the rocks.

"It's so good to see you, Jules," she said, when she returned. "You *are* coming with us, aren't you?"

Jules looked at Willis Ross and said, "Well, I hadn't planned on a boat ride."

"Might as well," the lawyer said. "We can talk up on the fly bridge after we get out to the ocean."

"The fly bridge is his refuge from women," Lou Ross said, when her husband walked forward to untie the bow line.

"*So* glad you're here, Jules," she said. "Hurry and talk business, then come on down so we can have a nice chin-wag."

"Sure," Jules said, then started aft to untie the stern line. She put her hand on his bottom and boosted him when he hopped onto the dock.

Jules had the feeling he'd be paying one way or another for his free legal advice, but that's how things work, he always said. Nothing was ever free, not advice, not even love, if there really *was* such a thing. Life was just one big whorehouse.

After Willis Ross eased the big boat out of the marina and they were powering slowly through the channel, Jules took a seat in the fighting chair, lifting his face to the sun. The lawyer's steering station was high up on the fly bridge, so the wind, the rush of water, the growl of the twin diesels, all made it impossible for Willis Ross to hear anything but shouts from where Jules sat on the open deck.

In a few minutes, Lou Ross appeared wearing a wide-brimmed straw sun hat with a scarlet band. She handed Jules a long-billed fishing hat, along with a generous glass of rum.

"Put it on, handsome," she said. "We don't want skin cancers on *that* baby face, do we?"

Jules usually didn't mind flirtations with older women. In fact, he'd thrived on them. Two of the investors his father had accused him of bilking were older divorcees, both of whom Jules had had to serve sexually in order to get their six-figure investments in a shopping mall that went belly-up.

He put the hat on and said, "Do I look like Papa Hemingway?"

Lou Ross laughed and said, "He was a notorious womanizer, Jules. Is the resemblance coincidental?"

Jules just grinned, and Lou Ross sashayed back into the saloon causing Jules to think: She's *way* past stretch pants.

He put his feet up on the gunwales while they cruised out the channel, passing a Sturgeon-class sub-

marine being demagnetized at the degaussing pier on
Point Loma's lee side. There was a Los Angeles–class
nuclear sub in one of the huge dry docks, the same dry
dock that caused a lot of jokes during the epic visit of
the Soviet fleet in 1990. The dry dock had been completely blanketed to prevent the Soviets from taking a
peek. This, when every Sunday of the year there were
thousands of camera bugs in everything from cruise
ships to rubber dinghies sailing past the dry docks,
snapping away like at high school graduation.

When the Bertram rounded the lighthouse at Point
Loma, Willis Ross pointed the boat out to sea in order
to clear the vast kelp beds that every local yachtsman
avoided. He got her cruising at thirty knots, and the
engines almost obliterated Lou Ross's voice when she
said to Jules, "Why don't you have lunch with me later
this week?"

"I'd love to, Lou," he said, "but I'm in the process of trying to sell my business and . . . you know
how it is."

"You're getting out of that dreadful toxic waste
thing? Good for you! Are you gonna retire?"

"I'd like to," he said, smiling. "But I'm barely
forty. I'm afraid I have a lotta years to work."

"Barely forty," she said, primping at her blowing
hair, for fear the wind might reveal the cosmetic surgery scars. "You *are* a baby, aren't you?"

"Maybe I need a mommy," Jules said.

"Maybe you do," she said peering coyly over the
lip of the glass. "Come on, let's go inside before the
skipper-from-hell opens up both engines."

Willis Ross steered the motor yacht northwest
after they'd cleared the kelp. The seas were very calm,
permitting him to cruise at thirty-eight knots without
buffeting the passengers below.

The main saloon had air-conditioning, an elaborate sound system and a video entertainment cen-

ter. The saloon was cabineted, draped and mirrored. Lou Ross stretched out on a peach settee and leaned her elbow on plum and persimmon pillows. Jules sat across the saloon in a barrel-backed chair done in tangerine and banana. When Lou Ross had replaced the factory decor everybody said she now had the world's most expensive floating fruit salad.

"I don't usually drink like this so early in the day," she said.

"Of course not. Neither do I."

"I think it's because you're here," she said.

"Oh?"

"You make me feel . . ."

"What?"

"Dangerous."

"I bet you *are* dangerous," he said, taking her empty glass and refilling it.

When he handed the drink to her, she took it *and* his hand, saying, "And naughty. Jules, you always make me feel naughty and young."

"You are . . ."

"Stop that," she said. "You know very well that I'm, well, *several* years older than you."

"Oh, I don't know about several," he said.

"Willis is going to Cabo San Lucas on a fishing trip next Thursday. He'll be gone for ten days."

"You're not going with him?"

"Are you crazy? I wouldn't spend more than a day on any boat smaller than the *QE Two*."

"What're you going to do for ten days?" He freshened his drink and sat down next to her on the settee.

"That depends," she said, "on several things."

He inched his hand closer to hers and said, "Such as?"

"Whether or not I'll be alone. What're you doing then?"

"Tying up the loose ends at my office."

"If a few loose ends could wait, you might like to consider a trip to New York. I've got some good theater tickets, and a girlfriend I'd invited can't come. I don't wanna go alone. Won't cost you a dime. Naturally, we don't want Willis to know about it."

"How many days?"

"Four. We can stay longer if you like. They take care of repeat clients at the Carlyle."

"Is that the hotel the Kennedys always stayed at?"

"Uh huh."

"Where Bobby Short sings in the café?"

"Uh huh, you've seen the Woody Allen movie. Interested?"

Jules was thinking about a lot of things. He did have plenty of work to do before the escrow closed, but maybe it could wait. There might be opportunity here. It was rumored that after Lou Ross's father died, she'd inherited enough real and personal property to be worth *twice* as much as her husband, and he was worth a bundle. There was no telling where this could lead.

And then he studied her. She was showing him a provocative boozy smile. With the rum hot in his belly, he thought she really wasn't too bad. He'd slept with a lot worse in his time, but only when it was advantageous to do so. He could manage Lou Ross quite nicely. Yeah, she wasn't all *that* old, Jules was convincing himself.

"Okay, but I think you should be forewarned: I have a morbid fear of flying . . . *coach.*"

"First-class all the way. And I wanna see you tonight, Jules." It wasn't an invitation, it was a command.

"Tonight?"

"Yes, tonight."

"Where? Why tonight?"

"At my condo. And tonight because Willis is going to a boring retirement party for a superior court judge."

"But is it wise if I come to your house?"

"I didn't say to our house. I said come to my condo. I bought it for an investment after my father died. It's *mine*, not *ours*."

"Where is it?"

"At the Meridian. Ever been there?"

"I've been *by* there a number of times, of course."

"Then you'll enjoy seeing it from the inside," she said. "Twenty-seven floors of good views and fabulous views. Mine's fabulous. On the bay side, of course. It's a getaway nest. Willis hates it. I love it. I have everything I want there, including lots of service and lots of protection. You could easily get used to it, Jules, if you're like me."

"I better go up topside and talk to Willis," Jules said. "He'll wonder what's happened to me."

"Eight o'clock, Jules," she said. "I'll have something for us. A light supper, maybe."

"Sounds perfect," Jules said.

When he climbed up to the fly bridge, he brought a fresh drink for Willis Ross. The lawyer looked surprised, as though he'd forgotten that Jules was aboard. As though he'd forgotten that anyone was aboard. Willis Ross was in his element, and Jules had no doubt that when the lawyer retired he'd set foot on land only when he had to.

They were well offshore by then, but the ocean-front homes along La Jolla's Gold Coast were large enough to be clearly seen and admired, even from that distance. As a lad, Jules had attended many parties in that row of homes, where ocean breakers would explode against offshore rocks and hurl foam and spray fifty feet in the air. Where well-to-do young revelers drank punch laced with hidden bottles of gin, and the green sloping lawns and ocean surf were bathed in white light. When you could not help but believe that youth and summer would never end.

Perhaps because of Jules's troubled look Willis Ross said to him, "Let's just enjoy the ride for a little while. Lemme get her turned around and headed back into the bay; then I'll put on my powdered wig and try to help you with your problem."

With a toss of his head toward the saloon, Jules said, "Is Lou okay alone or should I . . ."

"Don't worry about Lou," the lawyer said. "She'll be in the stateroom having her afternoon snooze any minute now. She can't stay awake after her noon cocktails."

17

While Jules Temple cruised unhappily in the placid waters of San Diego Harbor, Fin Finnegan foundered in the turbulent waters of show biz.

"I'm not surprised," he said to his agent when he received Orson's call at the police substation.

"I'm shocked," Orson said. "It wasn't too much dialogue for you, was it?"

"He's toast," Fin said.

"What?"

"That was the dialogue. He's toast."

"That was it?"

"I said it every way I could think of. I coulda done it in Uzbek, but it wouldn't of mattered. Can you get me a second chance with somebody that has better karma?"

"I don't see how I can go around her."

"Orson, I'm not asking to play Macbeth at the Old Globe!"

"I can try."

"In the length of time it took you to get me the last job, Russia turned democratic. Can you be a *little* more speedy?"

After his agent hung up Fin was even too depressed to wallow, so he called Nell Salter.

"Good day to you!" he said.

"By that delighted exclamation, this *can't* be Detective Finnegan," she said. "He'd be attending an A.A. meeting today."

"I'm sorry about last night," he said. "I don't usually . . ."

"Yeah, you said. You don't *usually.*"

"By way of apology, let's do lunch. Sorry, I was just talking to my agent. Let's *have* lunch."

"Too much work to do."

He tried another tack: "I was thinking about driving over to that waste hauling company. You know, Green Earth?"

"Why in the world would you do that?"

"Well, the stolen-vehicle report was made here at Southern, wasn't it? In my presence. So I've got a proprietary interest in this case. I think I oughtta talk to the truckers in more detail. There're a lotta part-time truckers and full-time thieves hanging around Angel's Café where the truck got ripped off. These Green Earth truckers might have a thought or two now that they've had time to remember. Like who they mighta seen there on the day in question."

"That's remote," she said.

"Sure, but it's worth doing because of the load they lost, isn't it? I mean, if I can get a lead on the suspect, I might find the stuff. The truck thief died from it, so maybe I don't want someone else to die. I thought you might feel the same way."

That neurotic little bastard was laying a guilt trip on her! And it worked! "Okay," Nell said, sighing. "I'll meet you at Green Earth in thirty minutes. But I *can't* do lunch."

"See you there," Fin said.

When he hung up, he opened his desk drawer

and gathered his electric razor, his shaving lotion, and his emergency toothbrush. He figured that after he did the cursory questioning of the two drivers, he'd be able to persuade her to have a burrito at his favorite Mexican joint on Palm Avenue where all the cops and Border Patrol *did* lunch.

They were well inside the jetty, cruising past a buoy where, on this sunny afternoon, three adult sea lions shared their space with two young ones. Every animal was asleep and did not stir when the yacht motored past them.

Jules and Willis Ross still sat quietly on the fly bridge, the lawyer looking up when they passed under the Coronado Bridge. It soared 246 feet above the water, and was dedicated in 1969 by then Governor Ronald Reagan. Since then, more than 150 pitiful wretches had leaped from it into the cold dark water.

After they'd passed the bridge Willis Ross slowed to watch the Navy SEALs practicing helicopter drops and pickups in the south bay. Only when he tired of it did he finally turn to Jules and say, "Okay, tell me your troubles."

"Not *my* troubles," Jules said. "Troubles belonging to the guy who's buying my business. Troubles from his other waste hauling company."

"Then tell me why I should be giving free legal advice to some guy I don't know."

"I'm asking you for myself," Jules said quickly. "Because if he gets in trouble with the EPA or the D.A., he might not be able to close escrow. That's why I'm so worried about what happens to him."

"Okay, as long as it's for you, gimme the whole scenario."

"Apparently a couple of his waste haulers, truckers with brains like insect larvae, *might've* dumped a load of hazardous waste that they should've returned to his yard for proper transfer to a disposal site. And somebody might get very sick from the dumped material."

"I'd say the truckers're in big trouble, but the owner of the company isn't in trouble unless he knowingly committed an offense. Did he know they were gonna dump it?"

"No, he didn't."

"Then I think he's okay."

"But there's a hitch. See, he'd improperly manifested that load of waste. He'd shown it to be one thing on the manifest when really it was much more dangerous than what he showed. And he was gonna haul it to an improper site and dispose of it in an improper manner. That improper site was also listed on the manifest."

"Improper? You mean, unlawful?"

"Let's say unlawful. But whatever happened, it occurred before he had a chance to transfer it to the unlawful site."

"Let me get this straight. The truckers just took it upon themselves to dump the stuff. Why?"

"Who knows why? They're scum of the earth, all of them. We're not sure why they'd do such a thing."

"Well," the lawyer said, "it's gonna look pretty bad for the owner of the business. He did some tricky stuff on the manifest, you say? It could be alleged that by *not* alerting his employees to what dangerous material they had, he'd contributed to their later actions of dumping what they couldn't have known was extremely dangerous."

"That seems very unfair to the owner."

"How sure are you that someone might get contaminated?"

"Let's say someone dies from it. Then what?"

"I know this much: Intentional mishandling that results in an injury or death can result in prison time, and some fines that'd scare even Ross Perot. I think your friend should talk to a lawyer. You can refer him to me."

"I'll do that," Jules said, "but tell me this, Willis. What if it was dumped out of our court's jurisdiction?"

"Where?"

"Say in Mexico. And let's say it's a Mexican citizen who gets hurt or dies. Does my guy still have to worry?"

"This is getting wildly speculative."

"Well, there's some evidence that his load could've gone to Mexico for illegal dumping."

"I'll tell you this as a practical matter, Jules," the lawyer said. "If the NAFTA agreement sails through the Congress of the United States under our sure-to-be-elected President Clinton and our green-as-grass environmentalist, Vice President Gore, I would *not* wanna be in your friend's shoes. Not if a Mexican citizen is injured by *our* hazardous waste that's been illegally dumped in *their* country."

"I see what you mean," Jules said.

The yacht had proceeded as far south as The Castle, a quixotic barge anchored in the shallows off Chula Vista. The barge had been constructed from surplus U.S. Navy landing crafts in the form of a floating castle with turrets at all four corners. The barge had served as a party-boat in good times and as a warehouse in bad times. Tied to one end of The Castle was a floating dinghy-dock littered with marine trash and guano, the gulls of San Diego Harbor being The Castle's primary users.

Jules looked at The Castle and felt a sudden chill. In its abandoned state it had taken on the look of a prison. Mini-Alcatraz!

Willis turned the *Peligrosa* around and headed to Glorietta Bay, throttling back, barely causing a ripple when he took the boat inside, passing the Naval Amphibious Base and pointing toward the Coronado Yacht Club.

Beyond the little club was the Hotel del Coronado, the Victorian fantasy resort opened in 1888 on one of the loveliest white sand beaches in all of California. The hotel now stood like a proud but seedy old aristocrat surviving on money from package tours, but in bygone glory days a dozen U.S. presidents had stopped there. Legend had it that in 1920 the-man-who-would-be-king was mesmerized there by a naval officer's wife whom he later courted and won, declaring to the world that he was renouncing the crown for the woman he loved. Perhaps the Del's greatest glory in more recent years was that it represented the Palm Beach resort in the film *Some Like It Hot*.

While gazing at the observation tower on the very top of the old hotel, Willis Ross said, "With all the hell being raised over not having adequate safeguards for us from *their* pollution, can you imagine the political outcry if it turned out that a Mexican citizen died because of the criminal acts of U.S. citizens? I think the D.A. or the U.S. attorney, or both, would file big-time charges against your friend."

"I see," Jules said. "Well, this is all hypothetical. Nobody knows yet if an illegal dumping really occurred, or if anyone suffered as a result."

The lawyer, who was used to friends offering all sorts of "hypotheticals" about dilemmas that *might* occur, took a business card from his wallet and looked Jules squarely in the eye. "Give him my name and phone number," Willis Ross said. "Your friend needs representation, my friend."

•   •   •

An accented female telephone voice said, "Mees Salter? Ees thees Mees Salter?"

"Yes, this is Nell Salter." Then the voice said something in Spanish and Nell heard a familiar male voice on the line.

"This is Doctor Velásquez, Ms. Salter," he said.

"Yes, Doctor, do you have news for me?"

"I have," he said. "We are certain that our patients were exposed to something very much like Guthion. And we have been able to talk to the younger boy, Luis Zúniga, age nine years."

"Good!" Nell said. "Then you know how it happened?"

"Yes, they found the drums on the ground behind a truck on a dirt road in *Colonia Libertad*. That is a very poor *colonia* by The Soccer Field."

"Yes?"

"The boys accidentally overturned the drum when they were prying it open and they were both soaked with the liquid. The older boy, Jaime Cisneros, age ten, had a history of asthma, so the material had a devastating effect on him."

"Is he still in a coma?"

"I am sorry to say that he died last evening just before midnight. He did not emerge from the coma."

"Oh, Christ!" Nell said.

"We expect Luis Zúniga to recover. He is a strong little boy."

"Christ!"

"Yes, I am afraid that too many of the children in the poor *colonias* do not survive to become adults."

"About the drums of hazardous waste, have you . . ."

"The authorities were alerted, and I have personally been advised that the drums are no longer where the boys found them, although there is evidence of the spill."

"Can we assume that the empty drums're being used by the local people?"

"Of course," Doctor Velásquez said. "Steel drums have many uses."

"Even drums with a skull and crossbones painted on the side?"

"These people, Ms. Salter, face far greater dangers than that in their everyday lives. That is what *they* would say."

"I hope I can find out if anyone besides the dead truck thief had a hand in this," Nell said.

"I hope so," he said. "Good luck."

"If I do I promise I'll try to have him prosecuted for causing the death of that child."

The line was quiet for a moment, then Doctor Velásquez said, "I do not want to sound cynical, but down here we do not believe that the American courts would care that much about a dead child. A dead *Mexican* child."

"If someone else was involved I'll get him into court. I swear."

"Yes, that is a good thought to keep," said Doctor Velásquez.

After hanging up the phone, Nell stared at her copy of the police report detailing the truck theft. Then she called Fin and told him that now she intended to take this investigation *very* seriously.

That afternoon, while Jules Temple was on his booze cruise in San Diego Harbor, Abel Durazo was licking the ear of the pregnant secretary at Green Earth Hauling and Disposal.

"Stop that!" she said, but didn't pull away.

"Okay, Mary," Abel said. "Where else can I leeck?"

"You little brat!" she said. "You're terrible!"

"We got time," he said. "One more months, then no more to make love. But we okay for now." He reached down and patted her belly.

"You really *are* terrible." She smiled when he nuzzled and kissed her neck.

"I need to make call to T.J.," he said. "Okay?"

"You're lucky Mister Temple doesn't check the phone bills," she said. "Or maybe *I'm* the lucky one. He'd fire me for all your toll calls."

"One more. Please?"

Mary was a plain dumpling even before the pregnancy, and she'd never been able to resist this handsome young hauler who might well be the father of her baby, for all she knew.

"Oh, all right," she said, "but hurry up. Mister Temple might come back."

Mary resumed her bookkeeping, not able to understand a single word of the angry telephone conversation that Abel had in Spanish with an employee of Soltero. But when he hung up he was smiling.

"I go to T.J. tomorrow," he said. "Maybe breeng back some perfume."

He slipped his hand inside the neckline of her maternity smock but withdrew it when there was the sound of footsteps on the stairs.

"Get outta here!" she said, and Abel scurried toward the back staircase. He turned in time to see a man and woman enter Mary's office. The man looked familiar.

"What'd you find out?" the ox wanted to know when Abel trotted across the yard with a lottery winner's grin.

"Soltero got money, Buey," Abel said. "Tomorrow he pay."

"What time we gonna meet him?"

"Like joo tell me, I say early. Hees man say we

meet late. I say no, my *compañero*, he scared of the dark."

"You little dickhead!" Shelby took a playful swing at Abel, who ducked, and feinted with a left hook of his own.

Then Abel said, "I say we go to hees house. Thees guy say no, we meet at Bongo Room, Avenida Revolución, fi' thirty."

"Five-thirty? Yeah, that's okay, I guess. In a bar, huh? That's cool. We ain't goin to no outta-the-way place. Not when we're collectin six grand from a crook."

"After we get money, we go all over T.J.," Abel said. "We get some tequila, some food."

"Some pussy?"

"Okay, no problem."

Shelby was wondering if he should score some meth down there or should he bring his own, when Mary opened the window of her office and yelled, "Abel! You and Shelby come up here! There's people here to talk to you!"

Fin Finnegan and Nell Salter were waiting in the office when the truckers entered by way of the back stairway.

Abel remembered where he'd seen the man as soon as the ox whispered, "The *cop!*"

Shelby Pate felt his anxiety level rising. These were older cops, real cops, not some little navy cop with cute tits and freckles on her nose.

"Can we use this office?" Nell asked the secretary.

"That's Mister Temple's office," she said, "but I guess it's okay."

Fin held the door and closed it after all four of them were inside.

Nell motioned them to the client chairs and she sat on the corner of the desk.

Shelby Pate admired her long legs, and thought that the bent nose made her look sexy, like a biker momma.

Abel wasn't looking at her legs. He was plainly worried, when Fin said, "This is Investigator Salter from the D.A.'s Office. She's helping me look into the truck theft. We were wondering, now that you've had time to think about it, could you tell us a little more about that afternoon at Angel's?"

"Like what?" Shelby asked.

"We tol' everytheeng," Abel said.

"Did you see *anybody* at Angel's," Nell asked, "anybody that you knew or had seen before? Maybe some out-of-work hauler? A lotta truckers hang around there."

Fin said, "Maybe you saw somebody there who mighta seen somebody else that was suspicious. Some trucker who'd already left by the time you'd finished your meal? Think about it."

Abel and Shelby each did an impression of honest truckers trying to think. Shelby actually started stroking his unshaven chin. His blue T-shirt was emblazoned in white with PUBLIC ENEMY.

Finally the ox said, "Naw, I can't think a nobody. How 'bout you, Flaco? Did you see somebody there that we knew?"

"Nobody," the Mexican said, shaking his head. "They all strangers that day."

"This is important," Nell said. "This is about a *lot* more than the theft of the truck."

Shelby felt his adrenaline surge. The shoes! They'd talked to that little navy bitch about the shoes! "Whaddaya mean?" he asked.

"We can say for sure now," Fin informed them, "that the man driving your truck died as a result of being exposed to the Guthion from your load."

"The thief, he die?" Abel asked.

"He *may've* been the truck thief," Fin said. "All we know for sure is he was driving a load of pottery from T.J. to San Diego and it cost him his life."

Enormously relieved that they weren't there to talk about *shoes*, Shelby bared his gap-tooth grin and said, "He kicked the pot instead a the bucket!"

Everyone looked at him but nobody laughed.

Well fuck *them*, he thought.

"Do you know about Guthion?" Nell asked.

Shelby said, "All we know is it's all bad shit."

Methyl-ethyl bad-shit, Nell thought. Even the people who handled hazardous waste didn't know much about it.

"All we do, we peek up stuff and breeng here to yard," Abel said.

"Take my word that it's *very* hazardous," Nell said. "That's why it was manifested for a disposal site out of state."

"Anyway," Fin said, "when you came out, the truck was gone. But was anybody *else* gone? Anybody who was there in the parking lot when you went inside?"

"There was lots a truckers around," Shelby said, looking at Abel.

In order to get a reaction about the missing cash, which anyone smarter than a Rottweiler would know these two had stolen from their boss, Fin asked, "And the five hundred bucks in cash that you got from your last pickup was in the glove compartment?"

"Een glove box, yes," Abel said to Nell Salter, who was looking at Shelby Pate.

"We thought it was safe there," Shelby said. "We jist wrapped the envelope full a money inside the two manifests and stuck the whole package in the glove box."

"And lock eet," Abel informed them.

"Naturally we *locked* it," Shelby said. "We thought

that was safer than walkin around with five hunnerd bucks in our jeans."

"Keep thinking about that lunch break at Angel's," Nell said, giving her business card to each young man. "Maybe you'll think of somebody you saw there. You see, this *is* much more important than a truck theft or even the fact that a suspect died driving that truck. Somebody else was exposed to that Guthion you were hauling."

That got their attention. Shelby Pate lost his innocent gap-tooth smile. Abel Durazo's jaw muscles started working.

"*Who?*" Shelby asked.

"Two little boys," Nell said. "They lived in a barrio in Tijuana called *Colonia Libertad.* One is nine. The other was ten."

"Whaddaya mean *was?*" Shelby Pate asked, heaving his bulk forward in the chair.

"The nine-year-old boy is expected to recover, but a ten-year-old named Jaime Cisneros is dead from spilling that drum full of waste all over himself."

"Dead?" Abel Durazo was stunned.

"He was a sickly boy," Nell said. "He had asthma, and his body wasn't able to fight off the toxicity. He died last night."

There was silence and then Shelby cried out, "This *sucks*, man!"

Both Nell and Fin were astonished to see his eyes fill!

Abel looked alarmed then. He said, "Our truck! Our poison! We feel bad! Real bad, don' we, Buey?"

"This sucks!" the ox repeated, taking off his hard hat and running his fingers through his lank, straw-colored hair.

"We feel bad, lady!" Abel said earnestly. "Maybe we worry now that we deed no' lock truck! Boy dead! We feel *bad*, lady!"

"*Did* you lock it or not?" Fin asked.

"I lock eet," Abel said. "I lock eet, I theenk. But now we upset!"

"I can understand that," Fin said, glancing at Nell. "Maybe you'll think of something since you know how important this is."

Shelby Pate asked Nell, "How old did you say the dead kid was? The one with ringworm?"

"Ringworm? I said asthma. He coulda had ringworm too for all I know. He was ten years old."

Shelby said, "This *sucks*, man! This *really* sucks!"

No one spoke for several seconds and then Fin said, "Is there anything else you'd like to ask us?"

"No, sir," Abel said.

Shelby Pate just sat staring at the wall and shook his head silently.

"You have my card," Nell said. "Call me if you remember anything. Anything at all."

Mary stared at Abel Durazo and Shelby Pate when they somberly trudged past her and disappeared down the back stairway. Abel didn't smile, wink, or even acknowledge her quizzical look.

When Fin and Nell emerged, Fin said to Mary, "You can tell Mister Temple that we've definitely ascertained that the drum of Guthion was responsible for the death of the man who was driving the truck, and at least *one* more person. A resident of Tijuana. He was ten years old."

18

After leaving Green Earth, Nell found herself following Fin's city car to the Mexican restaurant on Palm Avenue. He'd done it to her again. When she said she had to go back to the office, he said they had to talk about the case. When she said they could talk later, he said it was important that they talk now. When he suggested they have a business lunch, she said she still wasn't feeling well from the night before.

And then he said, "*Menudo*! Carmen makes the best *menudo* in the world. You can't have a hangover with a bowl of her *menudo* in your tummy."

"No," she said.

"I've got ideas about the case," he said. "It's important, Nell."

And she found herself wheeling into the restaurant parking lot, pulling next to Fin, who was parked next to a San Diego County Sheriff's car which was parked next to a Border Patrol four-wheel drive which was next to a San Diego P.D. patrol unit.

"Lineup," Fin said, indicating the police cars. "Answer when your name is called."

After they'd got seated and had ordered, Nell

tasted a tortilla chip with fresh salsa. The very first taste burned the tip of her tongue, but not unpleasantly.

"So what's your idea?" she asked, sipping her soda pop.

"That those guys *know* something about the dumping of the hazardous waste."

"What makes you think so?"

"Did you see the reaction to the news about the kid? Suddenly those truckers were giving off about as much eye contact as browsers in a dirty bookstore."

"Of course I saw it," she said. "But it could just be guilt from maybe having left their truck unlocked."

"Yeah, they coulda left it unlocked and be scared to admit it now."

"And feel guilty about it. You know about guilt. You laid some on me to get me down here."

"I really *do* care about this case, Nell."

"Of course they stole their boss's five hundred bucks," she said.

"That goes without saying."

"So maybe they just left their truck unlocked and they're scared, especially now that a kid's died."

"But I think I was looking at big-time guilt," Fin said. "Especially in Pate."

"I gotta admit, I sorta felt the same way."

"Yeah?"

"But it doesn't make sense."

"Why not?"

"What could they gain from dumping their load of waste in T.J.?"

"To get rid of it," Fin said.

"Why?"

"What if they . . . sold their truck down there?"

"Sold it?"

"Yeah, for, say, a couple thousand. They're gonna

be outta work. What if they took the van down where Durazo is connected and just *sold* it to somebody who needed to haul pottery north?"

"And then made a phony police report claiming it was stolen from Angel's?"

"Right," Fin said.

"It's possible."

"Sure it is."

"Why didn't they dump the load on our side of the border?"

"That's easy," Fin said. "They figured that down there, there'd never be a follow-up investigation that might nail them. They got so much mutant-producing waste down there that even one-cell animals can ride bicycles."

"I guess it's the only thing that makes sense if what we saw was a guilt reaction," Nell said.

"They dumped the drums in *Colonia Libertad* and they sold the truck to Pepe Palmera or to the pottery maker. When I met them on Friday night they claimed they took a taxi down to Southern to make the report. It sounded like bullshit at the time. Now I understand. They'd walked across the border."

"Okay, so now what?"

"I don't know, except the big guy might get the guilts so bad he'll phone us up," Fin said.

"Care to bet?"

"I don't think so. On another subject, how about dinner tonight?"

"The *menudo*'ll see me through," she said.

"How about tomorrow night? I'm cooking pasta and watching a Ross Perot infomational."

"A Perot-ista! I mighta known. You weird little guys stick together."

"Can you make it?"

"Call me tomorrow. I'll see if I'm well."

"Okay," he said. "And maybe I can talk you into voting for Ross. He's the only thing that can save our country."

"You think America's that desperate, huh?"

"Absolutely," Fin said. "The watershed event that signaled the imminent collapse of American civilization was the colorization of *The Maltese Falcon*."

Fin always felt particularly lonely for a few days after he didn't get a job that he'd read for. He talked about it with other failed actors. It was more than the sting of rejection that successful actors could attribute to the vagaries of the business, or to the artistic decline in the popular arts, or to the dietary habits of casting agents and producers who'd consumed too much arugula in recent years. The intense loneliness really stemmed from the fact that all failed actors had denial-free moments when they thought that all those schmucks might be *right*!

And that's where Fin's head was after the rejection by that *Harbor Nights* bitch who dressed herself in politically correct vegetation. But then, to be rejected again by Nell Salter after he'd practically offered to cook, cut and masticate her dinner, well, he was feeling intensely lonely.

When Fin walked into the front door of the substation, Sam Zahn was at the counter talking to an attractive young woman in a blazer jacket and winter-white skirt. Fin spotted the bulge of a handgun under her blazer, a very *big* handgun.

Sam Zahn said, "Fin, this lady's been waiting for you."

"I'm Detective Doggett, U.S. Navy, North Island," she said, putting out her hand.

That was quite a mouthful, he thought. He *knew*

she'd shake hands like a guy and she did. "I'm Fin Finnegan, a trusty in this gulag."

"Excuse me, sir?"

"Nothing," Fin said. "What can we do for you?"

"I already done it," Sam Zahn said. "I mean I tried to do it, but I can't. She's interested in shoes."

"So's Mrs. Marcos and the National Basketball Association," Fin said. He was *tired*.

"I wonder if you remember being present when Officer Zahn took a stolen-vehicle report last Friday? From two truck drivers?"

"Detective Doggett, it appears that this one's turned into a career-maker for me," he said. "Is it about the hazardous waste they picked up from the navy?"

"I told you, it's about shoes," Sam Zahn said.

"Did you happen to notice what the two truck drivers were wearing that night?" Bobbie asked. "On their feet?"

"On their feet?" Fin repeated.

"I can't remember," Sam Zahn said. "I prob'ly didn't even look. The huge fat guy musta wore boots. He was the biker type. Did you notice, Fin?"

"Can't say that I did," Fin said. "What in the world's that got to do with the hazardous waste from North Island?"

"I'm convinced that those two men stole a shipment of navy shoes from our warehouse when they were picking up the waste. We can now positively state that we lost about two thousand pair."

Fin gaped for a moment, and Sam Zahn said, "What's wrong?"

"Shoes!" Fin said. "Wait a minute, this is getting curiouser and curiouser. I might actually end up solving one! Big cans full of poison I don't understand. Grand theft from a warehouse, I understand *real* good."

"You *do* remember the shoes?" Bobbie said excitedly.

"No, I'm sorry," Fin said. "But we *have* to talk about this." He looked at his watch and said, "It's quitting time. Come on back to my office."

When they got there, Maya was just leaving. Everyone else had gone, and she looked Bobbie over, giving Fin a knowing smirk.

"This's business, Maya!" he said, and her look said, *sure.*

When they were alone Fin said to Bobbie, "This joint shuts down at five."

"I'm already on my own time," Bobbie said, "but I thought it'd be worthwhile waiting for you, sir."

He thought she was a great-looking kid. Wholesome, and corny as Kansas in August. Her navy formality charmed him.

"This is a very complicated case," he said. "Look, I live up in south Mission Beach, so whaddaya say I follow you back to the base. We can drop off your car and go somewhere and talk about it."

"Can't we talk now, sir?" Bobbie asked.

"Detective Doggett, I'm old, tired and cranky. I gotta have a beer. I'll buy you one, or I'll buy you a soda pop, or whatever. But let's you and me go to any old bar close to North Island, and I'll tell you a long story that might have something to do with your shoes."

"Well," she said. "Well . . ."

"We can have the suds on the base if you want. What's your navy rank?"

"Second class petty officer," she said.

"We can go to the enlisted man's . . . *person's* club. Whatever."

"I think I'd rather go to a civilian bar," she said. "Okay, sir, if you'll go to the main gate of North Island in thirty minutes, I'll be waiting there. What kinda car do you drive?"

"A Vette," he said with a hint of vanity. "I drive a white Corvette."

"Right, sir," she said. "See you then."

By the time that Jules got back to Green Earth, his secretary had gone home and the office was locked. He saw a few employees still in the yard, but most had gone.

Shelby Pate offered Jules his usual surly nod as he shambled toward the parking lot with Abel Durazo. Abel smiled at his boss and waved.

When Jules got in his office he found the usual phone messages relating to customers, and some written notes from Mary about billing. But there was another message in her handwriting that lay apart from the regular stack. And there were two business cards clipped to it.

The message said: "Mister Temple. The police were here talking to Shelby and Abel. They have traced more problems to our stolen truck. Two children in T.J. were contaminated. One has died. You can call the detectives tomorrow for more information. Can I reorder the new computer disks or do you want to do it?"

He looked at the business cards. The first belonged to Nell Salter, criminal investigator for environmental crimes at the District Attorney's Office. The second belonged to Detective Finbar Finnegan of the San Diego Police Department.

The message and the business cards took his breath away. Jules had to sit down. Abel Durazo and Shelby Pate had actually passed him outside and said nothing! What did it mean? What did any of this really mean?

He had to fight the urge to look up the address of that fat pig and that little Mexican and drive to their houses right *now*. Except that he had to get home and change for his "date" with Lou Ross. And no doubt, scum like those two would head for some hangout after work to get drunk or do drugs, so he couldn't find them anyway. What the hell did all this *mean*?

Jules Temple was right about Shelby Pate and Abel Durazo being at a bar. Abel ordered two Mexican beers and tried to talk about their dilemma, but the ox just wanted to drink tequila shooters and think.

Hogs Wild was a biker hangout in Imperial Beach, and there were six Harleys in the parking lot by the time the two haulers arrived in Shelby's battered Ford pickup. Almost every pickup in the lot had a gun rack inside.

The saloon had been the scene of some legendary brawls, including a few with sheriff's deputies. The bar mirror was cracked and taped in three places, and the metal shade hanging over the pool table looked like it'd been strafed by an M-16. The sawdust on the floor was not there to absorb beer, but *blood*. The jukebox may as well have been owned by Garth Brooks; you could sit there for an hour before you'd hear any other country singer. In Hogs Wild it was either country or heavy metal. The saloon was windowless and dark, day or night.

After his third shooter, the ox said, "I jist know it was the kid that tried to sell me the gum."

"Goddamn, Buey!" Abel cried in frustration. "It don' matter wheech one!"

"This ain't our fault, is it, Flaco?" The ox was *pleading*.

"No, ees no' our fault, *'mano*! We don' know a fucking thief steal our truck down een T.J. Why he no' dump the drums right where we leave truck? Right there een Rio Zone? Why he drives goddamn truck up to *Colonia Libertad* where peoples at? Goddamn thief! I happy he dead!"

"But the kid!" The ox actually choked back a sob.

That frightened Abel. "Buey, you stop! We get in beeg troubles! You keep talk like thees, we get caught!"

"Them shoes!" Shelby said. Then he signaled for another shooter. "I warned you about them shoes!"

"Stop thees, Buey!" the Mexican said.

Shelby said, "It *ain't* our fault, is it?"

"No!"

"We had no way a knowin this would happen."

"No way."

"But I feel *bad*, Flaco. I got this real bad feelin. It's in my gut. Like, it ain't never gonna go away. Do *you* feel like that?"

"I no' have time," Abel said. "Tomorrow we going to T.J. We going for our money. Buy drink, food, womens! Remember, Buey?"

"Yeah," Shelby said, staring into the mirror behind the bar. His image was fractured in that cracked and filthy mirror and the tape dissected his moon face. When the ox opened his mouth, the tooth gap made him look lupine. Shelby the wolf, he thought. He downed the shooter and quickly ordered another.

"You feel okay now?" Abel asked.

"I'm feelin better, yeah," he said. "I gotta get me some fear."

"What?"

"Cringe."

"What?"

"Meth. I gotta pulsate, then I'll be okay. Lemme have twenny?"

"Okay," Abel said, taking a twenty-dollar bill from a small roll in the side pocket of his jeans.

"I'll pay you back tomorrow."

"Okay, Buey," Abel said. "Tomorrow you be reech. I be reech too!"

The ox grinned at his partner, saying, "For one night we'll be rich. We'll prob'ly give it all to some Mexican whores after we drink about a quart a cactus juice."

Abel gave the ox a playful punch on the shoulder just as a voice behind them said, "They's a cantina right down the street, *amigo*. You can drink down there."

He wasn't quite as big as a cement truck and he sported the beard of a werewolf. He wore a cutoff gray sweatshirt and black jeans as grease-caked and filthy as Shelby's. His boots were savagely studded with metal discs, and you could shoot pool on his belt buckle. He was about Shelby's age and size, but his body mass looked concrete-hard.

"A little slack, dude," Shelby said, looking into the mirror at the leering widebody. "We ain't wantin grief."

"Then go on down the street with your little *amigo*. Them Messicans down there'll drink with you. Won't they, *amigo*?"

"Le's go, Buey," Abel said, standing up.

"We ain't goin nowheres," Shelby said, watching the bearded giant in the fractured mirror.

"Then I go home," Abel said. "I see you tomorrow, Buey."

The last time this happened, Shelby had let Abel go home, and settled for petty revenge by slashing the bike seat of the guy that ran them off. Shelby hadn't wanted to get it on with that other dude, but he felt differently this time. He felt that nothing would ever be right for him again.

The ox grinned at the mirror, and his missing tooth made him think again: Shelby the wolf. The fact was, Shelby Pate didn't care *what* happened to him. Not anymore. He'd become . . . transformed.

He turned on his stool and faced the monster looming over him. He said, "Kin we jist have our shooters, dude? Kin we do that without you goin turbo?"

"Sure you kin," the bearded biker said. "Down the avenue with the *other* Messicans."

The ox looked around for a moment. He was a nodding acquaintance of most of the bikers and rednecks in the bar, but this guy was the new gunslinger in town. Everyone watched with rapt anticipation, especially a pair of biker mommas in dirty T-shirts sitting at a corner booth. There'd be no taking sides. Nobody cared one way or the other who went to the E.R., just as long as *somebody* did.

Shelby said, "Tell me, Big Kahuna, how do your friends over there feel about it?" Shelby pointed to a group of neutral pool shooters who were watching and waiting.

The bearded biker turned his face toward the pool table and said, "Everybody here feels just like . . ."

He didn't get it out. The ox rose up with Abel's full bottle of Carta Blanca and smashed it across the eyes of the bearded biker. Shards of glass and beer pelted the pool players. The bearded biker grabbed his face and toppled back in one piece, crashing down like a boulder.

"You're mine," Shelby said calmly.

He kicked the bearded biker three, four, *five* times in the upper body. Abel heard ribs break with the second kick. The next one was in the kidney and the bearded biker screamed in agony, jerking his hands away from his bloody face, trying to protect his body. The next kick only made him whimper.

Then the bartender said to Shelby, "That's enough, dude. You learned him about life 'n times. That's enough."

"You kin pay the bill, Flaco," Shelby said, stopping the attack. "I need what I got fer some brews. I'm all overheated."

When Shelby and Abel were walking out of the bar, they heard the bartender say to the supine biker, "You want me to call nine-one-one or can you get your own self to the hospital, dude?"

After they were outside, Abel said, "Le's go, '*mano*! Le's get away!"

"Go on home, man," the ox said to him. "Take my pickup. I gotta git cranked."

"Get sleep tonight," Abel said. "We got bees-ness in T.J."

"Yeah, yeah, don't worry about me," Shelby said, turning to go back inside.

"Buey!" Abel cried. "Joo crazy? Don' go back een there!"

"Why not?" Shelby said. "Did you see them Harley honeys back in the corner? Them two with dirty hooters from hangin on the backs a bikers? They're gonna be all wet from seein that blood on the floor. I bet they *both* gimme a blow-job before the night's over. That is, if I kin score some cringe fer them."

When Shelby swaggered back into the bar, the bloody bearded biker was in a fetal position, and a customer was phoning for paramedics.

The ox showed the bartender his gap-tooth grin and said, "I fergot to ask. Do you validate parking?"

19

After he made a U-turn in front of the main gate, Fin watched in the rearview mirror as she sprinted across the street in her little red-leather pumps. Of course he revved the Vette, figuring that a kid like Bobbie would appreciate a muscle car. He leaned across to open the door, but she swung it open and lowered herself into the seat in a move as smooth as ice cream. Her cheeks were showing color from the offshore breeze.

"Cool ride, sir!" she said, with a smile that broke his heart.

What happened to it? *His* youth? What the hell *happened*? "It's a mean machine, all right," Fin said. "Whadda you drive?"

"I got a little Hyundai," she said. "Gets me around, is all."

"Wanna go down to that Irish pub in Coronado?" he asked. "Whatever it's called?"

She shook her head and her blond bob swung saucily, revealing flat tiny ears pierced with gold studs. "Too many sailors," she said. "I know a nice neighborhood restaurant up near Hillcrest. It's not a saloon though, if a saloon's what you wanted."

That surprised him. He thought she'd want to go to the nearest bar, humor the old geezer, and get the hell back to the barracks or wherever she lived.

"I got it up to here with saloons," he said. "Let's go uptown."

She directed him to a restaurant at Fifth and Hawthorne, where downtown bleeds northward into an older residential neighborhood, then farther uptown into the artsy and gay district of Hillcrest. It was too early for the dinner crowd, so Fin was able to park at the curb next to the canopy awning. Other than two couples drinking at a little entry bar, Fin and Bobbie were the only customers.

She'd surprised him by choosing an up-market, cozy restaurant, and she surprised him again when after they were seated in the dining room, she said to the waiter, "Bombay on the rocks with a twist."

"The same," Fin said. Then to Bobbie, "Detective Doggett, you *do* astonish me. I thought a sailor's cocktail'd be a bottle of Mexican beer with a lime sticking outta the neck."

"I drink my share a beer," she said. "But I had this boyfriend recently, he lived pretty good and taught me a lot about drinks and good restaurants. It's kinda neat to order a cocktail where there's a tablecloth and a flower and a candle on the table, right?"

"What happened to him?"

"Went back to his wife."

"I'm not married," Fin said, but Bobbie didn't respond.

"Whadda you do for fun?" he asked. "When you're on liberty?"

"I like water sports," she said. "Surfing, scuba, Jet Ski, any kinda water sports."

"I haven't surfed lately," Fin said, failing to say that the last time he'd surfed, you could still get your windows washed at a gas station.

"How come?"

He *loved* that. How come? It never occurred to her that at his age the icy ocean could even shrivel earlobes. "I got tired of it. And I hated the surfers at Windansea."

"I just surf in Coronado," she said.

"Yeah, well, in Coronado it's civilized. Up there in La Jolla you get a different breed of surf rat. Besides, I saw a great white shark out there and it really changed my mind about the sport."

"Wow! A great white?"

"I like animals and all, but I can't make a case for sharks. Only good thing about them is they draw no distinction between a harbor seal, an old truck tire, or a Windansea surf rat."

"I saw a few blue sharks," Bobbie said, "but never big daddy. You *sure* it was a great white?"

"It was big and aggressive and had two rows of big scary teeth," Fin said. "It was either a great white shark or Arnold Schwarzenegger."

Bobbie showed him a high-wattage smile he rarely saw on people his own age, and Fin felt a little shiver in his tummy.

"How long you been a police officer, sir?"

"Twenty-odd years," he said. "And I mean odd."

"You don't look that old," she said. And he could see she meant it!

"Can we get on a first-name basis? My name's Fin."

"Bobbie," she said. "Bobbie Ann. Sometimes they call me Bad Dog."

"I get it. Your initials. Bad."

"And Doggett. Bad Dog."

"I *like* it," he said. "On a young girl like you it's great. Bad Dog."

"I'm not that young," she said. "I'm almost twenty-eight."

Not that young. God! He was suddenly aware of his herringbone sport coat. Why didn't he wear his blue blazer? And his tie, a *rep* tie. Jesus, only guys older than gunpowder wore rep ties these days, and his was narrow. He was aware of his feet. He looked down in horror at . . . *wingtips!*

Her eyes followed his under the tablecloth, as though she was still looking for her black steel-toe high-tops. "Anything wrong?"

"Wingtips," he said with a weak grin. "Do you know anybody that wears them?"

"Never noticed," she said.

"I'm wearing them for a reason," he said. "I don't really *like* them, or anything."

"Could we talk about the case now, sir? I mean, Fin?"

He signaled for another pair of martinis even though hers wasn't half finished.

"Okay, here's the deal," he said. "This case has more wrinkles than Robert Redford."

"Who?"

"The Way We Were."

"What?"

"Butch and Sundance?"

"Huh?"

"The movie. You *musta* seen it on TV?"

"Oh, sure," she said.

"Robert Redford was Sundance."

"Oh yeah, I like old movie stars."

"You'll notice a lotta movie allusions in my speech," he warned. "I'm a professional *actor* as well as a cop."

"Yeah?"

"Uh huh," he said, "I've been in two feature films. Not speaking roles, but I was in them."

"Would I know them?"

"I don't think so. You didn't know Robert Redford."

"After you said, sure, I know who he is."

The waiter put the drinks down while Fin was deciding that the generation gap was insurmountable. So maybe he should talk about something boring like police work. He said, "The two truck drivers might very well be involved in the theft at your warehouse. We learned that the hazardous waste from North Island as well as some worse stuff from an agriculture supply house were dumped in T.J. And two little kids got poisoned. One's dead."

"Oh, no!" she said. Her brow knitted and two little creases formed between her eyebrows, the only two lines on her sweet young face. He *hated* making her sad.

"The other one's gonna be okay, we hope. Do you know anything about Pepe Palmera?"

"Who's that?"

"I better start from the beginning," he said, "or you're gonna be more confused than General Motors."

He never got headaches, at least not stress headaches, but he suspected that stress was causing the pounding over his left eye. Jules lay across his bed with the TV tuned to local news, but with the sound turned so low he couldn't hear the news readers.

Now there was a death—not the death of a truck thief whose demise on the bumper of a Greyhound bus might be considered good ecology—but the death of a *kid*. Mexican or not, jurisdictional problem or not, Jules realized that Willis Ross was right. At this time in history, during the debates over the NAFTA agreement, it could be disastrous for Green Earth Hauling and Disposal, and more important, for *himself*.

Jules thought he'd given Willis Ross a worst-case scenario: that two cretinous truck drivers had dumped hazardous waste for reasons unknown. Now he found himself being forced to consider every possibility, such as the notion that his drivers had certain plans that went all the way back to the North Island warehouse.

This made him begin thinking about the navy detective and the stolen shoes. Could those morons have stolen the shoes and delivered them to Tijuana? But if they had, why would they dump the waste? Why not just abandon the van and come back with their bullshit story about the truck being stolen? Or, if they felt they *had* to dump the waste, why didn't they dump it on the U.S. side? Why in a residential zone in Tijuana?

They must've had a hard time getting it over the border into Mexico, so why smuggle it down there just to dump it? The American authorities would presume that a Mexican truck thief would dump the load on the U.S. side and then drive the empty van to T.J. So if Abel Durazo and Shelby Pate truly dumped that load of waste in Mexico, they picked the goddamndest most baffling way to do it that Jules could imagine!

That this should be happening to him was an *outrage*, now when everything was going so right. Even this afternoon's stroke of luck boded well, getting close to a user-friendly old rich babe. All of it could be jeopardized by those truckers. It was more than a man should bear.

Jules sat up in bed. He had to stop this anguish. This was not like Jules Temple. This was what ordinary people did. He ordered events, and *controlled* them. What Jules's father had deplored in his son— his ability to live for the present and not stew over future consequences—was, in Jules's opinion, the key to successful living. If people truly were slaves to conscience they were handicapped and doomed to fail, that's what Jules believed. He'd seize the moment. He'd *deal* with those two if and when he had to.

Now he had other tasks, such as giving a recital tonight, an important one. Before showering, Jules laid out his deodorant, his after-shave, his cologne and hair gel. He decided to wear blue silk briefs for Lou Ross, but he hoped it wouldn't come to that.

After she got home that afternoon, Nell had a glass of vegetable juice and a bath. While she was watching the evening news she fell asleep on the sofa, and the short nap revived her. She looked at her watch and thought about Fin and that dinner invitation.

Nell had to admit she kind of liked the guy. Despite his horrendous marital history he was the sort she'd always liked: cute and not one to launch a sexual panzer attack. He'd opened doors for her and probably would've lit her cigarette if she was dumb enough to smoke. And he was semi-amusing, that was the thing she liked most.

And even if he *was* an emotional mess she thought he'd be pretty good in bed because he didn't take himself too seriously, except for the acting which nobody *else* could take seriously. All in all, he was the most promising guy to come her way in quite a while, if she disregarded any possibility of a long-term relationship.

He'd written his home number on the back of his business card, so Nell got her purse, retrieved the card, and picked up the phone. Then she decided it was humiliating. After all, she'd already turned him down, and anyway, he might not even be home.

A moment later, Nell picked up the phone, punched three numbers, then hung up. She poured herself a glass of wine, took a sip, and picked up the phone again.

She could say, "I was wondering if you might need some salad to go with the pasta?"

No, that was lame. She could say, "There *is* another angle about the stolen truck that's bothering me."

But what angle? Hadn't they explored every possibility?

She could say . . . oh, the *hell* with it! She dialed his number and got his answering machine.

Fin's theatrical voice said, "Hello, this is Fin Finnegan. If your call has to do with police or personal business, please leave a message after the beep. If it has to do with the performing arts, you may wish to call Orson Ellis Talent Unlimited, or leave me a message and I shall get back to you."

She hung up. Performing arts! *Such* a neurotic!

Nell opened a can of split-pea soup and read the latest issue of *Vogue*, cover to cover. The soup was more nourishing.

The valet-parking attendant took his Miata the instant he parked in the porte cochere of the twenty-seven-floor Meridian building on Front Street. A doorman directed him inside and a concierge met him at a counter in the lobby.

"Jules Temple," he said to the concierge. "Mrs. Ross is expecting me."

It wasn't until Jules was on the elevator that he thought how extraordinary it was that she lived on the thirteenth floor. He wasn't a superstitious person, but this *was* a residential high rise. He was still thinking about it when he rang her door chime.

He forgot about it momentarily when she opened

the door. Her hair looked like an Eva Gabor wig with highlights that weren't there in the afternoon. She was wearing a short red velvet dress with spaghetti straps and a deep neckline. It looked ridiculous on a woman her age.

"You look *wonderful!*" Jules said, pecking her on the cheek.

"I hope you like Szechwan," she said. "It's being delivered from my favorite Chinese restaurant in Horton Plaza."

"If it's hot enough," he said. "I like it hot."

"I never doubted that for a moment," she said, and Jules could see that she had an insurmountable cocktail lead.

The condo was tasteless enough to've been decorated by a Mafia wife. All it needed was a couple of candelabras, and a harp next to the pink marble fireplace.

While she was mixing him a vodka on the rocks, it came to him again, that worrisome moment on the elevator.

When she gave him the drink she pressed close and kissed him on the mouth.

"Mmmmm," he said. "You taste like gin. Sweet."

She smiled and said, "Take off your jacket?"

"In a bit," he said, "but tell me something."

"Sure, if it has nothing to do with age or money."

"This is the *thirteenth* floor."

She smiled and said, "We're not superstitious in this building. We have a thirteenth floor and I choose to live on it. Are *you* superstitious?"

"I didn't think I was," Jules said. "I'm usually too secure to worry about such things, but there're some bizarre goings-on in my life these days."

"Such as?"

"Things in my business that I don't understand. Inexplicable things're happening and I feel I'm losing control right when everything seemed to be crystallizing for me."

"Well, catch up with the drinks and you'll forget all about boring business problems. Come over here."

Jules followed Lou Ross to the view window. She took his hand and they clinked glasses. "See that?"

"Beautiful," he said, not taking his eyes off her.

She loved it. "The view, I meant. The glorious harbor view."

"That too," he said.

"One question from me and then we'll drop the topic of business," she said. "What *are* you gonna do when your escrow closes?"

"I have an investment idea," he said, "if I can scrape up a few partners."

"Willis told me you've had problems in the past. That investors've lost money with you."

"I lost more than they did. Hard times. It won't happen again. I've learned about plunging in too deeply."

"Sometimes plunging in deeply pays off," she said.

He grinned wryly, and said, "I'll remember that."

"If our friendship . . . *blossoms* as I hope it will, I might consider investing in your next project, Jules."

He leaned over and kissed her bare shoulder, saying, "You wouldn't be sorry." Thinking, she could use some fade cream for that liver spot.

"Don't try to con me, pretty boy," Lou Ross said. "I'm not a fool."

"Do I look like a con man?"

"That's part of your charm," she said. "I think we can be good for each other, but if I ever hear that you're involved in anything shady or remotely illegal, well . . . you *won't* be having any more Chinese suppers on the thirteenth floor. Nor will I entrust you with a dime of my money. Okay?"

Jules didn't like this at all. Losing control to a woman? An *older* woman? The kind he'd always been able to manipulate with ease? Her brown eyes didn't blink as they stared into his. She wore contacts, and up close, mood lighting or not, he decided she was at least sixty years old. Losing control to a goddamn senior citizen!

"Whatever you say, Lou," he said, trying to smile earnestly. "I've had feelings for you since the first time we met."

"I love a rogue," she said, kissing him again, touching his lower lip with her gin-flavored tongue, "as long as he's not *too* much of a rogue."

There it was again, the nagging little thought. He turned away for an instant and looked at the street below. "It doesn't bother you? Living on the thirteenth floor?"

"What's the matter, Jules?" she asked. "Are you afraid of omens?"

"Only lately," he said. "Something strange is happening."

"Is it mysterious?"

"Yeah, mysterious."

"Do you love mysteries?"

"I've always hated them."

"We can eat later," she said. "I wanna show you the master bedroom."

It was a nest of apple green and orange satin. The tufted chaise was covered in it, ditto for the king-sized bed, including the headboard. The drapes were done in canary taffeta, and there were some lovely Lalique pieces scattered about, but a nice alabaster lamp was lost in the mess of colors. When they stepped inside the dressing area she kicked off her pumps.

Jules did *not* perform well that evening. He couldn't stop thinking about the thirteenth floor. *Was it an omen?* Finally though, he blamed it on all the goddamn satin and the clash of vulgar tropical colors. It was like being trapped inside a coffin in Haiti.

20

Fin and Bobbie were having an amazed conversation by the time their third drinks arrived, and he was as amazed as she.

"Wait'll I tell Nell Salter tomorrow," he said. "Nell talked to Jules Temple on the phone, and we both talked to the truckers, but *nobody* told us about you!"

"It's obvious they didn't want us to get together," Bobbie said.

"The truckers I can understand," he said. "Your instinct could be right. They might be your shoe thieves, but what about Jules Temple? Why didn't he tell Nell about you? I'd say it was relevant that two different investigators were interested in Green Earth for two different reasons tied together by the same employees."

"Pretty weird stuff," she said, slurring the *s*.

"Wanna have dinner, long as we're here?"

"Super," she said, slurring again.

"My treat?"

"Dutch treat."

"I'll flip you for it afterward."

"Okay."

The restaurant was about half filled by then, and Fin signaled for menus. Bobbie was still wearing the blazer over her pink cotton shell. While reading the menu she started to take off the jacket, then remembered her sidearm and kept it on.

"I can take the gun to the car for you," he said, "if you're too warm in the jacket."

"It's okay," she said.

"A forty-five?"

"Yeah."

"Guess the navy and marines won't abandon the forty-five till they get Star Wars lasers."

"It's a pretty good gun though, the nineteen eleven model."

"Awfully big gun for . . ."

"Don't say a little girl, okay?"

"Why?"

"I don't want people to think a me like that. Do you know when you ordered the last drink you said, 'Ready for another, *kid*?' That's what you said."

"Did I?"

"I'll be thirty in a few years and I'm a good investigator. I don't have your experience but my forty-five's loaded and I got two extra magazines in my purse and I'm not a kid or a little girl."

Fin knew she was too polite and much too "navy" to have said that without a belly full of booze, but he was touched. "No, you're *not* a kid," was all he could say, and zing went the strings of his heart!

Then she grinned sheepishly and said, "But we're not allowed to carry it with a round in the chamber so I couldn't win a quick-draw contest with anybody."

After the waiter took their identical orders of sea bass, Fin decided that he might give an arm or maybe a leg to be ten years younger. Well, a toe maybe, the little one with fungus on it. If he was still forty he wouldn't feel that this infatuation was so preposterous. But of course the more he drank the *less* preposterous it seemed to be.

When she went to the rest room, he looked her over from the rear. She was a lot shorter than Nell Salter and maybe wore one size larger. Or did height have something to do with dress sizes? But she walked like a little athlete, and he was certain she had a very firm body. He *wanted* to be ashamed of himself.

The food came while Bobbie was gone, and he slipped his credit card to the waiter so she couldn't argue about paying. When she got back he stood up until she was seated. He could see that he scored big with that move.

"The fish is real good here," she said. "Not too much junk on it."

"I'm glad we came."

"Me too," she said, "except I always eat too much sourdough bread."

"Just be glad they still got the kinda joints that *serve* sourdough bread. My third ex-wife used to drag me to places where they sold you smoked-duck pizza topped with papaya, or ahi dunked in raspberry mango sauce. Anyway, you're too young to worry about calories."

"There you *go* again," she said.

"Sorry." Then to the waiter, "Bring us a nice bottle of white wine. *Not* Chardonnay. You pick it." Turning to Bobbie he said, "Okay?"

"Okay," she said.

"Chardonnay also reminds me of porcini mushrooms, tofu and blue-corn tortillas. *And* my third ex-wife who almost wrecked my health by smoking like Tallulah Bankhead."

"Who?"

"If I said Bette Davis would it make any difference?"

"Who's she?"

"Never mind," he said.

When the waiter brought the wine and a wine bucket, Fin said, "Let the lady taste it."

She smiled self-consciously, but performed the ritual she'd learned from her former boyfriend. She examined the cork and sniffed the bouquet.

"Real good," she told the waiter. "I *think*."

Fin was surprised at how much wine she could put away. She guzzled it.

When it was time for dessert Bobbie pointed to one on the menu and said, "You know what this is?"

He read it and said, "Crème brûlée. Yeah, that's outta style now, so let's have it. All it is, it's your mom's egg custard with burnt sugar on top."

"I got a theory about Jules Temple," she said after he ordered two of the desserts.

"What's your theory?"

"That he didn't wanna tell you guys about me because . . ."

"Because what?"

"Don't laugh."

"Okay."

"Because he's in cahoots with those two truckers. Maybe he planned the job."

Fin laughed.

"So much for promises," Bobbie said.

"I'm sorry, Bobbie," he said, "but I don't think somebody with a business as big as his would risk it for some *shoes*."

"Two thousand pairs. They're worth a lotta money."

"I know, but . . ."

"Okay, you're the old pro," she said. "You tell me."

"I can't," he said. "There're pieces here that just don't make sense, no matter how I figure it."

"The truckers stole the shoes, that much we know."

"That much we *think* we know."

"Same thing."

"Not exactly."

"Anyway," she said, "they stole the shoes and drove them to T.J. That's what we think now, right?"

"That's what I think I think," Fin said.

When the desserts came, she wolfed hers, forgetting about truckers and shoes. When she was finished there was a creamy little globule of custard clinging to her upper lip. It was so cute and she was so *young* that he didn't hesitate to reach across the table with his napkin and dab it off.

"Oops," she said. "I'm such a doofus when I eat stuff like . . . What's this called again?"

"Crème brûlée. My third ex-wife was a fad-food type. Used to drag me to a Vietnamese deli. In America they're called pet shops. I think I ate Rin Tin Tin a couple of times."

"What's Rin Tin Tin?"

"He was Lassie's role model."

Then she said, "You have such perfect table manners. Me, I eat like a sailor."

"You can thank my sisters for making me eat with the fork in my left hand, tines down. They trained me with a wooden spoon that was really a billy club. I was always having to sing or dance or recite poems for the entertainment of females. My childhood was a combination of *Great Expectations* and the Jackson Five."

"You gonna eat your dessert?" Bobbie asked.

"No, you can have it."

This time her smile had all the wattage of Las Vegas. Then she said, "You been married *three* times, huh?"

"So far," he said. "Maybe the last one cured me.

She needed a metal tag on her ear just so I could follow her migration habits."

Three ex-wives didn't seem to faze her. "Okay, so back to the case," she said, spooning out every last drop from his little dessert bowl. "They take the shoes to T.J. and sell them. Then they dump their load a waste down there."

"You got a problem already," Fin said.

"What's that?"

"They'd get very little money in T.J. for those shoes. Do you think Mister Jules Temple would risk his livelihood, his freedom, for such small profit?"

"You tell *me* then! How'd it go?"

Her eyes were bouncing boozily now, her pretty blue eyes. She wore no eyeliner, no mascara, and now her lipstick was gone. Fin thought she didn't need it, not with her robust good looks. He also thought she shouldn't drink any more unless he drove her home. "Do you live on the base?" he asked.

"No, I got an apartment in Coronado. Kinda expensive, but I like the privacy."

"But your own car's on the base, right?"

"No, I rode my bike to work today. I usually do when the weather's this good."

"Okay then, we can have an after-dinner brandy. I'll drop you at your apartment."

She smiled and said, "Yeah, my bike's okay where it is till tomorrow."

He'd forgotten how they smiled at that age. The old songs his sisters loved were right: This kid *beamed*.

"I wish I could solve your crime as easy as that," Fin said.

"If I had your experience I bet I could do it."

"Maybe I can come up with an answer by tomorrow," he said. "I'd like to impress you."

"You would? Why?"

"I'd just like to. I almost asked the waiter to call

my beeper number so I could jump up in the middle of dinner and look important."

"You *are* important!" she said. "You're a San Diego P.D. detective. That's what I wanna be when I leave the navy. And you're an actor. I think you're real important. People oughtta look up to you."

A helpless sigh in the face of her unabashed innocence. Fin actually felt himself blush! And he stammered when he said, "I wanna be a screenwriter *and* an actor when I leave the job. I wanna write the first screenplay in the last twenty years not to have 'Are you all right?' or 'Are you okay?' in the dialogue."

"Do they all have that in them?"

"Even the period films. *All* of them. The cliché of our age."

"Does stuff like that bother you?"

"People in the business oughtta get bothered by bad writing."

"In what business?"

"*The* business. You know? Show business?"

"I don't know anything about show business," she said. "You ever met Tom Cruise?"

"The guy twinkles too much. All that dentistry musta cost his old man more than four years at Harvard. You don't go for guys like that, do you?"

"You kidding?"

He tried to think of an actor his own age. Finally, he said, "Do you think Bill Clinton's attractive? Or Al Gore?"

"They're okay for *older* guys."

That did it. Fin thought he might as well take her home. Served him right, developing a case of vapors over a *child*.

"Getting late," he said, looking at his watch.

"Okay," she said, "but it's still early for me."

"Wanna go somewhere else?"

"My ex-boyfriend used to like to take me to this

place in La Jolla where they got some pretty good sounds."

"Live music?"

"It ain't dead."

"Hard rock?"

"Semi-hard."

Was that a double entendre directed at *him*? Was she laughing at this pathetic geezer, as old as Bill Clinton? How did he get *in* this soap opera anyway?

"I don't like La Jolla nightclubs," he said. "All those rich gentlemen from sand-covered countries get on my nerves."

"They don't bother me," she said. "They start slobbering down my neck I just say, 'Shove off, mate, and *salaam aleikum.*' I was in Saudi Arabia so I know how to handle 'em."

He decided to stop the charade, to show her who he really was, to see if she bolted.

"Could I take you to an *old* person's bar in south Mission Beach?" he asked. "They have music there too. Dead music of course. Could you stand it with the over-forty crowd?"

She took a good hard look at Fin. The *over*-forty crowd? She'd always been curious, hadn't she? He was more or less as good-looking as her ex-boyfriend, but of course Fin was even older. *Over forty.* Could he be the one to satisfy her curiosity?

"Okay, if I can buy you one a those brandy drinks, I forget what you call em. They're sweet?"

"B and B?"

"Can we still try to solve the case tonight?"

"You got a one-track mind."

"I buy the drinks, okay?"

"Buy me a drink, sailor? You bet," Fin said.

"That was a pretty sneaky trick," Bobbie said, when they were in his Vette heading for south Mission Beach. "Paying the bill when I was in the head."

"I told you I'd let you buy the after-dinner booze."

"We make good money in the navy nowadays. I can afford to pay my way."

"I know you can, but I can't help it. I'm an old-fashioned guy. My sisters made me do it."

Bobbie leaned back on the headrest, loosened the seat belt and scooted around. The streetlights glistened off her teeth when he turned to look at her. She said, "You really *are* a gentleman, know that? I got a lotta experience with sailors, even a little bit with the officers when they're not scared a getting caught fraternizing with enlisted personnel. Officers're not necessarily gentlemen, I can tell you."

"I was an enlisted man myself," he said. "I shoulda stayed in."

"Don't you like police work?"

"It's a living," he said, "but the theater's where I belong. I just did an important audition. In fact, the only reason I'm dressed like this is for the role of a dork in wingtips. Next time I get a stage gig I'll send you a ticket and you can come see me."

"I'd like to go see some plays," she said. "My boyfriend, before he went back to his wife, he was gonna take me to L.A. to see *Phantom of the Opera*."

"I'll take you. It's really good."

"You'll take me? Okay, but I'll pay for the tickets."

Fin was feeling woozy. The streetlights started swimming. His face felt hot and his pulse was up to a hundred, at least. And it was only *partly* because of the booze. The last time he felt like this he married the babe in the passenger seat!

A moment of panic, then he blurted, "I'm forty-five!"

"Yeah?"

"Does that shock you?"

"Why would it?"

"Take my word for it, Bobbie. Normal people get real goofy when they turn forty-five, but actors? We jump off buildings!"

"I thought you were about forty," she said. "Forty . . . forty-five, what's the difference?"

What's the difference? What's the *use!* He felt lonely for a moment, very lonely. He wished someone Nell Salter's age was sitting next to him. What's the *difference?*

"No difference," he said. "It's all the same."

She put her hand on his arm then, the first time they'd touched. She said, "I don't care if you wore wingtip baby shoes. I just wish you could forget about age. Is this what a mid-life crisis is all about?"

"No, this's what a mid-life *calamity* is all about."

"Well, just stop it," she said; then she unhooked her seat belt. "Speaking a forty-five," she said, "I *gotta* get this sidearm off."

"We'll lock it in the car."

"Are *you* packing?"

"Yeah, but I don't think we're gonna need a gun in the joint I'm taking you to. When their customers get in a brawl it's about as dangerous as two clowns smacking each other with pig bladders. I did Shakespeare once, when that's what we did. Hit each other with fake pig bladders."

Fin took the scenic route, driving past the Santa Fe Depot, a handsome train station in the Mission Revival style. It had been done well, so that the wood framing and stucco created the illusion of eighteenth-century adobe walls. Then Fin drove along the bay front, slowing for the nighttime tourist traffic. There was one cruise ship in port, and the three masts of the *Star of India* were outlined in white lights. Probably the oldest ship still sailing, the *Star* was christened on the Isle of Man in 1863, and had made numerous trips to and from Australia with other iron sailing ships of the era.

By the *Star of India* was a ferryboat that had done rescue work in the San Francisco earthquake of 1906. Across from the harbor side was the County Administration Center, Fin's favorite building, a 1930's beaux-arts landmark aglow with shafts of vertical light.

Fin was thinking how he was doomed to love everything old about his city and to scorn the new, when Bobbie interrupted his reverie to say, "It's a shame the Portuguese and Italians couldn'ta hung on to their fishing industry the way it *used* to be."

"I was just thinking how I like all that old stuff!" Fin said. "You read my thoughts."

"See, we got a *lot* in common," Bobbie said. "More than you think."

Fin crossed the San Diego River Floodway, driving past Sea World, and then across the Mission Bay Channel, that allows small pleasure craft to penetrate the 4,800-acre aqua park from the ocean side.

Bobbie said, "I think this is one a the most excellent things about this town. A huge water park right in the middle a the city!"

"Not like where you come from, huh?"

"Wisconsin? Not even!"

"Do you sit around in winter and ice-fish, or what?"

"Yeah, and we stay in saunas mostly, and talk with funny Scandinavian accents and whack each other with birch switches. In our spare time we *shiver*. Believe me, I've heard all the snowbird put-downs."

"So maybe you should stay in California when you leave the navy," Fin said, turning onto Mission Boulevard toward south Mission Beach.

The old roller coaster was lit up and operational since the. recent restoration. In Fin's youth, there was

a ballroom next to it where his sisters danced to the
big bands. He was feeling nostalgic, and would've
talked about those golden days in Mission Beach if
the woman next to him was Nell Salter, or someone
not younger than his handcuffs.

When they got to Fin's favorite gin mill they
were lucky to grab a parking space only half a block
away.

"You aren't expecting a trendy bistro, I hope," he
said, after they'd locked up Bobbie's sidearm.

"I've spent a little time in Mission Beach," she
said, "but mostly on the north side."

"Nothing up there but kids and derelicts," Fin
said. "Down here any derelicts you meet *won't* be
kids, just old geezers that sit around telling knock-
knock jokes."

As soon as Bobbie stepped inside she said to Fin,
"Wow! This is a *serious* saloon. Bet you could get a
terminal case of Smirnoff flu with this crowd."

"Or Napa Sonoma virus," Fin said, "if we stick to
wine like we should."

"Not in here," she said with a grin. "This is the
kinda place where you grog it up!"

It was a typical beach saloon: low ceiling, red-
wood paneling, and a large four-sided bar in the center where one could look across at alter egos and
always find somebody in worse shape than oneself.
There were many women drinkers, all of whom were
older than Fin. Two of the women had helmet-head
blunt-cuts, sprayed so they wouldn't ruffle in gale-
force winds or if they got conked by a beer bottle.

Even though California beach communities were
into outdoor sports and health, saloons like this one
were havens for those few smokers left. These people
had worse fears than death: *aging*, for instance.

Fin was in a semi-rollicking mood. He said to
Bobbie, "Until I ran into you today, I was feeling that

my life had the value of a disposable diaper, a used one. Now I think I'm ready for some fun. So where's my grog?"

Bobbie boldly wiggled through the drinkers standing two deep at the bar, and yelled, "Make a hole, shipmates!" The mustachioed bartender wore a tank top and shorts, and she said to him, "Two double brandies!"

An old coot sitting at the bar turned to her and said, "You old enough to drink brandy?"

Bobbie winked at the bartender, and said, "Make that one brandy and a double Roy Rogers on the rocks!"

This close to the election, there were lots of political debates going on in the saloon. Bobbie stood next to a guy who had navy written all over him. He was arguing with another old geezer whose belly was big enough to make the cover of *Vanity Fair*.

The old sailor said, "A liberal Democrat's always *against* capital punishment, but *for* killing fetuses."

"So?" the other geezer said, after a horrendous belch.

"It's not consistent. Don't you see that?"

"What's your point?"

"Mother Teresa's consistent. She doesn't wanna execute guilty murderers *or* innocent fetuses. *I'm* consistent. I wanna kill Death Row murderers *and* innocent fetuses as long as they come from the inner city and would probably grow up to be guilty murderers."

"What's your point?" the other codger repeated, belching again.

"I got more in common with Mother Teresa than *any* candidate does!"

Bobbie paid for the drinks, tipped the harried bartender a buck from her change, and wriggled back through the crowd to Fin, who was trying to play some not-so-oldies on the jukebox, even though it was impossible to hear the music over the din.

Bobbie looked at the dollar bills she'd been given in change and said, "Gnarly!"

Each was nearly faded to white. One was Scotch-taped.

Fin said, "Beach-town bucks. Those dollar bills've been in the pockets of shorts during surfing, swimming, Laundromat cycles, and maybe even bathtubs when their former owners were fully clothed."

Bobbie kept the limp rags of currency separate from her other money, intending to leave them as tips.

They began watching a woman with dye-damaged hair, who'd probably graduated from high school during Eisenhower's presidency, weaving in little circles with a geezer in flipflops, jeans, and a T-shirt that said "Canardly" on it.

Fin explained that all "Over-The-Line" players knew that it stood for "Canardly get it up." This as opposed to players in the other divisions like "Cannever," or "Canalways," or "Caneasy."

Bobbie learned that this saloon was an official hangout of the OMBACs, the Old Mission Beach Athletic Club—or if one preferred, the Old Men's Beach Athletic Club—a group that had made the zany sport of OTL world-famous since it began in 1954. Now, thousands attended the annual OTL Tournament on Fiesta Island, and money was raised for worthy causes while men and women tried to bat and catch softballs after having consumed enough Bacardi rum to make Puerto Rico not even *need* statehood.

The annual OTL Tournament attracted packs of aspiring models, actresses, strippers and other exhibitionists, who vied for the honor of winning the tit tournament, thus becoming "Ms. Emerson."

Bobbie was interested to find out that the most recent Ms. Emerson was an ex-marine her own age.

When she asked one of the old duffers why they called their beauty contest winner "Ms. Emerson," the geezer said, "Knock-knock."

Bobbie looked warily at Fin, but said, "Okay, who's there?"

The codger said, "Emerson."

Bobbie said, "Emerson who?"

The old coot said, "Em-er-*son* tits!"

Then all the fogies had a good snuffle and cackle, and Bobbie found herself with *three* Bacardis and *two* more brandies, compliments of the geezer gang.

Bobbie was told that some of the teams participating in the OTL Open Division had names like Dicks With Stix, Titty Clitty Gang Bang, and Tongue In Groove. The Women's Open Division had teams named No Flat Chicks, Our Team Sucks, Penis Envy-Not, and George, Stay Outta My Bush.

Bumper-sticker team names were plastered to the walls, alluding to Hollywood movies, such as, TWAT'S UP DOC?, HANNIBAL ATE JODIE AND SILENCED THE CLAM, DANCES WITH WOOL, and DANCES WITH VULVAS.

There were political statements stuck to the ceiling that said: ARKANSAS WOMEN ARE SO FAST THEY NEED A GOVERNOR PUT ON THEM, and a reference to Bill Clinton's ex-paramour, Gennifer Flowers: ROSES ARE RED, VIOLETS ARE BLUE, CLINTON INHALES FLOWERS TOO.

The motto over the smoky hamburger grill said, IF IT DOESNT GET ON YOUR FACE, IT'S NOT WORTH EATING.

On the door to the women's rest room Bobbie read, WE SNATCH KISSES & VICE VERSA.

By 11:30 Bobbie was ripped, and sitting in the lap of a retired San Diego cop called "Bub" who'd also been a commander in the U.S. Naval Reserve, thus bridging the two worlds of the two drunks at his table.

Fin's head was starting to loll, and he said, "That is *it*! No more *rum*!"

"Don't be a wuss!" Bub said. "You sound like one of those Secret Service guys last week chasing around after the vice president with spiders in their ears, saying, 'I can't drink when I'm on *duty*!' "

"They don't make Feds like they used to," Fin had to agree, scratching his chin but not feeling it. "Only reason the FBI and CIA even exist anymore is so every putz in Hollywood can make movies claiming their leading man is the target of government agents."

Bub literally bounced Bobbie on his knee like a child, and said, "Put on some tunes, will ya? But nothing by Ozzy Osbourne. It sounds like sea gulls chasing a trawler. And nothing by that crotch-grabbing, former human person, Michael Jackson."

"Okay, Bub!" Bobbie said, heading for the juke-box. Her cotton top was a mess from spilled rum. The former pink shell now looked like a paisley.

"I either gotta go home or make a dying declaration," Fin said to Bub, but he knew that before leaving there'd be the long sentimental goodbyes required in such places.

When she came back, Bobbie overheard an old redhead with big hooters whisper to Bub, "Do you like to talk dirty to your wife when you're having sex?"

Bub answered, "Only if there's a phone handy."

When Bobbie questioned Fin about the age of all the fun-loving fogies, coots, geezers, codgers, duffers and biddies she'd met in the saloon, he didn't know how to tell her that the oldest fossil in the joint wasn't fifteen years his senior.

All he could mumble in their behalf and his own was "Because of all their fun in the sun, crow's-feet are badges of honor. Sorta like the face paint on Alice

Cooper and Amazon headhunters. They're really not as antique as they look."

Fin was doing some shaky driving when they crossed the Coronado Bridge at 2:00 A.M. He had the radio tuned to a San Diego oldie station, and while Natalie Cole's old man sang "Too Young," he said to her, "My sisters made me sing that when I took guitar lessons. They thought I was adorable."

"You still are," she muttered drowsily, her eyes closed.

He glanced over, thinking that now she looked like a teenager. At the top of the bridge he saw the Suicide Prevention Hotline number, and thought: What is happening to me? Where am I going with my life? Do I have a life left? Where's the *Menopause* Hotline number? Does it get worse than this?

When they drove through the toll gate he said to her, "Time to wake up, kid, I mean, Bobbie. Open up your peepers."

"Huh?" she said, bolting upright.

"It's *not* a Scud attack," he said, "but we're in Coronado. Where do you live?"

She directed him to a house just off Fourth Avenue, and after he parked in front, he retrieved her .45 automatic. Then he opened the car door for her, and this time he had to pull her up by the hand. She staggered when she took the first step so he put his arm around her waist and walked her to her upstairs apartment in the rear.

She fumbled in her purse, and didn't object when Fin took the purse and rummaged for the keys. She didn't object when he unlocked the door and led her inside. Nor did she object when he put her purse on the kitchen counter, along with the holstered automatic, gun belt, and keys.

She *did* object when he pecked her on the cheek and turned toward the door.

In fact, still wobbly, Bobbie intercepted him and threw her arms around his neck, exploring his gold crowns with her tongue.

When he pulled away he knew he was in trouble. Gallantly, he said, "No way, kid."

"Don't call me kid."

Hoarsely: "No way. Not in your condition. Not in *my* condition."

Bobbie ran her hands under Fin's jacket and over his buns saying, "What condition are you *in*?"

"No way, Bobbie!" he said, even more raspy. "Your boyfriend went back to his wife, right? You're just lonely."

"Sure, but I don't have to hit on toll-booth attendants. I can find somebody *any* time I want."

"You'd be sorry tomorrow," he said.

"I never had an older guy," she said. "Besides, it's already tomorrow."

A croak: "I can't go the distance."

She stepped back then and said, "I can't believe it! You're the first guy ever turned me down!"

"I'm *not* turning you down," he said. "Just asking for a rain check."

"But why?"

That stopped him. His mouth was dry. His heart was hammering. His hands were shaking. He wanted to peel off that rum-stained pink shell right this second and fondle those Emersons for a week at least!

Instead, he said, "I can't take advantage of a kid . . . of a young *woman* that's drunker than a beer-hall mouse."

"You *are* a gentleman!" she said in amazement. "For real! The first one I ever met in California!"

Trudging out the door, he said, "I wish I had Jimmy Carter's home number 'cause I sure got a lotta lust in my heart!"

She popped her head out and said, "You really are! A gentleman!"

He was boozy and woozy and *full* of self-pity when he said, "I'm a combat veteran of the battle of the sexes, but somehow I can't bring myself to really use-and-abuse personnel of your gender. Because of my sisters! Those three babes have wrecked my entire life!"

When he got to the bottom of the steps she said, "Wait, Fin!"

He paused: "Is it about the rain check?"

"It's about the shoe!" Bobbie said. "I been forgetting to ask you all evening about the shoe on the dead guy's foot. Whazzisname, Pepe Palmera? What kinda *shoe* was it?"

21

Nell Salter had trouble going to sleep that night because of confusion, and mixed feelings concerning the neurotic cop, Fin Finnegan.

Bobbie Ann Doggett had difficulty sleeping because of her raging blood-alcohol level, and her astonishment at having met a gentleman in the state of California.

Jules Temple couldn't sleep because he was furious at the notion that he was losing control of his own life, and at his dismal sexual performance with Lou Ross. But finally, he blamed his failure on Lou's deteriorating body, and took a sleeping pill.

Fin Finnegan slept badly because of a plethora of emotions that involved Bobbie Ann Doggett, Nell Salter, his three ex-wives, and all three sisters. He had a momentary rum-soaked fantasy about living the remainder of his days in a monastery out near Borrego Springs, until he remembered that he'd still be a *forty-five-year-old* monk.

Abel Durazo was awake longer than the few minutes it usually took, because of the extreme violence he'd seen in the bikers' bar. And also because tomorrow he was going to collect six thousand dollars from Soltero. Abel had never had so much money at one time in his entire life.

Shelby Pate couldn't sleep at *all*. It was mostly because he'd snorted so much meth he was totally amped, and when he was like this he did all sorts of strange things, such as going out to his girlfriend's one-car garage and trying to take his truck engine apart and put it back together. Sometimes when he was wired he'd work on his Harley in the front yard under a droplight, or he might initiate a frenzy of hedge clipping until it looked like a herd of starving goats had raided the yard.

When he got like this, his neighbors would scream at him and threaten to call the cops, but they were tweakers too. They knew that Shelby was vibrating from having done a teener of go-fast, and that he'd chill pretty soon. Or else he'd flat-line, and they wouldn't mind that either.

There was another reason though, that Shelby Pate couldn't sleep, and it had nothing to do with the twitching and jumping and oscillating caused by the cringe. It had to do with the visit by Nell Salter and Fin Finnegan. It had to do with Shelby learning for the first time that they were hauling a very dangerous pesticide called Guthion, and that such a load should've been manifested for disposal outside California.

When Shelby had got home from the bikers' bar—long after the paramedics had hauled away the bearded biker with his guts kicked out—Shelby had crept into his girlfriend's closet and retrieved his leather jacket, the one he'd worn last Friday night. He removed both manifests from the pocket of the jacket and read them. The material from North Island was properly manifested for disposal at a Los Angeles refinery. Then he sat down at the kitchen table and carefully read the manifest from Southbay Agricultural Supply.

On line 11-a of the State of California Health and Welfare Agency form, the proper shipping name, hazard class, and I.D. number did *not* list a waste poison mixture of Guthion. It was listed as "waste flammable liquid," and specifically described as "weed oil and kerosene."

And on line 9, which required the name and address of the disposal site, the facility listed was a refinery in Los Angeles where Shelby and Abel had often hauled *ordinary* waste. There was no mention of a disposal site in Texas.

Shelby folded the manifest and put it inside a plastic sandwich bag. Then he hid the plastic bag inside one of his spare boots and took that pair of boots out to the garage. After that, Shelby fired up the power mower and started running it over the little yard until a next-door neighbor and fellow tweaker walked out of his house in his underwear at 4:30 A.M., and said, "Dude, if you don't stop workin like a deranged fuckin beaver my old lady said she's gonna burn your house down and that's a promise!"

The first one up the next morning was Bobbie Ann Doggett. The second was Fin Finnegan, only because Bobbie phoned him at 8:00 A.M. sharp.

Fin stared at the ringing telephone like he was Alexander Graham Bell's cleaning lady wondering what the hell that strange contraption *was*.

"Uuuhhhh!" he mumbled, after he worked it all out and picked it up.

"It's Bobbie!" she said. "I'm real sorry, Fin, but I could hardly wait to call!"

"Uuuuuhhh!" he said, afraid to raise his head from the pillow. "Bobbie, I'm near death! Please!"

"Don't you want a second opinion? Listen to me, Fin. The shoe? Whaddaya say we call and talk to the officer that found the dead guy's foot? Or maybe we could call the morgue?"

"It's Saturday, Bobbie! I'm on a day off. *You're* on a day off."

"But Fin," she said, "if the dead guy's foot was inside a black steel-toe high-top U.S. Navy flight-deck shoe, I'm gonna arrest those two truckers for grand theft!"

"Wait, Bobby!" he said, sitting up. Then, "Owwwwww!"

"What's wrong?"

"What's wrong? You drank as much, no, *more* than I did and you ask what's wrong?"

"I felt a little sick last night, but I went for a jog this morning and I'm fine," she said.

Youth. Communication was hopeless. "Don't go running off and arresting anybody," he said. "Lemme get up and find my head and make some coffee and call a priest for last rites. Then I'll phone the CHP and see if I can get in touch with the young officer who added to my present torment by going on a treasure hunt for a goddamn *foot!*"

"Okay, I'm at home and I'm ready to go to work," she said. "This'll be the biggest arrest I ever made. It's rad!"

"Rad," Fin said, hanging up the phone. Then, "Rad. Cool. Awesome. Ow, my freaking head!"

While Fin was trying to accomplish the most difficult task of the week, namely, locating the bathroom door, *another* urgent call was being made by an equally anxious caller.

"Here, pus brain," she said, "it's for *you.*"
Shelby Pate didn't know where he was. He didn't

know who *she* was for a moment, even though he'd been living with the woman for eighteen months.

He lay in bed and tried to focus, but couldn't. He heard the telephone voice saying, "Hello? Hello?"

He tried to put the receiver back on the cradle, but only managed to knock everything on the floor.

"Hello?" the voice said, more faintly.

Then Shelby felt himself being shaken by his hair. "Ooooooo!" he moaned. "You *bitch*!"

"Get up, puke face, and *talk* to him!" she said. "It's your fucking boss! I gotta leave for work now or I won't have a job and you'll have to support me for a change, you speed-freak asshole!"

And with that good morning, Shelby Pate's long-suffering girlfriend went off to her job as a manager of a pizza joint, leaving him to listen to that fucking telephone voice yammering at him.

"Hello? Hello? Hello? Goddamnit!" the voice said.

Disoriented, he picked up the phone and said, "Flaco, is that you? It's too early, man!"

"This is Jules Temple!" the voice said.

"What?"

"It's Jules Temple! Wake up. We gotta talk."

That brought him around a bit. He raised up on one elbow and said, "Kin I call you back, Mister Temple?"

"I just need a few minutes. It's important."

He couldn't find a pencil anyway, so he said, "Okay, I'll try to talk, but I was up late."

"It's about the cops that visited you yesterday," Jules said. "I got back to the office and found a note from Mary."

"Yeah?"

"What'd they want?"

"Kin this wait?"

"No, goddamnit! What'd they want? I gotta know! It's my business! You're my employee!"

There was nothing like a little jolt of anger to cut through the fog. "I *know* you're my boss," Shelby said.

"There seems to be a lotta interest in you two and that truck. What happened? Mary said a kid was contaminated from the Guthion."

His head was clearing more quickly and he said, "That's right, Mister Temple. From the *Guthion.*"

"That's a shame," Jules said. "But what else did they say? Did they find the drums? Did they find . . . *anything?*"

"No, Mister Temple," Shelby said. "They didn't say nothing about the waste drums. Whaddaya mean by find *anything?*"

"Well . . ." Jules hesitated. "Like the license plates, or registration, or any documents from the truck."

"They didn't say nothing about no license plates or registration."

"Anything else? Did they ask about anything else or mention *finding* anything else?"

"Like what?"

"Goddamnit, like the fucking manifests! Did they mention finding the manifests?"

"Which one?" Shelby asked innocently. "The one from North Island or the one from Southbay Agricultural Supply?"

Jules could have shot him dead. He could have plunged a knife into his throat. He could have pushed him into a vat of acid in the storage yard. But he took a long pause and said, "All right, did they mention the manifest from North Island? Like maybe they *found* it?"

"No, they didn't," Shelby said, and even through the hellacious methamphetamine and tequila hangover, he was starting to enjoy this.

"Did they mention the *other* manifest?" Jules asked very carefully, the way you'd talk to a lunatic chained to a wall. "Did they maybe find the manifest from Southbay Agricultural Supply?"

"No, they didn't say they found it," Shelby said.

"They didn't? Okay, I was just wondering, and . . ."

Shelby interrupted him: "But they *mentioned* it."

"What . . . did they say, Shelby?" Jules asked, with no emotion whatsoever in his voice.

"Just that we was carryin this real bad Guthion and it would have to be manifested for outta state. Texas, I think. That's what they said."

"And what did *you* say?"

"That we never pay no attention to what manifests say. Our job was to bring the stuff back to the yard and then you tend to it after that."

"Okay," Jules said. "Okay, was there anything *else* they said?"

"Just asked us again about how the truck got stolen. Like, whether we saw anybody we knew around Angel's when we went in for lunch. That kinda stuff. Cop stuff."

Jules was enormously relieved. Now he wanted to smooth things over with this halfwit, to keep Shelby Pate from thinking that there was any more to this than a routine call from a concerned employer.

"I'm sorry to be so abrupt and to call you so early," Jules said, "but you can imagine how I feel. A child died because our waste got dumped by some truck thief. It's not *your* fault. It's not *my* fault. Still, I feel very bad about it. You can understand, can't you?"

"Sure, Mister Temple."

"So that was it?" Jules Temple said. "They haven't found any paperwork whatsoever?"

The ox managed a little smile, even with a blinding headache. It was *fun* being clever, particularly since Shelby hated this cheesy son of a bitch with his manicured fingernails and thirty-dollar haircuts. A guy who never so much as got a palm blister in his whole life. Shelby said, "They asked again about your five hundred bucks."

Jules knew that this larcenous son of a bitch was rubbing it in about his money, but he forced himself to say, "And you told them the same as before? That the truck thief got it?"

"Right. That it was in an envelope wrapped up by the manifests inside the glove box. Where we put everything for safekeeping."

Jules persuaded himself to say calmly and casually, "In the glove compartment with the *two* manifests?"

"Right," the ox said, grinning now, because he knew that Jules Temple knew they'd ripped him off for the $500. And there was nothing he could do about it. Shelby *loved* this.

But he'd overplayed it again, just as he had with Bobbie Ann Doggett. As Fin Finnegan might say, he'd taken his performance clear over the top. But even if Shelby had had a clearer head he might not have been clever enough to manipulate Jules Temple.

"If I need to talk to you again, Shelby, I hope you don't mind if I call you?"

"Anytime, Mister Temple," said Shelby. "Anytime."

Then Jules hung up. The blood had drained from his face. He got up and began to pace. He went into the kitchen and poured a cup of coffee. His hands were actually trembling, and that was *not* like him.

That imbecile said that *both* manifests were in the glove box, but the day after the so-called truck theft, he'd told Jules that one manifest was on the seat in the cab and one was in the glove box. Now he'd forgotten about that lie.

It could be an honest mistake. Shelby Pate was

obviously hung over and more dimwitted than usual. *Maybe* it was an honest mistake, but Jules didn't think so. There was something about the way he'd said "Guthion."

Jules believed that Shelby Pate had read that manifest, and if he'd read it, he might still have it. Or at least he knew where he'd tossed it and he'd go find it, now that the cops had given those fools information that could put Jules Temple in prison!

But would Pate and Durazo risk jail themselves? They'd dumped the waste. They'd faked the truck theft. A moment's thought provided the answer. They could tell the authorities that they had no idea that the waste was anything more than what the manifest said it was: waste flammable liquid. They could cut a deal with the police, if it came to it. Jules knew he was about to be blackmailed.

While Shelby Pate tried to pull himself together by drinking hot coffee, Jules Temple, for the very first time in his life, began to contemplate an act of violence. He began to contemplate murder.

It was Nell Salter who got the next phone call of the morning, and she was surprised that it was from Fin.

"I got some news for you," he said.

"Was your pasta a success?"

"What pasta?"

"Last night. Pasta?"

"Oh, that. No, it's about our case. The guy that got killed in the hot truck was wearing a shoe that was stolen along with a couple thousand other shoes at North Island when our two truckers picked up the hazardous waste."

"What?"

"His cold foot was in a *hot* shoe!"

"Were you drinking again last night?"

"Yeah, but I'm sober now. The truckers *and* the dead guy apparently pulled a grand theft at North Island, then drove to T.J., then faked the theft of the truck. So this means they also dumped the waste!"

"Can we start from the beginning?"

"Not now, I gotta meet somebody. Are you willing to work on Saturday?"

"Of course not."

"But we might get lucky and make you a case for intentional dumping of hazardous waste resulting in deaths. I don't think you make a case like that every day, do you?"

The fact was, she'd *never* made a case like that, not for a dumping that caused *death*. Nell said, "Okay, where do I meet you?"

"At the front gate of North Island."

"Why there?"

"It's convenient for all three of us."

"Three?"

"We'll be driving down to Green Earth to have a talk with our two truckers, or we'll stake out their homes if they don't work on Saturday. We'll find those boys."

"Who's the *we*?"

"An investigator from the navy's gonna join us. She wants their shoes back."

After hanging up, Nell thought, *she*?

"You were right!" Fin said after he got Bobbie on the phone later that morning. "It took me awhile to get him, but the CHP officer that found the foot described *your* shoe to a T!"

"Out-standing!" Bobbie said.

"Don't go turbo on me," Fin said. "We gotta do a

few things. One thing we *should* do is wait till Monday when we're all getting paid for police work."

"What if those two dudes're working today? What if they dump another load a waste like they did the first one? Do you think they care about human life?"

"Just like every woman I ever met," Fin said. "A guilt maker."

"I think it's our duty to take those guys down as soon as possible. If you don't, I will!"

"Whoa!" he said. "Chill out, Bobbie. I'll meet you at the main gate of North Island at two o'clock. The D.A.'s investigator I told you about, she's gonna be there."

"Oh, then you'd already *planned* to do the right thing?"

"I mighta known. You've got a black belt in guilt-tripping."

At 11:30 that morning, Abel Durazo crawled lazily out of bed and fried himself some *chorizo* and scrambled eggs. He drank three cups of coffee and watched TV cartoons along with four of the kids belonging to the Guatemalan couple who rented him his room. He could've afforded better than a rented room, but he never squandered money. Abel sent $400 a month to his mother in Tijuana. She in turn wrote to him twice a week and prayed that someday they'd have enough so that he could return home and be with the rest of the family forever.

Before noon, Abel received a phone call from Shelby Pate, who said, "Kin you talk now, dude?"

Abel was puzzled and said, "We got problem?"

"We got a pot a *gold* waitin, dude, is what we got!"

"Yes," Abel said. "Een Tijuana."

"That ain't nothin!" said the ox. "I'm talkin about *big* money. Robo bucks. Humongous *dinero!*"

"You steel drunk, Buey?"

"A little bit, but I managed to get an hour's sleep. Let's meet and talk somewheres before we go to T.J."

"Okay, where?"

Shelby said, "Meet me where we got our truck stole."

"What?"

"At Angel's, you dumb Mexican!" Shelby said.

Abel giggled and said, "Okay, Buey, we meet at Angel's, but we don' stay too long. Maybe somebody steal my car!"

This time it was Shelby's turn to giggle. He said, "Meet me there at, say, three o'clock."

"Okay, Buey," Abel said, and hung up just in time to catch a Porky Pig cartoon. He liked the old cartoons best, especially Bugs Bunny and Daffy Duck.

Naturally, Bobbie arrived first, and she made sure that her bike was still safely locked up from the day before. She was wearing a raspberry, flannel-lined fleece stadium jacket that she got on sale for $29, along with Bill Blass jeans. The most expensive item on her body, next to her Colt .45 automatic, was her Gloria Vanderbilt lace-up booties that set her back $35. Bobbie had tried to dress for action in the event that the arrest of Shelby Pate and Abel Durazo got rough. Bobbie had been wildly excited all day and had gone jogging *twice* trying to calm herself.

Nell Salter arrived next, looked for a place to park her five-year-old Audi sedan, then decided to make a U-turn and wait at the curb for Fin's Corvette. While she was waiting she saw a young blonde in a raspberry jacket chatting with the navy sentry.

Fin parked on the side street, locked his Vette,

and while walking toward Nell's Audi, spotted Bobbie with the sentry.

"Bobbie!" he shouted, and she waved, then trotted toward Nell's car.

Nell was casually attired, but had invested more than Bobbie had. She wore a lavender silk blouse with rolled sleeves, pleated black stirrup pants, and black leather pumps. She had a black sweater vest in the car in case they worked into the evening.

Fin could see that Nell was not packing, but he figured that Bobbie would be loaded for rhino, and she was. When the three investigators linked up, Fin said, "Bobbie, this is Nell. Nell Salter, meet Bobbie Ann Doggett."

Bobbie showed Nell a big smile and shook hands vigorously. Nell gave her a half-smile and shook hands with less enthusiasm, especially when Bobbie looked so approvingly at Fin, who wore a blue cotton turtleneck, Dockers, and a white windbreaker.

Bobbie said, "You look *cool* in a turtleneck, Fin!"

"Hides a sagging neck," Nell said, dryly.

Bobbie thought that Nell was very attractive, but not in the usual way, not with that bent nose. Yet she was a mature woman who looked in charge of her life, and that was intimidating to a woman Bobbie's age.

Nell studied Bobbie and thought she needed to lose ten pounds. And Nell couldn't fail to notice how she fawned over Fin. He returned her fawning with a badly concealed "aw shucks" kind of foot shuffling. Nell half expected him to tug at his forelock. It was *pathetic*.

Before the conversation went very far, Fin said, "My Vette can't carry three."

Bobbie said, "My Hyundai isn't very comfortable."

Nell said, "We'll take my Audi."

"We need to go someplace and talk," Fin said.

"Not someplace where they serve alcohol," Nell said, looking purposefully at Bobbie. "Have you noticed that he *drinks*?"

Bobbie grinned at Fin and said, "No worse than a sailor."

Had to stay home and cook pasta? Nell thought. Yeah. She thought she might faint if it got any more revolting. He'd actually *blushed* when Bobbie giggled!

"I know what," Fin said. "There's a nineteen-fifties lunch counter on Orange Avenue. Let's go there for a burger and a coke."

"Out-standing!" Bobbie said.

"In-tense!" Nell said.

"What?" Fin said.

"In-credible!" Nell said. "Let's go hang *out*!"

"Is there something wrong?" Fin asked quietly.

"Of course not," Nell said, with the first of an afternoon full of smirks. "This is all so predictable."

The diner was a *real* fifties-style lunch counter, not one of the ersatz diners that've become popular in recent years. This one hadn't changed since We-liked-Ike, except for an occasional paint job, or a new sheet of Formica on the counter, or some new plastic on the revolving stools.

Fin sat between the two women and ordered a Coke. Nell ordered coffee and Bobbie ordered a large orange juice, and a burger with everything.

"Gotta replenish the vitamin C," she said, beaming at Fin and adding, "after last night."

Nell noticed that Bobbie usually placed her hand on his forearm when she spoke to him.

"This is *so* touching, I don't need sugar in my coffee," Nell said to the waitress in a stage whisper.

In that she was getting on in years, the waitress

turned her good ear toward Nell and said, "Excuse me?"

"Nothing," Nell said. "Everything's *swell*."

Nell also noticed that Fin deferred to Bobbie each time there was something to be explained to Nell during the fifteen-minute conversation. Nell learned about the theft from North Island, and that Bobbie felt it was very suspicious that Jules Temple hadn't informed them that there was a navy investigator interested in the case.

When Bobbie and Fin were all through telling the story, Nell stared into the bottom of her coffee cup and said, "This is a squirrely case and getting more so."

"I think it's clearing up," Bobbie said.

Nell said, "So Abel Durazo, Shelby Pate, and a deceased Mexican national named Pepe Palmera were in cahoots to steal the navy shoes, sell them in T.J. and . . ."

"*Along* with the truck," Fin added.

"Okay, so they *probably* sold the truck, or at least planned to use it to haul the pottery . . . Wait a minute. The pottery shop in Old Town? Do you think . . ."

"It's complicated enough," Fin said. "Let's not include him in this conspiracy."

"Okay, for now it's just those three."

"Why didn't Jules Temple tell you about me?" Bobbie wanted to know.

Nell smiled sweetly and said, "Maybe he didn't think you were that important, honey."

Fin shot Nell a dirty look and she returned it with a smirk, but Bobbie wasn't fazed.

"I can't believe he'd just think it was too trivial to mention," Bobbie said. "Do you, Fin?"

"I tend to agree with Bobbie," he said.

"Of course you do," Nell muttered.

Then Fin turned to Bobbie and said, "But still, I can't understand why Jules Temple would involve himself with the theft of two thousand pairs of shoes, not to mention going along with the loss of his truck."

"Maybe the truck's heavily insured," Bobbie said.

This time Nell leaned forward on her stool, looked around Fin, and said, "There's always a deductible on a policy, my dear, that *he* would have to pay."

Bobbie leaned over, looked at Nell, and said, "Of course! Since I don't have your many *many* years of investigation, I didn't think a that."

Fin interrupted quickly. "I think the faking of the truck theft lets Jules Temple off the hook as far as being part of any grand-theft conspiracy. Even if it's just one of *many* thefts involving these guys."

"Are those navy warehouses secure?" Nell asked.

"About as secure as Woody Allen," said Fin.

"True," Bobbie said. "They coulda pulled a lotta stuff outta our warehouses over a period of months."

"Jules Temple can't be part of *that*, Bobbie," Fin said. "It doesn't check out."

Nell looked into her cup again and said, "Yet . . ."

"Yet what?" Fin asked.

"What if his truckers're independent contractors as far as stealing is concerned, but in cahoots with their boss on something *else*?"

"Such as?"

"Such as dumping hazardous waste in Mexico, instead of Jules Temple having to spend the money to properly dispose of it."

"Yeah!" Bobbie said. "I *know* he's involved somehow. The guy's oilier than Kuwait."

"Could *that* be why he's less than forthcoming?" Fin asked. "He's a waste dumper?"

"Wait a minute," Nell said. "No, it doesn't wash. There were only a few drums involved here, and there're manifests to deal with, waste belonging to different customers on two different manifests. How would he explain to the EPA that manifested waste never got to its destination?"

"By claiming the truck was stolen?" Bobbie suggested.

"To save hauling costs on a few drums of waste, he's going to give up a truck? No," Nell said. "No."

"Okay, I give up," Fin said. "Jules Temple has nothing to do with anything. Durazo, Pate and the dead man were partners in a conspiracy to steal from the warehouse *and* to steal the truck. Period."

"Sounds right," Nell said.

Bobbie said nothing. She clearly didn't like anything about Jules Temple, including his goddamn haircut. All she'd say was "So let's go hook up the two truckers. The shoe on the dead guy ties them in good enough for an arrest, at least."

Nell nodded at Fin and said, "The porky dude'll rat off the little Mexican, I bet."

"Wait a minute!" Fin said. "Just when I got it sorted out another possibility jumped up."

"Go ahead," Nell said with a sigh.

"What if Pate and Durazo stole the shoes, but Pepe Palmera, a total stranger, stole their truck while they were having lunch at Angel's. Isn't that possible? Pepe Palmera got himself a cargo of waste and shoes, and he drove them straight to T.J."

"Then Pate and Durazo're telling the truth about everything except stealing the shoes from the navy?" Nell asked.

"Exactly," Fin said.

"But if they had nothing to *do* with Pepe Palmera, then how easy is it gonna be to connect them up with the shoe that was on his foot?" Bobbie asked.

"Not easy at all," Fin said, "unless they can be persuaded to drop a dime on each other."

"Shit!" Bobbie said. "They just gotta be involved in a conspiracy with the dead guy. *They* drove that truck to T.J. The two thousand pairs a shoes're in Tijuana and *they* know where at. *They* dumped the waste that killed that little kid."

"I'm getting tired of this," Nell said. "Let's go find those two guys and sweat them. First the big fat one, then the skinny Mexican."

Bobbie looked at Fin with anticipation. He looked back into her blue eyes for a few seconds and said, "Okay, sailor, but stay close to me. Hear?"

Bobbie beamed at him, and put her hand on his forearm.

Nell shook her head slowly, turned her face away, and said: "Dis-*gust*-ing."

The old waitress shuffled over and said, "It ain't *that* bad is it, love? I can make a fresh pot."

22

Abel Durazo didn't see the ox's pickup truck in the parking lot at Angel's Café so he thought Shelby wasn't there. But then he spotted Shelby's hog parked directly in front with four other Harleys, and on each bike was a hated helmet, now required by law.

When Abel entered he found the ox watching two truckers playing Pac-Man. Shelby's costume was designed to give off outlaw-biker death rays: black leather jacket, black jeans, studded boots, and a dirty gray tee with GRATEFUL DEAD in black across the chest. Instead of his usual loose and scraggly style, the ox had his dirty-blond hair tied back in a severe ponytail.

The ox showed his gap-tooth grin to Abel, threw a heavy arm around his partner's shoulder, and led him to a quiet booth where they ordered burritos and beer.

"Why we meet so early, Buey?" Abel asked, after the waitress was gone.

"I got some un-real *news*!" Shelby said. "We're gonna go into partnership with Mister Jules Temple!"

Abel Durazo had often thought that the ox might

someday just blow out all the wires in that massive skull, and now he feared it had happened. The Mexican looked around at all the various truckers, bikers, rednecks, and other lowlifes who used Angel's for various purposes. Several of them looked much more demented than the ox.

"Tell me one more time," Abel said carefully. "We going to be . . . *partner* weeth Meester Temple?"

"*Senior* partners," Shelby said, cackling. "Man, my life's become totally fucking *amazing*! I am in titty city, dude! I am gonna live in a meadow of meth! I am gonna reside in Harley heaven! 'Cept I ain't buyin no more Harleys. You ever seen that Honda Shadow eleven hunnerd? It ain't a fag bike like most a them. I'm thinkin about buyin me one. I'll buy you one too."

"Buey, you go crazy!" Abel said, with a sincerely worried look.

"If it wasn't fer you makin me steal them fuckin shoes, none a this ever woulda happened," Shelby said. "I am megafuckin stoked! *Totally!*"

"Okay, Buey, okay," Abel said soothingly, the way you'd talk to someone straddling the railing on the Coronado Bridge.

"Know that manifest? The one from Southbay? We was haulin *bad* shit, baby! And Jules Temple manifested it as not-so-bad shit, okay to take to L.A. fer ordinary disposal! Kin you see where I'm comin from, dude?"

"No, Buey," the Mexican said. "No."

"I didn't throw it away like you wanted me to. That manifest says we was haulin ordinary waste back to our yard for disposal at the L.A. refinery. But we was haulin *big-time* poison! And it killed the guy that stole our truck." Then the ox paused and the gap-tooth smile vanished. "And . . . and it killed that *kid*, that kid with the ringworm."

"We don' know eef eet was the one weeth the reengworms!" Abel said.

"Okay, but it killed a *kid*. On'y it wasn't our fault, was it, man?"

"No," Abel said.

"Anyways, that shit was illegally manifested by that cheesy faggot, Jules Temple. We never woulda let it outta our sight if we knew we had *real* bad poison, would we?"

"But Buey, we never look at manifest!"

"I know, goddamnit, but that's what we *say* to Temple. We say, we only did our thing in Mexico 'cause we thought we had ordinary waste!"

"He going to know we steal from navy."

"So what? Stealin shoes for guys like us is no biggie. Illegally manifested waste that *kills* somebody is the end a the fuckin world fer *him*!"

It was the first time that Shelby had ever seen Abel look scared. Flaco was a ballsy little dude, but for once he looked *scared*.

"I don' know, Buey."

"You don't know what?"

"Steal shoes, okay. Make report of stolen truck, okay. Tell Meester Temple we *partner*? I don' know."

"You jist lemme handle it, okay? You 'n me, we're fifty-fifty. I'll deal with Temple."

"He ain't like us, *'mano*," Abel said. "He deeferent people."

"No, he ain't like us. That bogus asshole don't know dick about the real world."

"Okay," Abel said, "but I scared."

"Don't be scared. Jist concentrate on the cool time we're gonna have tonight with six very *very* big ones that we're gonna collect from Soltero."

Then Abel broke into a grin. "Tonight, we have berry good time."

"There you go, Flaco!" said the ox. "Party *on*!"

"We go to T.J. now?"

"Pretty soon," Shelby said. "First we gotta stop by Green Earth before the overtime crew locks the fuckin place up."

"Why we go there?"

"I gotta git somethin."

"What?"

"Somethin I got in my locker. A derringer."

"Wha's that?"

"A little gun, dude. I ain't goin down there to Soltero without an edge. Don't worry, it's untraceable."

Abel said, "We get caught weeth gun in T.J., beeg problem!"

"I ain't gonna be talked outta this. I'd rather end up in the Tia-juana jail with those sphincter-stretchers stickin a cattle prod up my ass than meet Soltero without a backup."

"Buey," Abel said. "I scared now!"

"I know," Shelby said, "but I'm gonna make you *rich* and scared."

While Nell was driving down the Silver Strand from Coronado she couldn't stop thinking about how hard she'd worked on her hair that morning. First she'd ladled the mousse on her perm the instant she stepped out of the shower, then she'd combed it out ever so carefully, then she'd scrunched it up for twenty minutes until her do cried out: Tousle me with reckless abandon!

And Fin hadn't even noticed. He couldn't take his eyes off that *kid*. But of course that was typical. Why had she thought he'd be different from every other male person who walked the earth? Why was she even remotely concerned with what that three-time loser thought about her freaking hair?

For the first time, Nell Salter considered that it

might not be horrible to get old, not if mid-life agony ended then. She hadn't noticed that tension was causing her to goose the gas pedal.

Not until Bobbie, who was in the back seat, said, "Nell, I'm getting seasick."

Nell turned toward Bobbie and said, "You're a sailor, aren't you?"

From the corner of her eye Nell saw Fin turn toward Bobbie as though to say: Just ignore the old girl. She's a woman of a certain age.

"Doesn't the ocean look pretty today?" Bobbie said, to make conversation.

Nell didn't answer, so Fin said, "Lovely. Don't you think so, Nell?"

Fin saw Nell move her lower lip slightly and mumble something. He said, "I guess the surfing's okay down here, huh, Bobbie?"

"Not bad," Bobbie said. "I know a guy that lives in Coronado Cays. He lets me use his jet ski sometimes."

"How'd you meet him?" Fin asked.

"He's a cousin of a girl I did sea duty with," Bobbie said.

"Bobbie was in the Gulf War," Fin explained.

"In a very small way," Bobbie said. "Mostly we serviced the big ships. Nobody shot at us."

"Your country was proud of all of you," Fin said.

This isn't *fair*! was all Nell could think. First of all, Fin Finnegan wouldn't win first prize at the county fair. He was just a reasonably attractive person who made her feel . . . well, she didn't know *how* he made her feel. But he'd made her like him somehow. He hadn't seemed like a goddamn child molester! And that's all this Bobbie was really, a *child*. Bobbie had never stared into a magnifying mirror and seen Armageddon. *Her* cosmetic light didn't look like it was directed from the Point Loma lighthouse, revealing every goddamn sag and crease! What did *she* know about being a woman? And why was *he* sitting there gazing at her so doglike? The face of a goddamn golden retriever on a bag of kibble is what he looked like!

While passing Hogs Wild in Imperial Beach, Bobbie said, "The big porky one, Pate? He invited me for a drink at that place, I think it was."

Fin said, "Figures. It's the kinda joint where you can't decide if the patrons were raised by apes or wolves."

"What'll the navy say about you doing police work on your day off?" Nell asked, abruptly.

"I don't know," Bobbie said, "but if I bring back the guys that stole the shoes, I think . . . well, it's kinda weird to say, but I think they might be *proud* a me. I think *I'd* be proud."

Fin said, "You'd have a *right* to be proud."

"For chrissake!" Nell said to the roof of the Audi.

"It'd be a very big arrest for me," Bobbie said. "Maybe not for you guys."

"It *would* be," Fin said. "Those people murdered that little kid, as far as I'm concerned."

That made Nell shut up. No matter what she felt about Fin mooing like a calf over this girl, there was still *that* at the bottom of the whole business. They were trying to bring to justice some people who had directly or indirectly caused the death of a man and a *child*. She had to keep that in mind.

Abel and Shelby arrived at Green Earth in Abel's Chevy Nova long before the Saturday overtime crew had punched out. All the workers knew that the only reason they were getting the chance for overtime pay was because the boss had sold the business and had to get everything in order, even if it meant working the crew on Saturdays.

As Shelby Pate put it to Abel, "That cheesy prick pays overtime about as often as my old lady does my knob, and that bitch ain't gave me some knobbin since she told me she wants a *firm commitment*. I'm all faced at the time and I go, 'You want a commitment? Buy a vibrator, bitch.' See, the problem is, my old lady don't do meth. In fact, she don't do no drugs at all. You'd think she'd understand that a mixed marriage won't work."

Abel smiled, but didn't get it. He said, "We find good restaurant to eat tonight, Buey. We go to reech people's restaurant."

"It don't have to be a joint with ice cubes in the urinal," Shelby assured him. "Jist so it's clean and they ain't feedin us Mexican roadrunners and sayin it's rabbit."

"We find good place. I ask Soltero."

"I'm gonna feel a lot better about meetin up with that dude when I got my little twenny-five-caliber pal in my boot," Shelby said, and headed for the locker room, leaving Abel outside to chat with the overtime haulers.

After making sure no one was in the room Shelby unlocked the metal locker and reached up to the top shelf for the derringer, formerly owned by a Green Earth employee who'd been murdered by persons unknown in the Los Angeles riot during a visit to his aunt. When it had come time to clean out the dead man's locker and gather up his belongings, Shelby had taken the opportunity to steal the derringer, which was the only thing the hauler had that was worth stealing.

When Shelby came back out to the yard he whistled for Abel, and while they walked toward Abel's Chevy, Shelby said, "On'y thing that dead nigger did right was leave his derringer behind. Never yet met one a them North American porch monkeys that didn't have a hideout gun handy."

"We go to T.J. now?" Abel asked, hoping the ox had enough meth to last him. He *didn't* want to buy drugs in Tijuana.

"We're outta here, dude," Shelby Pate said.

"Hold it!" Bobbie said, as Nell was getting ready to pull into the parking lot at Green Earth Hauling and Disposal.

"What is it?" Fin asked.

"That Chevy that pulled out down the block there? Follow that car!" Bobbie said.

Nell said, "Where'd you see *that* movie? Follow that car?"

"It's *them!*" Bobbie said. "Pate and Durazo!"

"How can you tell from here?" Nell asked, but she accelerated and followed the brown Chevrolet.

"You sure?" Fin asked, as the car turned west toward I-5.

"I got twenty-fifteen eyesight," Bobbie said.

"Trust her," Fin said to Nell, and his head got jerked backward when Nell floored the Audi.

"Hey!" he said.

"Trust *me*," Nell said. "*I'm* driving."

After Nell got her temper and the Audi under control, Bobbie said, "Can I make a suggestion? How about we *don't* stop them. Let's see where they go."

"You're thinking of the shoes," Fin said.

"Two thousand pairs. They're worth a lot to the navy. Those dudes might lead us right to them."

"They're probably just going to some beer joint," Nell said. "Following them is a waste of . . . oh-oh!"

Abel Durazo's Chevrolet turned *onto* the freeway, heading south toward Mexico.

Nell had to hit the brakes when a Lexus cut her off at the on-ramp. "Bastard!" she said, then zoomed up to his bumper.

"You always drive like this?" Fin wanted to know.

The fact was, she didn't. She was a careful driver, proud of the fact that she'd never been in an accident, not even as a cop. Nell realized how unreasonably steamed she was. She was not going to let this neurotic *actor* and this *child* do this to her, so she slowed down.

Abel Durazo's brown Chevrolet was five minutes from the international border when Nell got close again. "I don't think this is smart," Nell said.

"Please, Nell!" Bobbie said. "Let's tail 'em across. They gotta be going straight to the guy that fenced the shoes."

Fin said, "This isn't like in San Diego, Bobbie. It's not possible to ring up the local constabulary and say come arrest our suspects and confiscate our shoes. That's another *country*."

"This is the point of no return," Nell warned when she got to the last turnoff on I-5 south.

"Go for it, Nell!" Bobbie pleaded.

"I say that's a good call," Fin said, and Nell saw him aim another one of those simpering smiles at Bobbie.

"*Good* call," Nell muttered, dropping behind a Toyota Corolla that was in the same lane as Abel Durazo's Chevy, just as it crossed the international line.

The instant they were on Mexican soil, Shelby reached down inside his left boot and withdrew a bindle of meth. Abel glanced over nervously when the ox unfolded the paper and snorted the meth into both nostrils. Then he licked the paper.

"Wanna try some cringe?" Shelby asked.

"No, I don' wan' that stuff. Leetle marijuana good for you. No' that speed. Bad, '*mano*."

"Thing it does for me is, it makes me harder than a tax return. I could do the Sisters of Mary or the whole Mustang Ranch when I got some go-fast in me. So you better find us some *babes* tonight."

"I try," Abel said.

"It's my old lady's fault," Shelby said. "That bitch could douche with battery acid and never feel it. Cold. She's *cold*, man. She says she wants a baby! I says to her, 'You'd end up with a frozen fetus.' A womb or a tomb, in her case it's all the same thing. She's *cold*."

Abel Durazo looked at his watch and said, "We going to park down by *Frontón* where they play the jai alai. We going to walk for leetle while. We going to be late."

"Why?"

"I wan' Soltero to wait. Let heem wait teel seex o'clock. We eemportant peoples too."

Shelby was feeling the methamphetamine rush. He grinned and said, "You may end up bein *glad* I brought my little chrome-plated pal along."

"Be careful, Buey. We een Mexico."

"You don't hafta remind me," said the ox.

He looked with trepidation at the lanes of cars crawling along beside them, all heading into the center, some for a Saturday night on the town. Many of the Mexican cars had religious medals or good-luck amulets or rosary beads hanging from the rearview mirrors. This troubled Shelby. He didn't want to admit it to Abel, but all those dangling charms and trinkets and religious symbols bothered him.

"Voodoo," he finally said.

"Huh?"

"All that fuckin shit hangin from the mirrors. Like *voodoo*, dude. My bitch is a Catholic and she wears a medal and talks about Holy Ghosts and all that voodoo shit."

In that Abel didn't understand the ox most of the time, he just shrugged and smiled.

"This is the first time in my life I've driven to T.J. without buying Mexican car insurance," Nell said.

"Most U.S. policies cover you twenty-five miles from the border," Fin said.

"If something happens to this car . . ."

"It sure is a *nice* car," Bobbie said. "For a while there everybody thought Audis were like Christine in the Stephen King movie. The car from hell that took off when you stepped on the brake."

After Nell drove across the Tijuana River, Fin said, "They're turning down Avenida Revolución."

"Predictable," Nell said with disgust. "They're not going to see their fence. They're going to a skin joint for a cheap night out."

"We've come *this* far," Bobbie said. "We can't give up."

Abel drove down Avenida Revolución and parked by the *Palacio Frontón*, the Tijuana landmark where jai alai players from Spain and Cuba join the Mexicans in the art of hurling hard rubber balls from wicker baskets lashed to their wrists. The *Palacio* was huge, with Moorish arches and a fountain in front near a statue of a jai alai player leaping in the air.

Abel had once tried explaining the game to the ox, but Shelby was a lot less interested in hearing about a goat-skin sphere that travels 180 m.p.h., than he was in knowing that he could wager on the men, like they were horses or greyhounds.

Abel was directed to a parking place by a kid in a Dodgers baseball cap, and after Abel parked, Shelby gave the boy five dollars, telling him to watch the car.

"We geev the boy too much," Abel said.

"So what? We're gonna be rich," Shelby reminded him.

The Mexican kid then ran toward a Cadillac driven by an elderly American and waved the guy toward a parking space near Abel's car.

Shelby Pate wondered if under that Dodgers cap the kid had ringworm.

Momentarily losing the Chevy in the bumper-to-bumper traffic on Avenida Revolución, Nell wheeled into the *Frontón* parking lot just to turn around. She practically ran over Abel Durazo, who had to jump out of her way!

"Kee-rist!" Fin said, turning his face away while Bobbie ducked down in the back seat.

"He didn't recognize us!" Nell said, speeding toward the rear of the parking lot, ignoring the man who was trying to direct her.

The guy yelled something in Spanish, but after Nell parked, Fin jumped out and handed him ten dollars. The guy nodded and said, "Okay, okay," and allowed the Audi to stay where it was.

The three investigators followed Abel and Shelby at a distance of half a block while the truckers strolled through the weekend throngs. The sun had begun its quick autumn descent, after which the city would come to life in all its vibrance.

Shelby stopped at one of the leather shops at the corner of Calle 5, to check the prices on bomber jackets.

"I make you good deal," the shopkeeper said.

The shopkeeper was about Shelby's age, with a

barrel of a torso. He wore a fake Rolex and fake
diamond rings on both hands, and had the thickest
black hair Shelby had ever seen.

Shelby said to the guy, "I saw one back there in
that other joint for fifty bucks less."

"That ees no good leather. No good," the shopkeeper said. "You like thees one? I sell to you, fifty
dollar off the price. Okay?"

"I'll keep it in mind," Shelby said, but the man
followed him toward the sidewalk.

All the shops were wide open to the masses on
the avenue, and when they were disappearing into the
crowd, the man yelled, "Seventy-five dollar off the
price!"

"Damn!" Shelby said to Abel. "That's a good deal,
ain't it?"

Abel shook his head and said, "After we get money we go to *good* place for jacket. Don' worry, Buey."

"Kin we stop fer a tequila?" Shelby asked, looking
at Abel's wristwatch. "I'm goin shithouse waitin fer
the fuckin little hand to get on the six."

"Okay," Abel said. "We got time."

A man walked out of a saloon that had a glass-
covered collection of photos on the door, pictures of
curvy bikini-clad women dancing on a stage.

"Come!" he said, taking Shelby's arm. "Good
show here, *amigo!*"

Shelby turned to Abel and said, "Whaddaya think,
dude?"

"Okay," Abel said. "But lousy dancer. No good.
Lousy."

There was a large elevated stage in the center
of the barroom, with twenty tables surrounding it.
Booths lined two walls, and the third wall was tak-
en up by a long bar. It was dark, dank, seedy and
wet.

Shelby said, "Gud-damn, the fuckin floor's covered with water jist like that street up there where Soltero's momma lives. Ain't there no plumbers in this fuckin town?"

The floor was so uneven that the puddles only settled on one side of the saloon, so Abel led Shelby through the darkness to the far side where exhausted-looking women in frumpy dresses tried to smile at passing male customers.

One of them looked at Shelby and patted the plastic bench next to her.

Shelby said to Abel, "These babes're *thrashed*. I'd rather get cranked and jack off. That way I can have anyone I want instead a these bowsers, right?"

Abel said, "We go to *good* bar later."

They took a seat at one of the tables next to the stage, where Abel had to shoo away two blowsy women. Shelby was busy looking at the redheaded "dancer" on the stage and didn't pay attention when Abel ordered two double tequilas and two beers.

She wore hip-hugging black shorts, white cowboy boots, and a red tube top. Shelby figured she was forty, but Abel said she was no more than thirty. She was already forming serious cellulite, and up close, Shelby saw a surgical scar across her abdomen. It looked like someone had hand-troweled the pancake makeup onto her face.

Three times during the performance, she lifted the tube and showed Shelby her sagging tits. He stuck a dollar bill inside the waistband of her shorts every time she did it, and went "Wooooo!" ending in a giggling, high-pitched snuffle.

Her number consisted of sliding each foot six inches back and forth out of time to taped soft-rock music that Shelby couldn't identify. After a thirty-minute set she shuffled off the stage and disappeared into a closet-sized dressing room.

Shelby slipped another bindle out of his boot and

dropped his head below the stage level. When he came back up he downed a tequila and sucked the juice from a Mexican yellow lime protruding from his beer bottle.

Then he grinned and said, "My old lady got better hooters, but I bet that dancer's a nicer person. Right now, I'll settle fer anything wet and warm with a pulse."

Abel looked at his watch, drank his tequila, and said, "We go now, Buey."

Fin Finnegan got up from his stool at the opposite end of the long bar, put three dollars next to his glass, and followed the truckers out into the vanishing twilight.

Nell and Bobbie spotted the truckers and quickly turned their backs, examining a sidewalk display of black-velvet paintings: Madonna, Elvis and Batman. Nell picked up Batman and turned it toward the light inside the shop.

Abel and Shelby walked directly behind her, and she heard Shelby Pate say, "Know what, dude? This town ain't *half* as grimy as L.A., and it's gotta be a *lot* safer, right?"

Fin trotted up to Bobbie a few seconds later, saying, "Let's give it no more than an hour. Okay?"

"Then what?" Bobbie asked, as Fin went scurrying after the truckers.

"Then we go home and we bust them Monday morning like responsible *mature* investigators," Nell informed her.

Nell and Bobbie had to trot to keep up with Fin, who was threading his way through the early Saturday evening mob of U.S. teens and young adults who descend on Tijuana to get drunk, slam-dance in nightclubs, fight, bleed, vomit, and in general, have a wonderful time.

23

The thing was, nobody would do a *serious* investigation into the death of a Mexican citizen on Mexican soil, Jules was certain of that. He was *not* going to have to face federal officers, or San Diego police, or even that busybody bitch from the District Attorney's Office. It would just play itself out and pass from his life. A pity that the Mexican kids had been contaminated, but there was nothing he could do about it. Everything would work out just fine.

Sitting in the hot tub, Jules took a sip of Scotch and for a brief instant convinced himself that things simply couldn't go wrong. Except that there were several layers to the rotting onion that Shelby Pate could drop into his soup. In the first place, if Southbay Agricultural Supply was brought into it, Jules was sure that Burl Ralston would panic and confess. For an agreement to testify, the authorities might give immunity to the old bastard. They might even grant immunity to the idiot truckers who caused this whole misery. That, in order to convict a real environmental threat: the *owner* of Green Earth Hauling and Disposal. Jules could become a sacrificial lamb to the green administration of Clinton-Gore: a prosperous and greedy waste hauler who illegally manifested hazardous waste that ended up killing a child of the Third World. Good press for the new administration.

Jules thought about offering Shelby Pate $10,000, more than that imbecile had ever seen in his miserable lowlife existence. Jules might even raise it to $20,000 if he could be guaranteed that both Durazo and Pate would maintain their silence. But what if they turned over the manifest to Jules only to blab to the authorities at a later time? Burl Ralston would then be contacted and he'd spill his guts the first time a cop mentioned jail. If Burl Ralston had a fatal heart attack it would be very helpful to Jules's predicament. If Shelby Pate and Abel Durazo died suddenly it would be a time to *rejoice*.

If Jules paid extortion money, what would be his assurance that six months down the line he wouldn't get a visit from Pate and Durazo showing him a photocopy of the manifest? A little something they'd set aside for a rainy day. The fact was, Jules's only real safety lay in the destruction of the manifest, Pate, and probably Durazo, in that order. There was no other way. How could he come this far, with his entire life about to be transformed, only to let it all be controlled and ultimately doomed by two morons?

Even though he had no experience whatsoever with acts of violence, Jules Temple felt certain that he could do what he had to do. They had forced this course of action. There was only one question left in his mind: *How?*

Abel and Shelby were working on their second drink, but still Soltero hadn't arrived. The Bongo Room was a cut above the last bar they'd visited. At least this one had some bamboo paneling nailed to the walls, and some blinking colored lanterns hanging from the ceiling. There was a similar stage and a similar long bar, and all too similar women sitting in booths and tables, not looking hungrily at gringos with bucks, only looking shabby and *tired.*

So much so that Shelby turned to Abel and said, "I think they feed downers to the babes around here. Or maybe they're all shootin that Mexican tar heroin. Now that's bad stuff. Me, I never even shot meth. I'm scared a needles."

With that he leaned over and snorted what was left of a bindle of methamphetamine.

"Hey, Buey!" Abel said. "We got work to do!"

"I kin handle it, dude," Shelby said. "Anyways, I think there's somethin wrong with this cringe. I ain't feelin a rush."

But Abel knew that was a lie. The ox was twitchy. He kept looking around, twisting up his cocktail napkin, blinking, sniffling.

"Hey, baby!" Shelby yelled to the waitress. "Bring us two more mega shooters!"

After the tequilas arrived, a man slid into the seat beside Abel and said, "I am buying your tequilas, please."

"What're you, a fag?" Shelby wanted to know.

The man smiled and spoke to Abel in Spanish. Shelby recognized one word that was uttered several times by both men: *Soltero.* Abel looked like he was getting mad, but the man raised both palms as if to say, "It's not my fault." Then he got up and left the saloon.

"What the fuck's goin on?" Shelby demanded.

Abel said, "He say we see Soltero een one more hours at club by *pasaje* on other side of Revolución. He say we see Soltero there."

"Hope it's better than this joint. One hour?"

"Ees okay. There good theengs to buy down below avenue. Many many shops down there. We go now and look at leather jacket. We *stop* dreenking tequila."

Shelby said, "Know somethin, dude, when we git our money tonight, I might jist reach over and snatch that Soltero's ponytail right off his skinny little head, that's what I might do."

Abel watched in dismay as the ox gulped the last tequila and reached inside his boot for his stash of meth. Abel Durazo was getting a very bad feeling and wanted to get outside *pronto*.

This time Nell and Bobbie were ready for them when they came out of the bar. Abel walked, Shelby weaved.

"He's amped," Nell said to Bobbie.

She and Bobbie were standing next to a donkey cart. The sad-eyed animal was painted black-and-white like a zebra, and gringo tourists wearing huge sombreros posed for photos while seated in the donkey cart.

"Where's Fin?" Bobbie wondered aloud.

Bobbie looked worried, and that made Nell ask, "Do you two have something going or what?"

"Whaddaya mean?"

"Whaddaya *think* I mean?" Then Nell added, "Of course it's none of my business except I hate to see a girl like you get all messed up with a guy like Fin."

"A guy like Fin?" Bobbie said, just as he came outside, looking the wrong way.

Then Fin spotted Shelby reeling across Revolución, barely dodging traffic. Fin followed after them with Nell and Bobbie bringing up the rear.

Now that it was early evening young Americans were milling everywhere, stopping only long enough to buy more beer cans to toss from car windows. A dozen drunken kids were hanging from the patio of a restaurant directly over their heads, yelling, "Cool it, Pancho!" to a harried traffic cop on the corner.

"Let's move outta the way," Bobbie said, "before one a those dweebs hunks a bellyful on our heads."

"Keep an eye on Pate and Durazo," Fin said. "Something's going down. A guy came in and talked to them."

"Probably a pimp," Nell said.

"I don't think so," Fin said. "The conversation was very . . ."

"Intense?" Bobbie asked.

"Right," Fin said. "It was very intense."

"They're just shopping, for chrissake," Nell said. *"Intense."*

Since they now had more time to kill, Abel wanted to keep the ox out of bars. He'd never seen his partner so wild-looking, not even on the night when he'd kicked the biker senseless.

"We got lotsa time," Shelby said. "Let's go git our knobs jobbed!"

"We walk, Buey!" Abel said. "Joo are drunk already."

"Me, drunk? Are you mental? I kin drink two quarts a that cheap tequila and not even feel it!"

"Too much speed," Abel said.

"Naw, this ain't even good cringe," Shelby said. "I'm jist mellow."

Abel said, "Le's go see jacket, Buey. We go down to *pasaje*. Good down there."

Shelby was getting twitchier. He was wrinkling his nose like a hungry rabbit. He jerked his head this way and that every time he spotted something that gleamed, sparkled, or shone. He was blinking and snapping his fingers. And he'd started sweating.

Shelby's anxiety level climbed in relation to their

descent down the steep concrete stairway into the narrow passageways below the avenue. Shops were jammed cheek by jowl in a rabbit warren of arcades. There they sold *ponchos* and *sarapes* and papier-mâché birds as big as a human being, and velvet paintings, jewelry, souvenirs, curios and leather goods galore. Shelby stopped for a moment and played with a dangling Bart Simpson puppet. Everywhere he looked there were Bart Simpson dolls and figurines. He was getting light-headed and staggered more.

An old Indian woman with a face like a walnut, all bundled inside a *sarape* with violent stripes, startled Shelby by clicking castanets in his face. She laughed at him toothlessly, and a small boy next to her shook some hissing red maracas at him, hissing like rattlesnakes. "Good price, meester," the boy said, and Shelby feverishly wondered if the kid had ringworm.

"All the peoples own their shops." Abel tried to talk to him, but the ox was getting dizzy and wasn't listening.

He wanted to stop for some cringe, but Abel made him walk. Shelby was afraid to get left behind, and he started feeling a sliver of panic behind his ear somewhere. It was like a shivery cold blade, and he was breathing faster in huge gulps.

Everywhere there were *piñatas*, and puppets and cardboard dancing figures in the shapes of skeletons and witches and goblins.

"Guess they celebrate Halloween here, huh?" Shelby said, leaning against a block wall to steady himself, his Grateful Dead T-shirt damp and sticky.

Abel saw that the ox's face was flushed and his pupils were dilated. "Tomorrow ees *El Día de los Muertos*," he said. "Day of the Dead. For two days the dead peoples they come home."

"Whaddaya mean come home?" The ox just couldn't stop blinking and twitching. He didn't *like* this voodoo shit. And he couldn't get enough air down there.

"We tell them welcome home. We burn candle at the cemetery and we put many flower on the path to their house. We feex altar for them. Berry eemportant day."

"I don't wanna see no dead relatives," Shelby said, looking around at a life-sized witch hanging at eye level. He had an urge to kick that bitch clear off her broom!

"Eet ees no' so sad eef there ees a day when the dead ones can return. My *mamá*, she see my *papá* every year. Eet ees true. The dogs bark always on the Day of the Dead. The dogs, they know."

"What the fuck do they do when they come back?"

"We put out the bread for them. Sweet bread and chocolate and salt. They eat and they watch over their family. Then they go back to the graveyard. The leetle dead childrens they play weeth the toys we leave for them. We make the bread eento leetle animals for the dead childrens. My mother, she always puts out the *mole*. My father use to love *mole*. And some beers for my dead brother. He use to like beer. We have lots of beers and tequila in the cemetery on *El Día de los Muertos*."

"I seen them cemeteries on TV," the ox said. "They ain't like ours with our little flat stones. You got humongous stones with pictures of the people on them and fences around these sorta walk-in graves. It looks like Munchkinland. Bunch a creepy little houses for dead people."

"Ees berry beautiful our cemetery," Abel said. "Many colors and pretty stones."

The ox said, "You people're Catholics, ain'tcha? I thought Catholics ain't allowed to believe in that pagan zombie shit."

Abel said, "We *Católico* but we use to have Indian gods long time ago. They was berry strong gods, *'mano.*"

They started strolling again. Colors and exotic shapes swirled around Shelby Pate. The colors of Mexico were too vibrant, the lights too hot. He stumbled into a Ninja Turtle *piñata* made of cardboard. His body temperature had gone vertical and he was nearing meltdown.

Abel said to him, "Joo don' do no more speed, Buey! I *tell* you!"

They found themselves in a passageway where there were less exotic shops selling Guess? and Ralph Lauren, and Fila. Shelby calmed down a bit, and stopped at a display window full of soft Mexican gold jewelry.

"Hey, dude!" he yelled to Abel. "I gotta buy somethin fer my bitch!"

But Abel had walked ahead and had turned the corner past a very narrow passageway where shopkeepers had installed overhead flashing colored lights, like in the Bongo Room.

Shelby lost sight of Abel for a moment and staggered into the wrong passageway. The smell of new leather overwhelmed him, conjuring images of dead animal carcasses. The winking colored lights bedazzled him. The passageway got too narrow! The colors of Mexico kept blazing away at him! Skeletons and witches dervished all around!

There was another Indian woman squatting in the passageway. Her bare feet looked like they'd never been washed. A little boy with her was even grimier. On a spread-out blanket was a handful of chewing gum, and the little boy said to Shelby: *"Chicle? Chicle?"*

Shelby Pate bellowed, "Noooooo!" and started running away from the boy into *another* passageway.

And he still couldn't find Abel. And the colors—the swirling vibrant Mexican colors—were enveloping him!

Then he whirled and saw a man moving toward him in that demon cloister. The man was his age, perhaps older. The man was three feet tall. He did not walk on legs, but on stumps that ended six inches below his buttocks. The stumps were padded with leather for "walking." The most grotesque part was that protruding from between his stumps in front was a tiny deformed bare foot. At first, Shelby thought it was a Halloween prank. A fake foot sticking out between the little man's stumps. But when the man plodded past him he saw *another* foot protruding from between his stumps in the back. Two deformed bare feet which would never support a human being—growing out of what should have been his thighs!

"How'd you get like that?" Shelby cried out to the little man. "Did they dump poison in your momma's water supply?"

Of course the man didn't understand Shelby, and may not even have heard. He just plodded on. Shelby followed him. He watched the little man laboriously climb every step, one stump at a time, toward the avenue above.

"WAS YOUR MOMMA POISONED OR WHAT?" Shelby bellowed.

He was reeling now, and he pawed at the concrete wall of the passageway for support. His hand pressed not concrete but a molded plastic face: a death's-head. Lining the wall for a distance of twenty feet were the faces of death, like the skulls painted on the drums of poison.

He was hollering for Abel when the young Mexican appeared and grabbed him by the arm, saying, "Why you yell, Buey? Wha' happen, *'mano*?"

"Oh, man!" Shelby blubbered. "Where you been?

I got lost! It's weird down here! Get me back up to the world!"

"I tol' joo, Buey. Speed mess up the brains!" Abel said.

Fin, Nell, and Bobbie had split up, with Bobbie trailing behind Shelby Pate. She'd witnessed his extra-ordinary behavior: flailing at *piñatas*, running in terror from a boy selling chewing gum, yelling gibberish at a pathetic legless man. He was hopelessly drunk or wired on drugs, or both.

When Shelby and Abel wandered along the last passageway, Fin joined her and he said, "Don't follow there. Wait'll they climb the steps."

"Was that Pate doing the yelling?" Nell asked when she joined them.

"Yeah," Bobbie said. "I got a feeling he isn't doing much for U.S.-Mexican relations."

"You shoulda seen him at the Bongo Room," Fin said. "He enters a joint like a Molotov cocktail."

Nell asked Fin something that she was curious about. "What goes *on* in those nightclubs?"

Fin said, "The animal rights people who never appreciated what women used to do for the welfare of Great Danes and burros apparently have had their way. Their stage shows're about as racy as a high school assembly."

Shelby Pate was drenched and popeyed by the time Abel led him up the concrete stairway.

"I feel like there ain't no more world up there!" Shelby said as he climbed, looking at a patch of sky as gray as ashes.

"The world ees there," Abel said, "but joo won' be een the world berry long eef joo don' stop the speed."

When they were halfway up the steps, Shelby started taking in massive gulps of air. Suddenly, he grabbed Abel by the front of the shirt and said, "You gotta tell me, dude, about them dead kids! If you put out toys 'n cake 'n stuff, how do ya know the kid's gonna find the right house?"

"The dead peoples, they know, *'mano,*" Abel assured him. "Ees hard for them to remember the way but they weel find eet. They find their way home."

Shelby held on to his partner and said, "Will that kid come home tomorra? Will he get to see his momma again? That kid with the ringworm?"

Abel cried, "Goddamn, Buey! I get seek and tire' of goddamn reeng-worms! I don' wan' to hear no more goddamn reeng-worms!"

"But *will* he come home, Flaco?" Shelby demanded, with inflamed horrified eyes.

24

The traffic on Revolución was nearly bumper-locked. Young Americans hanging out of car windows were whistling, clapping, yelling, thumping on car doors, flipping the bird at pedestrians, cutting off cars, mooning any female older than twelve, and spewing the contents of their stomachs onto the streets of a country they considered third rate and Third World.

In short, it was a scene that might be replayed in just about any U.S. city if the police were underpaid, underfunded, undermanned, undermined, and as desperately corrupt as the police of Tijuana.

At the corner of Calle 5, two U.S. servicemen in civilian clothes with telltale whitewall haircuts were involved in a punch-out with three students wearing UCLA sweatshirts. Fin stopped to watch for a few seconds, then turned to Nell and Bobbie and said, "That's a mismatch. UCLA students're for Clinton, and everyone knows that white Democrats can't fight."

"Who're you voting for?" Bobbie wanted to know.

"Perot, of course," Fin said. "He's not a professional politician."

"Neither was that other nut, Rasputin," Nell said, "but he still managed to wreck his government."

"Perot's not a bad choice," Bobbie said. "He was a navy man."

"Puh-leeze!" said Nell, but then she spotted trouble, and said, "Uh-oh. One of our boys needs to call nine-one-one. Or *nueve-once*, as they might say down here."

Shelby Pate had just become one of the hundred or so Americans who would throw up on the streets of Tijuana that evening.

"Gross!" Bobbie said. "He's hunkin all over the sidewalk!"

"Let that be a lesson," Fin said. "Stick to high-grade tequila. And none of that stuff with a worm in it, even if you're sure the worm's dead."

Nell said, "Wonder if he's puking up live animal parts, or what?"

After Shelby got finished vomiting, he and Abel continued to weave their way along Revolución, pausing only for Shelby to terrorize a bunch of college kids. They were blocking the sidewalk and encouraging a frat brother to do a semi-striptease for the benefit of a coed hanging out the window of a restaurant overhead. The stripteaser danced to heavy-metal sounds coming from a boom box that could knock the fillings right out of your mouth.

Bobbie said, "They're all trying not to notice Pate."

Fin said, "Only reason anyone *ever* risks eye contact with a guy like that is so they can describe him later to a police artist."

Nell said, "I hope little Juliet dumps her chamber pot on Romeo while he's boogeying."

The investigators watched as Shelby Pate staggered up to the striptease kid, grabbed him by the neck, and sailed him like a Frisbee into the traffic lane, where another carload of college types had to brake to keep from running him down.

While Abel pleaded with Shelby to move on, the

ox planted his size 13 EEE's and glared at all the other students. They took a gander at this blazing destroyer in his nightmare costume of biker black, and suddenly started to get extremely interested in shop items, such as silver buckles, Mexican blankets, and velvet paintings of Michael Jackson's gloved hand.

Nell said, "Before the night's over I bet he just about wrecks any chance of ever getting elected to public office."

Bobbie said, "Wonder what's it like for Durazo, being on the town with that nonevolved mammal?"

"About like being circumcised with draft beer as an anesthetic," Fin said. "He's doing his best to get killed."

"Not quite his best yet," Nell said. "But he'll flat-line before he's much older."

Bobbie said, "Dudes like him'll violate *any* law, including gravity. A walking reign of terror."

Fin said, "I bet he's never changed those jeans. Just puts on a different rocker T-shirt and away he goes."

"He'd be easy to buy for," Nell said.

The truckers stood looking in the window of a pharmacy where a line of worried, hopeful, or frightened Americans were buying Retin-A, minoxidil, and AZT over the counter. Then they moseyed around the corner and vanished.

The three investigators ran to the next corner but Abel and Shelby were nowhere in sight.

Nell crossed the street and discovered a narrow passageway. Ten feet inside the dark passageway was an arch lit by a pencil of neon. It said, SOMBRAS.

"Find something?" Fin called out.

Nell yelled, "This must be a nightclub or restaurant. Let's try it."

"Are you two packing?" Bobbie asked, when they stood at the mouth of the passage.

"No way," Nell said.

"Not on your life," Fin said. "If we got caught down here carrying concealed weapons, they'd just say: Badge? I don't want to see no steenking badge! And we'd end up in the Tijuana jail. They don't want *any* foreigners being armed."

"I'm packing," Bobbie said, looping the purse strap over her shoulder. "And I'm *glad*."

She led the way down the corridor between two windowless concrete walls of neighboring buildings. They walked perhaps thirty feet before they heard music. The closer they got, the louder it got. Not the heavy metal blaring on Revolución, this was Mexican folk music.

Then they found themselves in a small open patio with a fountain in the center and a pepper tree in a tile planter off to one side. Double wooden doors with huge iron pulls separated them from the festive music inside.

Fin opened the door and Nell took a peek. A white-haired proprietor in a dark blue suit and a pale blue necktie said, "Welcome to Sombras. How many een your party?"

Nell turned to Fin, who said, "If they're not here, we've lost them anyway. Might as well go on in."

Nell said to the proprietor, "Did a large man in a black leather jacket just come in with a small Mexican gentleman?"

"Yes," the proprietor said. "They are een the back at Señor Soltero's table. Shall I take you there?"

"No, he's just a person I used to know," Nell said. "We'd prefer a table in the front."

"Very well," the proprietor said. "Follow me, please."

The restaurant seated about eighty people. There was a second fountain inside, constructed of multicolored Mexican tiles. All the tables were solid walnut, as were the chairs, high-backed with tasseled yellow seat cushions. The tables were covered with yellow tablecloths except for those where patrons were just having cocktails. Each table was lit by a huge candle inside an onion-shaped, emerald-colored glass bowl. Three guitar players strolled among the tables singing old favorites.

But the restaurant was not a quiet place to dine in that the bare floor was made of twelve-inch squares of tile with a patina and color of old saddle leather. The wiring inside the low ceiling was concealed by thin reeds lashed together, and lanterns dangled throughout, low enough to make tall men duck their heads.

The patrons, both Mexican and American, were not ordinary tourists, and all were very presentable, with the exception of Shelby Pate, who may as well have been wearing light bulbs.

The investigators spotted the truckers with three other men in a tiny alcove toward the rear of the room.

"We're okay here in front," Bobbie said. "It's too dark for them to make us."

Fin excused himself after saying to Nell, "Order me whatever you're having, and a Mexican beer."

After he had gone to the rest room, Nell ordered three of the house special plates, consisting of a chile relleno, a tamale and a chicken taco.

The waitress was a stunning girl, perhaps eighteen years old, wearing an off-the-shoulder, lace-topped cotton blouse and a red full skirt. Her red shoes were fastened with ankle straps, suggesting that she probably doubled as a dancer.

"That order's safe enough for everyone," Nell said.

"Don't worry about me," Bobbie said. "I haven't had much Mexican food, but what I've had I really like. I'm experimental in everything."

"You *must* be," Nell said.

"Whaddaya mean by that?"

"Fin," Nell said.

"Look, this is only the second time I've been with him!" Bobbie said.

"Me too," said Nell.

"Really? I don't believe it."

"Now whadda *you* mean by that?"

"It's easy to see you got feelings for him, big-time."

"What?"

"One woman to another," Bobbie said. "It's easy to see."

"Me? Fin?"

"I don't blame you," Bobbie said. "He's cute, and he's *so* nice. A real gentleman, in a way. I can see how you might feel. But honest, we're just friends, is all."

Nell wanted to deny it, but the words wouldn't come out. This child was in-furiating! Calmly, she said, "Bobbie, I don't know what to say about that except that I would rather spend my life arranging flowers and pouring tea in a geisha house than be hooked up with that neurotic cop!"

"I know," Bobbie said, sympathetically, "but we can't really follow our heads, can we? Not when our hearts're pulling us in another direction. Toing-and-froing, right? I know how it is, Nell."

Nell didn't get a chance to respond in that Fin returned to the table just as the waitress brought the beer and margaritas. They were hand-shaken margaritas, not gringo slush.

"*Salud*, as they say in these parts," Fin said, raising his beer bottle to each woman, with a lingering look at Bobbie.

The strolling guitar players came closer to their table, singing "Guadalajara." When Bobbie turned to look at the musicians, Nell whispered to Fin, "Did you tell her about your very low sperm count?"

"Nell!" Fin said, shooting a quick glance at Bobbie, but she wasn't paying attention to them.

"And that you give blood regularly?"

"Nell, what's wrong with you?" Fin whispered. "She's a sweet kid!"

"They *all* are," Nell said. "Sweet. When they're *kids*."

Fin whispered, "Do you have some sort of . . . *problem* with her?"

Nell smiled, but only with her mouth, and said, "Not at all. It's very predictable."

"What is?"

"Life is," she said.

"My whole life's been a failed effort to please women!" Fin blurted to a strolling guitar player, who didn't understand a word. "Is this a smoke-free zone or can I just set fire to myself?"

They'd already had two drinks, yet nothing had been said about the money they were owed. Before they'd entered, Abel had tried to warn the ox not to be pushy by telling him that Mexicans were patient, and that Soltero had chosen an elegant restaurant, so he might be playing the gentleman. And that Soltero would talk about money only when he was good and ready.

But after his second double tequila, Shelby wanted action. He only had one more bindle of meth and was needing it. He slipped it out of his boot and put it in the pocket of his Grateful Dead T-shirt, then watched the guitar players and twitched.

One of Soltero's companions was the man who'd approached them in the Bongo Room. The other was short but very burly, with a mustache so long he could've used it for a chin strap. He had a deep scar on the side of his neck, and a piece of his left earlobe was missing. From time to time, Shelby glared at this scarred mustachioed Mexican, but the man kept his eyes on Soltero or on his drink.

Soltero wore a double-breasted suit of gray silk and a charcoal shirt buttoned at the throat, with no necktie. In fact, Abel thought he dressed a lot like their boss, Jules Temple, but he was several years older. Soltero's ponytail was pulled back more severely than Shelby's, and was gray-flecked.

Soltero asked dozens of questions, both in Spanish and English, about the business climate in San Diego, and the politics of the presidential election, and if Abel would be interested in hauling other loads from San Diego to Tijuana and sometimes in the other direction. His English was only slightly accented, and his hands gestured gracefully.

Just when Shelby thought Soltero was going to talk about money, he said, "And now it is time to eat."

He had preordered two kilos of carnitas—marinated pork roasted on a spit. The waiter brought another large plate that held homemade flour tortillas wrapped inside a red tasseled napkin, a bowl heaped with cilantro and onion, and yet another brimming with guacamole. Finally, a bowl of homemade salsa arrived.

"I believe our American guest will not be disappointed," Soltero said, smiling at Shelby. "The salsa is made special for me."

The food looked, smelled, and tasted delicious. Abel bolted it down, but when Shelby was on a methamphetamine rampage like this, he didn't want to wreck his edge. Shelby picked at his food, but drank two more tequilas. Then he got up and lurched toward the rest room to snort the last of his meth.

Fin said to the women, "Oh oh, Pate's heading for the john. The men's room's about as wide as a Cuban cigar, and he's listing to starboard. It'll be like docking the U.S.S. *Ranger* in a car wash. Listen for a collision."

Bobbie said, "My twenty-fifteen eyesight tells me that if that guy with the slick suit and the pony-tail doesn't like you, instant emigration is in order. What're we gonna do if they all leave together?"

Nell looked at Fin and said, "You're of the hunter-gatherer gender. Whadda we do?"

"I think we try to get their license number and call the Mexican state judicial police on Monday. That's all."

"For what?" Nell asked.

"To ask if they'll search his house for shoes," Fin said.

"Fat chance," said Nell. "He probably has a broth-er or a nephew or a cousin *running* the state police. Or else he owns a few of them."

"No matter what happens, I've really enjoyed this day," Bobbie said. "It's the most fun I've ever had as a detective." When she said it she put her hand on Fin's forearm, as was her habit by now.

"I've had a great time too," Fin said softly. "You're as good a partner as I've ever had. You're a smart little detective."

Nell mumbled, "Me, I'm so dumb I better run home and memorize the encyclopedia. Well, maybe just A through G tonight."

When Nell turned toward the singers, Bobbie whispered to Fin, "She has an *attitude*."

Fin whispered back, "It's her *age*. They're all about as easy to understand as black holes in the galaxy, light-years away."

When Shelby got back from the rest room, he was barely able to sit in his chair. He'd done the last of the meth and was turbocharged and getting paranoid. He kept looking from one to the other. The little Mexican glanced at him with amused detachment. The burly one with the Zapata mustache continued to watch Soltero as though Abel and Shelby weren't even there. He'd nursed a beer for an hour, but had eaten more than his share of carnitas.

Abel peeked at his watch more than once, but Soltero was in no hurry at all. The tequila and salsa heated them up and Soltero unbuttoned the first two buttons of his shirt.

Shelby's body temperature had shot up like a Patriot missile, but he didn't seem to notice the flow of sweat. He was too busy fiddling with the fork, folding and unfolding the napkin, looking from one man to the other, checking inside his boot for meth that wasn't there anymore. If there'd been a television in the place, he'd have taken it apart and put it back together by now.

When the coffee was served, Shelby ordered what would be his final tequila of the evening. Abel had given up counting, but was certain that the ox's tequila intake could only be measured by the liter. Moreover, Shelby was blinking so hard you could almost hear it. That was when the mariachis appeared.

There were seven of them in black waistcoats, black trousers, red string ties: two trumpets, two violins, two guitars and one bass guitar. They did not play the traditional mariachi tunes that American tourists loved. Instead, they began by playing an old Mexican piece.

The music had a haunting quality; Fin thought so at once. So did Bobbie. They put down their coffee cups and listened. The restaurant din quieted and the crowd became subdued.

Bobbie said, "There's a sadness about that."

Nell said, "I've heard it before. It's about death, I think. No, wait. It's about a lost soul."

Soltero smiled at Shelby Pate, who had suddenly become enraptured by the music. All the mariachis were facing the far side of the room where there was a dark alcove near the kitchen. They played and seemed to be looking for something in the darkness. And then from that black alcove came the answering sound of a muted trumpet. And a small boy, attired in the same costume as the men, stepped into a little blue spotlight.

The proprietor came to the table when Nell signaled, and he said, "Yes, señora, you have a question?"

"What's the name of this piece?" she asked. "I can't remember."

"Ah!" he said. "Ees beautiful, no? Ees called 'Niño Perdido.' "

Soltero leaned over the table when Shelby Pate asked, "Why's that kid all alone over there in the dark?"

Soltero whispered, "The music is called 'The Lost Child.' You see, the boy is trying to answer the other trumpet voice that calls for him."

As the music played, the little trumpeter moved slowly through the darkness, toward the other trumpet's call, followed by the blue spotlight. The Lost Child *wanted* to be found, but could not find his way. The muted sound of his trumpet would sometimes grow faint as he moved in the wrong direction, away from the searchers.

Suddenly, Shelby Pate shouted, "Gud-damnit! Why don't somebody jist go *git* him? He wants to come home! He wants his momma!"

Heads jerked toward Shelby Pate. Diners were stunned. Even the burly man with the Zapata mustache turned to gape.

Abel said, "Eet ees only music, Buey!"

But Shelby Pate stood up and knocked the heavy walnut chair crashing to the tile floor. Everyone in the restaurant turned toward him. Some diners stood to see what was happening, but it was so dark now they could only see a towering shadow figure inside the alcove.

"He's movin away!" Shelby cried. "They gotta *git* him! They gotta show him the way home to his momma!"

The proprietor ran toward the disturbance, but the mariachis kept playing. The lead trumpet kept calling for The Lost Child, but The Lost Child was wandering, and his trumpet grew more muted.

The proprietor stepped into the alcove and said, "Señor Soltero! *Por favor!*" Then he put his hand on Shelby's arm and said, "Please, sir, you are frightening everyone!"

But Shelby looked at him with eyes full of terror and grief, and said, "He came home for the Day of the Dead! Don't you git it?"

The burly man with the Zapata mustache got a nod from Soltero, and for the first time that evening he spoke in English.

He said to Shelby, "Joo dreenk too much, *amigo!* Le's go out to the fresh air!"

Shelby shoved him so hard he took the platter of carnitas with him crashing onto the floor.

Then Abel leaped up, yelling, "Buey! Buey! Ees okay! Outside! We go outside!"

By now most of the diners were on their feet.

People were whispering, gesturing. Several men came forward.

The mariachis, including the boy, had stopped playing. The lights remained dim, but Abel Durazo, with his arm crooked through the arm of Shelby Pate, led the ox toward the door.

"We can't follow yet," Fin said. "Give them a few minutes."

He and Nell kept putting money on the table to pay for the food and drinks until Nell said, "That's enough."

"Lemme go alone!" Bobbie said. "He's so tanked he won't recognize me."

"Watch yourself!" Fin said. "Durazo isn't drunk. He might make you."

Bobbie nodded, and put her purse strap over her shoulder on the way out.

"Should I have let her go alone?" he asked Nell. "Can she handle it?"

"Of course not," Nell said. "Women don't have testicles, we have ovaries. We keep forgetting that."

After the disturbance was over, the diners went back to eating, and the mariachis stopped searching for The Lost Child. The musical interlude had ended for the time being.

Abel Durazo led Shelby Pate back through the passageway toward the busy street, with Shelby bouncing from one wall to the other as he tried to negotiate the narrow corridor. Soltero and his companions stood in the small patio for a moment, whispering in Spanish, paying no attention to Bobbie when she walked past them on her way out of Sombras.

When she emerged onto the street the traffic from pedestrians and cars had totally clogged Revolución.

Most of the deafening noise came from young Americans screaming at the top of their lungs. Not at anything in particular, just screaming. Bobbie saw Shelby Pate leaning against a wall, rubbing his face as though he couldn't feel it. Abel Durazo stood in front of him gesturing wildly and yelling things she couldn't make out.

Bobbie walked directly behind Abel and when she was nearly at the corner, she ducked into a doorway to observe them unseen. She was startled by a whimper and looked down at a bony, mangy, flea-bitten mongrel dog, chewing on a sandwich wrapper and looking at her fearfully.

The three Mexicans emerged from the passageway and joined Abel Durazo and Shelby Pate. Then all five men crossed the street and got into a Ford Explorer. By the time Bobbie could cross, the car was already into the traffic and gone. She was sure that it had California license plates.

Abel and Shelby sat in the back seat with the mustachioed Mexican. Soltero sat in the passenger seat, and the small one drove. Abel was crushed between the burly Mexican and the ox. He couldn't move either arm until he managed to squeeze his body forward. They drove for ten minutes without talking.

Shelby was very still now, and Soltero said soothingly to him, "The drugs and the tequila do not go well together."

Abel wasn't sure that the ox even understood what was happening, and he said in English to Soltero, "I theenk my *compañero* would feel better eef we get our money now and go home to San Diego. Yes, I theenk that would be the bes' theeng."

"Of course," Soltero said. "But I had to get you away from Sombras. The proprietor was going to call the police."

"Yes," Abel said. "But now eef joo can drive us to my car and geev us our money, please?"

"Of course," Soltero said.

But the little Mexican kept driving away from downtown and oncoming headlights were becoming infrequent.

Abel said, "Señor Soltero. We wan' our money now!"

"Stop," Soltero said to the driver, who pulled to the side of the road.

Shelby looked around. They weren't in the city center anymore. It was quiet out here. There were some houses nearby that looked as though they might be lit by kerosene lamps rather than electricity.

Soltero said, "I want us to do business in the future, but I do not want you to create any further disturbance tonight. That is why I have brought you out here. In case your friend makes a disturbance there will not be a problem."

For the first time in twenty minutes, Shelby Pate spoke. He said, "Why the fuck would I make a disturbance? You intend to pay us our money, right?"

"Certainly," Soltero said. "But there is a problem."

Shelby looked at Abel and said, "What *kinda* problem?"

Soltero withdrew an envelope from the pocket of his jacket. He handed it to Abel Durazo, and said, "There are eighty fifty-dollar notes. I hope you are pleased."

Shelby said, "*Four* grand? You owe us *six* grand!"

Abel could smell the ox. His body odor was powerful, and when Abel's hand brushed against Shelby's, the ox's hand was clammy.

Abel was terrified. He said, "Ees okay, Buey!"

"No!" Shelby said. "Fuck, *no*! We got *six* grand comin!"

"I thought I could sell them to my contact for several dollars a pair, but I could not," Soltero said, reasonably.

Shelby said, "And you got no profit for yourself, right?"

"Not very much," Soltero said. "I spent most of my profit on your food tonight."

"Okay," Abel said. "Okay. Ees okay, Buey!"

"Sure," Shelby said, very quietly. "Sometimes things don't work out."

Abel had heard that tone once before, when the ox had smashed the bottle of beer across the eyes of the bearded biker. Abel was petrified.

Then Soltero yelped! Shelby had grabbed his ponytail with his left hand and jammed the derringer against the bone behind Soltero's right ear, saying, "Tell your pals to get outta the car or I'll put one right between your runnin lights!"

The driver reached under his jacket, but Soltero yelled, "No!"

Then Soltero said something in Spanish that Shelby didn't understand, and his friends opened the doors and got out slowly.

"Buey! Don' do eet, Buey!" Abel pleaded. He was afraid to even touch the ox for fear he might pull the trigger.

"Get out, dude!" Shelby said to Abel. "You're drivin!"

"Where?" Abel cried.

"Back to our car," Shelby said. Then he released Soltero's hair, but reached inside Soltero's coat pocket, removing his wallet. Then he said, "Take that fuckin watch off!"

Soltero removed his gold wristwatch and handed it to Shelby Pate, who put it in the pocket of his leather jacket. Shelby said, "We're gonna take Señor Soltero with us and make sure he ain't got some hideout money. Then we're goin home. If this's a *real* Rolex maybe it'll make up for what he owes us."

"Crazy!" Abel whispered. *"Crazy!"*

But now there was nothing Abel Durazo could do except go along. He stepped out and started to open the front door. Soltero's men stood in the headlight beam, whispering.

Then the small one moved out of the light and came toward Abel, saying in Spanish, "The keys. I have the car keys."

Shelby said to Soltero, "Jist relax and this'll be over before ya . . ."

"Aaaaaaahhhhhh!"

A loud sigh. It sounded to Shelby like Flaco was taking a badly needed piss. Then Abel looked in at him through the side window of the car.

His eyes were white in the moonlight. "Buey!" he cried. "Buey!" Abel's right hand came up to the window and smeared it with blood.

Soltero hit the door handle and fell out onto the roadside. Shelby heaved himself out just before three explosions shattered the bloody glass!

Abel staggered around the car toward Shelby, clutching the steel that protruded from his belly. Then his hands relaxed and he toppled onto the road.

Shelby bellowed and stood over Soltero, who held his palms up to ward off the bullet. Soltero was silent when Shelby kept his promise and fired the derringer point-blank, right between his running lights.

Then an orange fireball exploded at Shelby from the other side of the car. . . . The explosion revived him. . . . The fireball seemed to blow him down. . . . He lost the derringer. . . . He got up and ran!

The two Mexicans screamed to each other in Spanish and Shelby heard footsteps padding after him. He kept going, running up the hillside, plunging into the mesquite, plowing through it! In a few minutes the Mexicans' voices grew fainter.

There were two rows of houses on the hillside, and an open field off to the right. There were no streetlights on that hardpan road, not one. Shelby started for that open area but stopped in horror!

Through the darkness, strange shapes loomed up from the earth. . . . Crypts and gravestones . . . Figures moving among them . . . Flickering candles floating as though through the air . . . It *was* a graveyard! Shelby screamed and ran the other way.

He doubled back again and scrambled up a desolate hill, away from houses and cars, away from tombstones and flickering candles. Shelby ran into the blackness of the night, which was not nearly as terrifying as those flickering floating candles.

When Fin and Nell had left the restaurant they'd found Bobbie waiting at the mouth of the passageway. She'd described the Ford Explorer and told them she didn't get the license number, but was sure it was a California plate. Then, with nothing further they could do, the three investigators had headed for Nell's car in the parking lot of the *Frontón*.

The traffic leaving Tijuana was unusually busy for early evening. The vendors were out in force, and they walked between the traffic lanes hoping to interest the tourists in pottery, leather belts, blankets and plaster figurines.

An old woman in a shawl shuffled among the throng of vendors. She had nothing to sell. She was bony and stooped and so badly wrinkled it would be difficult to say she *was* a woman were it not for her shawl and long dress. On her feet she wore the remnants of a man's shoes.

Bobbie thought of the mangy starving dog in the doorway, of how the dog had whimpered in fear. She reached into her purse and handed the old woman a twenty-dollar bill.

Shelby Pate was hopelessly lost and there was no one to light his way. No one to call him with a golden trumpet. No mother to await him on the Day of the Dead. He was exhausted, panicked, battling wave after wave of hysteria. He'd sometimes hallucinated when he'd snorted this much methamphetamine, and he thought he might be hallucinating now. He wasn't sure that any of this was real.

He was lying on a dusty hilltop in the darkness and could hear dogs barking, and children shouting in the distance. Out in front of him he saw a road traversing a lonely ridge. A vehicle moved slowly along the road and someone was searching from the vehicle with a flashlight. He was certain it was Soltero's men hunting him. To kill him with a knife the way they'd killed Abel Durazo. Or to belly-shoot him and let him writhe in agony.

Then he saw a silhouette of a *boy* coming his way out of the darkness! It was all he could do to keep from screaming! Shelby pressed his face into the earth. When he raised up the child was still there. The child moved without a light, seeming to float through the night. Then the phantom boy vanished into a small tunnel, into the darkness.

Shelby heard a voice down the hillside behind him. It sounded like the Mexican with the Zapata mustache. He got up and ran, *staggered*, after the boy. Toward the fearful tunnel, and whatever lay beyond!

When Shelby got close he could see that it was not a tunnel but a hole in a tall metal barrier. There was an opening chopped clear through, but he was so fat he almost couldn't follow the small boy through the hole. He ripped his jacket and cut his hands on the rusty metal. He got stuck for a moment and began to weep, but kept wriggling, finally getting his hips through, tearing his jeans, bloodying his legs. Then Shelby got up and limped across a desolate plateau in the moonlight.

He heard the sound of Mexican music from a boom box far off to the left. He heard voices chattering and laughing off to the right. But there were no lights, none at all, only an occasional dagger of moonlight.

Shelby looked for the boy but couldn't find him. Then he tripped and fell, rolling down a dusty hillside. When he got up, he couldn't run anymore. His legs wouldn't obey him, and he heard a sawing sound, realizing it was coming from himself. His breathing sounded like a hacksaw cutting through steel pipe; a screeching raspy saw-blade was buried deep in his chest. Shelby Pate was sure he would die then, there in the devil's gorge.

An English-accented voice said, *"Arriba las manos!"*

Shelby dropped to his knees. In a way, he *wanted* to die, to get it over with. A flashlight beam struck him like a club. He was blinded. He put his hands up to his face.

A voice said, "Hey, Phil! This guy's an *American!"*

Five minutes later, Shelby Pate was handcuffed and sitting in the back of a Bronco, heading toward the Chula Vista Station of the U.S. Border Patrol.

25

It was nearly 11:00 P.M. by the time Nell's car arrived back at the main gate of NAS North Island.

Before she parked, Fin said, "I was thinking about stopping someplace in Coronado for a nightcap. Anyone wanna join me?"

"Not me," Nell said. "I've had enough for one evening." She didn't say enough of *what*.

"I'm a little tired," Bobbie said.

"Okay, guess I'll have to go it alone," Fin said.

Almost in unison, both women started to indicate he shouldn't drink alone. They both stopped, and Nell said, "You go ahead, Bobbie. I've really gotta run along."

Bobbie said, "No, I just didn't want Fin to have to be by himself. Why don't *you* join him? I gotta wash my hair and do some ironing."

"Well, I won't be stopping," Nell said.

"I gotta run along home," Bobbie said.

Fin said, "All this indecision makes me wanna just go home and improve my mind. Maybe I'll stop and buy that new book by our country's greatest living naked author, Madonna."

When Fin and Bobbie got out, Fin said, "We'll all team up right here at noon on Monday, right? I'm sure we got enough to arrest Durazo and Pate based on the navy shoe on the severed foot. But I think somebody should positively identify that shoe as being from the stolen shipment. Okay, Bobbie?"

"That'll be done first thing Monday morning," Bobbie said. "I'll go to the morgue myself."

"After seeing Pate in action tonight, I'm more convinced than ever he'll spill his guts," Nell said. "The guy's a complete psycho in addition to being a doper."

"I can't *wait* till Monday!" Bobbie said.

"But you *will*, won't you?" Fin said.

"I'm not gonna go off and do something stupid," Bobbie said, mischievously. "Like moseying back down to T.J. and staking out Durazo's car to see what the gang was up to."

"That'd be about as smart as Julius Caesar moseying on down to the Senate to see what Brutus and the gang was up to," Fin said.

Bobbie said, "Don't worry. I'm going straight home, Sherlock."

"Okay, Watson," Fin said. "See you Monday."

Bobbie kissed Fin on the cheek and said, "I wanna be just like you when I grow up."

He stood watching her drive off, when Nell interrupted his thoughts, saying, "Good night . . . Sherlock."

"Give her a break, will ya?" Fin said. "She's just a kid."

Before she could stop herself, Nell blurted, "Why don't *you* give her a break. She's obviously *ga-ga* over the big-city detective. Or is it goo-goo at her age? Kee-rist, you're old enough to be her . . ."

"Big brother."

"Father."

"I'm only . . . seventeen years older."

"Like I said: *father*."

Fin didn't say anything for a moment. Then he said, "Forty-five is a real tough time for an actor, Nell. She just allows me to pretend I'm not over-the-hill. That's all she does for me."

While he was walking away, Nell said, "Still wanna have that drink?"

Four separate Border Patrol agents had a crack at Shelby Pate that night. Their questions varied slightly. His answers not at all, usually delivered in a monotone. The chase through the darkness had sobered him a lot, but he was still twitching and perspiring as he sat in the interrogation room.

The last agent to question him was almost as big as Shelby. He gave Shelby a can of Pepsi and said, "We've checked your record. You've been in jail a few times."

"Not for running drugs over the border," Shelby said. He tried to focus on his questioner's eyes, but his own eyes kept leaping away of their own volition.

"That's a nice watch you got."

"My mother gave it to me."

"You're loaded on something, aren't you?"

"Did some drinking early in the evening."

"You're loaded on something *else*."

Shelby said, "I already told the other guys, a taxi driver offered to take me to a whorehouse up in the hills somewheres. And when I got there three Mexicans tried to mug me. See these cuts on my hands and legs? I was lucky to get away. I was lucky you guys found me."

"And how'd you know where to get through the fence?"

"I jist followed the shadow."

"What shadow?"

"Jist a little shadow that went through the tunnel."

"What tunnel?"

"It turned out to be a hole in the fence. A little boy jist went through it."

"And what happened to the little boy?"

"He got lost, I think."

"Did you ever see him again?"

"I never did. I hope he found his way home, is all."

"We think you were carrying a load of drugs and got ripped off passing through Deadman's Canyon. That's what we think."

"Is that what you call that place?"

"It's what the Mexicans call it. The Canyon of the Dead."

"Then maybe it was a ghost that took me in the tunnel," Shelby said, and his eyes popped wide. "I think maybe it *was*."

"What tunnel? You mean the hole in the fence?"

"Yeah. I thought I was going into hell when I went in that tunnel."

"Then why did you go?"

Shelby Pate said, "I thought I *belonged* in hell."

The Border Patrol agent left him alone then, and later said to his supervisor, "The guy's whacked out on drugs, but I don't think we really have anything. He probably got burned trying to make a drug buy, and *did* have to run for his life. What'll we do with him?"

"He's sober enough now," the supervisor said. "May as well cut him loose. He's obviously a nut-case as well."

Shelby Pate called a cab to pick him up at the Border Patrol station. When he was delivered by taxi to

Hogs Wild, he was mildly surprised that nobody had stolen the helmet off his bike, a common occurrence at that time of night.

There were still a few bikers in the bar, and two mommas having last call. He recognized one of the bikers, a little guy with a scraggly fringe of red hair down to his shoulders. The biker was trying to persuade one of the mommas to ride home with him.

Shelby interrupted them by tossing a gold Rolex onto the bar. "Gimme an eightball and five hunnerd bucks and it's yours," he said.

The biker picked up the Rolex and took it over to the broken sconce next to a jukebox rocking with the thud of heavy metal. The biker examined the gold bracelet more carefully than he did the watch itself, then said, "It's genuine."

"Good call," Shelby said. "Deal?"

The guy handed back the Rolex and said, "I can give you a teener and two-fifty. That's all I got."

"Deal," Shelby said. "Gimme."

Ten minutes later, Shelby's bike was roaring toward the pier at Imperial Beach. And twenty minutes after that Shelby was lying on the sand, sweating and shivering. The methamphetamine made the crashing surf sound like the roar of howitzers. Shelby burrowed into the sand to escape the explosions and to find some warmth. He spilled as much of the meth as he snorted. He lay on his belly and rooted, licking the meth and tasting sand in his mouth.

He was like a giant crab burrowing on his belly on a mist-free night, when a dagger of moonlight inflicted agony on his sensitive eyes.

The Coronado pub was full of Navy SEAL team members who were trying to drink the joint dry before closing time, those who weren't busy trying to pick

up one of several young women who were there to
be picked up by the strapping young sailors.

Fin and Nell took a table in the corner after order-
ing a cognac.

He said, "Here I am, dying of a mid-life crisis,
and I have to pick a joint where everyone thinks aging
is like AIDS: It can only happen to people who aren't
careful."

"Wonder if Bobbie comes here," Nell said. Then,
"She's a pretty good kid, I guess."

"You sure didn't seem to like her much."

"I don't know who or what I like lately," Nell
said. "This is a cruddy age, isn't it?"

"I gotta admit, I've had a good week though.
Getting to know both of you."

"Both of us?"

"I know you a lot better than I know Bobbie."

"It didn't look that way."

"Was I giving her coy glances?"

"You looked more coy than Princess Di. Middle-
aged men who want a woman their own age are so
rare they could get on the next Geraldo."

"Having a young girl pay attention to me made
me a little goofy."

"It's a cruddy age," Nell said, patting his hand.

"You just *touched* me!" he said.

"Does this mean I get to wear your class ring?"

"Wanna go to the beach tomorrow?"

"Why the beach?"

"I wanna see you in a bikini. Got one?"

"A woman my age wears a *one*-piece," she said.

"Okay with me. Wanna go?"

"Whadda *you* look like in a swimsuit?"

"It ain't pretty," he said, "but I can build a mean
sand castle. I got lots of experience building castles,
most of them in the air."

"Okay," she said, "let's go to the beach tomorrow."

•　•　•

They were drifting and floating away from him, all the dark shadows holding flickering candles. They were leaving him and he was trying to scream: "NO! NO! I'M ALIVE!"

He couldn't get the words out because the dry acrid dust of Mexico was in his mouth and in his nostrils. He was slowly suffocating in a grave under a tall tombstone with a portrait of a boy on it. The boy was Shelby Pate, ten years of age. It was *his* tombstone!

Then a shadow figure approached. It was a woman in a shawl. She might've been the mother of the boy with ringworm. She looked down at his grave, and he tried to scream: "DIG ME UP! I'M ALIVE."

All she did was shriek at him. His ears were full of the dry dust of Mexico, and she shrieked inside his skull. The *unearthly* shrieking!

Gulls shrieked and screamed and wheeled above him. He opened his eyes and stared at a sky inflamed, at a dawn red as blood. The sound of surf thundered in his ears and he gagged on the sand in his throat. He whimpered and sniffled, and clawed his way out of a dune of drifting sand.

When he sat up his hair and face were white with sand. He didn't know where he was. A gull hovered in the sky above him, like the Holy Ghost. Shelby covered his eyes and sobbed, swallowing back his terror. It wasn't until he spotted the remains of his bag of meth lying beside him that the phantasmagoria retreated and he knew he was still *alive*.

By the time Shelby Pate had snorted enough cringe to get control, and by the time he'd located his bike parked in a vacant lot close to a coffee shop, it was nine o'clock Sunday morning.

He was a fearful sight, with his loose stringy hair

full of sand, with dried blood on his hands and on his face, from thrashing through the fence at the international border. He shuffled toward the coffee shop, and a street person loitering outside took one look at him and went scuttling away. After three cups of coffee, Shelby thought he was ready to go home.

Bobbie went for a jog along Coronado Beach in her shorts and T-shirt on Sunday morning. There were lots of hardbodies out, both male and female. It was a dry morning in that a Santa Ana was blowing in from the desert.

Coronado was Bobbie's favorite beach. She started her run along the sand beside the Coronado Shores high-rise condominiums, a.k.a. Taco Towers because so many wealthy Mexicans from Tijuana owned condos there. She ran north past the Hotel del Coronado, zigzagging through sand dunes tufted with ice plant. She ran north all the way to the Naval Air Station golf course, beside which dogs were permitted to run free on the beach and play in the surf with their owners.

She stopped to watch a dog catching a Frisbee, then paused again at the golf course. Although there were lots of navy personnel on the links that day, she didn't spot anyone she knew. Then she stopped to say hello to the lone sentry on the beach, where public access was divided from the navy land. After that she turned and ran as hard as she could all the way back to the Towers.

It was a strenuous workout. She arrived home, showered, ate a bowl of cereal, and read the paper. It was very hard to concentrate on the boring election coverage. She went to her file folder and removed the copy of the San Diego police report she'd been given by Fin. Bobbie got out her county map book and pinpointed the addresses of Abel Durazo and Shelby Pate. She was dying to know if they'd come home after having driven off with the Mexican who no doubt was the fence for stolen goods.

Bobbie did not dare admit to Fin or to Nell what she still believed in her heart: that Jules Temple was involved. They'd just scoff, and keep repeating that a guy like Jules Temple would *not* be stealing navy shoes. Still, there was something about him that made her know he had something to hide.

Impulsively, she picked up the phone. If Abel Durazo answered she'd hang up. If anyone else answered, she'd wing it.

A child said, *"Bueno?"*

"Do you speak English?" Bobbie asked.

"Yes."

"Is Abel Durazo there?"

"He's not home."

"Where is he?"

"I don't know."

"This is . . . somebody from his job. I need to talk to him. Did he come home last night?"

The child yelled something in Spanish, then came back and said, "My mother says no, he didn't come home last night."

"Thank you," Bobbie said.

After she hung up, she thought about calling Fin, but of course he'd tell her to cool it till Monday. He'd make her feel like a rookie cop. Like a *kid*.

She picked up the phone and called Shelby Pate's number. A woman answered.

"Excuse me," Bobbie said. "Is this Shelby Pate's residence?"

"No, this is *my* residence. Who's this?"

"I have to speak to him. Is he home?"

"No!" the woman said. "He *ain't* home! So he's out fucking around on you too, huh? Are you one a the speed freaks from Hogs Wild?"

"Sorry," Bobbie said, getting ready to hang up.

"If you see that scum sucker, tell him for me he's *outta* here! Tell him I threw his fucking clothes out in the street at eight o'clock this morning!"

After the line went dead, Bobbie immediately called the Tijuana Police and talked to four different people to whom she gave the names of Abel Durazo and Shelby Pate. She got an English-speaking woman on the line, who said, "Who are you inquiring about?"

"Shelby Pate," Bobbie said. "I'm a detective with the U.S. Navy. I'm just trying to find out if he's in jail, or in the hospital or something."

The woman said, "You gave another name. What was that name?"

"Durazo," Bobbie said. "Abel Durazo."

"One moment please," the woman said.

When she came back on the line she said, "Do you have a pencil? I have another number for you to call."

Bobbie was excited. Maybe they *were* in jail, and maybe it had to do with being caught selling two thousand pairs of shoes! When she rang the other number she was given over to a man who spoke nearly unaccented English. "This is Rojas," he said. "Who do you wish to learn about?"

"Shelby Pate," Bobbie said. "I'm a detective with the U.S. Navy at North Island. And also I wanna know about Abel Durazo. Are they in jail, or what?"

Rojas said, "I am with the state judicial police. Do you know Mister Durazo very well?"

"No," Bobbie said. "I'm investigating his *possible* involvement in a large theft of navy shoes."

The Mexican cop said, "We have a murder victim in our morgue with the name of Abel Durazo on his California driver's license and on his *pasaporte.*"

"Good god!" Bobbie said. "How about Shelby Pate?"

"No, but *another* man was murdered. A man

named Porfirio Velásquez Saavedra, better known to us as Juan Soltero."

"Is he a receiver of stolen property, by any chance?"

"Yes, and other things. It appears that they killed each other. Durazo was stabbed, and then must have got off one shot before he died. A derringer pistol was found beside him."

"Could you go to the home of the dead man and search for two thousand pairs of U.S. Navy shoes?" Bobbie asked, and then she had a long conversation with Rojas concerning her investigation.

After she hung up she dialed Fin's number, but got his answering machine. She dialed Nell's number and got *another* machine. She hung up and experienced the longest afternoon of her life. She called Fin and Nell no less than fifteen times, leaving several messages for each of them. The messages sounded progressively more impatient and more excited.

After spending three hours on Mission Beach, most of it under a beach umbrella, Fin and Nell decided to go to his apartment to shower and change for dinner.

"And to do *what?*" Nell asked, after he made the suggestion.

"Ride the roller coaster," Fin said.

"I haven't ridden a roller coaster in twenty years," she said.

"I ride it every once in a while. It's very nostalgic for me. When I was a kid my sisters used to take me for rides with their boyfriends. I sat between them usually. The boyfriends hated my guts."

They were lying under the umbrella when he'd asked her. He thought she had a terrific body, for a woman of a certain age. She thought he had pretty good buns, but ought to work on his tummy.

Late that afternoon, after eating a hot dog and a hamburger, Fin Finnegan and Nell Salter rode the Mission Beach vintage roller coaster, raising their hands in the air and screaming as they sped down the dips, losing themselves for a while in lovely memories of their lost youth.

When Shelby arrived home he found some of his clothes in the driveway. Some were in the street and some were on the little patch of grass in front of the house. He parked the Harley, jumped off and ran to the front door, discovering that his key no longer fit the lock.

He started banging on the door, yelling, "Bitch! You better open this fucker or it's goin *down!*"

His next-door neighbor, the tweaker who'd interrupted him when he'd been trying to landscape the neighborhood, opened his window and yelled, "Hey, dude! Your old lady said to tell you she went home to her momma!"

"She changed the fuckin lock!" Shelby hollered.

The tweaker said, "She told me you ain't got nothin in the house no more. She threw everything out. By the time she told me, there was people from down the street stealin *everything.* I got some a your stuff in my garage. You kin come get it."

Shelby ran to the tweaker's garage and jerked it open. His camouflage jacket was there, and his extra helmet. He ran inside his own garage and pulled things down from the shelf: every box, every tool, every auto part. The boots were *gone!*

He ran back outside and said to the neighbor, "My boots! I had some *boots* in the garage!"

"Didn't see no boots," the tweaker said. "I saved

your shirts and some jeans and I got a bag full a your sox. Them greasers from down the block, they got your boots, I guess."

The ox just gaped. Finally he said, "You shouldn't *never* steal somebody's shoes."

"That's cold, dude," the tweaker agreed.

Shelby said, "Some Mexicans got the firin squad for takin a man's shoes."

"What firin squad?"

"They got shot."

The tweaker said, "Dude, you shouldn't be doin that crystal so early in the morning. You ain't talkin sense."

"You shouldn't *never* steal somebody's shoes," Shelby Pate informed his neighbor. "It's the worst mistake you can ever make."

Bobbie Ann Doggett was beside herself with excitement. She thought about calling up the assistant director of security at North Island, but she knew he'd say what Fin would say: "It'll all keep till tomorrow. Till you're on duty and can work in a proper investigative environment."

What *could* she do now anyway? Nobody was going anywhere. Abel Durazo was on ice, and so was his Tijuana contact, Soltero. Shelby Pate might also be lying in a Tijuana alley with a knife in his ample gut.

Jules Temple would be coming to his place of business tomorrow as usual, none the wiser as far as his employees' fate was concerned. And how was she going to tie Jules Temple into all this? She *wasn't*. Not unless Pate was still alive and willing to talk about it.

So far, everyone who'd come in contact with those navy shoes had ended up dead. Her boss would probably tell her that if she recovered the shoes, the navy ought to send them immediately to Saddam Hussein.

Bobbie sat and tried to read a magazine, cooling her heels until three o'clock. Then she rang up Fin and Nell once again. Bobbie was going bughouse.

After she hung up, she got dressed in jeans and a T-shirt and strapped on her shoulder holster, concealing it under her most comfortable cardigan. Then she grabbed her purse and map book and headed for the house of Shelby Pate in National City.

She drove her Hyundai slowly through the ethnically mixed, working-class residential neighborhood, a district with lots of homeboy spider-script sprayed on all the walls. His house was easy to spot. It was the only one with the front door kicked off the hinges. The small yard was littered with articles of clothing, and a Harley hog sat menacingly in the driveway, aimed at the street.

A fleeting memory occurred to Bobbie. The director of security had once warned her that women in police work frequently take great risks because they don't want to call for backup from the men until they're sure they need it. But by then, it's often too late. He'd warned that many female cops had been needlessly injured and even killed, for fear of seeming to be the damsel in distress.

He'd finished reading the paper, but found that he couldn't concentrate on the Sunday talking-head shows blathering about Tuesday's election as though everyone wasn't already certain that George Bush was history. Jules had never cared anything about politics. He sat, channel grazing, when the phone rang.

"Hello," he said, thinking it might be Lou Ross with details about the New York trip.

"It's Shelby Pate, Mister Temple," the voice said.

Jules was astonished. He caught his breath and said, "Yes?"

"I gotta talk to you today."

"How'd you get my number?"

"Abel got it for me," Shelby said, "a few days ago."

"How'd he get it?"

"From Mary," Shelby said. "He was fuckin her."

"I see," Jules said. "What do you wanna talk about?"

"Money," Shelby said.

"I see," Jules said.

"Want me to explain?"

"I don't want you to explain on the telephone," Jules said. "I'll meet you somewhere."

"Where?"

"At my office."

"Be there at one," Shelby said.

"I simply can't," Jules said. "I can be there by five-thirty. That's the best I can do."

"Okay," Shelby said. "Five-thirty."

"Will Durazo be with you?" Jules asked.

"He had an accident in T.J.," Shelby said. "He ain't never gonna be with me again."

When Jules hung up, he was paralyzed with rage. His heart was pounding. His mouth was very dry but at least his hands didn't shake. He was pleased that his hands didn't shake. He'd always been able to control stress to a remarkable degree, hadn't he? He was pleased that his mind had worked so quickly under fire. He'd told that pig to meet him at five-thirty because he knew instinctively that he'd be better off after dark. Whatever happened, it should happen after dark.

Jules hadn't clearly formulated a plan yet, but Shelby Pate was forcing him. He wasn't exactly making it up as he went along. He already had ideas, but they weren't crystallized. Abel Durazo *wasn't* coming back? That was *great* news. There was only Pate.

Jules looked at his watch. There was plenty of time to go to Green Earth and make preparations. Hazardous waste could be stored for a long time if he did it properly, and he certainly knew how to do that in order to sidestep government regulations. There was a stack of drums containing diesel fuel, and some containing etching acid that he'd been holding until he had a sufficient load. He'd put Shelby Pate into one of those drums.

Then it would be a matter of borrowing a boat from someone at the club. Maybe a runabout on a trailer. He could haul it to the yard and dolly the drum onto the boat; then he could launch the boat and dump the drum a mile offshore. He could do it as soon as Monday, or wait till the weekend. That might be best, doing it on the weekend. Then he could stay out and do some fishing just to *prove* something to himself: that Jules Temple did not panic. That Jules Temple was once again in control of his own destiny.

But he quickly dismissed that plan. The more mundane but less dangerous way would be to dump Pate's body in the vicinity of a bikers' bar like Hogs Wild, and let it be found. Let the police think he'd died as he'd lived, at the hands of some other lowlife scum.

26

"It's possible that I've been running away from my three sisters all my life," Fin said to her.

He was sitting on the sofa eating his second bowl of butter brickle ice cream. His bachelor apartment, a block from the sand in south Mission Beach, had been thoroughly cleaned and tidied up by Fin on the chance that he'd be successful in persuading Nell to come home.

She was seated at the kitchen table finishing her second bowl.

"Why would you spend your life running away? Are they so awful?"

"Actually, all three're smarter than me. And each managed to have a happy marriage to guys that weren't millionaires or senile or comatose. The youngest one's recently widowed and she got herself a good job, recession and all. They have nice kids and they're successful in life. Me, I'm a failed actor, a failed cop, and the world's worst marriage prospect."

"So're you saying you always marry women who *aren't* like your sisters?"

"Actually, I came to that conclusion just after I met you."

"Whaddaya mean by that?"

"You remind me of my sisters."

"I thought they kicked ass and took names."

"They did. It didn't work, but they kept trying."

"Did it ever occur to you that you waste a lotta time on self-pity?"

"That's exactly what my sister says."

"Which one?"

"All three."

"Are you a junkie that can't stop?"

"Probably," he said, "unless I finally get involved with somebody who's like my sisters."

"I thought your first wife, the good sergeant, kicked your butt from time to time."

"Yeah, but she did it for her own amusement. My sisters did it to make me a better person."

Nell got up and went to the refrigerator for more ice cream. "The hell with calories," she said.

"With that bod, you can afford a few calories."

"Looks like I'm doing it again," she said.

"What?"

"Getting involved with a Peter Pan policeman. Your favorite song is 'Someone to Watch Over Me,' right?"

"What's wrong with that?"

"A woman my age would kinda like it the other way around, even in these modern times."

"Hillary Clinton wouldn't think so. Who're you voting for on Tuesday?"

"Since you got me all mixed up I'll probably vote for Perot."

"I'd rather not talk politics."

Nell sat down next to him on the sofa, and said, "I'll bet your sisters spoil you rotten. Want some of my ice cream?"

"Does this mean we're . . . *involved?*"

She didn't answer, but she put down the bowl and scooted closer.

"The thing that drove me wild was your broken nose," he said. "It's *so* sexy."

"My most masculine feature," she said.

"I *told* you I was probably gay . . ."

"Except for the sex part," she said. "Right?"

"Riiiiiiight," said Fin Finnegan.

Jules was tired, but quite satisfied with his day's work. He felt he looked cool and collected in gabardine slacks and an oversized cotton shirt with a yachting crest on the pocket. He wore the shirt for the freedom of movement he'd need during the action he'd planned. Instead of tasseled loafers, he wore boat shoes, for traction on the greasy asphalt in the truck yard.

Jules almost went back out to the yard again, but that was pointless. It would work or it wouldn't. He was ready or he wasn't. He had a small liquor cabinet in his office, so he opened it and poured himself a shot of Scotch. He held the glass of Scotch in a half-extended arm. His hand did *not* shake.

Bobbie was parked at the end of the cul-de-sac half a block from Shelby Pate's house. He'd have to head in the other direction if he left. Bobbie simply had to know *where* he'd go if he left his house on a night when his crime partner lay dead in a Tijuana morgue.

She knew that what she was doing was foolhardy, and that her boss would go cosmic if he found out about it. She knew that Fin and Nell would react in a similar fashion, but she believed that Shelby Pate might hook up with the man who'd masterminded the theft of the navy shoes if only to tell him that Abel Durazo had been killed. Any meeting with Jules Temple would help to cement her case, or at least assist in the interrogation after they arrested Shelby Pate on Monday morning.

At 4:45 P.M., he lumbered through the open doorway. He propped the dangling door in place, but didn't bother to secure it with nails. He didn't pick up any of the clothing that was strewn all over the property. He got on his bike, put on the black helmet, and roared away, not noticing the Hyundai that was never far behind.

At twilight, Shelby Pate parked the Harley in the parking lot of Green Earth Hauling and Disposal. He thought Jules Temple hadn't arrived because his yellow Miata wasn't in front. But he looked up at the second story and saw a light on in the boss's office so he rightly assumed that Jules Temple had parked inside the truck yard.

Shelby wondered why the boss would do that, and while Shelby was wondering he removed a paper from his pocket and took a hit of meth. He already had a buzz, but he needed a little boost. Then he was ready.

He slid a buck knife inside his belt and made sure it was accessible. He would've preferred a gun, but it was too late to go shopping for one. He wasn't really worried though, because even if Jules Temple went shithouse when he heard Shelby's terms, what could he do? The dude needed the manifest. He didn't know that the manifest was gone—gone with the fucking boots!

Shelby strode through the unlocked front door and climbed the darkened stairs, hearing music coming from a radio in Mary's office, and when he got to the landing, he looked in.

"I'm in here!" Jules Temple's voice came from his own office.

Shelby followed the voice and found his boss sitting at his desk, apparently signing payroll checks.

"Maybe you'd like to sign one a them fer me," Shelby said, without smiling.

"What the hell's this all about?" Jules demanded. "And what's this about Durazo not coming back? What happened?"

"Stabbed by some dudes in T.J.," Shelby said, plopping down in the client chair in front of Jules's desk. "He's dead."

He wore the same clothes that he'd worn to Tijuana the night before, except for a change of T-shirts. His hair still had sand in it. He was as unshaven and scruffy as usual, and he stank to high heaven. Jules curled his lip when he smelled him.

Shelby's black T-shirt said BLACK SABBATH across the front, in blood-red letters.

"Are you sure he's dead?" Jules asked.

"When I left him he looked dead. He could come back tonight though."

"Is that a joke?"

"This is the Day of the Dead," Shelby said. "Flaco might come home to his momma if she puts a bottle a beer out for him. Flaco loved beer."

"I may be dense," Jules said, leaning forward on his elbows, "but I don't understand you."

"It don't matter," Shelby said.

"So why did you wanna see me?"

"Since you're here that means you got a general idea," Shelby said.

"None at all," Jules said.

"I got something that belongs to you."

"What's that?"

"A manifest. One *you* made out."

"I make out lots of manifests," Jules said.

"Not like this one. There's no manifest like this one."

"Did you and Durazo steal from North Island?"

"Yeah. A couple thousand pair a shoes."

"You fucking *idiot!*" Jules couldn't help blurting it.

"I ain't in no mood fer that," Shelby warned. "I came to do business."

"You say it's *my* manifest? Then give it to me."

"In time," Shelby said.

"Do you have it with you?"

"It's in a safe place," Shelby said.

"I wouldn't want anybody else knowing my business," Jules said. "You live with a woman, don't you?"

"The bitch threw me out."

"If anyone *else* knows about it, I wouldn't be interested in doing business with you."

"Nobody knows," Shelby said, " 'cept you and me."

And *that* sealed Shelby Pate's fate. Jules Temple didn't believe that this freak was savvy enough to arrange for a third party to hold the manifest. Jules believed that the manifest was probably in a bedroom drawer or some obvious place, and that it would be thrown away when Shelby Pate's property was disposed of. After his death.

Jules certainly believed that he'd have to pay Shelby Pate for the rest of his life and never *see* the manifest anyway, if he were to succumb to blackmail. So as Jules saw it, he had nothing to lose and everything to gain by proceeding with his plan.

But things were moving too *fast.* He needed one more drink, and then it'd be dark enough. Then he'd be ready.

"Tell me about Durazo," Jules said. "Tell me about his death. It's terrible."

"He died. There ain't no use talkin about him. There ain't no use thinkin about him. I came here to talk business."

"There's plenty of time to talk business," Jules said. "But I'd like to send a check to Durazo's family in Mexico. I think he had a family in Tijuana, didn't he?"

"I don't wanna talk about no fuckin *dead* people," Shelby said.

Jules could see those dilated pupils even from across the room. Jules had to placate the monster. He glanced at his watch. It was nearly late enough. *Dark* enough.

"He was your friend, wasn't he? You wanna help his family, don't you?"

"I wanna help *me*!" Shelby lurched to his feet.

Jules felt a jolt of fear and panic. Those wild eyes! His immense size! "Wait a minute!" Jules said. "Calm down! I just asked for the sake of the man's family. Okay, okay, we'll talk business."

Shelby sat, but leaned forward, as though he might leap across the desk and strangle Jules at any moment.

Jules said, "Do you want a drink?"

"No," Shelby said.

"Do you mind if I have one?"

"Let's talk *business*, dude."

"Okay, but I need a drink."

Bobbie was supercharged when Shelby Pate parked his bike in the lot of Green Earth Hauling and Disposal. She drove her car around to the side street looking for Jules's car. Not knowing what he drove, she could see the rear end of a yellow car in the corner of the truck yard. He was the yellow roadster type, that's for sure.

She parked, got out, and walked up to the locked truck gate. Why had he put his car inside? Why not park out front where he could enter the building through the main door? She decided that possibly he had to enter through the back door because of a preprogrammed burglar alarm. On the other hand, maybe he didn't want his car to be spotted by someone driving by. It could be that he didn't want anyone to know that he'd been at Green Earth Hauling and Disposal on Sunday evening. They might be plotting another theft.

He'd managed to stall long enough to get a glass of Scotch in his hand, but he hadn't returned to his desk when Shelby Pate said to him, "I'm gonna need some long-term unemployment insurance and you're gonna give it to me."

"How much . . . *insurance* did you have in mind?"

"I ain't a greedy dude," Shelby said. "Say, fifty grand."

"If I give you fifty grand, you'll give me back my property?"

"Why not?"

"Would you give me the property *first*?"

"*After* the check clears."

"I see," Jules said, knowing that fifty thousand dollars would only be the first installment.

He glanced at his watch. It was as dark as it would get. He took a sip of Scotch. There was a moon, but it was mist-shrouded.

Bobbie, standing outside the gate of the truck yard, was surprised to hear the roadster's engine turning over. It was very dark now, and the rear of the car was barely visible. Who could be starting up the car?

Jules pressed the button on the remote control inside his belt, and said, "I'd like to be certain that you'll keep your . . ." He was interrupted by the sound of the engine in the yard below, easy to hear because Jules had left the window open.

Shelby turned toward the window, and said, "Somebody's out there."

"That's my car!" Jules cried. "I parked it in the yard! Somebody's stealing my fucking car!"

Jules got up, ran around the desk, leaped over the outstretched legs of Shelby Pate and hurtled down the stairway.

Shelby got up and moved to the window to look out. The little yellow Miata was parked behind one of the trucks, and all Shelby could see was the rear bumper.

He saw Jules running across the yard yelling, "Hey! Hey, you asshole!"

Bobbie Ann Doggett was stunned when Jules Temple came running out the back door of the building hollering his head off! At first she thought he'd spotted her, and that *she* was the asshole he was screaming at. She ducked back behind the concrete wall and was ready to get the hell out of there before the cops arrived and mistook her for a prowler.

Then she heard Jules Temple cry out in pain!

Shelby Pate stuck his head out the window when Jules screamed: "Ohhhhhh!"

• • •

Bobbie sprinted along the sidewalk heading for the front door of Green Earth, every neural fiber on red alert! Somebody in the truck yard was *attacking* Jules Temple!

Shelby scrambled down the back stairway in the darkness, and ran into the yard, a thought whistling through his brain: Just his luck if Jules Temple got his throat cut by some nigger car thief!

He *really* wished he had a gun now, but he drew the buck knife from his belt. He held it like a hammer and charged around the truck expecting to find somebody killing Jules Temple.

Shelby didn't exactly feel the crowbar so much as he heard it. Then he collapsed like his spine exploded. He was slumped against the front fender of the yellow Miata when Jules grabbed the collar of Shelby's leather jacket and tried to drag his massive body away from the car for another clear swing.

Shelby flopped onto his side, blood flowing into his eyes, when Jules stepped forward, holding the crowbar like an ax. Shelby was sure that he could hear the mournful trumpet, sure that they *would* call The Lost Child home. When Jules swung the bar a second time. And yet again. Jules stopped when the target got spongy.

She didn't blunder out into the darkened truck yard like Shelby Pate had done. She stood inside the building peering out, unable to see anything across the darkened yard except the rear of a yellow Miata. She hadn't heard a thing since Jules had cried out. The .45 was in her right hand and she was cursing the navy regulation that forbade them to carry it with a chambered round. She had her left hand on the slide, but didn't want to draw it back and rack one into the chamber because the sound would be heard in the stillness of the truck yard.

Jules was proud of himself for not having panicked when it came time to do it. He turned off the ignition with the remote control, thinking giddily that he should write a testimonial to the manufacturer that it *does* work from up to three hundred feet away!

He hadn't needed to resort to his more desperate plan if this one had failed. There beside him on a shelf in the storage shed was a 9mm Beretta. Two years ago, he'd bought the pistol from a former employee who'd no doubt stolen it. "Mister Beretta is the finest Italian I've ever known," that employee had said when the money changed hands.

If Jules couldn't have physically handled Shelby Pate, he'd been prepared to shoot him down. And if gunshots had alerted anyone, he'd been prepared to say that he'd surprised a thief in the truck yard who turned out to be an employee. A very unsatisfactory plan that hadn't been needed after all.

Jules uncovered the empty fifty-five-gallon drum. The dolly and forklift were ready. He only had to get the body into the drum and the drum forklifted into the bobtail van. He was extremely glad that Shelby Pate had ridden his motorcycle. He was going to transport the bike and the drum to the vicinity of Hogs Wild and dump the body and the bike on the street. If Shelby had driven his pickup truck it would've meant using a taxi to get back from the dump site. This was infinitely better.

He'd have to do a good job cleaning up the blood, that's for sure. He'd had no idea that the human head contained so many blood vessels. Jules would have to hose down the ground, and the Miata, and even the truck next to it. The drum was needed in case something happened en route: a traffic accident for instance. No loose ends.

Jules was stepping into coveralls and Wellington boots when he thought he heard something: like a foot scraping on the asphalt in the yard. He stopped and listened, but there was nothing.

Now for the hard part. Jules realized this would not be easy, but he hadn't guessed *how* hard it would be. The dead weight of Shelby Pate made it like trying to lift a water mattress. Jules turned the drum on its side and wedged it against the truck wheel. He got the feet and legs inside, but when he got on the ground and pushed against the shoulders, the corpse wouldn't budge. He had a panicky thought that maybe Shelby Pate was too big to fit inside a fifty-five-gallon drum and he'd have to forklift the bloody heap right onto the floor of the van.

Then Jules dragged the body back out of the drum, but he slipped in the viscous puddle of blood and engine waste. Jules bumped his head on the fender of the truck, and soon was panting, sweating, cursing. He got the corpse turned 180 degrees by using the blood on the asphalt as a lubricant. He got the head and shoulders inside, but he couldn't get the drum upright without the forklift.

He'd decided to give up on the drum idea when a woman's voice cried out: "WHAT'RE YOU DOING?"

Jules jerked around! He could make out a small figure in the darkness. . . . He spun toward the shelf, slipping and sliding in blood. . . . He grabbed the Beretta.

Bobbie used her left hand to rack one in the chamber as two round fireballs roared at her!

Bobbie dropped to her knee . . . Jules crouched

behind the little yellow roadster ... Bobbie crawled toward the back of the truck, toward the bloody heap that used to be Shelby Pate.

Jules leaped onto the hood of the Miata and a fireball flamed down at her! She aimed wildly and three huge fireballs roared over his head.

The massive blasts from the .45 terrified Jules! The rounds ripped into the waste drums behind him and high overhead, drums that were stacked twenty feet high.

Two streams of etching acid from those highest drums fell in a lazy arc, eighteen feet through the air, splashing onto the head and face of Jules Temple. He raised up *screaming.* ... He ran straight at the crouching shape. ... The scalding acid etched his flesh!

Bobbie Ann Doggett experienced what many a law officer before her had experienced during gunfights: tachypsychia. She had tunnel vision ... could only see a black shadow. ... It moved in super slow motion. ... If she'd been thinking, and not reacting, she'd have thought she had all night to raise her .45 in a two-handed combat grip ... to aim for the silhouette, because it was all going ... so ... *slowly.* Then Jules fired three more rounds!

In an instant, Bobbie dropped to the kneeling position—aimed directly at those fireballs—and unleashed two huge slugs from a distance of twelve feet.

It was like Jules Temple slammed right into a concrete wall. The .45 slugs blasted open his chest and Bobbie watched him shudder and crumble, still in slow motion, unaware that she'd experienced yet another phenomenon common to law officers in gunfights, by releasing about 290 cubic centimeters of urine from her bladder.

Jules lay sprawled across Shelby Pate with wide staring eyes, his face blistering from the waste acid that, by law, he should've disposed of. Except that Jules Temple had been trying to save the acid until he had a larger load . . . in order to skim a few bucks.

Bobbie Ann Doggett didn't move a muscle until the smell of acid and cordite and blood was all but lost on the Santa Ana wind.

27

"You're not a failure at *everything*," Nell said, sitting on his bed with the top sheet wrapped around her. "I'm happily exhausted!"

He was wearing the new polka-dot boxer shorts that he'd been *hoping* he'd get to show her. He'd already showered and wiped down the shower stall with his towel; then he'd wiped the sink and the mirror.

He began tidying up the bedroom until Nell said, "Fin, put away the Dustbuster. They already made the Joan Crawford story."

Then he came over to the bed, sat down, and kissed her lightly on the nose, saying, "I adore that bent beak."

"I might just keep you as a love slave," she said, tracing his chin dimple with her fingernail. "I only hope you weren't *acting*."

"If I was I deserve an Oscar," he said.

"Can I come back tomorrow?" Nell asked. "For an encore?"

"Okay," he said. "Can I cook that pasta for you?"

"Yeah, but I have to leave by Monday morning

if only to keep Bobbie from using a flamethrower on Jules Temple and everyone he knows."

"I was thinking," he said. "Forty-five *ain't* such a cruddy age after all, is it?"

They looked at each other for a moment; then they nodded their heads, and Fin said, "Yeah, riiiiiight."

The phone rang, and Fin reached across Nell to pick it up. "Hello," he said. Then, "Yes, this is Finnegan. Yes? Bobbie Ann Doggett?"

Nell jumped out of bed and started looking for her panties and bra as soon as Fin snatched a pencil and pad from the nightstand drawer and said, "Yes? What? No! WHAT?"

When he hung up, he could only gape at Nell for a moment. She was getting into her jeans when he said, "That was a sergeant at the Chula Vista Police Department! Bobbie's blown away Jules Temple!"

Thirty minutes later, Fin's Corvette squealed into the parking lot of Chula Vista P.D. He and Nell ran into the station, where they found a tall man in a green sweater and chinos standing in the lobby with a uniformed Chula Vista P.D. sergeant.

The tall man said, "You must be Detective Finnegan and Investigator Salter?"

Fin nodded and said, "Where is she?"

"Talking to detectives," the tall man said. "This is Sergeant Harvey. He was the first one on the scene."

"It was pretty gruesome," the cop said.

The tall man said, "I'm Captain Fontaine, USMC. Assistant director of security at North Island. I got to hear most of the story when Bobbie told it to the detectives. All about how you two've been working with her. I wish she'd told me."

"She was going to on Monday," Nell said.

Fin stared for a moment and said, "I guess this means she was right all along about Jules Temple."

Captain Fontaine said, "Yeah, looks like he was involved in a conspiracy to steal from our warehouses."

"It's just *incredible!*" Nell said. "A man like Jules Temple stealing shoes?"

"Maybe they stole a lotta things from us," the marine said. "Who knows how long it's been going on. We assume Temple and Pate had a falling out over sharing the loot, and Temple decided to kill him."

"She shouldn'ta been there," Fin said, shaking his head, utterly bewildered.

"No, but that's the way she is," the marine said. "When we took her on, I said to my boss, 'This little sailor's gonna be an *amazing* detective.' "

"But I don't get it!" Fin said. "Why would Jules Temple steal *shoes*? Why would he commit murder? Kee-rist! This is more mysterious than the register at the Show 'n Tell Motel!"

The marine said, "Maybe he just wanted more. Don't you read about big Mafia guys getting nailed for some petty little offense? People like that can't do anything legit. But I don't have to tell *you* about people like Jules Temple."

"Face it, Fin," Nell said. "With all our police experience it was so simple it took a kid to figure it out."

That's when the marine broke into a grin wider than the Halls of Montezuma. "That *kid*," he said, "is one gung-ho, stainless-steel, U.S. Navy issue, baaaaaaaad dog detective!"

Later, when they were alone in the police station lobby waiting to give their statements, Fin said, "Well, if Ross Perot doesn't get elected next Tuesday, I'll write and suggest he drop Admiral Stockdale as his running mate in ninety-six. Bobbie'll probably be an admiral by then and ready for public office."

"I'm gonna call the psychic advisory network," Nell said. "The high priestess tarot pendant holds the key to all that is hidden and mysterious."

"I'll never figure it out," Fin said. "I guess I got no talents whatsoever. So maybe I should go to law school?"

"Wanna go to the beach next Saturday?" Nell asked. "You're pretty good at building sand castles. Then we could go to my place afterward so I can find out if tonight was a fluke or if you have real love-slave potential."

"Okay," Fin said, "it's about the only way I can still get applause, I guess. And I been wondering, do you think it's remotely possible that you might share the rent with me someday? I mean, if I promise not to do something zany like marrying you?"

"Share rent where? In south Mission Beach?"

"No, I got roaches you could lasso for prize money with a number on your back. I was thinking maybe we could share your place in Pacific Beach. That way we could save a few bucks for our old age, which is right around the corner. I don't wanna be living alone when I can't even spoon chicken soup down my own neck."

"Here I go again," Nell said with a sigh. "I'll think about it and give you an answer after I feel you *perform* one more time. Which, by the way, I keep thinking about."

"I wish I could invite you to share my place, but there's barely room to turn around if you leave toenail clippings on the floor. Which of course I don't do. But if I did you could smack me with a wooden spoon, which coming from you I'd probably appreciate."

"Can you really cook?"

"Yes indeed. And maybe I can't promise you a satellite dish on your roof, but I wouldn't take up much space 'cause I'm not very big and all my belongings fit in a couple of those handkerchiefs my sisters always made me carry. Can't you decide now? I'm getting *real* anxious, especially since I'm fighting an old compulsion to propose marriage right this minute."

"Before I decide," Nell said, "do you know of any good support groups for stage mothers?"

28

The next day, *El Día de los Muertos*, the mother of the thief, Pepe Palmera, honored his memory at the graveyard. She brought flowers, and a photo of him that she'd put inside a cheap pewter frame. She gazed at his photo for a long time that day.

The mother of Porfirio Velásquez Saavedra, a.k.a. Juan Soltero, spent the day praying on her knees to the Virgin of Guadalupe while a mortician negotiated with family members for the price of a splendid funeral, as befitting his position.

Abel Durazo's mother did not put out a bottle of beer or anything else for her son's ghost. She was so shocked and grief-stricken to have learned of his murder that she was disconsolate, and refused to leave her bedroom.

The mother of Jaime Cisneros baked some sweet breads for her lost little boy. Also, she put out a few of his favorite toys, along with his asthma inhaler, even though her husband said that it seemed foolish to leave an inhaler for their dead son. Jaime's twelve-year-old sister, Socorro, swore that she saw Jaime that night, walking along the path that leads from *Colonia Libertad* to the north, and crawling through the hole in the fence like thousands before him.

Epilogue

Three months after the resolution of the strange and baffling warehouse theft conspiracy that led to the deaths of two Americans and four Mexicans—during the first weeks in office of the forty-second president of the United States—the new owner of Green Earth Hauling and Disposal received a communication from Sacramento inquiring about some waste that had been manifested from NAS North Island but had never arrived at a disposal site. The mid-level bureaucrat in Sacramento was informed by telephone that the load of waste had been stolen along with the waste handler's copies of the manifests, and that the stolen load included a drum of Guthion from Southbay Agricultural Supply.

That same civil servant then telephoned Burl Ralston at Southbay Agricultural Supply to ask why in the hell he'd mailed them a donation to the American Red Cross, but not his manifest copy for the Guthion that later went with the stolen truck. Burl Ralston explained that his entire office had been disrupted by his secretary being off sick, and that he'd sent all sorts of documents to the wrong places and made a thousand stupid mistakes with paperwork. He guessed that his copy of the Guthion manifest had probably gone to the American Red Cross and was now lost forever.

Burl Ralston apologized, and told the civil servant that he was seventy-four years old, and was making so many mistakes he thought it was time to retire to a little place he was thinking about buying in Mexico, just south of Rosarito Beach. He told the bureaucrat that with the NAFTA agreement apparently a done deal, the Baja Peninsula might just end up being a kind of Mexican Riviera. And that any sharp American would be wise to take advantage of the Mexicans while he still could.

ABOUT THE AUTHOR

JOSEPH WAMBAUGH, formerly of the Los Angeles Police Department, is the author of fifteen books—*The New Centurions, The Blue Knight, The Onion Field, The Choirboys, The Black Marble, The Glitter Dome, The Delta Star, Lines and Shadows, The Secrets of Harry Bright, Echoes in the Darkness, The Blooding, The Golden Orange, Fugitive Nights, Finnegan's Week* and *Floaters*—all of them outstanding best-sellers. He lives in Southern California.